I0826558

EMERALD SPIRE

EMERALD SPIRE

LESLIE O'SULLIVAN

CITY OWL
PRESS

EMERALD SPIRE
Rockin' Fairy Tales, Book 5

Cover Design by MiblArt. All stock photos licensed appropriately.

Edited by Lisa Green.

For information on subsidiary rights, please contact the publisher at info@cityowlpress.com.

Print Edition ISBN: 978-1-64898-554-6

Digital Edition ISBN: 978-1-64898-555-3

Printed in the United States of America

PRAISE FOR LESLIE O'SULLIVAN

"As full of heart and soul as the music it describes, Crimson Melodies drew me in with a fresh take on a classic tale, masterfully combining celebrity and monster romance vibes to give me everything I wanted and more!" — S.C. Grayson, author of *Beauty and the Blade*

"Submerging readers into a fantastical world, *Wild Azure Waves* is a love story swimming with music, mysticism, and magic." — *InD'tale*

"*Pink Guitars and Falling Stars* is a fast paced and very engaging read, with a constantly evolving main character and a colorful cast. The adventure wraps up nicely, and ends with a hint of what is next in the Rockin' Fairy Tales series. This is a great read if you are looking for an action-packed modern fairy tale with aspiring rock stars who fall from the sky." — *Paranormal Romance Guild*

"*Gilded Butterfly* is a unique and magical mashup of fairy tales, Shakespeare, and lore, unlike anything I've read before. At its heart, is a beautiful story about family, the destructive power of chasing fame and money, and the healing power of love. The twists, turns, and magic sprinkled throughout create an engaging story that brings a new kind of fairy tale to modern Hollywood." — *Megan Van Dyke, author of Second Star to the Left*

"*Pink Guitars and Falling Stars* is an interesting take on the story of Rapunzel...O'Sullivan has definitely nailed the initial animosity between Justin and Zeli. As they become closer, the relationship jumps off the page and morphs beautifully. There are awesome love scenes with a lot of description which pull the reader right in and keep a tight grip... A fascinating remix of a popular fairy tale with some very sexy differences. One to add to the e-reader and to be read list!" — *InD'tale*

"With wickedly clever wordplay, fresh and lovable characters, and an utterly unique take on a classic fairytale, *Pink Guitars and Falling Stars* is one of the swooniest romances I've ever read. You'll be cheering for B.A.S.E. jumper Justin to help Zeli escape her tower in the heart of Hollywood's twisted music industry and fall equally hard for their chosen family on the Boulevard. A romantic, heart-in-your-throat read!" — *Sarah Skilton, author of Fame Adjacent*

"Leslie O'Sullivan's narrative style in *Gilded Butterfly* celebrates truth, love, and heritage, and reads as pure poetry from the opening line until the end." — *InD'tale*

"*Pink Guitars and Falling Stars* reads like glitter and stardust, like a song of the heart set free and realizing every dream." —*Fairrryprose*

Pink Guitars and Falling Stars is a winner of a 2023 Gold Author Shout Reader Ready Awards "Top Pick."

Hot Set is a 2023 Holt Medallion Winner for Mid-Length Contemporary

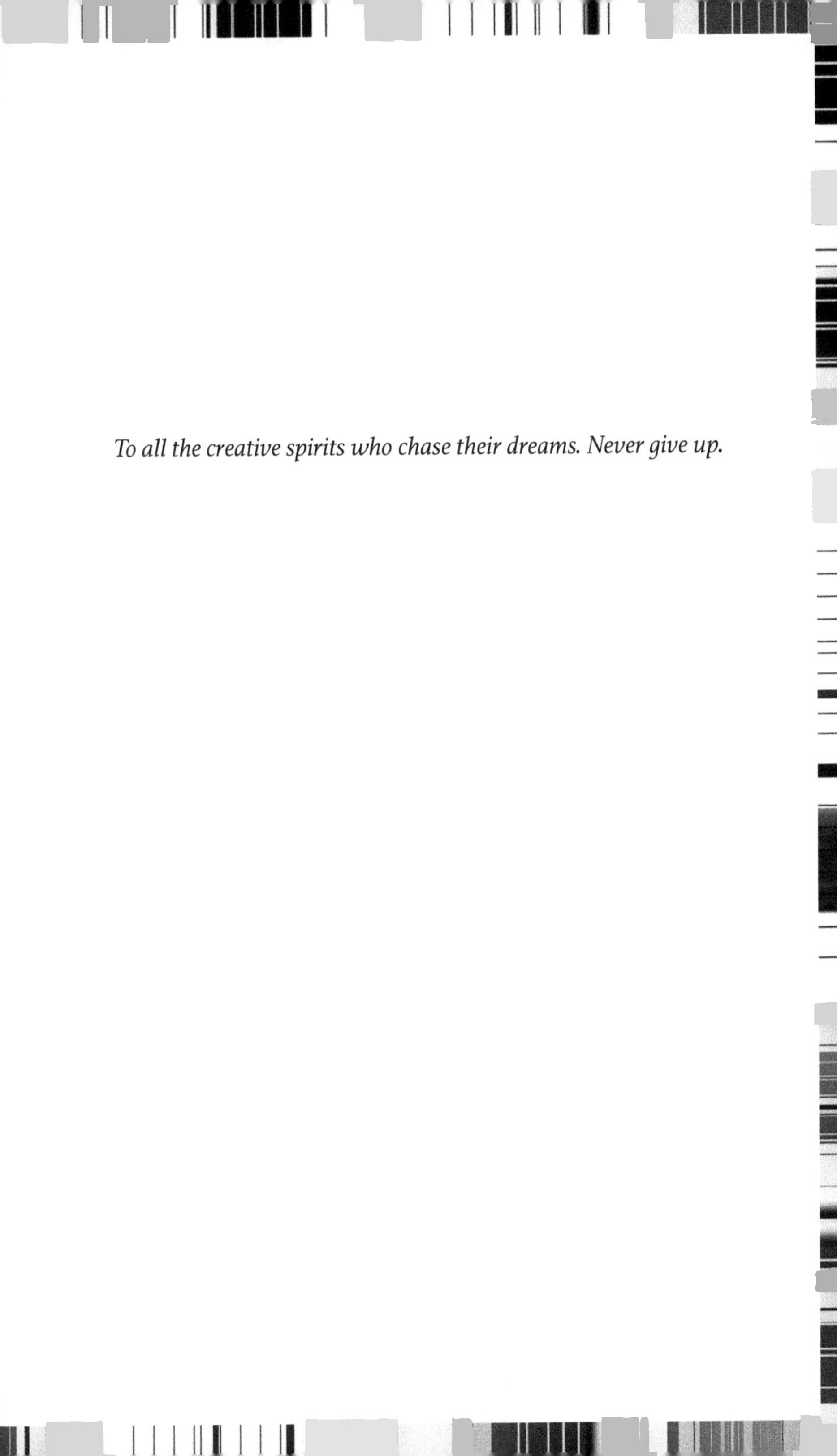

To all the creative spirits who chase their dreams. Never give up.

ROCKIN' FAIRY TALES

BY LESLIE O'SULLIVAN

Pink Guitars and Falling Stars

Gilded Butterfly

Wild Azure Waves

Crimson Melodies

Emerald Spire

“To say the truth, reason and love keep little company together nowadays.”

-Bottom, Act 3 Scene 1, A Midsummer Night’s Dream, William Shakespeare

PROLOGUE

AURORA

Call me a "cocktail magician." Management wants us to use the kitschy, flirty title they've assigned to those of us designing fancy themed drinks for Stalk, the much buzzed about LA hotspot. The set-to-debut premier nightclub sits atop the Emerald Spire complex in the dead center of Hollywood. The only way to access the place at present is via the glitzy steel and frosted-glass elevator currently holding me prisoner.

What I'd give to possess even the tiniest bit of real magic to calm my queasy stomach as I white-knuckle it inside this ultra-high-speed cylinder of mayhem to clock in at work. Give me sky, clouds, the horizon, or anything natural besides the smear of floors screaming by.

Today is the final brainstorming session to finalize cocktails for Stalk's elite gala opening night drink menu. We have to lock it down so there's time to order the exotic ingredients we need from Europe and Asia.

I've prepped several new proposals for enticing sips that all pay tribute to Hollywood, such as the *Hotel Caliwood Haunt*, a blackberry and lime infused vanilla whisky poured over a bed of tiny butterscotch beads that promise to fizz for the life of the cocktail. The *Rampion Records Tower* boasts a frozen bed of champagne topped off with layers of pureed blood orange, strawberries, a peach/kiwi blend, and pulverized chilis to add a surprise kick.

I'm in major *impress the boss* mode. Stalk is my ticket to solid employment as long as I don't screw anything up during this final prep period leading to the club's whammo premier gala. One perk of the job is a front row seat for the big night's talent lineup. I'll be in the same room with Justin Time and Zeli from Rampion Records, Chorda and Midas Lear from Golden Pipes, and Rai Cloud and Azure Tempesta from Cloudpath Music. The real kicker is the hitmaking Benedict and the Boulevard Bunch from Caliwood Inc., who recently rebranded back to B & B +3 since vocalist Beatrice Sharpe reappeared after her year-long celebrity vanishing act.

Priceless inspiration for my own musical dreams.

I strum an invisible guitar to calm my nerves. I'm more than willing to tolerate nausea-inducing rocket ship elevators and spoiled celebrity clientele for an even bigger reason than a steady, well-paying job. Once a month, Stalk will audition amateurs to perform as warmup acts for the high-octane talent booked on Tuesday nights. Their professional vs. ammie gimmick is an homage to the now defunct Summer Number One annual singing competition Rampion Records used to host every June.

I'm determined to see my name, *Aurora Herman*, or maybe simply *Aurora* to come off more mysterious, on the club marquis as one of the first warmup singers. It's time to start taking musical risks and jettison the specters of my past that have constantly made me question my self-worth. A buzzing bee of anxiety flits through my chest, asking...

Do you have the courage?

I've always been better at building up others instead of myself.

Before I have a chance to contemplate anxiety's question, the gut-twisting elevator eases to a stop. The frosted tint of its walls becomes transparent as the curved door swishes open.

My step falters at the sight beyond the elevator. When I step out, instead of the plush emerald carpet leading to Stalk's entrance, a shadowy forest greets me.

I turn back, but the damn turbo tube's glass door *whooshes* into place. This elevator is not one to stick your hand in to stop it from closing unless you're willing to bid your fingers farewell. With a *huff*, I growl an over-enunciated voice command into the chrome post next to the elevator.

"Pick up for Stalk."

A cheery automated voice answers. "*Estimated arrival time approximately fifteen minutes. Please stay behind the emerald glitter circle while you await your ride.*"

Ugh. I shouldn't have been so hasty to leave the elevator. This central lift is the only one currently in use to reach the nightclub and other attractions with soft openings in progress. Any day now, the ring of exterior glass elevators with killer views of Hollywood will go operational, leaving this one as an exclusive and much quicker non-stop ride to Stalk.

A flicker of light off the glass cylinder catches my eye. I whip around to stare into the fake forest. Since I'm stuck here, why not snoop for a few minutes?

As soon as I step beneath the outstretched boughs of the closest tree, it begins to glow a faint silver. I press a tentative hand against the bark to sample its strange glittery texture. Twinkling lights like shiny flecks of metal trickle up its trunk until every leaf is outlined in dazzle.

"Wow." The tree looks sculpted from actual silver. It's breathtaking.

Off to my left, a second flicker of light draws my attention, but when I turn, it vanishes.

Strange.

I brave a single step onto the path that leads into the trippy forest next to the shimmering tree. The moment my toe touches the dark road, the ground flashes so brightly, I have to cover my eyes. In seconds, the blaze settles into a lovely, illuminated path.

Is this place ten ways of weird or wonderful?

Underfoot, a meandering trail of diamonds twinkles beneath a sheet of thick glass. The undersides of unlit branches and leaves beyond the tree I brought to life, catch the path's glimmer, giving the illusion they're bobbing in an invisible breeze. The diamond path's brilliance beckons as if saying, "*Take the next step*."

Curiosity prompts me to oblige. As soon as I step fully onto the diamonds, my skin begins to tingle. When shivers bubble along my spine, I quickly yank my foot off the path. Sounds that could be quiet giggles or merely the tinkling of bells erupt from several places deep in the trees.

I rush away from the unlikely woods to the known quantity of the elevator. As soon as I'm no longer within the arms of the forest, the woods fade back into shadows. The tree I touched loses its light, and the diamond path degrades to a grayish blur.

A heaviness in my chest accompanies the dimness. I reapproach the tree and touch it again. Its glow of precious metal elegance returns. I brave a few steps along the path of trapped diamonds. The tingling resumes as before. This time it's more akin to a gentle tickle than a painful zap. As I venture farther, cup-shaped petals of shimmery teal pop on like a string of holiday lights to line the pathway.

This place is delightful. I make out outlines of other dark treasures that could be flowers or willowy trees. Pleasant sensations simmer in my chest, tempting me to awaken more of the forest with my simple touch.

"*Estimated arrival time thirty seconds. Please stay behind the emerald glitter circle while awaiting your ride*."

Curse the elevator's timing. I'm powerfully drawn to linger in this discovery of mine.

Reluctantly, I skip out of the forest. My departure shuts down the woodsy light show. I search the chrome post next to the lift to note the floor so I can return and explore further, but there's no number listed. Odd they haven't finished marking the floors so close to the Emerald Spire complex's official opening. Maybe this attraction isn't going into operation at the get-go. I'll ask my boss, Mr. Cinnabar, about the forest. It would be a blast to be one of the beta testers for such a fantastical attraction especially if its managers are paying for the effort.

"*Rider, you will have twenty seconds to enter the lift.*"

As promised, the elevator door slides open. A heartbeat before I'm sealed inside, a tiny dancing light jumps from tree to tree like a manic firefly. Instead of giggly bells, voices sing in a quirky melody.

"*We'll be waiting, Aurora.*"

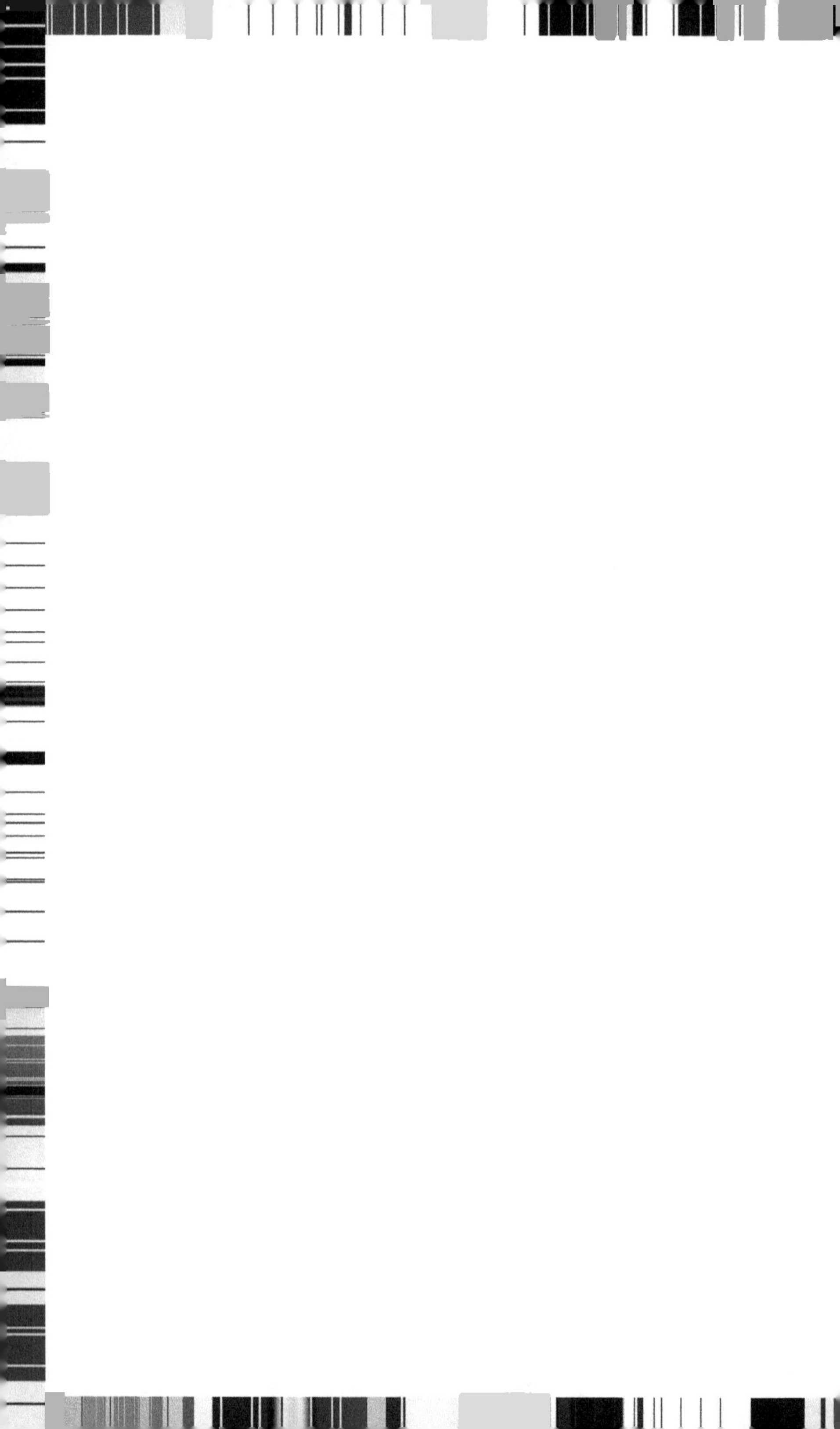

1

MAYHEM

TEK

I WOULD KILL TO HAVE MY WINGS BACK. IN THE AFTERMATH OF *THE Great Salting*, I disobeyed the king and queen to flit through our Griffith Park kingdom on the slopes of the Hollywood hills in search of even the smallest bit of habitable space left in my fairy coterie's domain. My dismay at the total desecration of my homeland from the Brineborn Fairy Coterie's curse scrambled my wits. I flew smack into a branch and dropped spine-first into a pile of salt.

On that fateful day, the toxic white crystals dissolved my glorious wings.

If we had foreseen the repercussions of declining the Brineborn's offer of a royal betrothal would court catastrophe of this magnitude, perhaps the past might have been rewritten. My Folk would still be singing their merry songs from treetops and dancing along the well-trod paths of our rightful home. Oh, to feel the beat of my wings in flight, matching those of my heart.

A curse did wreck the land we praised, one hundred years of torture raised.

Today, I'm summoned for a fresh infraction. I wish I had those wings to flee far from the regal rage tumbling in a multi-colored fog out of the Arborborn Coterie's throne room all the way to the palace's grand entrance. Butterflies that usually dance through the flowers lining the way to their majesty's doorstep, dip behind favorite blooms to avoid the storm surge conjured by the displeased royals. My fluttery friends needn't fear. The combination of King Cinnabar's ire and Queen Citrine's disdain seek a distinct target.

Me.

The twinkling metallic grain of the ornate main steps to the palace carved from the massive trunk of an ancient silverwood tree is a cheery contrast to the brewing anger inside. For the beat of a hummingbird's heart, I glance down the pebbled royal road to the village and consider postponing this confrontation. The sign for Wulfenite's Pub creaks on bronze hinges, catching a lazy sunray. I puff a wistful breath. If only the friendly and gregarious establishment was my destination. I'll have greater need for the pub after my audience with my prickly monarchs.

Jet, the king's muscle-bound personal guard, materializes from the furious fog. He's in formal copper armor, an indicator mine will not be a casual audience with the royals.

"Tek Goodfellow, the king and queen grow weary of waiting." Jet's curt gesture bids me pass into the palace.

"I need no escort, good Captain Jet. On and on I go. See?" I point to my feet and take an exaggerated step to the top of the stairs.

To irritate Jet for my own amusement, I transform into a ball of light to lumen travel. Bopping around in this form is the single mode of fairy transport left to wingless me. I dart into the palace, along the corridor, and through the seam between the throne room's massive doors of braided copper oak studded with shiny lapis lazuli pebbles.

Once inside the royal chamber, I switch to my fairy body and read the room.

Grim.

So very grim.

The goldenrod and bronze veining of the walls doesn't flow in its usual tiny rivulets through marble. Instead, the streaks are frozen in place, stilled by the combined anger of the royals. Every blossom on the climbing hydrangea and loops of wisteria draping the chamber is clamped shut, protecting their cheery colored petals from the impending royal blow.

My king and queen may be locked in an emotional stalemate with one another, but they are excellent at double-teaming a target when occasion calls for it.

Today, I am the occasion.

I give a single bow of the head before approaching the thrones. There's no harm in showing, despite popular opinion, I am capable of respect. The pair sit with rigid posture on their seats woven of branches adorned with a hundred varieties of delicate crystalline leaves. The palette of green-hued decorations on their thrones are treasures I gifted the royals after managing to salvage these reminders of our home before the salt-laden wind tainted everything from earth to treetop in our Griffith Park kingdom. I ready the defense of my generosity on the tip of my tongue to illustrate my loyalty if my audience with the regal duo turns dark.

"Careless fool," snaps Queen Citrine, skipping any formal preamble. Her eyes glow electric lemon instead of their usual sunflower shine as she glares at me. Eschewing the flowy, meandering grace of a fairy queen, her body snaps toward me like a newly released bowstring.

I may have gravely miscalculated the depth of shit I'm in.

"The mortal woman you thoughtlessly drew into our realm will seek the Pristine Forest again. Not one of their race possesses the willpower to be satisfied with a single glance at fairy brilliance." To punctuate the point, every inch of floral trim on Citrine's lavender gown flares with a pop of light to emphasize her rage.

Keeping my gaze lowered, I decide the best plan is first to

pretend to absorb then immediately ignore the flurry of reprimands the king and queen will unleash on me. Who gives a pixie's damn if I used one witless mortal as a plaything and allowed her a glimpse at our fabulous jewel?

My fabulous jewel.

I claim one hundred percent credit for the Pristine Forest's magnificence as both contributing architect and caretaker of the Emerald Spire's design.

I had barely begun to enhance her human sight to perceive our world when I detected enchantment of the wood reflected in her gaze. In that breath of time, I pondered whether she had needed my interference at all to behold the Pristine Forest, then dismissed the thought as folly.

I bow until my chin touches my chest to hide a grin. It had been worth the amusement watching the Aurora woman's befuddlement when she took her first steps into the Spire's fairy dimension. As an unexpected bonus, I was surprisingly touched as the glory of our realm shifted her wariness into wonder. It's not often their dull race interests me, but something about Aurora egged me on to let her explore deeper than good sense allowed. A single glimpse should have been enough to blow her mind and make her flee to the elevator, but she showed no fear at the strangeness of our world.

I will admit my delighted laughter resounding through the fairy forest to catch her attention and the "*We'll be waiting, Aurora*," tease was over the top. No matter, her human rants of silver leaves and diamond pathways on an unmarked floor of the Emerald Spire beanstalk tower will raise questions regarding her sanity, not lead troops of humans to our fairy doorstep.

A spike of magic jerks my chin up, and I'm forced to look straight into the sepia eyes of the king. They've shifted closer to black, a sign his anger teeters on ballistic.

"You took an oath, Tek Goodfellow, to protect this temporary realm of our Arborborn Coterie against any foe," growls the king.

"One human woman is hardly a foe. It was but a fleeting lark she was able to see the forest."

Cinnabar stands to take a menacing step forward. "No doubt your careless magic supplied this ability."

"Most eyes we open with our gifts do not see our world clearly. This woman was an anomaly, nothing more. Without my aid, I doubt she will ever again behold our realm." I do not dare reveal that the merest wisp of my magic had been summoned before the forest was clear to Aurora.

Perplexity as to the true influence of my magic on the human again captures my thoughts until the king lifts his palm, and my feet leave the floor. I rise until I'm eye to eye with his seven feet of unrelenting fairy beefiness. Vain as he is, every inch of hairless, sienna elm-colored skin not covered by his copper chainmail tunic, wears a light sheen of oil. The king literally glistens with power.

I let the magic do his bidding even though with one snap of my fingers, I could stretch, matching his size until we're eye to eye. I've learned from experience it's best to let him flex his kingly muscles when he's pissed.

The king's tone is iron. "Is this latest disobedience born of your tattered intelligence or willful defiance?"

My skin begins to heat. I see reprimand was only a small plate starter. Insults are the main course on today's menu. If they're meant to encourage cowering in addition to my obligatory grovel, it's not happening.

I muster my version of a growl. "Was it my tattered intelligence that bartered effectively for the spell stones?"

A muscle in King Cinnabar's jaw twitches, and he drops his hold on me.

I float to the floor and roll my neck from side to side with exaggerated movements that fill the chamber with a series of loud pops and cracks. The royals never skip a chance to put me in my place for any infraction no matter how minor. They detest being beholden to me for the existence of our current home, especially

Queen Citrine to whom I'm an aphid on a rose. "Was it tattered intelligence, Your Majesties, for me to work in conjunction with the *Verdant Promise* spell stone and create a realm for us in this Emerald Spire?" I sweep an arm to take in our surroundings.

Their stillness tells me I hit a bullseye on the nerve I was aiming for.

Queen Citrine pinches the bridge of her nose. "For nature's sake, Tek. Your purpose was clearly stated. Follow the fiery arrow to the tree it pierces and then speak to the fairy lord within." She narrows her gaze at me. Her disdain distorts the air between us. "Had you followed our royal instructions, we'd enjoy a home within leaf and bough instead of this unnatural ostentatious monstrosity."

I call on willpower not to bark a laugh. Ostentatious might as well be the queen's middle name.

I forgo any semblance of groveling and stand tall. Well, at least my standard five and a half feet. It's a convenient height for slipping in and out of situations unnoticed, and I can easily adjust as needed. "Royal instructions that would have resulted in that reclusive crackpot telling us to fuc..." I catch myself in time before straying into full throttle disrespect with coarse human curses. "... fend for ourselves."

I reach into the pocket of the green and gilded leaf-patterned tunic I wear in our fairy dimension and remove eight shiny multicolored stones, each the size of a forget-me-not's center. Closing my palm, I shake them. Using magic, I amplify the sound of their clatter.

"Enough," roars Cinnabar. He returns to his place at Citrine's side. "You've made your point, Tek Goodfellow."

I slip all but the green half-pebble into my pocket. "Have I?" Lifting the pretty rock up to the bobbing strings of shining flower garlands above us that illuminate the throne room, I smile. The halved stone glows in emerald glory. I tilt it to and fro, its reflection playing across the thrones.

It's a petty move, but I will insist the royals acknowledge what I've done for them, for our coterie.

"Take heed, Tek," says Cinnabar.

Even without his warning, I sensed I may have veered too far into disrespect. I do honor my king and queen, but a man can only take so much of being treated like a naughty child. Still, avoiding the full force of their wrath is the prudent move.

But per my monarchs, I possess tattered intelligence.

The king cocks his head, piercing me with a glare to temper my attitude. "Lest you forget, by creating the Spire heedlessly without consulting us, you forced us into a bargain with unsavory magic-gifted mortals. Without their powers joined to ours, we could not dwell in the human realm undetected."

Damn. He's got me there.

King Cinnabar dips his chin, never taking his gaze from mine as magic pricks my skin with his warning. He voices a proclamation. "The Emerald Spire is both a blessing and a curse for our coterie. Fragile peace with magic humans is ever a risk."

He thrusts the fact of our vulnerability like a spear through my ribs. I'm weary of the constant cut no matter how truthful. Partnership with magic mortals, foul as it may be, is not a new thing. Magic sees magic. Our kind has interlaced with magical humans for eons in too many earthly places to count. This is merely one dealing among thousands over time.

In our present homeless predicament, bargaining with the local magic wielders to alter human perception was essential to explain the existence of a giant beanstalk sprouting over Hollywood Boulevard and to mask its hidden fairy dimension.

"Enough distraction," barks the queen in her command voice. "I demand you acknowledge the seriousness of your lack of judgement with the wandering human, Tek Goodfellow." She narrows her eyes until only a bright lemony glow escapes from between her lids. "A penance is due for your callousness with the mortal."

They do not fool me. My game with the human woman is but the latest excuse to inflict punishment for defying my monarchs and procuring spell stones instead of leasing fairy real estate for our temporary homeland from a nutter they bade me to treat with. I've no doubt the embittered creature would have stuck us in a fetid swamp or barren dust lands for our efforts.

I hold up one finger. "I acknowledge I bartered the fairy eaglet to the limping dryad for her eight spell stones."

Cinnabar throws me a warning glance for my pushback, but I'm intent on having my say.

I hold up two fingers. "I acknowledge you wished the rare bird to go to the certifiably insane and notoriously duplicitous fairy lord who dwells in the spindle tree."

Citrine bares her teeth. "He is a worthy lord with lands that would have served us better than our current situation."

I meet her glare and hold up three fingers. "I acknowledge my unquestioned obedience would have denied us a temporary home in direct proximity to our rightful kingdom."

Cinnabar's gaze darts to his queen then quickly returns to me as he gives his head a subtle shake. He closes his eyes when I raise a fourth finger. The king knows there's no stopping me when I've worked up an impulsive head of steam.

"I acknowledge it is our current proximity that will provide immediate knowledge when the Brineborn Coterie's salt curse laid upon our homeland is no more."

The queen braces her hands on the arms of the throne as if preparing to spring at me when I raise my fifth finger.

"I acknowledge when that glorious day is upon us, we shall be perfectly situated to instantly reclaim our ancestral lands before any wandering fairy coterie overtakes our rightful realm."

I press my open hand to my heart and bow. There's a blur of vibrant yellow, lavender, and copper as the queen lunges for me and the king intercepts her. He hisses words I cannot hear into her ear before the pair retake their thrones.

I belong to a proud and arrogant folk, but a little gratitude here and there wouldn't label them as softies.

Cinnabar grunts, clearly reaching his limit with me. "Nevertheless, Tek Goodfellow, your actions with the mortal woman clarify the necessity for a punitive reminder you are bound to regal rules."

I close my eyes and shake my head. The king and queen are right. My creation of the Emerald Spire doesn't give me blanket amnesty for screwing up. It was never my intention to endanger my folk by giving Aurora a peek at our realm, but I can't argue the validity of the royals decreeing it so.

Facing them with my chin up, I ask. "What humiliation shall I expect?"

I wait, but the rulers of the Arborborn Coterie are silent.

The buzz of a lone honeybee searching for open blooms is the sole sound in the throne room as the royals fix their non-blinking eyes on me in our game of fairy chicken.

Without answering my question, the king fades into a column of gray and black whirlpools while the queen bursts into amber flames. Their faces are last to vanish. Twin expressions of abject disappointment in me are a fist to the gut.

"Goodbye to you too." Typical. They'll force me to stew over every unsavory possibility before announcing my sentence. I let loose a growl of frustration and transform into a ball of scarlet light. The color telegraphs my boiling anger. Despite the velocity limitations of lumen travel, being pissed adds enough speed to smear the air around me.

The king and queen can't stand the truth that cocky Tek Goodfellow created the Emerald Spire. They prefer to take credit for every good and decent act on behalf of our fairy coterie.

I speed out of the palace and through our village. The massive trunks of metallic silverwood trees each housing a fairy shop or eatery, line either side of the pebbled main street. The tumultuous air I create around me knocks over an entire bench of ridiculously gaudy shoes in front of Carnelian the Cobbler's place.

"In trouble again, Tek?" shouts Carnelian, shaking a shoe at me.

"Apologies," I call as I flit away.

A fine fellow would stop and help him with the mess, but I'm too enraged by the royal claw marks through my ego to be of any use. The talented craftsman is one of our most adept at masking his fairy countenance. Carnelian's bauble-heavy shoe designs make him a sought-after craftsman by Santino Fedele, who runs Fedele Costumes on Hollywood Boulevard and several of the studio wardrobe departments. I cross my eyes for luck Carnelian won't report my infraction to the royals.

Seething with frustration at Citrine and Cinnabar for stringing me along instead of being forthright with my punishment sets my mind ablaze, intensifying the blaring red of my luminosity. If I'm already drowning in royal disdain, why not revel in more mischief?

My lips tighten into a mirthless grin. "What shall I do to scorn the two?"

Striking directly at fairy royals is idiocy but indirectly tormenting them promises some satisfaction. I snap my fingers as an idea sparks. King Cinnabar and Queen Citrine masquerade as key human players running Stalk to amuse themselves as well as placing them in a strategic position to keep a close eye on the magic mortals whom they're in league with. I'll pull a prank or two and muddle the final preparations going on for the highly publicized opening gala of Stalk, the trendiest nightclub at the very top of the Emerald Spire. Nothing too damaging, just enough to irritate. Oooo, how my monarchs will squirm when their meticulous plans skitter oh so slightly off the rails.

I zip past the end of the village and head toward one of the handful of gateways between our dimension and the human realm. Beneath me on the Field of a Dozen Shimmers, a group of fairy children whack a buttercup ball the size of a melon with silverwood branches in a game of hurling. I find them an irritating swarm of gnats in need of disruption. I alter my lumen trajectory to dive among them.

A boy spots my approach. "Tek is fire red," the child screams, and they scatter.

Feeling spiteful, I dart straight to the ball and ram it. The golden yellow sphere rockets into the forest bordering the field, effectively ending their game.

"You're an ass, Tek," lisps a sassy young fairy girl no taller than my navel as she shakes a diminutive fist at me. The even smaller girl next to her begins to cry, and my heart shrinks with shame.

Chastened Tek.

I'm every bit the villain they accuse me of being.

In a flash, I retrieve the buttercup ball and toss it to the kids. I slow, hovering above them. "Sorry, little petals. On and on you go."

I am an ass for taking my ire out on littles. After raining some of my signature mayhem over Stalk to properly scratch my anger itch, I'll bring them a basket of lemon ginger tarts from Beryl's Bakery.

Soaring into the woods, I aim for the carved door at the base of a coralberry tree that opens directly to the Stalk nightclub. I shift to human form as I switch realms. I come in too hot and slam out of the shadows straight at the counter behind the bar. Before I can stop myself, I collide with a blender whirring at high speed. It flies off the base, spilling its contents over the white button-down shirt of the female bartender next to it. She jumps backwards as if she can escape the tsunami of bright blue liquid.

I snatch the now empty blender from the floor.

"Dammit," she chokes out. The furious glare of eyes as brilliant emerald as the Spire itself, finds me at her feet. "Who are you?"

I refrain from magicking the stain away and nearly blurt her name.

Aurora.

2

BLENDING

AURORA

"What the hell, Tek?" My fellow cocktail magician, Demetrius Lysand, shouts at the human battering ram who ruined the new recipe I was perfecting. Of course, Mr. Fussy scrambles away before any of the liquid carnage stains his uniform.

I stare at the man kneeling at my feet who extends the blender pitcher up to me like a sacred offering. How have I never seen this Tek person at the club before, but Demetrius knows him? He must be connected with the more businessy aspects of the bar Demie dabbles in with Mr. Cinnabar.

If I'd met this guy, I'd certainly remember that hair. His head is covered in fifty or more tiny braids. As I look closer, it's clear the strands aren't braids at all. They're tightly woven springs the color of the delicious brown bread from my favorite Irish pub on Hollywood Boulevard, with tips the color of a golden sunset. Nearly every corkscrew of hair is draped over the top of his head to cascade down the left side of his face. His skin is a beautiful shade of golden caramel. Exotic is the word my brain lands on for this agent of disaster.

My not-so-crisp and not-so-white anymore uniform shirt and black vest are splattered with sapphire gin stains from neck to waist. Even my black tie with the embroidered Emerald Spire beanstalk crest is doused in a blue wash.

"Wow, just wow," I groan.

"I'm so so so sorry," says Tek. He stands and nearly slips on a square of black-and-green marble floor tile that costs more than I'll make in a lifetime. The guy offers me a weak smile. "Lost my balance."

"Balance my ass," says Demetrius. "You barged in like a crazed lunatic, *errand boy*."

Demetrius's *large and in charge* demeanor is one of the things that initially drew me to him. He offered me an alluring blend of strength and caring, a winning combination in a partner. In my *choose to see the best in people* somewhat rose-colored glasses philosophy, I believed this man may have been the shot at stability I'd been yearning for. It's hard to pinpoint exactly when his strength shifted into control and caring became a smothering possessiveness.

I hate it when Demie mounts his high horse, which is often. I've been tiptoeing around his moods that have increased in direct proportion to our thorny intimacy issues. He's still technically my boyfriend, but instead of our relationship aging like one of the fine wines Stalk offers, it's a watered-down, free casino cocktail.

Demie's dingy blue eyes shoot Tek a familiar look of scorn that sets my teeth on edge—yet another sign I've hit my limit with his entitled rich boy attitude.

A burnt apricot flush bursts across the caramel skin of Tek's face as he glares at Demetrius. Our visitor recovers quickly, tapping a finger against his full bottom lip before pointing at his insulter. "Interesting. The hired help calling me *errand boy*."

"Allow me to educate you, pal. Cocktail magician is up here." Demie stretches his arm above his head. "Being Cinnabar's lackey is…" He lowers his gaze, pretending to search the floor. "Sorry, I can't see that far down."

I'm appalled at Demie's boorishness. Why is he being combative? Previous run-ins with Tek? No matter, it doesn't give Demetrius the right to be a jerk. I'll quiz him later about his history with Tek. Right now, I feel the urge to play peacemaker.

"Let's cool it, okay. I'm sure it was an accident." I reach a hand to help Tek up. "Hi, Tek. I'm Aurora Herman, one of the cocktail magicians here at Stalk." I wince at my use of the lofty title instead of just saying bartender. God, I sound as hoity-toity as Demie.

Instead of taking my hand, Tek continues to hold the pitcher to me. I jerk my chin at the sink. "Put it—"

My gaze locks onto a disaster. "No. No. No." I cry, clocking the decanter of thick honey-brown liquid knocked on its side and cantilevered over the edge of the counter. The last dribble of syrup flows in a sticky river down cabinet fronts to pool on the tiles. "My Westwood Blue and Gold."

I reach for Demie's tennis-toned forearm. "Please tell me I'm wrong, and that wasn't the last of our brandied honey."

He jumps backward before my drippy blue fingers soil his uniform.

"Sorry, Demie."

He sneers at Tek, who attempts to be helpful by rinsing the pitcher in the sink. "You're not wrong, Aurora. There's no more of your fancy honey. I planned to get the okay from Mr. Cinnabar to order a whole case of it if we conquered the cocktail." Demie and his sour expression move to the other side of the bar away from the spillage. "I'm taking my break."

Demetrius grabs a sack out of the bar fridge with our sandwiches from the deli on the New York-themed fifth floor. Demie storms to a table near the place where Stalk's circular windows face the Hollywood hills.

"Fuck all," I say and join Tek at the sink to wash my hands, hoping to hold back frustrated tears. For hours, I've been fine-tuning the Westwood Blue and Gold cocktail, sapphire gin with a descending spiral of the thickened brandied honey suspended through its middle. With a smidge of ice blended into the gin, I finally made it thick enough to hold the golden curlicue intact. If this is truly the last of the bespoke honey we import from the UK, I won't be able to get a new supply in time for Stalk's opening.

I shiver from distress and the aggressive AC assaulting my wet clothing. Tek leans his shoulder against mine, not caring I'm a wet blue mess. There's a welcome tingle of warmth where we touch.

He hands me a towel. "More for me to apologize for, I see. If you're speaking to me, I assume you've figured out I'm Tek. Tek Goodfellow, personal assistant to Mr. Cinnabar and Ms. Citrine."

I accept his offering. "Didn't know they had one." This explains Demie's bluster. Tek has an in with the big bosses, a position that silver-spoon Demetrius Lysand believes he should occupy.

I flash a smile, determined to counterbalance Demie's rudeness. "Happy to meet you, Tek." I sigh louder than I intend. "Despite your unfortunate entrance. I'm surprised our paths haven't crossed sooner."

The man's laugh is almost a giggle. "I'm a behind-the-scenes kind of guy."

I stare at him. The cheerful giggle and his voice seem familiar, but I can't place them. I suppose Tek has one of those sunny personalities that makes you feel you're already acquainted.

"Speaking of which..." Tek leans in to whisper in my ear.

His warm, buttercream frosting scented breath tickles my skin. Someone's been to the Emerald Spire's five-star bakery floor. I could use the comfort of a custard-filled éclair from Jean Pierre's Patisserie right about now.

"I may or may not have access to Cinna—Mr. Cinnabar's private stores."

I swivel my head so quickly, we brush noses. I pull back a little. Our proximity gives me a front row seat to eyes that add to his exotic vibe. His irises are a dark rust color with tiny dandelion-colored sunbursts around his pupils. I'll bet if I asked where he's from, he'd give me the name of an enchanted island in a sun-drenched sea.

We study one another for a moment before Tek swipes a finger through the pool of brandied honey on the counter. His tongue darts out to lick his fingertip. Those strange eyes roll skyward as he murmurs. "Good stuff."

"Rare stuff," I say.

He waggles thick eyebrows. "Rare is not impossible." Tek darts into the storeroom behind the bar as fast as he crashed into the club.

I can't help but smile at the weird ball of energy I've just met. Since I'm already saturated and sticky, I clean up the mess while I mentally flip through my catalogue of other cocktails I need to finesse before we commit them to the menu.

Peeling off my soggy apron, I call across the club. "Demie, I'm going to wardrobe to get a fresh uniform. Will you stick my sandwich in the fridge?"

He waves a hand, never raising his focus from the game on his cell. I lose faith my Reuben has any chance at survival. It feels a sacrilege to sit at one of Stalk's brushed nickel and black granite round tables while lounging in an unspeakably comfortable basil-colored leather chair and eat a pedestrian deli lunch when typical culinary club fare consists of microscopic servings of unpronounceable trendy foods.

Demie has no problem making himself at home in such luxury. A cutting-edge club is my high-end, Beverly Hills-raised boyfriend's element. He's only slumming it here as a cocktail magician for a summer before he starts his MBA in the fall.

My pretentious beau wears fighter pilot sunglasses as he lunches to cut the glare of sun spearing through the nearly 360-degree UV windows set within their gleaming black metal frames. The glass circle curves around the edges of an onyx and green, Italian marble tiled floor so highly polished the brightness of light reflecting off of it should come with a blindness warning. Working here is like being a prop in a design magazine's photo spread.

Stalk is not a daytime place. It was created for the darkest of nights, and patrons so ridiculously famous, they insist on blending anonymously into the club's shadows.

I've seen the reservation lists. I'll be serving the who's who of everyone from Hollywood to the moon.

But not forever. Here in a club that pierces the clouds, I'm going to get my big break. Cocktail magician, Aurora Herman, may make a name here for her libation creations, but my true splash will come when the right people hear me sing. And every one of those potential dream makers will walk through the doors of Stalk.

"Babe, before you go, bring me a sparkling water."

The correct answer is *get your own damn water*, but I take the path of least resistance and grab one of the green bottles from the glass-front refrigerator behind the bar and walk it over. I'll salvage my Reuben and placate Demie. Win-Win.

After tucking my sandwich out of sight on the bottom shelf of the fridge, I take the grand curved staircase of black marble shot through with green veining down one floor to the main entrance of Stalk. The opulent foyer and upstairs bar share the non-windowed wedge of the nightclub's giant circle. I could use the employee back stairs to wardrobe, but once Stalk opens, I won't have the chance to play fancy lady descending. That is until I am a ridiculously famous singer who can always get a reservation at this bazillion-star club.

After donning a fresh uniform, I head back to Stalk and find Tek sitting on the smoky quartz bar swinging his legs. The moment he sees me, the quirky dude jumps down brandishing a large bottle of dark honey-colored liquid aloft like it's the FIFA World Cup.

"You didn't," I say, skipping across the room to him.

"I did," he says, bowing as he hands me the bottle.

"Tek, you are positively magic."

He snorts as I gingerly accept the fluted glass decanter and walk it to the bar.

Tek follows me. "May I watch?"

I set the brandied honey on the counter far from the edge and raise a hand to stop him from getting any closer. "From a distance."

"That's fair," he says and moves away.

I open my mouth to call Demetrius over as I grab the sapphire gin to recreate the cocktail. He's leaning back in a chair, earbuds in place, wavy summer-kissed brown hair mashed against the chairback. "And there rich boy sleeps while I do keep, the design we sought from turning to rot," I grumble.

Tek perks up and dances closer, eyes twinkling. "I love a good rhyme."

His humor is infectious, but Demie won't appreciate Tek's positive energy. "Please forget the stupid rhyme. Hazard of being a songwriter." I dump a cup of crushed ice into the blender and top it off with two jiggers of gin.

As soon as the blender begins to grind, Tek stage-whispers to me, nodding to Demie. "And he's a fool who shuns delight, of inspiration shining bright."

"Nice," I say.

"Your rhyme is fine, but how are you at riddles?"

A corner of my mouth sneaks up. "Love 'em."

He taps a finger against his lips. "Guess my birthday."

"March first."

He laughs in his merry way and shakes his head. "Wait for the riddle."

"Hit me."

Tek's eyes sparkle. "Double the second prime in line. Then skip ahead twice eight plus the starting gate for the date."

I chew my bottom lip. The second prime is three, which doubled makes him a June baby. Skip ahead twice eight is sixteen plus the starting gate. Hmm, does he intend three, the prime, or six, the double for the gate? It must be three since that's technically the start of his riddle.

"June nineteenth."

Tek claps his hands. "Most say April and get the date wrong because—"

I point at him. "They think two is the second prime."

"But one isn't a prime," we say together and then smack a high five.

Tek bounces as if his feet are springs. "You riddle me back."

He's so much fun with more childlike energy than I've seen in any man. I wonder how old he is. Mid-twenties I'd guess even though his face is as soft as a pre-whiskered teen. I wish Demie had more of what appears to come naturally to Tek. It's tempting to fall into a game of rhymes and riddles, but I'm on a deadline. This is the last week to nail down my new drink designs before the opening night menus go to the printer.

I gesture to the blender. "I need time to think of a good one." I pulse the blender one last time and pour the icy blue transparent slush into a small bowl-shaped specialty cocktail glass. I dip the end of a drink syringe into the brandied honey and lightly draw out a thread of thick gooey goodness. Next, I plunge the long hummingbird beak-like extension of the syringe into the bottom of the thickened gin, depressing the plunger while gently lifting at the same time. With well-practiced timing, I twist upwards through the center of the drink to create the perfect spiral. The gold cyclone bobs suspended within the mixture. My heart pounds as I set the syringe on the counter and wait to see if my golden thread will dissipate.

"Yes. Yes. Yes." I give a quick twirl when it stays intact. "A rim of blue sugar with a slice of lemon and the Westwood Blue and Gold is on the menu."

"Now who's magic?" says Tek.

I'm tempted to grab him in a hug of appreciation for saving the day when I'm gathered against a familiar skinny chest. I slap the arm pinning me. "Demie, I've told you, not at work." He doesn't give a damn about losing this job for unprofessional conduct, but the work is vital to me.

Demie dots my cheek with a kiss, reaching over my shoulder to grab the drink. Once he has a hold of the glass, he lets me go and chugs a big gulp. "Needs the sugar."

His knee-jerk thoughtlessness is why I hate sharing shifts with him. Lately, I'm not too keen on sharing much with him, even though from outward appearances we are still a couple.

He offers the drink to Tek. "Want a sip?"

Tek doesn't temper his sour look. "We are not on cocktail-sharing terms, Mr. Lysand."

Here we go again with the friction. "Demie, aren't you working a half day? Go ahead and head out. I'll clean up."

"Trying to get rid of me, babe?"

Oh, if he only knew.

Demie grabs my hips to pull me close again and spins me in his arms. Lips crash into mine as a rich-boy smooth hand threads through my hair. I shove him away.

"Not cool, Demetrius." He's pissing on his territory for Tek's benefit. As if Tek did anything to provoke Demie's jealous streak. Judging from Tek's compact gymnast bod, sailboat weekend Demie wouldn't stand a chance in a real fight between them.

"Come on, babe. I know you dig it when I'm aggressive like the guys you bunked with in crazy town."

Tek's eyebrows shoot up at the mention of the notorious enclave of homeless teens just off Hollywood Boulevard. My hands ball into fists, and I try to keep my cool. "Leave now, Demetrius."

He smirks at me. "I'll save it for later."

I want so badly to tell him to fuck off, but not in front of Tek. Who am I kidding? I lack the gumption to break it off in public...or in private.

I remind myself Demie's been good to me.

Mostly.

His nasty little digs concerning my past are a constant reminder he hasn't quite convinced himself I'm good enough for him. Aurora Herman is still his charity project. Privileged rich boy gallantly falls for the lower-class gal. How very Prince Charming of him.

The disgust in Tek's expression prompts me to blurt, "Consider yourself off the clock where I'm concerned tonight as well, Demetrius."

Demie's suntanned face turns blotchy as he rocks a glare before blasting into the storeroom with such violence, I'm afraid the round frosted-glass window in the door will shatter. Oh, I'll hear about this later.

I lean both elbows on the counter and drop my face into my hands. I'm humiliated. Hopefully Tek will get a clue and leave me alone.

"And you're with the guy because...?"

I take a deep breath and straighten up. "You're not seeing him on his best day."

"And you're apologizing for the guy because...?"

I shake my head. "Look, Tek. I appreciate you bailing me out with the honey, but I don't know you well enough to discuss my personal life. I'm sorry you had to see our argument."

He dances from foot to foot. His buzzing energy isn't as charming as it was a few minutes ago. Can't the guy sit still for a second?

"I can say with certainty your boyfriend is an ass."

So, we're doing this. I should defend Demie, but he was an ass. Probably not for the first time where Tek is concerned if the tension between them is any indication. "I take it you and Demetrius have met before."

Tek circles his eyes. "Yep, with the same less-than-pleasant pleasantries. Let's just say Demie-poo doesn't relish receiving Mr. Cinnabar's instructions through me." He bobbles his head back and forth while jabbing a thumb to his chest. "The errand boy."

Demie-poo? I'd love to see Demetrius's reaction if Tek launched the condescending cut in a face-to-face. Maybe I'll give Tek's barb a whirl during our next argument. Hell, that could be the straw to send Demie-poo running from me. Easier if he leaves the relationship rather than me giving him the boot. Less complicated. If I initiate our end, he could turn stalkery out of spite. Working together would be unbearable.

I pull at a strand of my blond hair, still tinged blue from the gin explosion. "I wasn't very nice either." I stare out the window at the Hollywood Sign. "And I hate being mean." I rub the dull ache in my stomach guaranteed to follow any confrontation.

Tek sidles in next to me and leans an elbow on the bar. "That was you not being nice?" He clicks his tongue. "Ha. Nope, not even close. You were exponentially kinder than the ass deserves."

Tek's fixed stare makes me nervous. "I'm not comfortable talking about Demie behind his back. Let's change the subject."

"Tell me tales of crazy town."

I turn toward the counter and pound my fists onto it. "I can't believe he threw my past at me."

"If it's so, inform the ass such a topic is off-limits."

I whirl to face Tek. "I, I...never mind." Impromptu couples therapy with a stranger is outside my personal boundaries.

"We all have pasts with blows and bruises, Aurora."

Tek's expression is soft, caring. Nothing this sweet has been directed at me for a long time. It punches a hole in my privacy filter. I've got no one to confide in when it comes to the Demie situation. Tek did witness a less-than-flattering portrait of my relationship, the not-so-rosy status of Aurora vs. Demie.

I carefully meet Tek's gaze and see nothing but openness with tinges of kindness around the edges. Squeezing my eyes shut and holding my breath until my temples ache, I make the decision to confide in him since I desperately need to unload. It's not as if the two of them will engage in a dishy chat. "I, I think I'm ready for Demie to become one of those fading bruises, but I'm shit at confrontation."

Everything about his look says that he gets me. I stare back, wanting to believe it. Tek reaches out as if to cup my cheek when a sharp female voice fills the room. "Tek Goodfellow, Ms. Citrine wants you in her office."

Tek stiffens. His spunky demeanor vanishes as he meets my gaze. "On and on I go. I only wish it were not so." With the corners of his lips downcast, he follows Tourmaline, one of Ms. Citrine's willowy, fashion-forward assistants who's clad in a matching dusky pink pencil skirt and blazer. They move with identical graceful gaits through the grand entrance of Stalk, ballet dancers leaving a stage. Is fun-loving Tek mocking Tourmaline's showy exit, or is that truly the way he carries himself when he's not jittering like a puppy?

I stare after them. I wonder why I haven't encountered Tek before if he's Mr. Cinnabar and Ms. Citrine's personal assistant. An errant notion hits me. If he's been around a while, how well does Tek know the Emerald Spire? Is it possible he's aware of the silvery forest installation I stumbled upon? I'm dying to go back and explore the dazzling venue, but damned if I've been able to find the right floor again.

Once they're gone, I pull out my phone and scroll through the Spire's website. Restaurants, theaters, other clubs, indoor and outdoor theme parks including the tallest open-air roller coaster in the world, business and residence floors, and even spaces still available for lease or coming attractions show up on the locator. No teaser for an enchanted woodland feature. I've haunted this metallic beanstalk on every break and even after hours late into the night, but I've never found the forest again.

With a dramatic sigh no one will hear, I dump the cocktail into the sink to make way for my next experiment. Glancing at the carved silver archway that marks Stalk's threshold, I think about Tek and smile. "Goodbye for now, my strange new friend. I'll eagerly wait 'til we rhyme once again."

3

SUMMONS

TEK

Aurora.

Her name swirls through my mind, a woodland breeze gentle enough not to disturb a single leaf.

"Aurora," I whisper to taste it on my lips and capture the warmth rolling over my tongue.

Wistful Tek.

I'd been fascinated by her boldness since the night she ventured into the Pristine Forest. Now that I've interacted with her, my curiosity is on fire.

Am I the only one?

I crank my jaw side to side, pondering Cinnabar's choice to use mortals in coveted positions such as drink designers in a fairy enterprise. Sure, humans are a layer of masking for us, but does Aurora intrigue the king's licentious nature? Thoughts of Cinnabar touching Aurora burn and churn in my gut.

I pray my concern is unfounded.

For once, as annoying as it is, I'm grateful for the rift between the royals, and their edict of sexual restriction. It protects Aurora from becoming a target for the king's lust. The royals forbid one another from taking a member of the opposite sex to their bed while they are at odds. The queen is limited to her ladies and the king his male conquests until the pair of arrogant, stiff-backed monarchs settle their long-standing feud over progeny. Only then will they once again partake in marital carnal pleasure with one another.

I huff. Given their history of energetic fulfillment with partners of either sex, the king and queen clearly feel no urgency to mend their differences. Still, our coterie must endure their majesties' prickly undertones and short tempers inflamed by sexual tension. Thank the seasons they didn't extend the ban to us all.

Away from mortal eyes, Tourmaline, my fairy escort, shifts into a dazzling splash of fuchsia light. Her lumen energy rolls over the thin scars of my missing wings.

"Poor, Tek. Do you miss them?" Before I can answer, her touch sneaks to other parts dear to me as she purrs through a pout. "Do you miss my talents, lover?"

I squirm out of reach and blow a kiss. "You know the queen doesn't share, Tourmaline, and she's already not my biggest fan."

Lights of lilac, mint, and muted cobalt splash around me as the queen's other personal attendants join Tourmaline. One by one they tease my body with sizzle and suggestions.

"Kisses, kisses for my lips," coos Chalcedony's blue glow.

Not to be outdone, Galena's lilac light flares between my thighs, teasing my cock. "Take me to your bower, sweet Tek."

Peridot pops into her human form, lightly grinding her sinuous fairy hips against mine as she reaches around to grab my ass. "Taste my nectar first, naughty knight."

I gently remove my body from Peridot's tempting overture before my perky cock escalates into full arousal from heated recollections of the bed sport I've shared with each of these delightful fairies. All so lovely, so giving. They were my first forays into pleasure, and I fell a little in love with them all. I'll never understand the rigid morality of mortals when there is an endless variety of sweetness in life to be savored.

Not a one of these fickle temptresses ever returned my affections. I suspected they had been sent by my parents as had a similarly strikingly gorgeous trio of fairy men with physiques as chiseled as Cinnabar to school me in the menu of sexual possibilities. I was a willing pupil with each partner but ultimately discovered I preferred to expend my energies with the females of our coterie.

Chalcedony is next to assume her mortal body. Before I skip free, her hand strokes the growing bulge in the front of my jeans. "Dear Tek, is but a knavish lad, born to make poor females mad." I defy any man or woman, mortal or fairy not to combust under the attention of this quartet of ephemeral beauties.

The silk of Chalcedony's sleeve flows under my T-shirt, ticking my skin. "Surely you don't want Queen Citrine to see you in such a state."

The mention of my dick and the queen in the same sentence kills my hard-on. I snap into an amber ball of light to put a stop to their wandering and oh so tempting touches. "Enough, my gorgeous temptations, who instead of your true names I will from this day forward call Hemlock, Foxglove, Nightshade, and Snakeroot as you poison my previous longings for you with impossible promises."

The four fairies titter at my barb.

"We knew better than to fall in love with a flighty fellow such as you, Tektite Goodfellow," says Tourmaline.

"Our crystal hearts are not yours to break," says Peridot in her singsong voice.

I spiral around the group, eager to change the subject. "What does the queen want with me?"

Peridot and Chalcedony discard their human form until we are five colored pinpoints of light moving toward the fairy door artfully carved within a shadowed curve of the silver grand archway, the same passage I barreled through earlier to nearly destroy Aurora's fine work. I glance around to confirm we are out of Aurora's sightline. Her back is to us as she huddles over the bar, focused on her latest drink design.

If Aurora looked up now, she'd assume we were nothing more than delicate reflections against silver in the day's fading light. To my surprise, the fairy quartet bypasses the door to our dimension and leads me down the hallway that houses Stalk's executive offices.

Odd. Fairy business is traditionally conducted in our realm.

The four fairy lights bob in front of Cinnabar's office. From behind the closed door, Queen Citrine's voice rips through the air. Given her furious tone, my escorts retreat in streaks of light. I wish I could do the same. The sight of me disgusts the queen on a good day. When she's in a mood, my life becomes a dank pit of misery.

"A mortal, Cinnabar. How dare you?"

My heart degrades to a pulpy mess. Does the queen refer to Aurora, pecking at my suspicions about Cinnabar's motivation to hire her? I like my new friend and cannot stomach her falling victim to the king's lust.

A disheveled and confused Captain Jet lookalike squeezes into the hallway, suit coat draped over his arm. My narcissistic king prefers men wrought from the same mold as himself, echoing the brawn and stamina factors of his make-up, taking self-love to a new level. With relief, I reach around the latest royal conquest to close the door.

I doubt I'll ever truly understand my king's amorous proclivities. Cinnabar is clever and wily. Surely, he must desire bedmates with brains as well. Then again, the intellectual bond of his relationship with the queen is as fertile as ever. Perhaps their constant bickering sates his mind while his chosen treats only serve to quench his lust.

The disoriented plaything stares at me. Feeling charitable, I snap my fingers in his face. "Quitting time. You've worked all day as well as played and now it's time to go away. Once off you go, you will not know the happenstance this day did sow."

He dons his jacket. I'm nothing but air to him as he picks his way down the hall.

On and on I go. My attention returns to the battle behind the door. When I step inside, Queen Citrine lifts a finger topped with a deadly sharp nail, making it clear I'm not to interrupt. The king tucks in his shirt and moves to buckle his pants as she rakes a claw-like hand in the direction of his genitals.

"I am adding an addendum to our agreement. Take no mortals be they man or woman to your bower, Cinnabar."

"Ah, then I have not broken your addendum." He fans an arm over his office. "For this is not my bower." He snatches her hand and presses it to his bare chest. "Never fear, my heart beats only for you, light of my darkest night." Cinnabar's other hand slides up her neck into her hair. He eases her head back and slowly lowers his mouth to hers. In the breath before a kiss, he growls, "No addendum. If they possess a cock, they're dessert wherever I choose to partake."

When she bites his lower lip, they literally fly apart.

Queen Citrine plants her palms on the king's desk. With straight arms, she leans toward him, rage flaring in her eyes. Their sexual tension ignites flicks and flares of stinging white light around the room. One hits my arm, and I cry out from the burn. If they would just fuck each other and make up, life in the coterie would be much easier. At least in my case.

I saunter to one of the chairs facing the desk. "Shall I come back later?" I flip through an imaginary datebook. "I believe I'm free at moonset."

Queen Citrine stands tall in regal glory, glaring down her nose at me while the king buttons his shirt. He settles into the high-backed leather chair behind his desk as she stalks toward me. "We have decided upon your punishment for luring the mortal woman into the Pristine Forest."

"Bring it on," I say, fully aware the royals detest casual mortal speak.

The queen eyes me with the same disgust she'd spare on an overcooked acorn pie. "If you desire to renew our approval, you will acquiesce to spend one of those precious spell stones you hoard like a stunted tree stump troll."

Muscles beneath my missing wing scars tense. The fact that the spell stones only answer to me is the one thorn in Citrine's side more irksome to her than my existence. The queen doesn't hide her satisfaction in insisting I spend one as my punishment.

I clutch the stones in my pocket to protect them. "I assume you have one in mind."

Her eyes shift between lemon and sunflower, telling me she attempts to control her anger and is losing the battle. "*Pearl Tear*," she says.

The corners of her mouth rise at my wide-eyed reluctance to part with a spell stone until she's fully smiling at the cleverness of her scheme.

Cinnabar steeples his fingers. "We need its powers of obfuscation to cloak our magic mortal associates when they enter Stalk."

Citrine purses her lips. "The sorcerer and his witches wish to be in attendance during the nightclub's soft openings in the run-up to our premier. A powerplay to flaunt the belief that they are our equals." She mock spits on the floor. "Imbecilic peons."

The king sneers, leveling his gaze at me. "And there will be too many people circulating through the club between now and then for the vermin to come out of their hole undetected."

"I understand the strategy of hiding your unfortunate bedfellows." I switch my focus from one royal to the other. "But if I shield the magic mortals from view, you won't know what they're up to."

The monarchs wear matching predatory grins. "Ah, but you

will, keeper of the spell stones," says the queen. "Is it not true you hold sway over your baubles?"

Their ask becomes clear. "So, my punishment is to be a jolly game of hide and spy."

Cinnabar smacks his hands on the desk. "Yes, master of mist and mischief. This is a gentle punishment, Tek Goodfellow. Surely you do not object to tricks well known to afford you sport."

The queen wrings her hands. "We must hear every plot and dealing that passes between the vile quartet who call themselves Dark Vinyl Artists."

I pop my lips. "Trust issues from the pair of you? How unexpected."

They both glare at my sarcasm. Citrine is first to speak. "Have you not yet learned in your multitude of sun circles trust between fairy and magic mortals is a rapid road to doom?"

Cornered Tek.

I sense arrows from her quiver of insults about to be loosed in my direction, so I suppress my urge to be an ass. "I will be your spy, but it cannot compromise my duties to tend to the well-being of the Emerald Spire." Being the keeper of the spell stones and co-architect with magic in the creation of our beanstalk comes with responsibilities.

Cinnabar pins me with a stare. "Are you not capable of serving both your monarchs and gardening well the Spire?"

Damn him. As thorough a trickster as I am, he plays on my desire to be of value to both my king and queen as well as nurturing our temporary home.

Citrine crosses her arms. "Well, Tek Goodfellow? Will you surrender the *Pearl Tear* and complete the task put before you as your penance?"

Each gift from the limping dryad I expend tips the power balance in the royal's favor as I lose clout spent stone by spent stone. I scrape teeth over my bottom lip. The loss of one more still throws the advantage my way.

I whistle and give a curt nod. This task offers a bit of fun, and my penance could be infinitely worse. Confinement, banishment from Stalk and therefore the intriguing Aurora, or restrictions on lumen travel would hold more bite. Surely there's sport to be had in this punishment. I shall look for opportunities to wreak havoc on the magic mortals even as I steal knowledge of their machinations. I bow. "Yes, majesties. I accept my sentence."

Cinnabar stands, grabbing his suit jacket from a rack in the corner. "Enchant the table to the left of the main archway so it appears empty to all but fairy eyes. We shall make certain no one but the magic mortals inhabit that table." He pins me with a serious stare. "Tek, guard well their blindness where you are concerned. They must be unaware of your presence." The king shrugs into his jacket. "With this task, you serve your king and queen with honor."

The king proffers his arm, and the queen accepts it. Instead of dismissing me, they leave without a backward glance as if I'm in any doubt how little I matter to either of them. My fairy hearing picks up the *snick* as they pass through one of the doors, leaving the human dimension for our fairy one.

I cross behind the desk and sit on Cinnabar's mortal leather throne. I've got plenty of time to kill before Aurora leaves for the night, and I attend to the business of enchanting the magic mortal's table. I'm tempted to return to Stalk and watch her work. I'm drawn to her complexity. How can she be full of wit yet fall into witlessness in the company of Demetrius the lout? What is his hold on her I cannot see?

Oh, nature's justice, does she love him?

Love tolerates much. Proof of this is the bond between my king and queen that does not shatter despite the constant skirmishes they wage against one another.

It sickens me to dwell on the image of Aurora in the arms of Demie the fool. I spin in the chair to face the window. One of the massive leaves of the Spire glitters in the setting sun. If the mortals could see the living beauty of this beanstalk instead of its metallic disguise, their hearts would burst with wonder. That is why it is my duty to keep its true nature hidden from their fragile understanding. I created the Emerald Spire, and I owe it to my people to guarantee it continues to flourish until we can return to our homeland a hundred years from now.

I always feel at my best when showering nurturing magic over every leaf and vein of the Spire to keep our hidden realm thriving. Conquering the pull to seek Aurora, I move to the open office window. In a blink, I am only light, leaping into the dusk.

4

AFTER HOURS

TEK

I FINISH CROONING MY FAIRY SONG OF STRENGTH AND SUSTAINABILITY over every inch of the Emerald Spire from ground to cloud.

Peaceful Tek.

Tending the beanstalk always restores my sense of wonder and joy. If she could, Queen Citrine would strip me of the responsibility and hand it off to one of her favorites to rob me of this bliss. I smirk with the satisfaction of knowing as long as the Spire is our home, the queen is beholden to me.

Standing atop the highest tapered curl of its main stalk, I stare down at my magical handiwork. Below me a shimmering haze of gold encompasses the Spire. Within the elegant shroud, myriad bursts of starlight erupt around leaf and stem to generate a layer of ethereal brilliance. Some are the pinpoints of nurturing magic I scattered between the branches while other flashes in the nimbus are my fairy brethren lumen traveling throughout our kingdom.

I pity weak human vision that prevents mortals from reveling in the Spire's magnificence. They only see a gargantuan tower of reflective green steel fashioned after a legendary human fairytale beanstalk.

I buried the limping dryad's magic deep within the earth at the bottom of an abandoned construction site on Hollywood Boulevard. Speaking the incantation to awaken half the powerful stone enchanted our marvelous home into existence. Had I summoned its full force, all of Hollywood would have been lost beneath a tangle of root and branch. Fairy magic laid bare.

The *Verdant Promise* spell stone partnered with my vision to conjure curvatures and trailing tendrils to fully capture the authentic flow of organic flora. Magic is after all, a master of creativity.

Moonlight paints a silver-blue streak along one side of the Spire. I pull the white *Pearl Tear* spell stone from my pocket. "Time for some fun, my friend."

When my gardening is finished, I fly from the pinnacle of the Spire down to a leaf the size of a soccer pitch whose tip reaches toward ocean. I long to linger here in this place of refuge where I come to plan mischief or escape the bitter scrutiny of the queen, but there's no time to spare. Moving to the petiole, where leaf cleaves to branch, I approach the private doorway I created between the fairy and human realms. As I prepare to pass into mortal territory, my tunic reassembles into jeans and my favorite T-shirt.

The fairy door empties me into the end of the hallway outside Cinnabar's office. Traipsing its length toward Stalk, I pass a series of fairy enchanted doors leading to restricted suites the royals set aside for their private guests. I nearly trip on a burst of magic escaping from beneath the one closest to the club.

They're in there—the magic mortals. Unable to resist, I lay an ear to the curved top door that leaks magic.

"Ach." I leap away with a cry and grab my suddenly bloated, throbbing ear. There is a spell afoot. One preventing access to the dealings within.

I whisper-hiss at the carving of a fully flourishing grapevine carved into the door. "A bite and sting will not prevent determined souls to circumvent secrets hiding through the portals of high-handed magic mortals."

I grow new appreciation for my duty to spy on these presumptuous necessary evil humans we're beholden to. I'm tempted to add my own mischievous magic to the powers of the *Pearl Tear*. It would be gratifying to see the sorcerer and his witches weep tears of sharp-edged glass to nick their pretty faces whenever they cross the barrier of the spell stone's influence. I abandon the notion, imagining the displeasure such a prank would raise in my king and queen once the mortal spellcasters cried *foul play*.

The royals are most adamant we do not overtly appear to taint the partnership between our fairy coterie and the magic mortals. For the Emerald Spire to thrive, our unfortunate symbiosis must endure to keep uninvited eyes averted from our realm.

My ear returns to normal size as I skip along, craving the peaceful stillness of an empty Stalk. Soon the club will be abuzz with patrons enjoying the uninterrupted starlight streaming through the circle of windows.

I cross beneath the entrance arch when I hear a female voice purring the first notes of a melody. Which one of Citrine's favorites waits to torment me, or worse, summon me once again into the presence of the queen. I've had my fill of royalty today.

The voice cuts off, and I freeze, hoping the lovely lady didn't hear my approach. Then again, a quick tryst with no emotions involved could ease a bit of my pent-up frustration with the monarchs. Naw, the amorous fairy would accept my cock then spill every detail of our liaison to the queen, who would in turn find a way to ridicule me. Citrine never bypasses the chance for a Tek-taunt.

I'll fly back to my leaf then return when the space is fairy free. I close my eyes, preparing to snap into lumen travel, when the blare of a media announcement sounds from the club.

"Do you have what it takes to be Saturday's Star?"

Using incomparable stealth, I peep into the club. Aurora leans on the counter halfway down the bar. She stares up at the flatscreen that's poised above rows of liquor bottles backlit by the imitation of a starfield enhanced by fairy magic to set the spirits within aglow.

Why is she still here? Demie's comment about Aurora's history of living on the streets comes loping back to me. Is she slumming at the club? Sleeping in the changing room?

Andres Andrews, the blond California beach body MC of Golden Pipes Record's weekly singing competition show, *Saturday's Star*, crooks a finger at the viewers. Midas Lear, president of the label, concocted the copycat program to compete with Rampion Records' *Weekly Number One* vocal smackdown.

I pinch my lips to forestall a giggle, savoring the potential for mischief when musical mucky mucks from top record labels will gather here for Stalk's high-profile opening. I imagine the fun in plaguing them with strategically placed inappropriate invisible touches to be credited to a nearby patron. Reactions to under the table brushes of a fingertip along thighs or hot breath on the back of a neck will prove amusing.

Puckish Tek.

Perhaps sprinkling a little magic in cocktails to prompt out-of-character actions would give me a giggle or two or ten. I ditch the impulse. Messing with Aurora's creations might reflect badly on her. That is something I refuse to do.

Kudos to Cinnabar for weaving surreptitious fairy bargains to lure the top brass competitors from Rampion, Golden Pipes, Tempest Tunes, and Caliwood Inc. to invest in Stalk. My king created a perfect pipeline to book top name acts at our cozy little nightclub here in the sky. If I had any sense, which is debatable by many, I would devote more time learning bargaining savvy from Cinnabar. Lessons for later. At present, I'm keener to know what Aurora is up to.

"Our top three extraordinary talents, whom you know well from this

season's Saturday's Star, will perform as the warmup acts for Stalk's chartbusting headliners: Zeli and Justin Time, Rai Cloud, and B & B + 3 to name a few who are set to dazzle at the club's extravagant grand opening gala."

I try to read Aurora's expression to see where her musical fangirl proclivities lie. The woman gives nothing away. Will she go full groupie for Benedict Boyd or Rai Cloud? My nose scrunches at the thought of Aurora shaking anything for those rockers.

"Strap in, my friends, 'cause here comes the catch. There is still one spot waiting to be filled for the musical warmup team."

Andres circles his lips into an exaggerated O and slaps the sides of his face.

"Amazing, right? But you already knew that. I'm ready to spill the tea on how you, yes you, could be the final singer to join the team. Saturday's Star and Citrine Fairley, the talent coordinator for Stalk, will join forces to hold an open mic night during one of the club's soft openings to see who is worthy of the coveted spot."

Another power play from my queen. The woman thrives on controlling others.

Andres waggles a finger at the camera.

"No, no, I'm not talking about slumming it in a line for hours under a blazing Hollywood sun to audition like the days of the old Rampion Summer Number One. This is much more civilized. You'll submit footage convincing us to swoon over your performance. Our Saturday's Star talent team will screen and choose finalists to advance to the open mic night where Ms. Fairley and our people will bestow the honor on the worthiest performer. Jump to the link on our website for all the requirements and instructions on how to get your voice heard."

I duck behind the arch as Aurora points the remote at the flatscreen and powers it off. Ah, she's a *Saturday's Star* addict. Blending into the shadows, I wait for her to head down the grand stairway so I can use *Pearl Tear* to cloak the table.

She doesn't. Leaf rot, it's past nine o'clock. Once the club opens, this will be prime time, but during the prep period she's on-site after hours. I hate the thought of Aurora having no home and secretly living here in the Spire. My lumen glow wavers around me in dolorous blue on her behalf.

I'm on the verge of bursting in on her when a mechanical rumble begins low enough only fairy hearing could detect it. What is the woman up to?

I rub my recently blighted ear. Curiosity is my worst vice. I tiptoe to the arch and peer inside. The circular stage in the center of Stalk rotates in leisurely revolutions. It's designed to give the occupants of every table an equal chance to come face-to-face with the performer.

To my surprise, Aurora leans into an empty mic stand, lips nearly touching the place where the microphone would be. Her eyes are closed as she slowly raises and lowers her arms as if they're floating. The purr I heard earlier flows from her lips, meandering through the air straight to my core. Her contented note becomes a sustained growl then she breaks into song.

"I follow you to shadow,
Seeking promises you gave.
But once the light had vanished,
Lost truths my heart did crave.
The currency you bartered,
To crush my loyal soul,
Deceived a willing spirit,
A diamond turned to coal.

Love me once.
Love me twice.
Love 'til stars arise.
I long to see sweet yearning,
Reflected in your eyes."

This is a new-to-me Aurora, a sensual Aurora, laying her emotions bare. This is an Aurora I cannot look away from.

"Out I cry to powers blind,
To overturn deceit...

Aurora's song continues to bathe the room in sorrow. Not a melancholy, but rather a sultry sound that makes me pity whatever idiot inspired the song.

Love me once.
Love me twice.
Love 'til stars arise.
I long to see sweet yearning,
Reflected in your eyes."

Does she sing of Demetrius or some other imbecile who was blind to her value?

Blind to her value.

The thought rocks me. I know this decrepit state all too well. I am necessary yet valueless to my king and queen. Is that how the bastard Demetrius causes Aurora to feel? I'll boil the blood in every vein until he cries for mercy. This newborn connection between Aurora and me calls to my spirit. I take one step, then two, closer to her. I thrum with the urge to take Aurora in my arms and confess every weakness. Strange surety that she would understand them all seizes my soul.

What is this mortal doing to me?

I still my skittish thoughts long enough to land on a single question. Was Aurora watching *Saturday's Star* as a fan or for a different purpose? Perhaps she dreams of being chosen for the contest. What else could a woman singing to an empty club want but fame?

Thankfully, the turntable's rotation positions her away from me.

I steal a moment to recover my wits before I stroll into the club proper. "Well, if that isn't the most depressing song I've ever heard."

Aurora's head whips around. She falls out of sync with the turntable and nearly stumbles.

"Tek. What are you doing here?"

I execute a spin and point to her. "Turn your question right around."

She looks flustered as she steps onto the control to stop the rotating stage. "The song is not depressing. It's soul-searching, full of longing."

I force myself to walk slowly toward her. "Hmm, maybe the lyrics, but your delivery says drive a stick in my eye and pour me a drink."

"Exactly. You clearly don't understand what a torch song is."

"Oh, but I do." I step onto the stage. "It's about wanting..." Another pair of steps brings me so close to Aurora, we're nearly touching. With a feather-light caress, I glide my fingers up her arm.

Aurora's breath catches, but she doesn't move away.

My gaze falls to her slightly pursed lips, plump and inviting. "... what you can't have."

Heat leaks from her body, raising a sensual shell around us.

"Dare me to want you through the lyrics, Aurora." I won't confess she's already achieved that. I swallow hard and drop my hand. "When you sing your torch song, turn it on its head. Don't just whine over a tool who dumped you. Make every man and woman in the audience believe your former lover is a fool for losing you. Invite them all to your bed to prove it."

Aurora doesn't blink, hanging on my every word.

"Stoke fires of yearning and the longing to touch." I twist a strand of her hair, the color of honey mixed with sunlight, around my finger and brush her cheek softly with my knuckle. Aurora sips a breath but does not discourage me. I reach to free another tendril from her bun on the opposite side of her lovely face to match the first freed lock.

With no attempt to hide the husky desire in my voice, I continue. “Encourage their lust to thirst for the delicate silk of your skin.” I trail a fingertip along her jaw, under her chin, and down the front of her throat, reveling in the way her blush follows the trail. A sizzle springs along my finger then straight to my groin. My breathing becomes heavier as I fall prey to my own seduction.

“A torch song should be exquisite torture for that which is forbidden.” Sealing my gaze to hers, I slide my finger from the hollow of her throat to the heated skin at the top of her chest. Hooking my touch just inside the collar of her shirt, I ease her nearer but not close enough for her to feel my robust cock knock as the randy fellow pleads to join the game.

I breathe hot breath across her face with my next words. “Send your audience to their knees begging.” I’m already there. At the slightest provocation, I’ll drop down in front of her and tuck my head beneath her dress.

She exhales, and her deliciously balmy breeze slides across my lips. They tingle, encouraging me to capture that sweet, puckered mouth with my own. Fairy allure gives me an advantage to attract, but this woman oozes her own enticement. I hunger for her kiss.

Then Aurora blinks, taking a step back to wipe away our almost-moment and waves a dismissive hand at me. “I don’t need your critique.”

I’m stunned. How did she resist? Was hesitation my downfall? The failure must be mine. No mortal can escape a fairy seduction. I cover my bewilderment by leaping off the turntable and take a gamble. “Oh, but you do if you want to catch Citrine’s eye for the warmup spot.”

She steps off the stage across from me. With each step I take toward her, she counters with one of her own to maintain distance between us. We stalk around the circle.

“I’m fully confident in my talent, thank you very much.”

I lock my gaze to hers. “I’m not talking about talent. It’s your presentation that comes off too nice-girl.”

Aurora delivers a potent evil eye. "I am nice."

"You need to be…" I bust out my smokiest bedroom face and dip a shoulder in her direction. "Passionate." The tip of my tongue slowly strokes my bottom lip.

"Nice girls can be passionate." She fusses with a strand of golden hair that's fallen loose.

I swap smoky for unabashed lust as Aurora's single gesture starts my body pulsing with want. If she'd have me, I'd show her what a fairy deems as passion and take her right here center stage. I could make her beg for me. In my pocket, the *Fire Melon* spell stone heats beneath each stroke of my thumb. If I use it, she will want me, lust for me, trade her every need for mine. I rip my hand from my pocket to break contact with the stone.

Not Aurora. No, no, not so. I won't use a spell on her. Too easy. Winning her on mortal terms is the more entertaining path.

I justify the connection I feel with her this night as fate's fanciful tease. I shall rise to its challenge. My growing arousal approves of the promised prize.

I do so love a game.

This can be nothing more. Aurora is certainly not a viable option in my life. My gut tells me this woman could never be happy with one whose nature is as fickle as a fairy. We are merely to be destiny's folly—a game. Still, a very pleasant endeavor. One I am determined to win without using fairy wiles. Victory shall be to gain Aurora's amorous attentions without spell stone or magic.

She stares at me in silence, waiting for my reply to her pronouncement.

My lips quirk up as I ready my retort, the first move of the game. "Then let's show everyone privy to your torch song just how *nice* you can be."

Aurora raises a brow.

"Let me coach you."

5

COACH

AURORA

I GAPE AT TEK. "*YOU* COACH *ME*?"

"Advise, direct, refine, all of it."

The idea is nuts. Who is this guy? My skin still burns from our close contact. His description of what a torch song should be, and his fingertip dipping dangerously close to my breasts lit a fire in my belly. He intrigues me for sure, but tingles along the nape of my neck advise caution.

"Care to share your musical qualifications, Tek?"

He retreats to a chair, leans back, and crosses a bare ankle over his jean-clad knee. "I know my way around a song."

I study him. Maybe he's not full of crap. He is Ms. Citrine's assistant as well as Mr. Cinnabar's. Perhaps part of his duty is to work with talent.

I nod at the stage. "Sing for me."

Tek's head wobbles and his collection of corkscrew strands dance. "I'm not the starving artist looking for a big break."

Arrogant ass. "Who says I'm starving? This job pays damn well."

He faces me, elbows to knees, and leans forward. "Then why are you living here in the Spire?"

An arrogant assuming ass. "Who said I live here?"

"Well, do you?"

I huff. "Of course not."

"Do you live with Demetrius?"

"Oh, hell no." I smirk. "He wishes."

Tek tilts his head as if confused, never taking his gaze from me. "Where do you live?"

I shake my head. "You're avoiding the issue. Sing for me, Tek. Do you really know your way around a song, or are you full of shit?"

"If you want a shot at being in the talent lineup, Aurora, let Citrine in on your dream." In the next instant, he gives a sudden jolt and shakes his head. "No, no, not so. I reclaim my words. It is wiser to avoid giving her information to leverage against you. Citrine is unpredictable, a mercurial being with thorns."

Damn, this guy is incapable of talking in a straight line. There's clearly no filter between his brain and mouth. Is there bad blood between Tek and Ms. Citrine? Who hasn't this guy pissed off?

Not me.

Not yet.

I suppress a snort. Unless I count our first meeting when he destroyed my drink design and doused me in sapphire gin.

I drop into the padded leather chair next to him. He wants to help me. I'll give him credit for that, but all the prying...

"Let's stay on topic. Why do you want to help me, Tek?"

He ponders the question before reaching for my hand. "Your voice is the loveliest I've heard in countless sun circles."

My hand slides into his, a perfect fit, so unlike the way Demie's paw feels as if it's caging mine. We sit for a moment, holding hands and watching one another. "Sun circles?"

"Years," he says quickly, looking a little flustered. "I'm being poetic."

I release his hand. "Thank you for the compliment, but I'm not going to take you on as a coach because of your clear talent for sweet-talking. Sing, Tek, and then we'll chat." Rising from the chair, I gesture to the stage.

Tek slaps both hands on his knees and then stands. In a single leap, he's center stage. "Any requests?"

"Surprise me." I cross my arms and perch on the edge of a table, preparing to call his bluff. This should be interesting.

Tek clears his throat then tugs down his oddly shiny gold T-shirt where it's ridden up to expose a thin strip of rich dark skin. His gaze finds mine and he begins to sing.

From his first note, I swear the floor disappears and is replaced with stardust. Glittering lights from outside pierce window glass and streak across the club. My body seems to float, illuminated by sparkles as Tek sings. His voice is sweeter than the brandied honey he brought me earlier. I close my eyes, forbidding other senses to intrude upon the delicate sensation of his voice weaving through me. How can this man's song caress the depths of my spirit? I never want him to stop singing and cause his essence of lightness and joy to disappear. If magic was real, it would be Tek's voice.

To my disappointment, the song does end. Stalk may be silent, but I continue to sway, still captured by the melody of Tek's song.

"Aurora?" His hand lightly grasps my elbow.

"Oh, wow." I stare into his reddish-brown eyes with their unusual citrus flare. "That was..." I search for a word to do justice to the beauty of his song. None worthy enough come to mind. "Out of body."

Tek smirks. "Good enough to earn me the coach job?"

I lay my hands on his chest. "Mister, if you can teach me how to affect an audience anywhere close to what you just did to me, you're in."

We pause in each other's touch. It's gentle and...intimate.

With a warm smile, I move away. I don't want to hurt his feelings or send false signals. Even though I'm ready for an exit strategy in my relationship, I am still officially with Demetrius. These break-up things must be done in the right order—an ending before a new beginning. I pat my cheeks to return to a rational mind.

I narrow my gaze at Tek. "Why aren't you auditioning for the warmup slot? No one is going to come close to your...your..." I want to say magic, but I don't want to open myself up to ridicule.

Tek snorts. "As if Cit—Ms. Citrine would let me near the stage."

The urge I felt earlier to get to know him better resurfaces with a jolt. There are a million questions I want to ask him about his singing, his life, why he's here. It's only fair for me to answer some of his. "I rent a room in a house near Griffith Park," I blurt. "Where do you live?"

He leans to one side then the other as if the movement helps him decide what to say. "That is a hard question to pair with an honest yet fulfilling response."

Am I off my nut to be attracted to this vague, flighty guy? I humph. Anyone who sings like Tek, no matter their secrets, can definitely elevate my performance. I think back on my days living in Rand Diggs's dormitory for youths he rescued from the street. It's hard for me to revisit that period of time before I transitioned from despair to hope. Does Tek share a similar challenge?

I go for a change of subject. "You work for both Ms. Citrine and Mr. Cinnabar, right? Do you think Mr. Cinnabar would be cool with a cocktail magician going for the open mic slot? Maybe it's weird to even mention it and..." I pull the clip from my bun, letting my hair fall free. "I'm not entirely comfortable around him." An errant thought sends a not-unpleasant shockwave through me.

But I'm quite comfortable around Tek.

I use the curtain of my loose hair to hide the surprise on my face. This man blew into my life like a cyclone today, yet his presence attracts me more than Demie's ever did.

"How so, how so?" asks Tek in the singsong cadence that often crops up in his speech. I wonder if the habit is part of his musical identity.

Out of the corner of my eye, I catch him reaching a hand toward the hair falling across my shoulders. He quickly retracts the movement before making contact. "Sorry. Your hair looks wonderfully soft." He smiles sheepishly when I frown at him. "Cinnabar troubles you?"

I debate for a moment whether I should come clean about my history with Stalk's boss. Tek's non-judgey, quizzical expression feels like a safe space. "Confidentially…" I twirl my hand at him.

He copies the hand twirl. "Of course."

I take a deep breath and decide to trust him. "He came on to me at my previous job. I was a server in a private room at Cityscape. Do you know it?"

He wiggles more than nods his head. "The snooty place next to the observatory on Mount Hollywood."

We settle into chairs near the stage. "That's the one." I stare past Tek's shoulder. "Every time I passed, he'd find an excuse to touch me and ask personal questions. When I deflected, he changed the topic to the specialty cocktails I improvised for everyone in his group."

I peek at Tek to find his smooth caramel skin flushed with a plum tint.

I bite my lip as the rest of that evening comes flooding back. "He lingered after his party left, making sure I saw him tuck a hundred-dollar tip under the edge of his dessert plate. Before I knew what was happening, his lips brushed my ear while a hand found my ass." I debate for a hot second to tell Tek everything then forge on. "He invited me to join him and continue *serving* him. His pervy suggestion was the final straw. I told him to fuck off and keep his hundred bucks."

Tek's eyes widen. "You did?"

I shrug. "Nice girls are capable of dealing with assholes."

Tek chuckles.

"When I attempted to storm away, Mr. Cinnabar offered me the cocktail magician gig here at Stalk and promised to keep his hands to himself."

Tek crosses his arms. "It was a bluff and a test. The boss wanted to see how you dealt with assholes. He never intended to sleep with you."

"Should I be insulted?"

He laughs. "Not at all. His tastes run to the male flavor."

"Huh." I twist my lips. "I got the impression he was into Ms. Citrine." I should shut up. It's not right to dish about our mutual employers. "Sorry, I didn't mean to cross a line."

Tek waves me off. "They're a complicated duo."

I glance at my watch. Shit, I've got to get going. The show at the Boulevard Theater will be letting out soon. I need to claim my territory on the sidewalk near the entrance before the final curtain. I practically jump to my feet. "So, Tek. If we give the coaching thing a go, how will it work?"

"We'll meet at your place."

I snort. "That'd give Demetrius an aneurism. Sorry, my room is a no go. The people I rent from have noise rules. What about your place?"

Tek scrunches his brows and fixates on Demie instead of our coaching logistics. "You aren't going to call it quits with Demetrius? Didn't you tell me this afternoon it was time to shed him?"

I drop my head back. I certainly spilled my guts to Tek before we'd even known each other a single day. "I, I'm working on it."

"Is his lovemaking not fulfilling?"

I glare at him. "Jeez, do you have any filters? That is none of your business."

He shrugs. "If the sex is bad, it's a legitimate reason to end things and damn the fallout."

"I'm not discussing this with you."

Tek clearly isn't listening to my protests. His gaze darts around the room. "From what I've seen, he lacks respect for you. In my experience, disregard extends to bed play."

I clap my hands to draw his attention back to me. "Stop. I don't need an evaluation of my personal life. Let's focus on the coaching."

"You'll sing better without him dousing your light."

Everything he's saying rings true, but it's wrong talking about my impending breakup with a guy I've just met. I blow out a breath. "Tek, seriously. Shut up about Demetrius."

He claps both hands over his mouth. "Yes, yes. Shutting up is for the best." He removes his hands and gives me twinkle-eyes. "I enjoy a good pry. One of my favorite vices."

I want to dig into what those other vices might be. No time for it tonight. "Let's settle coaching logistics."

He fans an arm across the stage. "Meet here, after the crew leaves."

I'm already on the move to grab my stuff from behind the bar. I changed into street clothes while I was waiting for Stalk to clear out. "That works. Everyone but me is usually gone by eight o'clock. Can we start tomorrow? My timetable is pretty tight."

"On and on we go," says Tek with a little hop.

Such a bizarre dude.

"Great. See you." I sling my guitar case and tote bag over my shoulder as I head toward the arch.

Tek skips up next to me. "Where are you going? I will walk with you. The Hollywood night is ripe with vandals."

I appreciate how considerate this funny fellow is, but I don't need another guy hovering over me. "I'm not going far. No creepy alleys."

Disappointment darkens his face.

"You're sweet to offer." On an impulse, I lean in and kiss his cheek before leaving him behind. I half expect him to skip along next to me and keep peppering me with questions, but he hangs back. I'm weirdly disappointed.

What a strange day. What a strange man.

The elevator rockets me to street level, and I stroll through the balmy Hollywood night with Tek on the brain. Memories of his indefinable voice fill me with a lightness that's bypassed me for quite a while. I smile. It's not his voice alone. His entire presence manages to siphon off a litany of my stresses.

Tek's intrusive questions about why I'm still with Demie hold up a mirror to a situation I can't avoid any longer. My odd new friend offered unlooked for validation to the gut feeling it's well past time to end my stale relationship. I suck my bottom lip. Ugh. No matter how sensitively I present the concept of our split, Demie will fight me.

Ahead of me, the lights of the theater marquee brighten the night. It's time to ditch sullen Aurora and rev up performer me, the musical artist Tek boosted with his vote of confidence. The fact he's willing to coach me says at least one person besides me thinks I have a real shot at open mic night. If Tek can help me achieve a fraction of his musical magic, my chance may become more than a dream.

6

OPUS

TEK

OH, I AM GOOD.

Jumping from tabletop to tabletop in Stalk, I sing.

"Tek is tricky. Tek is wise.
My songs of love claim willing sighs.
A silken touch, a hungry kiss,
Charms both lad and beauteous miss.
To my bower they will run,
From dark of night to rising sun.
Alas they cry when kisses wane,
And all too soon they'll come again."

Offering to coach Aurora gives me an open invitation to spend time with her. Woo her. Win her. When I sang for her, I saw my magic dance across her skin and quickly pulled it back. She is one person, mortal or fairy I refuse to trick into my bower.

Loud and bitter voices from the private fairy doors remind me of my task. The magic mortals approach.

From the depth of my pocket, I free the *Pearl Tear* spell stone. It pains me to part with any of my treasures, but this is my penance, and I will obey my monarchs.

Laying the precious white stone in the palm of my hand, I gently blow on it. The stone melts into a glistening pool of liquid pearlescence. My next breath changes the substance into steam. I whisper, freeing the spell.

"Around this table you will go,
Obscuring sight from friend and foe.
While magic mortals weave their spells,
Silence reigns outside their shell.
There is but one to see within,
'Tis I who witness tales they spin."

Pearly haze envelopes the table. I guide the blur with my hands until it encompasses enough space to accommodate the circle of chairs. With a flick of my wrist, I send offshoots of mist along a path the Dark Vinyl Artists, those vile magic mortals, will travel between their suites and Stalk. This barrier will prevent them from being seen. Once I've shaped the spell, I press my palms together and speak the words the limping dryad promised would solidify the actions of the spell stones. Ones I haven't uttered except to the *Verdant Promise* when I created the Emerald Spire.

"All is well, enact the spell."

There's the faintest hiss in the air, and the mist disappears. In its place, a distortion wavers where I've placed the parameters of the magical shield. It will be imperceptible to all but me, the spell caster. A pang in my heart mourns the loss of a spell stone. When the limping dryad bound her magic to me, she warned I'd lose a droplet of my soul's merry nature whenever a stone is spent. It is the price of activating their power.

I've lost two spell stones in the king's service. I vow this will be the last of my treasures to suffer such a fate. By allowing Aurora to glimpse the Pristine Forest, I opened myself up for Cinnabar to foist me into this potentially precarious situation. I rub a finger under my nose to stifle a snort. Was the royal play all along to weaken me and steal my magic pebbles? The joke would be on the monarchs. As part of the deal with the limping dryad, the stones obey only me.

Be it threat or truth plain told, this Tek shan't fear the warning bold.

No matter the accuracy of the dryad's portent, each stone exacts its unique cost. I fell into exhausted bliss after creating the Emerald Spire. Expending *Pearl Tear*'s magic weaves a warp of loneliness through me, bordering on pain. I've created nothing of beauty with my action tonight.

I station myself in the shadows next to Stalk's entrance arch to greet the mortals. Tendrils of metallic magic slither in front of them, guards clearing the way for their masters. I count four writhing strands of icy blue light. One watchdog for each unsavory human. It's impossible to decipher which power bearer casts the seeking spell?

The foul threads circle my body, attempting to taste potential threat. My magic repels the inquisition. I will remain invisible to the approaching storm of undesirables until I choose to reveal myself. I grin, anticipating the surprise on their faces when who they assume is a lesser fairy steps out from behind the arch to greet them.

A smallish woman with a face as beautiful and ageless as my kind, squints into the shadows of the arch. I douse my magic even more so I'm as insubstantial as the air around me. Her gaze sweeps over me but doesn't stick.

"We're clear," she trills and bounces into the club. Her white sequined minidress swishes from side to side. Someone is ready to party. The faint shimmer of icy light surrounding her is like in color to the probing strings of magic that preceded them. This must be the enchantress, Tressa Divine, heartless bringer of light and ice who Cinnabar warned me never to cross. Of all the Dark Vinyl

Artists, her magic poses the greatest potential to break through fairy shields.

Not tonight.

My king briefed me earlier on the threat level each individual fiend may hold against a fairy. In my role as the king's doer of unsavory deeds, he clearly planned for my life to collide with the sorcerer and his witches.

"Last one to the open bar is a sucker," says a woman with cherry red hair, wearing a deep purple catsuit that over-accentuates every curve as she rushes through the arch. My foot itches to stretch long enough to trip Rubata Lear, the AWOL singer daughter of Midas Lear, president of Golden Pipes Records. This one had a bad girl reputation even before she aligned herself with the Dark Vinyl Artists. Of the four, as Cinnabar predicted, I sense her magic is weakest. There will be jolly games to be played with the Lear witch.

I lick my lips, and remind myself per royal instruction, no matter how seductive the package, interfering with a magic mortal is forbidden. Rubata may ooze lust, something I usually enjoy, but Aurora's face is the one that flickers in my thoughts.

I blend farther into the dim when the last two breach the entrance arm and arm. A glow of imperiousness to rival Cinnabar and Citrine swirls around the pair in sinister waves of plum and obsidian. Sometimes fairy sight is a burden rather than a gift. Seeing the darker side of these mortals' natures sours the stomach.

Sulaa Kylock, the sea witch, clutches a gold trident necklace resting in the hollow of her throat against skin the color of polished teakwood. Oversized oval jewels, like three-dimensional tattoos, adorn her well-defined upper arms and shoulders. Each disc generates a swirl of jewel-toned light. I wonder what creature she trapped to illuminate her baubles.

The sea witch peers into the empty club then speaks in low tones. "Do we trust the fairies to keep us hidden?" Even suppressed, her voice is commanding. A twinge of fear pings deep in my belly. Given the bodily might obvious beneath her sleeveless, metallic sheath dress of azure and gold, this witch could fit the qualifications for one of Cinnabar's inner circle of guards.

Danger.

Sulaa doesn't pose the biggest threat of harm to my kind, but no doubt her magic still leaves a mark. I swallow my concerns of sea witch magic. Cinnabar pointed out Sulaa is far from the ocean, her source of strength. Whatever her potential under the waves, it is diminished here on land.

Her escort, a man of considerable height, but not enough to rival Cinnabar, brings Sulaa's hand to his lips. "Never trust a fairy, my lovely witch, but we hold this particular band in check. They are as beholden to us as we are to them."

Here is the charred heart of the magic mortals, Grant Gothel. My fingertips tingle, reminding me he is a dangerous fire-wielder who's grown in power during his exile. Not long ago, he ran the empire of Rampion Records, but his crimes and ill-deeds drowned him in ruination. According to Cinnabar, it's not Gothel's flames, but rather his scheming mind and obsession with revenge that cement his reputation as a viper.

I've seen Gothel before in Cinnabar's office as they debated the intricacies of their fairy/mortal symbiosis. Something about him is different tonight. I stare, reassembling my memories of him, and land upon the change. Gray currents have begun to pepper the slick black strands of hair upon his head, the only outward sign of stress in the sorcerer's poised façade.

In a whoosh, the Lear woman blows by me, never glancing my way as she slides behind the bar, Aurora's bar, and starts to grab bottles. "Come on, Claude. Mix me a cherry Cosmo."

A protective streak heats along my spine. I don't want these lesser humans messing around in Aurora's domain.

"Take care, Rubata," says Gothel, catching the arm of a man who attempts to maneuver past him. Oooo, Gothel doesn't like this guy. For a hot second, I expect him to shove the man out of the club.

"Caution is key," growls Gothel. "We must be shadows, leave no trace. Our reign shall be a whisper, a fear one dreads but cannot name."

Five mortals? Who is Claude? There's no sense of magic surrounding the man in jeans and tank top decorated with a surfboard logo, a casual contrast to the upscale dress code worn by the other four. Rubata's pet perhaps? The scornful look on his face telegraphs discontent.

Sulaa and Gothel stride the last few steps into Stalk with an air to equal the self-importance of any fairy royal.

I decide to give them a show and snap into my lumen form. They both startle as my amber light pops into being near the arch, a quick shift any fairy child can manage. On one point Gothel is correct—never trust a fairy.

I make a show of bobbing through the air and blocking their way before I inhabit my human form and execute a courtly bow not even the queen could find fault with. "Tek Goodfellow, aid to the royal court of the Arborborn Coterie, at your service. Queen Citrine and King Cinnabar will be among us momentarily."

Gothel appraises me. His wrinkled brow telegraphs annoyance. "They send their boy lackey as messenger?"

I chafe at his dismissal. Moving into the light of Stalk, I fluidly adjust my form to raise myself eye to eye with Gothel and consider sprouting an ample tuft of chest hair to peek above the top button of my white dress shirt. Dropping into another more exaggerated bow, I deepen my voice. "I haven't been a *boy* for some time now, but I thank you for the compliment."

Gothel's head quirks to the side, suspicion roiling in his onyx eyes. "Fairies," he grumbles under his breath.

"Allow me to lead you to your sanctuary." I sweep an arm toward the enchanted table with a black and gold *reserved* sign in its center.

The group moves warily into their Tek-made privacy.

I dart ahead and rap twice on the tabletop. "Within these

confines, you shan't be seen. For glancing eyes, this sign they'll glean." I wave at the arch. "I've extended shield betwixt door and table. Your silent presence will be stable."

Rubata sneers. "You fairies and your rhymes. It's not as charming as you think." She takes a glass from Claude's hand. "It's insipid."

"Who's the doof?" asks Rubata's mortal toy, shooting me an unpleasant look.

The Lear witch drapes an arm around his shoulder and holds her drink to his lips. "Wipe the worry creases off your face, babe. He's not joining the team."

I'm dying to blow a kiss at Rubata just to rile mortal Claude, who is clearly excess baggage in the magical group.

"You're Cinnabar's spellcaster?" says Tressa, pulling my attention from the barflies. She gives me a side-eye, then approaches slowly and reaches to lay a finger on my shoulder. "Why didn't I sense your magic?"

"Perhaps a touch is what you need to find me in the dark." When I lay my palm over her finger, she yanks it away. I treat her to a smile that's melted the resolve of many a fairy mistress. "A person is entitled to their secrets. Wouldn't you agree, Ms. Divine?"

"On that point, I believe we are all in accord," says Cinnabar, striding through the arch with Citrine on his arm.

At first, I'm surprised to see my monarchs in human business attire. Clearly, they won't treat these mortals to the magnificence of their true forms. The snooty demeanor of the Dark Vinyl Artists makes belief in their own superiority quite apparent.

I pinch my lips between two fingers to trap a laugh. Considering fairies lesser or even equal to this bunch? Ridiculous. Magic or not, these humans are fools.

The queen frees herself and saunters over to Tressa. She captures one of the enchantress's white-blond curls between her fingers. "Soft as the first snowfall."

The enchantress titters and primps. "Kind of you to say."

Citrine trails a finger across Tressa's shoulder. "You are pure loveliness this evening, my dear."

Swallowing my laughter nearly chokes me. Of the she-witches, Tressa is the closest to Citrine's type—wispy, flowy, and gorgeous. The enchantress has no idea the queen is considering her as a potential acquisition to her clutch of attendants. Citrine's flattery is a power unto itself. Unwittingly slipping under a royal fairy's spell would swiftly demote Tressa Divine from enchantress to royal concubine. Her mind and magic both would be stripped away. Vanity has been the undoing of many of Citrine's targets.

Cinnabar approaches Gothel with an outstretched hand. "Is the subterfuge to your liking?"

They shake as Gothel nods appreciatively. "The extension of the shield to our suites is an excellent addition to our initial plan. Yours, I assume?"

Without so much as a glance at me, Cinnabar waves an arm toward the hall and fairy doors to steal my thunder. "We wish you to have as much freedom of movement as possible while still maintaining concealment."

As in the royal we, not the Cinnabar and Tek we. Why did I entertain the notion I'd receive even the meagerest speck of acknowledgement for using my *Pearl Tear* stone? Who's the fool now?

"Shall we leave our attendant Tek with you to serve your needs?" asks Citrine.

What is she on about? I'm supposed to vanish yet not vanish. If they ask for me to stay—

Oh.

My wily queen can compare what the Dark Vinyl Artists say in front of me and when they think me gone. She means to seek duplicity on which to sharpen her blade.

Gothel is first to take a seat at their charmed table and appears to ignore Citrine's question. He steeples his fingers and gazes up at Cinnabar.

Ach, the hubris of the dark vinyl man. The sorcerer telegraphs that even in repose he assumes himself superior to my king, a being who could crush him with a passing whim. If he had any inkling the repercussions disrespect could unleash, Gothel would be hiding under the table instead of drumming his fingers on polished black granite.

"So, Cinnabar…" Gothel shifts his gaze to be inclusive. "… Citrine. Have you given thought to our discussion of expansion? Now that this magnificent edifice is close to completion, we should consider where we will *sprout* our next endeavor."

Roiling fire burns in my chest. Expansion would entail using the second half of the *Verdant Promise* stone to build another spire. *My* stone. How dare they? Their disregard for my relationship with the stones is one more indicator of how low I exist in their esteem.

As if sensing my rising fury, Cinnabar flicks a finger in my direction. While still engaged with Gothel, my king sends a ribbon of invisible calm to curl around me. Within it is a whisper for my ears alone.

Your spell stones' safety is ensured for these mortals 'tis but a lure.

Sulaa stands behind Gothel resting her hands on his shoulders. How cozy are the Dark Vinyl Artists with one another? We in the Arborborn Coterie celebrate lust and sensuality, but I haven't always found it thus with other magic folk.

Perhaps sex is an area I can exploit with these undesirables for my amusement.

Citrine opens her arms with the grace of a butterfly. "Shall we not all revel in our marvelous achievement before forging on to the next?"

"Just so," says Gothel, flashing an appreciative smile at the queen.

What mortal says, "*Just so*?" A pretentious ass. I'm over this polite banter. I want to get on with spying and earn a modicum of respect back from my king and queen.

Cinnabar darts a warning look at me. I realize I'm swiftly

swaying from foot to foot in my frustration with their cordial pace. "None of the staff except Tek here are present, nor will be until morning. You are free to enjoy the club without concern."

Sulaa slithers into the chair next to Gothel. "Excellent."

Tressa gazes at Citrine. "Your hospitality is noted."

"Our pleasure," says the queen and dots a kiss on the enchantress's cheek. I do admire Citrine's skill at seduction. She's turned Tressa gooey and primed for whatever the queen's future plan for her may be.

"We'll be off then." Citrine keeps her focus on Tressa while she takes Cinnabar's arm.

A chilly distortion bearing the tang of salt wavers through the air as Sulaa stares at me. She's checking to see if her magic affects me. I will not give her the satisfaction of a shiver as an inelegant tone spills across her lips. "Take your errand boy with you." The sea witch smirks at Claude. "We have our own."

No witch or sorcerer spares me a glance as I trail after my monarchs. Once we've rounded the corner, the queen pulls her arm free from the king and hisses in my ear. "Do not make a mockery of your task." Without giving me time to respond, she melts into a lemony lumen sparkle and flies through a fairy door.

Cinnabar doesn't follow. Instead, he sets a hand on my shoulder. "This task is the means to lessen her disdain for you, Tek."

"Lessen not lose?"

He inhales until his broad chest expands and then allows the air to leak out. "I am sorry she constantly takes her displeasure out on you."

I shrug. "On and on we go. I also wish it was not so."

"Mind your wits," says Cinnabar and transforms into a thousand dark swirling whirlpools of shadow before following his wife.

My leaf of repose calls, but I've a job to do. Waving a hand in front of my body, I discard my human form in favor of a transparent fleck. Floating back through the arch, I settle on the lip of a brushed nickel accent high on the wall above the magic mortal's table.

For an hour, they bandy nothing of interest or consequence for my royals, gabbing on and on about Stalk and its opening night gala. Claude sits at the table next to the quartet, obsessed with his phone. While the group downs two bottles of wine, I almost fall asleep until Rubata's whine of a different sort grabs my attention.

"Brandy Winter should compete for the open mic spot in the *Saturday's Star* roundup." With a shimmy, the red-haired bombshell transforms into the guise of a blond beauty and pops to her feet. She starts to belt a song, but Gothel shakes his head and motions for her to sit.

"In time, Rubata. In time."

She sits, pouting. Without a pause, the redheaded Lear witch is back. I cover my mouth to muffle a snort. If there's any being less trustworthy than a fairy, it's a shapeshifter.

"Patience," Gothel purrs. "With Opus back in play, we'll soon be supplying all the talent here, you among them."

My ears prick up. What in the cricklewood bark is Opus?

He nods to Tressa. "Thanks to your intervention, the Golden Harp is soon to come into her talent. She will be the first rising star of the rekindled Opus crop to elevate Dark Vinyl Artists to the top of the music mainstream. Paving the way for you as it were."

Rubata crosses her arms. "Play favorites much, Grant?"

Gothel's mouth curls into an acid grin. "I play the odds I can win, my dear Rubata."

Is that what he calls fucking up so badly he went to prison and is now forced to exist in shadow? Definitely a flawed perspective.

"How do I know you won't pluck another pair of singers from your new Opus project to steal our place? You promised that Claude and I would be the duet to rise as Dark Vinyl Artists' first hitmakers," she says, gesturing at the non-magic mortal.

Sulaa emits a groany grumble. "Consider appearances besides

your own in a mirror for once, Tressa. Claude's taint needs to fade a bit more before the Dark Vinyl Artists' parade him out of..." She clears her throat and glares. "...retirement."

I finally put an identity to the face of their tag-a-long. Claude was one of the lead singers of the rock group Benedict and the Boulevard Bunch, Caliwood Inc.'s golden boys who are all over the music channel constantly playing on the club's flatscreen. They were top of Cinnabar's list to headline at Stalk's opening, even after the shakeup that ousted Claude from the group once its lead female singer, Beatrice Sharpe, reappeared.

The Lear Witch glares at Gothel. "Don't you dare cancel Brandy and Claude's set at Stalk."

Gothel waves her off. "As long as you disguise your plaything, I will allow it."

With a huff, Rubata stands. "I see how it is. You're back-burnering me while you obsess over creating the next Zeli with your Golden Harp." She twitches one shoulder forward and frowns. "We know how well you succeeded with your first traitorous protegee."

Gothel's olive skin blanches. Oooo, the witch hit a nerve there. This is getting good.

His grin shifts into a sneer. "I am one to learn from mistakes."

Tressa examines her fingernails. "Take a page from the Book of Gothel, Ruby."

"Claude," snaps Sulaa. "Get Rubata another drink. She's getting testy."

With a scowl, their rocker manservant slips the phone into his pocket and follows Rubata to the bar.

Gothel drains his wineglass and turns to Sulaa. "Where are we on a new teacher for the Harp? Her talent has matured past that husk of a vocal coach you enchanted."

Opus—Golden Harp—Vocal Coach. I sense undercurrents of trouble in these juicy tidbits I'll soon share with my royals. I wish to coax more details with my magic, but it's too risky. If the enchantress senses me, I can't complete my assignment and earn favor with the king and queen.

"No one sings more beautifully than the fairies," says Sulaa. "Do we dare approach them for a musical tutor?"

Gothel's eyes narrow as he taps his bottom lip. "Tempting, but we must begin to move away from our obligations to Cinnabar and Citrine if we're to..." He leans in, beckoning the others to do the same. Rubata returns to the fold and the four magic mortals are close enough to mingle breaths.

I hold my own breath in anticipation as Gothel scans the room, confirming they are alone. "...collapse our bargain with them."

I slap a hand over my mouth in the nick of time to suppress my gasp.

Collapse the bargain. No, no, not so. Foul fiends indeed.

Luck rides my back. Here is the blunder I've been waiting for. Treachery directed at my king and queen. The flame-wielding sorcerer knows not that he just ignited the fire that will consume him.

To the royals I go.

7

SIDEWALK DUETS

AURORA

I almost blow my sidewalk gig after lingering too long with the intriguing Tek. A bead of sweat tickles my ear thanks to the sprint from the Emerald Spire. Under the glow of the Boulevard Theater's marquee, I practically bowl over my friend Robo Robbie.

"*Aurora Express*, arriving on Track One," he says, catching my tote bag as it slips from my shoulder.

"You're a miracle worker, snagging my spot," I say, circling my finger in the air around the sought-after location for my post-show, boulevard performance.

"You know we got you covered," he says with a wink.

"Which of Rand's guests did you cheat out of tonight's cut?" I have a standing deal with Rand Diggs to give a portion of my night's take to whoever he sends to the theater to secure my sweet sidewalk stage by shooing off other street performers. I always appreciated the way he called those of us he'd rescued from the streets *guests*. Rand insisted on the term to signify we had a future beyond our stay in his hostel-type dormitory.

"I'm injured," Robbie says, smacking a hand over his heart.

"The guest was generously compensated to abandon his post." He nods at the neon blue rings of the Rampion Records Tower glowing off in the distance. "I was hanging with Justin at work after hours. When I noticed the time, I decided to mosey on over and check in with you."

I free my guitar from its case. "I'm honored you descended from your lofty tower to visit, brother," I tease.

He nudges me playfully. "I'm never too far away to hear you sing, sis." He zips open my tote bag and sets up the handy and very portable unit he designed for me, complete with mic, speaker, and backing tracks. I do prep breathing to compose myself for the performance.

If I actually had a brother, Robbie would be my first choice. We met while living in Rand Diggs's dorm, both of us with dreams beyond getting off the streets. Robbie's breakthrough came first when Rand connected the budding tech whiz to Hollywood Boulevard businesses. Those connections led to my sweet friend hitting the bigs working for Justin Time and Zeli at Rampion Records. With his savvy and huge heart, he deserves success.

He kneels to connect my guitar to the mini speaker then studies me. "Things good with you, Rora?"

I think of Tek and his promise to help polish my song for *Saturday's Star*. "Very good."

Robbie tilts his head. "Very good, huh? Care to elaborate?"

I debate for a hot second then spill. "I'm going for the *Saturday's Star* contest, to try and earn a spot in Stalk's opening night warmup act gig."

He stands and snatches me in a hug with my guitar as the center of our sandwich. "Yes. You're finally embracing your inner dragon slayer and going for the bigs."

I kiss his stubbly cheek with a loud smack. "I'm not going to let this chance slip by."

Robbie sets the guitar into the case and grips my upper arms. "Rand always knew there was more to you than meets the eye."

I snort. "He said that about all of us."

Robbie doesn't laugh. "Seriously, Rora. He once confided in me that he sensed an indefinable quality in you that the world needed more of, a...goodness that could too easily be snuffed out if you weren't given a chance. He was determined to get you out of shadows as quickly as possible."

"I owe him everything."

Robbie nods. "We all do." He chews his lip, thinking hard. "Once, Rand swore he saw a glow around you, and not a metaphoric one as if the brightness of your nature was tangible."

I gently whack his shoulder. "Now, you're just making shit up."

Robbie doesn't smile. "Take him at his word, Aurora. Your kindness, that goodness Rand believes in, is not your weakness."

I kiss his other cheek. "I'm trying to believe that, my dear Robo Robbie, but it's hard to translate that into a life plan."

"Give me the word, Rora, and I'll hook you up with Justin and Zeli."

Shaking my head, I reclaim my guitar. "Your generosity is over the moon, truly, but I want to do this on my own."

With his sneaker, Robbie slides my tote against the bottom of the giant show poster on the wall behind me. "They're super chill about helping friends."

"I've never even met them."

"Friend of my friend is a friend. You know how the Boulevard family works."

I adjust one of the strings on my guitar. "Let me earn this, Robbie."

He raises his hands in surrender. "Just sayin'."

There's a hint of hurt in his expression. I know his heart is in the right place. He's always been a giver, but the stubborn part of me needs to see how far I can go without a crutch. If I can't conquer the *Saturday's Star* hurdle, why would Justin and Zeli think I'm worth their time? My inner voice tells me if I score the spot at Stalk's opening, it'll prove I've got the chops to be a pro.

"This isn't a hard no, Robbie, just a not yet."

His features relax. "You know I want only good things for you."

"I know. I love you for that." I wish Demetrius was capable of leading with his heart the way Robbie does. For a while, I thought Demie might be. It's depressing my perception of him was so completely flawed. In my dark moments, I'm afraid my proclivity toward the kindness Rand saw is gullibility in disguise.

The rumble of the crowd spilling from the theater is my cue to boot my inner doubt beasties back into their cave for now. I shake the hair off my face, start my backing music, and pluck a few notes to draw their attention. I've got the timing down perfectly. I wait until the first wave pours around the edge of the theater foyer and hits the sidewalk to bust out my first song, an upbeat tune to capture their attention. Once I follow with a killer ballad, which draws them in closer, they're hooked.

I adore street performing. It's such a rush when people still on a high from whatever musical they've just seen stop and take in my set. I don't judge a successful night by the cash in my guitar case, even though that's always a welcome perk. A high bar is when my audience blocks the sidewalk and spills around the corner.

Tonight's weeknight crowd has the energy vibe of a weekend. They're bopping to the rhythm of my song. A pair of couples near the corner are dancing. Thankfully there's no Santa Ana wind tonight, so the bills piling up in my guitar case don't blow away. Since most people don't carry cash these days, Robbie made me a nice QR code sign for people to deposit tips straight into my account. He even set up an auto-reply thank you.

As onlookers add their voices to my finale, I wish Tek were here. My new coach could witness the effect I'm capable of having on an audience. I'd prove to him I've got the goods to score the open mic slot.

The crowd joins me enthusiastically for this final song—the showstopper from the musical they've just enjoyed. I love capping off their evening by reigniting the magic.

From around the corner where a second group waits at the stage door for autographs, I hear a swell of voices. I shoot a questioning look at Robbie, who lingers at the edge of onlookers. His eyes widen and he stabs two fingers down the side street. A second later, the leads from the show, Josh and Cassandra, round the corner to join me in an impromptu concert.

The adrenaline rush adds new shadings to my voice as we harmonize as a trio. They've done this a few times before. It's always dreamy to sing with them. A flood of cell phones tilt to catch our tune. I sense a blue-ribbon tip night.

When the song ends, Cassandra poses for selfies and blows us a goodbye kiss. Robbie offers a wiggle-finger goodbye and heads off. To my surprise, Josh leans in so I can hear him over the hubbub. "One last a cappella eleven o'clock song duet?"

My voice comes out in a squeak. "Me—with you?"

He slings an arm around my back. "If you'll have me."

I look past his finely chiseled jaw to a pair of earnest, hot cocoa-colored eyes. His generosity touches me. He usually sings this song with Cassandra on their drop-by visits. I've learned every note from watching, as mesmerized as the onlookers when these stars contribute to my humble sidewalk concert. To stall while I get over being choked up, I take a swig from my water bottle. After removing the guitar strap from around my neck, I prop the instrument against its case.

Josh pats my shoulder and then hums a starting note in my ear. We ease into the beginning of "When We Again Shall Love," his character's epiphany moment. People who'd begun to move away, gravitate back toward us. My voice adds feminine grit to his soul-smashing confession.

"How could the moon be so cruel?
How could the sun become my doom?
Our waning song foretold a plight
That my soul could not accept.

It is not time to end our song.
I will find you.
I will fight.
The sun and moon will smile anew.
When my folly is erased.
Wait for me.
I will sing our perfect song.
And spirit's fire will blaze
When we again shall love."

I match him emotion for emotion. It's transcendent living in the raw sensation of this song. The lyrics are about not giving up. I heed the message and let it soak into my soul. As we near the final phrases, he grabs both my hands and stares deeply into my eyes. Our performance sparkles through my body like a falling star.

The gathered theatergoers erupt with appreciation when we finish. Josh brushes a gentle kiss to my lips to stoke the applause and hopefully my tips, then whispers in my ear. "Nicely done, Aurora."

We stand side by side signing programs. My tiny flicker of fame sends waves of confidence crashing through me. Eventually people peel off for their cars or an after-show drink.

Josh gives me a final hug before heading to his car. "See you soon."

What a night. I wish I could take a longer beat to revel in the rush of this amazing experience, but the boulevard can change from friendly to unfriendly in the flip of a switch. Vandals lurk in the shadows, clocking a mental tally of my take. Fading away with the dwindling theater folk before the night creepers can pounce is key. I'll call for a ride down the block in front of the Hotel Caliwood where the lights are bright and a predictable late-night crowd mills around outside.

As the theater marquee clicks off, I sling my bag over one shoulder. There are still two or three clusters of patrons chatting about where they'll go grab late dinner while gushing over the show. When I reach for my guitar case, it's already been retrieved by long, thin fingers I know all too well.

"My Aurora, singing with the stars. Impressive." Riker Reese steps into the glow from boulevard traffic. He's dressed in a Boulevard Theater usher's uniform. His gaunt face beneath wavy brown hair still wears the hungry look of the streets.

I cringe at his use of *My Aurora*.

"Thanks." When I try to take the case from him, he nods down the block.

"I've got it. Let me walk you." He moves next to me, settling a hand on my lower back. There was a time in Rand's dorm when I craved the feel of Riker's touch and the way it excited me. Before I fled the nightmare of my aunt and uncle's house, there wasn't time for boyfriends or the back seats of cars. I focused on survival.

Once Rand gave me a safe place, Riker offered attention that naïve me thought was romantic. We'd go for walks along the boulevard, and he impressed me with his stories of surviving on the streets of Hollywood. His bigger-than-life persona drew me in. It was like having my own personal superhero to teach me how to dodge vandals and other unsavory aspects of our tenuous existence.

The night he kissed me for the first time was a fairy tale with the Hollywood Sign glowing in the distance. Riker taught me the pleasure of a deep, wet kiss and the thrill a calloused knuckle scratching the eager peak of my breast. We arranged mutual late lunch breaks and took full advantage of the empty dorm in the early afternoons while our fellow *guests* were away doing odd jobs. There was a strict no sex rule in the dorm, which added more excitement to our furtive tangles. Riker was my first, but I definitely wasn't his. As he began to steal his satisfaction without a care for mine, I woke up to the reality that what I first took for passion was him using me as often as possible to satisfy an itch.

Not long after that, I got the gig at the high-end restaurant and was able to get my own place. The move allowed me to fade from Riker's life and avoid the kind of breakup confrontation I'm tragically inept at. Unlike my genuine friendship with Robbie, Riker never tried to find me or stay in touch, confirming the fact I'd been nothing more to him than a convenient place to park his dick.

I try to relieve him of my guitar case, but he guides it out of reach. "It's my first week at the theater. What a surprise to find my ex supplying post-show entertainment."

I itch to correct him.

You mean your ex-fuck buddy.

The person who meant nothing to him beyond an occasional hookup.

"Come on, Riker. I'm hardly your ex."

His gaze bores into me. "You disappeared."

"How long did it take you to notice?" Wow, that came out easily. I hate that my tone hints I actually give a crap. "It doesn't matter."

I'm not going to linger in the dark having this conversation, so I head to Hotel Caliwood. If he hasn't let go of my guitar case by the time we get there, I'll flash my pal, Bertram the night doorman, *help me* eyes. Crap, all the cash from tonight is in the case. I wouldn't put it past Riker to take off with my guitar and the money.

"Get a drink with me, Aurora. Let's catch up. I hear you're doing fucking great." He jerks his chin toward the Emerald Spire in the distance. "Stalk is literally top of the world." Riker gazes dreamily at the metallic beanstalk.

I take the opportunity to rip my guitar case away from him. The pissed look he flashes gives me the creeps.

"I've got to go." My thoughts flash to Tek. I wish I'd invited him to come with me. I'd even be grateful for Demetrius's presence, although I think one intimidating look from Riker would make him soil his ridiculously overpriced linen slacks. Not Tek. I sense he would stand up to Riker's bullshit.

Riker schools his face back into a friendly expression. He lays a hand on my arm, and I force myself not to pull away. "Okay. I get it, but what do you say to giving an old friend a leg up?"

Of course he wants something. Riker is a taker. People like him are the biggest danger to people like me who are givers to the point of our detriment. I pull away and start walking down the boulevard.

"If you're asking me for money, Riker, that's a hard no. I work my ass off for everything I have."

As we pass under the neon sign of the *Sunset and Vinyl* bar, I see his lips press together as if he's working overtime to hold back. When he twists his mouth into a tight smile, I speed up.

"Look, Aurora, all I'm asking is for help to get me a foot in the door at Stalk."

The nerve, the raw gall of this guy. He uses me, doesn't give a shit if I'm alive or dead, and then wants a favor. "You are unbelievable." I wonder how many jobs Riker's pissed away in the past two years.

"Come on, Aurora. For old times."

I jab a finger at Hotel Caliwood across the street. "I'm going to walk to the hotel. And you..." I hitch my thumb back to the theater. "Go that way."

He reaches for me, but I slap his hand away—hard.

"Ouch. Damn, Aurora."

"Listen up, Riker. Never show your face at my sidewalk gig again. I swear if you do, I'll get you fired." He may see it as an empty threat coming from me, but I'm banking on the fact he needs the theater job. Riker knows Hollywood Boulevard is a smaller community than most folks realize. The shitiot must know Rand Diggs has connections with the theater. He could easily get Riker kicked out on his ass. In fact, to hell with being ambushed again. I'm going to call Rand tonight and rat my not-an-ex out.

Spinning away from him, I dash between the cars blocking the crosswalk and book it to Hotel Caliwood. Instead of lingering on the front steps to call a ride, I approach the grand glass front doors.

Bertram, the night doorman, shoots me a concerned look as he opens the door for me. "Everything all right, Aurora?"

I glance over my shoulder to see if Riker followed me. He's expertly blended into the shadows of the boulevard like the vandal he is. Breathing heavily, I drop my head. Once I catch my breath, I slowly raise my chin and grin at Bertram. I did it. I found the strength to send Riker away instead of letting him guilt me into helping him. Tek would be impressed. I'm surprised at how eager I am to share this bit of news with him. Or maybe not. My past with Riker is a chapter I'm ready to send into the vault for good.

"It is now, Bert."

"Are you going in?"

I retrieve the phone from my pocket. "Nah, calling a car and keeping you company while I wait."

He lets the door swing closed. "I'm not going to turn that down."

Delight simmers in my chest at my small victory. Destiny gifted me tonight to prove I can stand up to men who believe it's easy to use me. I've got to take responsibility for the sticky encounter with Riker since I didn't show enough strength in the past to make him think I wasn't a pushover. It's good to discover I actually have a functioning backbone. A tiny bead of warmth dances inside my chest. Ditching Riker tonight suggests I'm capable of mustering oomph a second time and ending things with Demie.

8

FEUD

TEK

I CHECK THE THRONE ROOM FIRST. FAIRIES FLIT ABOUT AT ANY GIVEN hour, be it sunlight or starglow, so there's every chance the royals are attending to Arborborn Coterie business or indulging in revelry while the human realm slumbers. Even though the fragrances of coralberry wine and roasted apple sausage cling to the air in the throne room, tonight's festivities have ended—at least my brethren's public activities. No doubt, many a bower sway and steam beneath the moon.

I hum in appreciation to belong to a coterie that mostly adheres to a coda that the sweetest sensual pleasures are best enjoyed in private. We are a cut above the classless Brineborn who flaunt their ecstasy indiscriminately in roving orgies along the Malibu shoreline. Not to say we completely avoid indulgence at festivals calling for less discreet entanglements. I smile recalling one particularly athletic midsummer's eve atop sprawling meadow grass and buttercup buds with the fair Tourmaline.

For a fleeting moment, I wonder what Aurora would make of fairy excesses. There's a tenuousness about the way she faces life that may not be a happy match for the more intimate of our practices. Then again, perhaps she's never dipped deeply enough into the well of sexual adventure to glimpse its myriad delights. A hum resonates deep in my chest. Oh, if I were to be the fortunate one to lead her into such an experience.

As much as I ache to collapse in my own bower, it's vital to report the Dark Vinyl Artists' stink of treachery to the king and queen.

The news I must share is far from positive. My lumen light shines a deep violet, the color of anticipation with a shading of dread as I fly to Cinnabar's dwelling. I knock the pattern of two raps, silence, three raps, silence, and then a single rap on the trunk of the massive rowan tree to identify myself, but the door into my king's glen does not appear. I gaze up into a canopy of coppery leaves, each shining with a warm internal glow, and sigh. He is not here. I'd much rather meet with the royals in Cinnabar's open woodsy chamber instead of the queen's personal flowery hideaway. I'm at my most vulnerable when we're on her private turf.

I repeat the knock without much hope and am again unanswered. Steeling my ego for a shower of disapproval, I fly from the loamy comfort of Cinnabar's wood to the Pristine Forest. Alighting onto the diamond road leading to Citrine's royal bower, I return to the vision of wonder on Aurora's face when she started down this same glimmering pathway.

Naughty Tek.

It's true I brought Aurora to the edge of the Pristine Forest for amusement, but there was another motive. I wanted to rankle the queen. A human breeching the border of Citrine's royal bower delivered an unpleasant prick to her royal haughtiness.

The silver-white and gemstone motif is pure Citrine. Her presence bathes these glossy woods in her radiant glow. The queen illuminates and her domain reflects. She intends to exude warmth and light, but all I feel is cold.

I hear their voices before the monochrome palette of the

Pristine Forest shifts to the multi-colored pastel elegance of Citrine's private arbor. The queen is not alone. Haunting, beautiful tones of Chalcedony's voice mix with the sugary trills of Tourmaline and Galena. Weaving through their melody is the steadfast harmony of Peridot. Their notes flow between the hanging vines of gold, magenta, and pink bougainvillea curtains marking the entry to the queen's bower. The blossoms are lovely to behold but touch them unknowingly and hidden thorns invade your flesh. Not unlike the queen herself.

It's not only the draping flora that halts my progress. I know well a song of seduction. The queen and her ladies are imbibing in the ambrosia of one another's bodies. Interrupting, even for news as vital as mine, is a danger. I do not dare make myself known and must slip away as silently as a spring morning mist.

Stealthy Tek.

Before I make my exit, the song of the queen's favorites begins to work its power on me. I'm blissfully familiar with the skilled fingers and lips of Citrine's intimates. I allow my imagination to hearken back to previous love-play I've enjoyed with these fairy charmers. Currents of sensation flow beneath my skin, sending a rush of blood away from my brain to an all-to-eager location below.

No, no, not so, it's off and away Tek must now go.

As I turn to flee the lure of my former lovers' songs, I connect with a chest of stone.

Cinnabar.

He sets hands on my shoulders and turns me back toward the lascivious symphony. "We are unseen here in shadow, Tek Goodfellow. Drink freely from this beauteous portrait of indulgence."

I pull away mortified, not only to stumble unwittingly to where the queen is entertaining, but to be caught. Turning from her bower and the activities beyond, I mutter. "I would never watch when the queen is involved. That violation would leave a scar more painful than my missing wings."

"Too true. I applaud your denial." He takes in my flushed face. "Poor Tek. It appears you are not unaffected by the music of love freely given. Since you will not see, allow me to paint the picture."

Cinnabar drags me closer, blending deeper into the vines. His voice wafts over to me in a barely perceptible whisper. "They are creatures of silk and breath. Each of the four favorites wears a transparent sheath, hiding no detail of their fair forms. All glow with the unique color of their crystal hearts as they float around their regal lover. Who can resist these maidens? The perfect pink of Tourmaline, Galena's lovely lilac, Peridot's seductive sage, and Chalcedony's blushing summer sky blue?"

I scrunch my face to trap a laugh. Maidens the four are not, but it is a tribute Cinnabar bestows the compliment. The fairy women are lithe and lovely but purity is a virtue they've long left behind.

When the king releases a low rumble of desire, I squirm and attempt to slink away. "I shall seek you out at a more opportune time."

Cinnabar licks his lips. "My queen welcomes the worship of her favorites. Oh, that such invitation would be mine."

I wave my hands. "Stop. Your narration will stain my mind. I will hear no more."

Moving farther from his rogue voyeurism does not free me. The king's magic roots me to the soil. Dark spirals dance across his skin as he spears me with his gaze. "There is nothing as graceful as a woman bestowing the perfection of feminine love upon another woman. We men take women like brutes, Tek. Women share desire as poetry. They are delicate foam rising from a frothy sea."

I banish memories of my lusty romps with the four fairy favorites. "Your Majesty, I beg you, let us decamp to where we may speak freely. I have urgent news."

The loud snap of his teeth sets the bower vines trembling.

"Cinnabar!" shouts the queen. "You ogling bastard. Show yourself."

When I try to shift to lumen form and retreat, Cinnabar's magic forbids it. With a throaty laugh, he parts the vines and drags me into the queen's bower. "I was teaching Tek to appreciate the sensitivity of feminine lovemaking."

The rush of heat carrying Citrine's furious voice blows my hair back. "As if this vile spawn isn't the very image of you already!"

Here we go. My least favorite place to be is wherever these two decide to go toe-to-toe with me in the middle. It's obvious the four fairies attending the queen share my urgency for escape. They brush swiftly past me as a quartet of colored lights.

I eke out words through a nerve-tensed windpipe without looking at her majesty who may yet be unclothed. "My queen, my intention was not to interrupt, rather I've come to report alarming news from the magic mortals."

"And did you *come*, Tek Goodfellow, spilling yourself alongside this rogue of a king who enjoys the sport of sullying my bower blooms as he spies?"

The unnatural thought disgusts me. I slash an X with my hands still not looking at her, drop to a knee, and bow my head. "Absolutely not, Your Highness. On my life, I would never practice such unforgivable disrespect."

Cinnabar chuckles. "Beloved wife, you mistake my appreciation as intrusion. Your love-play is balletic, melodic, rhapsodic, poetic, a rare masterpiece to be envied and admired."

I'm surprised at the notes of true earnestness with no undertones of scurrilous innuendo in the king's praise. He indeed holds his queen's passions in great esteem, almost reverence.

The queen launches fiery words. "You are a common thief, Cinnabar, stealing the earnest delights of others."

The queen's amber magic sizzles through the air, raising goosebumps along my skin. I hear the familiar swish of a skirt. A quick peek brings relief as I confirm she wears a dazzling gown of braided sunflowers. Citrine combs fingers through her limoncello-colored hair, arranging it over her shoulders.

Cinnabar drifts to his queen, slinking until his body is flush behind hers. Must they always force me to play the observer to their sensual teases?

When his nose burrows under her carefully placed shining strands, clearing a path for his kisses, and a brawny dark arm wraps around her waist, I study the vines overhead.

"Never question my desire for you, loveliest of all beings."

The king's raw tone makes me dip into leave-taking bow. "Majesties—"

Ignoring my overture of farewell, the queen whirls on Cinnabar, grabbing his cock.

"This treacherous shaft will never fill me with your trickery again."

His wince suggests she's given him a good squeeze. The king is not deterred as he removes her hand and kisses it. The heated look passing between them lacks the character of two who refuse to share a bed. Desire radiates from them, thickening the air in the queen's bower. They bat attraction and revulsion back and forth like a shuttlecock in their standoff of forced abstinence from one another.

Cinnabar purrs into the queen's ear. "When we once again taste the delights of one another, my queen, I will sire the child you dream of."

Wordlessly this time, I slowly back into the bower vines eager for escape.

"Our business with you is not yet concluded, Tek Goodfellow," says the king, fanning an arm in my direction while never taking his gaze off Citrine.

The magic laced through his words root me to the bower as deeply as any flowering vine, forcing me to continue bearing witness to their encounter. The queen slides her lips across the king's cheek with counterfeit tenderness ending in a bite to his ear. Cinnabar roars in pain.

The queen points a dagger-sharp fingernail at the king as she shoves him away. "Your promises are as empty as a rotted bloodmelon."

Cinnabar's face glows the color of a heated brick. "I promised you a princess to pamper and pet and fully intend to honor my oath. Your condemnation of my kingly inclination to first sire a son is the offense here. Never did you explicitly forbid such an outcome. The bitterness that divides us is based on tainted understanding."

A thin branch, the color of Cinnabar's skin, appears in the queen's hands. "An oath can be broken as easily as a promise." She snaps the wood in half and tosses it over her shoulder. "Twisted words. Twisted intentions. This is why you are banned from my bed." Her eyes flare as she flings a hand at me. "I will not suffer another of your useless misadventures in my womb."

That's a new one. I've been a disappointment, a blight, an affront, and a disaster among other rank flatteries from my queen, but never a misadventure. I think I prefer this new title to the others, better to be any kind of adventure than a blight.

Cinnabar beckons me to stand beside him and lays a hand on my shoulder. "Stop tormenting Tek. He deserves more regard than you deign to offer."

The queen glares at me. "For what—every foul trait you've stamped upon this duplicate of his father?" She pulls me from the king's grasp so I stand apart from him. Citrine slowly circles me. Each taunt delivered with more disgust than the last. "Addiction to misdeeds? Duplicity? Arrogance? Self-indulgence?"

Cinnabar raises a hand along with his voice. "Enough. You disown the prince for no other reason than your wrath with me."

Ugly shifts to hideous as my title is thrown into the fray. The royals only acknowledge their ownership of my existence when rage and retribution are the daily specials on their menu. My entire body buzzes with the need to snap into lumen form and flee.

Citrine copies the king's volume and every blossom in the bower quakes. "Untrue. I reject him as the deceptive result of our coupling." She seizes my chin in her wicked grip. "Where is the mother in the son? You conjured this counterfeit to infect my womb."

"You deny what you choose not to see. Queen Citrine of the Arborborn Coterie is woven into every strand of his sun-kissed hair, the flair of gold in his eyes, his wit and complexity of thought. These are your gifts to our son, not mine."

The queen waves a dismissive hand at him. "Tek Goodfellow is nothing but your puppet on a string, Cinnabar, a product of your hubris. You allow him to remain unschooled in the duties of a royal son."

The king spreads his arms wide. "A royal son, excellent. Do you hear, Prince? Your mother acknowledges you."

Citrine's eyes flash electric lemon at his comment. "You twist my meaning." My father's satisfied smirk enrages my mother even more. Tiny puffs of amber steam escape her fingertips.

"Ha, my dearest queen! I do not. There is no ambiguity here. As I am his sire, you are his bearer."

The origin of my interpersonal issues is no mystery. I'm a prince of their blood who is forbidden by his own mother to use his title. An unwanted prince, a weapon used in the bitter war between my royal parents.

"Stop tormenting him, Citrine. Do not blame the prince for our estrangement. Embrace the truth of your longing. You yearn for a princess, and I am the sole vessel to fulfill such desire."

My mother's features distort as if she's ingested poison. She storms up to my father, her face inches from his. "I do not trust your seed."

He grasps her upper arms. "Then trust my vow."

The queen shakes her head slowly. Her body melts from rigid rage back into the airy quality in which she moves through our realm. "You have not earned that trust." She cups my father's face in her hands.

What I'd give for a drop of that tenderness tossed in my

direction. If their standoff ever ends and my queen gets her princess, perhaps she'll thaw to her firstborn.

Dreamer Tek.

Cinnabar rests his forehead against his queen's. "What must I do to soften your hard heart?"

I don't want to hear the answer in case it involves me. My mother's heart may be hardened, but mine is battered from a lifetime of living as the prince that shouldn't be. I've never doubted the passion and love my parents hold for one another. It is a burden to be the wedge in their story.

Stupid me believed when I procured the spell stones, my mother would begin to see my value, but I remain nothing more than evidence of my father's perceived betrayal to her. Expecting her love was too lofty a dream. Over decades, the expectations of a boy have been whittled down to the disillusion of a man. Hope of a mother's affection reduced to the tiniest fragment of a wish that I possess even a small morsel of value to her.

Cinnabar's whisper is laced with desperation. "Is there still true love, Citrine, as has always existed between us despite your current grudge and ire?"

The queen slides her hands under the king's black mane of curls and looks him in the eye. "What is this true love you speak of? Mortal love? The elevated love our kind enjoys? Or is the love you proclaim merely a myth that fades into mist?"

While they coo and postulate the meaning of love's curse, which I am pledged to avoid lest I end as they have, I decide to counter the queen's contempt for me by withholding my information until morning. Call me passive-aggressive. I've learned from the masters.

I'm halfway through the vines when Cinnabar calls me back. "What news do you have for us, Tek."

They move past their emotional loop-de-loop that decayed my mood. My queen's assessment of me downgrades from disgust to boredom. They are my monarchs first and only acknowledge parenthood when I'm needed as fodder to fuel the combustion between them. I'm duty bound to fulfill the penance they've saddled me with and report the troubling news of the magic mortals' plans.

"This puppet..." I slap a hand to my chest. "...discovered Gothel and his witchy cohorts entertain intentions to sever the pact with the Arborborn Coterie."

Royal eyes flash, his as flaming coals and hers as a bolt of lightning. If they but glimpsed such proof of true fairy power, the Dark Vinyl Artists would scurry into safer ratholes than the one they inhabit now as our guests in the Spire.

The queen claps her hands and the bower shakes. "Speak."

Would it kill her to add *prince*, *Tek Goodfellow*, or nature forbid, *son* to her command?

"No details were discussed but do not doubt they exist in Gothel's labyrinthian mind." I cock my head to the side. "They spoke of a Golden Harp that seems to be a key piece in their strategy to best Your Majesties."

The king and queen exchange a glance laden with information I lack, so of course I pry. "You know of this Harp? Is it the empire building collateral they believe it to be?"

Citrine snaps her head in my direction. "Of course, we know of *her*, fool."

The king begins to pace, trampling the bluebonnets and butterscotch trumpet flowers strewn across the ground. "Ah, this completes a picture." He taps his bottom lip. "Gothel sees the girl as the catalyst to his rise from the flames."

Citrine's wings flutter as she flies to light on her bed of sweetgrass and posies. "The fiend is no phoenix. We must steal the Golden Harp to lessen their power. We cannot risk any weakening of our agreement with the Dark Vinyl Artists until our homeland is free of blight." She runs her fingers through her shining hair. "Since I could not trust my *husband*..."

I flinch at the venom she injects in the word.

"...to fulfill his oath to charm his seed to create the princess I desire, perhaps the Golden Harp will suffice. I will claim her as my daughter by other means." The queen wears a dreamy look as she contemplates fulfillment of her wish. When I fidget, waiting for her to rejoin our chat, she glares at me. "You bring us nothing more of value?"

I slide clenched fists behind my back to hide my sign of insubordination. "They spoke in nothing but vagaries about besting you."

As the queen strokes the wavering petals of the flowers surrounding her, they burst into full bloom. Glittering flecks of pollen dance above them. "If I seduce Gothel, I will conquer him and siphon off his secrets."

Cinnabar's roar causes every newly opened blossom in the bower to snap shut. "Faithless woman, you dare to dishonor the pact between us and lust for another man beneath your gown?"

I'm surprised to glimpse a heartbeat of fear in my mighty mom's expression. Cinnabar's rage is fucking terrifying, but so is hers. She darts across the bower to take him in an embrace.

"My king, no man could ever satisfy my hunger as you do. Therefore, it is pointless to invite one to my bed for pleasure. This would be for preservation of the coterie."

Onyx cyclones quiver across the king's ebony skin. "You will not break the agreement. I take no other woman, and you take no other man until we are reconciled."

Citrine smacks his chest. "Calm yourself. I shan't seduce the sorcerer. Our pact stands. You keep to your passion playthings, and I shall do the same." She trails a finger between her breasts. "Although mine are infinitely dearer to me than the kaleidoscope of cocks you use for nothing more than fleeting amusement."

I tire of listening to my parents' repartee about their sexual exploits. "Do you need me here for your royal banter?"

Cocky Tek.

The exasperated looks they flash me zip my lips.

"Perhaps we don't need the magic mortals as our conduit to the human world," says the queen as she sways. "The Golden Harp's magic may serve as the sole connection we need to bind our realms while we linger here in the Emerald Spire. She is innocent and pliant."

My moral compass is as flighty as that of my parents, but it still bothers me when they target guileless non-fairy folk to fuel their manipulations. If this Golden Harp is innocent and pliant, she doesn't stand a chance if my mother chooses to acquire her.

Is the unexpected niggle in my gut an inkling to protect the one they call Golden Harp from Citrine? I suppress a snort. Doubtful. Rather, the niggle suggests potential satisfaction in thwarting any plan of my mother's.

The king juts his chin in my direction. "Go now, Tek Goodfellow. Keep watch on the magic mortals. We will think on your report."

I bow and gladly slip into lumen form to leave. The feeling of exhaustion that always overtakes me when I get tangled in my parent's volatility wicks through my body. As I fly from the queen's Pristine Forest to the far corner of the Sassafras Glen where I keep my bower, my mind drifts to a more pleasant topic—Aurora. Spending time with someone who shows me warmth and kindness will be a nice change from my thorny place in the fairy pecking order. She is my sweet secret.

Once tucked under a blanket of woven cowslip petals, I fall into dreams of torch songs and Aurora's laugh.

9

TORCH SONG

AURORA

I CHECK MY INVENTORY AGAINST THE INCOMING ORDERS FOR THE millionth time while I hide in the stock room waiting for the club to be deserted.

What I'm really doing is stalling in the hopes this will be the night Tek finally reappears.

I reluctantly agreed to let him help me fine-tune my audition song, but *coach* hasn't shown up for a week. There have been no signs of him hovering around Mr. Cinnabar or Ms. Citrine. I wonder if they fired him. It wouldn't surprise me if Tek's frenetic energy rubbed them the wrong way. I may be the only person around here who finds it charming.

Thank goodness Demie took the week off to go gallivanting with his parents at their digs in Hawaii. He invited me; more proof he's clueless about my waning feelings for him. It was the perfect moment to break it off, but the words wouldn't come. I need to jot them on paper and rehearse as if ending us is a new song I'm learning.

I thought confronting Riker would buoy my courage to take the plunge. It brought me a single step closer to the finish line, but not across it. I begged off the Hawaii trip, insisting I couldn't squander any of my valuable prep time to perfect our collection of cocktails for Stalk's opening. In truth, I'll need every moment to create a kickass video for *Saturday's Star*.

I peek into the club. It's as still as the predawn moments I cherish in my Hollywood Hills hideaway. I revere that first breath of day before the birds begin their sunrise melodies when I slip out of bed and head to my favorite bench in Griffith Park. I think of it as my charmed seat of inspiration. Thoughts about work and Demie fade away, and I concentrate on my art.

I've already changed out of my work uniform into a sleeveless, calf-length summer dress that flatters my curves while still giving me room to breathe. It makes me feel sexy. Sexy me to sing a sexy torch song. I've never attempted to entice Demetrius with this dress, but I'm surprised by how eager I am for Tek to resurface and see me in it. Is the flutter in my chest simply about Tek's opinion of my new torchy look or something else?

I wait another handful of minutes. It appears there will be no resurfacing tonight. I set up the small travel tripod I found at a thrift store. Tonight, I'm going to record myself singing as a trial run. Making the actual video here in Stalk is a no-go. It would reveal my unsanctioned, after-hours sneaking into the club and might work against me.

Too bad. The space is designed to be an acoustic dream. I'll tack my quilt and blankets to the wall of my closet at home to fashion a recording booth then fancy up the video with the magic of graphic and songwriting apps.

I face the mic, roll my neck, and shake my arms to loosen up. After trying a couple of different positions, I settle on my version of an alluring pose and start the song.

"I follow you to shadow,
Seeking promises you gave.

But once the light had vanished,
Lost truths my heart did crave.

"Is this your chosen body language for, 'I'm hot' or 'I hurt my back'?"

I jerk into an almost military stance, ready to rail at Tek for both startling and insulting me. "Look who decided to grace me with his presence, *coach*."

"Oooo, Aurora spice is worth the price of staying away before we play." He melts out of a dim corner of the club then saunters to the edge of the stage. Tek's gaze takes the slow train up and down my body.

My heartbeat goes nuts as I attempt to craft a clever comeback. "I saved a dose of fiery spice, to shower a rogue who...dammit, I'm too pissed at you to rhyme. You ditched me for over a week."

Tek joins me on the turntable and to my surprise, takes my hands in his. There's the tiniest spark when we touch, probably from the static he built scuffing his shoes along the tile floor.

"Forgive me, Aurora. I've been embroiled in..." He pauses as his gaze rests on the table closest to the bar. "Family business that knocked me sideways. I lost track of the days."

My anger fades, and I squeeze his hands. "Oh, I'm sorry. I should have asked before unloading on you. Are you okay?" I feel terrible for snapping at him.

He brings my hands to his lips and kisses the back of one and then the other, lingering long enough for me to appreciate the damp heat of his mouth. "Let me be the sorry soul. I tend to have issues with time. Even a rogue should be capable of manners."

"Where is your family? Are they far away?"

"No, no, not so. They live here."

The jaunty little phrase he constantly uses irritates me, and I pull my hands from his. My face heats as anger seeps back across my skin. "You've been here all week and couldn't leave me a fucking note?" I huff. "You know, I've been just dandy without your help." I make a shooing motion with my hand. "Goodnight, Tek."

When I hop off the stage to adjust my tripod, he's right there with me, jabbering. "I've been called flighty and thoughtless, which are not wrong. I'm working on it." He pinches a lock of my hair and stares at it before lifting his gaze back to mine. "Is there perhaps a second chance for me bobbing below your anger?"

I'm mesmerized by the brightness in those damn gorgeous eyes that ooze vulnerability. I don't want him to leave, but he can't think it's cool to take advantage of my time either. It sucks to be a pushover, but I want someone in my corner for this audition.

"Not if you're going to blow me off again."

Tek draws an X across his chest. "Cross my soul to meet your goal."

His rhyming is completely goofy, but damn if it doesn't attract me to him. Must be the songwriter in me.

I cross my arms and fix him with a stare while I craft my own rhyme. "Promise me you'll now stay true, and I will sing my song for you."

Before I realize what's happening, he licks his lips then drops a kiss on mine. Even though the barely there pressure sends a thrill through my chest, I push him away.

"The bargain is struck," he says, a jolly twinkle in his eyes.

My fingers fly to my mouth. "A handshake works just as well." I glare at him. "Try asking first next time."

Tek gives me a sly look. "But hands are not nearly as fun as lips." He leads me onstage. "I will honor your request for permission in future. Now, we work. First posture."

Given his previous insult about my body language, I suppose it's a decent starting point. Stretching my leg to tap a toe onto the turntable control, I nearly topple. Tek clamps my thigh to catch me. He wraps an arm around my waist, pulling me close. A pleasant haze surrounds Tek's body, like gentle summer sun soaking into skin. For a long beat, neither of us moves.

Tek steadies me on the stage. "Pardon me, pupil, there was not time to request a touch before preventing your tumble."

I ease my body out of his grasp to stand before the mic, pleased he acknowledges my boundaries. Ones the embarrassing foreign wellspring of desire building inside me is tempted to amend. With Riker, I'd known the pull of newly awakened lust. The attraction to Demetrius was born of seeking a steadier connection. I have no experience with this raw magnetism streaming between Tek and me.

Clearing my throat, I adjust the mic. Does he feel the pull too or is it just me? Maybe it's the novelty of attention from a man so different from my previous lovers that sparks my enticement for him. I need distance if I'm going to concentrate on my performance. "Go stand over there," I say and gesture toward the bar. "I'll sing then you can critique."

"It's a challenge to see your face from there."

I shake my head. "You'll make me nervous if you're too close."

He licks his lips. "I want to knock you off base. Get to your raw material then rebuild you as a siren."

If I'm going all in with this coaching agreement, I should give over to him. The sexuality and magic that filled this room when Tek sang is exactly what I need to create for the video.

He bends to look me in the eye. "It's safe to let loose with me, Aurora. Break the dam to drown your audience in longing."

Nodding, I give him a tight smile. "That's the goal, but it's not my default."

Tek pats my cheek. "Then let's get to work resetting you, darling."

His *darling* carries a bite. Not the condescending *darling* or *doll* I've heard countless times as a server. Tek says it with an undertone of *I want to see you naked*. What is it about the man that lights me up so fast?

Tek drags one of the leather-padded chairs close to the stage to perch on. Pointing a finger at me, he chirps, "Hit it."

I do some prep breathing and lip fluttering warmups that rivet Tek's attention to my mouth. Forcing myself to ignore his interest and stick to the lesson, I reach for the sound unit next to me on stage and start my music.

Before the end of the first phrase, Tek shouts at me. "Relax your shoulders." After a handful of lines, his next correction comes. "Lean forward. Sing to me."

His constant interruptions are damn distracting. I stumble on the lyrics.

"Stop. Stop." He pounds fists to the sides of his head.

If this is his style of coaching, I'd rather take my chances without him. I'm stiffer than ever and a thousand times more self-conscious.

Tek smacks the arm of the chair. "I know," he says, voice brightening. "Try the song with your eyes closed. Feel the lyrics flowing through your body."

I start the music again and shut my eyes. It is easier to infuse emotion into the song without him shouting random suggestions. When I finish, I wait for his analysis. He's silent as he chews on his bottom lip.

"Hmm," is all he says.

"Helpful," I say, stuffing as much sarcasm as I can in my tone.

Tek flips all the corkscrew strands of his hair to one side as he continues to gaze at me.

I huff at him. "Care to share or will you just stare?"

My rhyme shakes him out of his stupor. "I'm trying to separate the threads in my head and pluck out the best ones." He pretends to draw one of these "threads" from behind his ear and dangle it in front of his eyes. After a moment of contemplation, he grins then mimes tossing the invisible strand aside. "My conclusion. I saw docile, compliant Aurora. Now, show me the edgy street-dweller Aurora buries inside."

"You want me to sing as if I'm scared shitless." I glare at him.

"Convey to the audience I'm starving and don't know where my next meal is coming from? That buried version?"

He bounces in the chair like a kid with a new toy.

"There's the Aurora I'm looking for. Snap and spice and nothing too nice."

I shoot him an exasperated look. "Earn your keep, coach, and tell me exactly how to pull that off." It stings that the grit I tried to infuse in my lyrics isn't raw enough for Tek.

"There's the sass. Now sex it up."

I growl. "By—doing—what?"

Tek is still while his gaze bores into mine. "If you'll allow it, I'd be willing to employ a more hands-on teaching methodology," he says in a low rumble.

Dammit. The intensity of the simple phrase and the tone of his voice set off the beginnings of a different type of rumble between my thighs. What he manages to do to me with only words and innuendo is exactly the reaction I need to inspire in an audience.

"Define *hands on*, Tek?"

He's out of the chair and onto the stage in a flash, standing close enough to share his alluring warmth again. "I'll take it slow as on we go. If lines are crossed, give Tek a no."

I raise an eyebrow at my frenetic friend. "Are you capable of slow?"

At his hint of a smile, a dimple appears near the corner of his lip. "When the occasion calls for it."

"Let this be one of those occasions." When I nod for him to get on with it, he slides in behind me, gently tucking his chest against my back.

"Yes?" he asks.

"It's fine."

It's not much more than a simple hug, but this first move of Tek's tactile coaching sparks enticing tension through my body.

"Will you allow a touch more so that I may make my point?"

"Quit stalling. I'll tell you when it's too much."

When his hands run down my sides to settle on my hips, my legs tingle, and I'm afraid they're not going to hold me up. I'm mortified by my slight shiver he can undoubtedly feel.

He leans over my shoulder, and a whisper tickles the shell of my ear. "Green or red light?"

My voice is breathy as I answer, "Yellow."

His low chuckle shoots a current of heat through me. When I turn my face to ask him when he plans to allow me to actually sing, we're so close his adorable pillowy lips graze the edge of my eyelid.

He increases the pressure between us. "What are you feeling, Aurora?"

Equal parts shy and turned on as hell.

Tek may project youthful energy, but his solid chest and the strength of the arms brushing my sides are all man. The flush of my heat mingles with his. I'm seconds from spinning in his arms to slide my hands under his shirt then grip that inviting lower lip between my teeth.

"Shall I continue to awaken your sultry core?"

My sultry core is screaming for him to continue. "Maybe just a little more."

Fingers find their way to my stomach and travel upwards, his knuckles barely grazing the lower curve of my breasts. I'm breathing hard. The faintest of sighs escapes at his teasing touch. I'm tempted to sneak my ass backwards just enough to discover if there's any sign he's as aroused by the effects of his coaching as I am.

I should banish him back to his chair, but a tug of curiosity keeps me silent. What will these sensations do to my performance?

"Now sing, Aurora."

My voice is breathy. "With you..."

"Yes, with me touching you."

Do I have the wherewithal to deliver a song with these lusty ripples running through me? Sensing my hesitation, Tek rubs his fingertips down my arms and guides my hands to the mic. He brings it to my mouth.

"Sing your emotions," he purrs, returning his hands to my hips as he sways us oh so slowly side to side. Tek's voice alone immerses me in a near trance.

I find enough breath to let words flow past my lips.

"Love me once.
Love me again.
Love 'til stars arise.
I long to see sweet yearning,
Reflected in your eyes."

"Let your song beg for how you want to be loved, Aurora. Listen to your body. What does it want?"

I want Tek to press me against the great glass windows of Stalk, raise my skirt, and take me until I scream his name.

Am I so desperate for the fire of mutual passion that his simple touches set me off like this?

We continue to move together and without conscious effort, the timbre of my voice shifts into a deep, almost throaty moan. I'm slightly aware he's set the turntable in motion. There's sensual longing in every note as my core becomes a coiled rope of fire. My song begs for the climax my body craves.

Tek eases my shoulders so my back arches. "Do not be afraid to flaunt your beautiful breasts for the audience. Fill every man and woman with desperation to taste you."

Holy hell, this man chases my shyness, driving me to be as suggestive and brazen as a torch song requires. I ache for him to act on his suggestion and practically moan the next note. Singing to the splashes of stars outside the windows, I use my body to enhance the performance as we slowly rotate on the stage.

"Out I cry to powers blind,

To overturn deceit.
Return the joy I do believe."

As the words spill out in the sultry haze Tek coaxes from me, I'm exhilarated. Intimacy issues with Demetrius make me question my desirability, but in Tek's embrace I feel every bit the wanton vixen the song requires.

Tek moves my hair aside to rub his nose along my jaw. "Alright?" he asks.

I lay a hand on his cheek to show my permission for this new touch. His simple contact sparks urges in me that can only benefit my delivery.

"Yes, my naughty Aurora. Moan for them. Purr and plead."

His voice drips with the lust I feel. "Fuck everyone in the room with your song."

I rest the mic close to my breasts, still rocking to Tek's delicate swaying rhythm. I'm a new Aurora, an erotic Aurora with emotions and wanting laid bare. This is an Aurora I can no longer deny.

I don't recognize my own voice as the last note rolls across my tongue.

Digging his chin into my shoulder, Tek growls in my ear. "And that, my beautifully carnal Aurora, is how you sing a torch song."

The bubble of lust and longing my song created fades. I spring off the stage away from Tek. Judging from the stinging heat, my face surely flames fire-engine red. Mortified, I turn away from him. "Well, that was..." I lay my cool hands on the sides of my face.

"Intense?" says Tek with lilting humor in his voice. He follows me across the room and lifts my chin. "It was splendid."

I smile, yearning to savor the taste of his lips a second time. What would he do if I asked? "Your style of coaching is..." I search for the word to do justice to what he's done to me. "...unique."

"Let's see if it works. To the stage, my temptress," orders Tek. "Incinerate me with desire." He pinches the fabric of my skirt. "By the way, this dress has me halfway there."

I can't tell if he's teasing me into the mood or if he's serious. Either way it's working. The pulse starting up again between my legs is the perfect reminder of what my song is meant to do. Taking the stage once more, I let the memory of Tek's body moving against mine infuse the song.

He sits closer to the stage than any guest ever will be once the club opens. As each rotation brings me to face him, his expression grows hungrier, and I know I've hit the seductive mark. Whoever this libidinous Aurora he awakened might turn out to be, I can't wait to get to know her better.

10

REFLECTIONS ON A LEAF

TEK

WHEN SHE FINISHES HER NEXT GO AT THE SONG, AURORA STOPS THE stage from rotating. It's not the only thing spinning. Like a burst pipe, my magic surges out of control, splattering around the room in bursts thankfully invisible to Aurora. I'm unhinged by her voice, her body, and her acceptance of my admiring touches. Even though temptation overpowering discretion is one of my favorite vices, I'm determined to practice better restraint. If this woman wants me, it can have nothing to do with fairy coercion. I will not make love to Aurora until I know she wants me without magical interference. Doing so loses me the game she has no idea we are playing.

Respectful Tek.

Now there's a twist.

Aurora stares at me with raised eyebrows. "Well?"

My voice is still husky with lust. "Excellent sophomore effort."

She frowns. "That's all you got?"

"Do you want me to go into detail?" I squirm to relieve the bulge still pressing against my zipper.

Even in the low light I see her apricot skin burn. She checks her watch. "I have a little more time. Shall I go again?"

For nature's sake. If she gets me any hotter tonight, I'll need to fly out the window to avoid giving in to my cock's relentless begging.

"I think you get the idea. Why don't you work out moves on your own then show me tomorrow."

Her tongue slides across her lips. The moisture shines in the light from the bar. Oh, what a treat it would be to kiss those dark pink beauties beyond a friendly peck.

She hops off the stage and comes to sit next to me. "No specific suggestions?"

I can't tame my wandering fingers as they brush a tendril of poofy hair over her shoulder. "More of the same, beautiful. More of the same."

Aurora leans an elbow on the table, worry lines popping across her forehead as she stares at me. "I need to ask you something."

My muscles tense, sending a pinch along the tender strips of my missing wings. Is she going to confront me about the hard evidence of impropriety in my pants? Evidence that deflates as I stress over her next words.

She drops her head, focusing on the tabletop. "It's really *out there*, but since you work for the bosses, I suspect you know more about the Emerald Spire than I do." Aurora's eyes peep at me through her curtain of hair.

So maybe this isn't a confrontation concerning the tenting of my jeans by an ornery dick. "I enjoy a good *out there* question."

Her shoulders sag as she barely shakes her head. "This may sound nuts..." She steels herself and looks me in the eye with an expression of *listen up*. "Okay." Her chin gives a cute little bob before she launches in. "A couple of weeks ago, the elevator stopped on a super weird floor. The whole place was a silver, glassy, diamond forest with sparkles in the trees and tinkly little voices."

I grit my teeth, trying not to take offense at my voice being called tinkly.

"I took a few steps along a path and it lit up. I swear it knew I was there." She studies me for signs of ridicule.

Pressing my lips together, I dip my head for her to go on.

"I've searched every floor of this damn Spire, and I've never been able to find it again." She leans closer. "Have you seen it? Did Mr. Cinnabar or Ms. Citrine ever mention a place like that?"

The urge to tell her everything bubbles inside me.

Yes, Aurora, I know it. It's the Pristine Forest where my mother the queen of the Arborborn Coterie of faeries, Citrine, keeps her bower. I lured you there for my own amusement and am now paying the price by spying on a sorcerer and three witches. Any more questions?

"They've never said anything to me about a fancy forest." I pat her hand. "The Spire is a massive complex. Except for the popular attractions of amusement parks, theaters, and clubs, no one knows what else hides within its leaves and branches."

She presses her back to the chair. "I was sure Spire management would know, but when I went to the sales office to ask, they looked at me like I was batshit crazy."

Before I realize I'm doing it, I've clamped a hand on her thigh. "Don't beat yourself up. Your mystery is probably a Hollywood contrivance, like a top secret celebrity hideaway or even a movie set that's already been dismantled."

Her gaze drops to my hand, but she doesn't pull away. There is definite heat seeping through the fabric of her dress.

"I'd rather it was real."

My heart crumples a bit at her disappointment. I don't want a single drop of sadness to flow through her beautiful body. "What if I help you look, Aurora?"

Why did I say that? The king and queen will slap me inside a silverwood trunk for even suggesting such a thing. Magic itches across my skin in warning.

She's a mortal, Tek Goodfellow. Tread carefully.

I concentrate on reining in my skittering power and miss her response. "What?"

Her hand rests on top of mine. "Rora. My friends call me Rora. I accept your offer."

The touch and invitation raise my already brimming level of temptation when it comes to her. I squeeze her leg. "Let's wait until after Stalk's opening and then we'll—"

"You'll what?" Demetrius steps through the entrance arch. His gaze immediately locks on our hand stack on Aurora's thigh.

She jumps up like her ass is on fire. "Demie, you're back in town."

They meet each other halfway between our table and the arch. Aurora stops short of touching him, but Demetrius, the tool, throws his arms around her, hands cupping her ass, and yanks her hard against him. He attacks her with kisses while her arms hang limp at her sides. After a moment, she gently guides him away and clears her throat, glancing at me.

"Figured you'd be working late. I thought I'd walk you to the theater," says Demetrius, sliding an arm around the delightful curve of her lower back I recently had the pleasure of pressing up against. "I didn't expect to find this joker hanging with you."

My magic escalates from an itch to an ache as it begs to be released. I want to send Demetrius flying across the room into one of the high pub tables with a scorch or two across his pretty boy skin.

Aurora is flustered as she looks between us. "I, uh, Tek..."

"Tek what?" says Demetrius, accusation simmering beneath every word of his nasty look.

I want to shout at Aurora to break it off here and now with the ass. It's not my place to butt in no matter how badly I want to obliterate Demie with a generous dollop of acid from a bitter widow vine. Rora wouldn't thank me. In fact, I could mess up the possibilities brewing between us with such a dick-wagging move. Sadly, it's not in my nature to silently stand by and not cause at least a little friction. "I'm coaching her on a song for her audition."

The color drains from Aurora's face as she shoots me wide *shut up* eyes. Interesting. It appears Demie-poo is unaware of her *Saturday's Star* opportunity.

Demetrius puffs out his chest and enters my personal space, ignoring every mention of Aurora's audition in favor of harassing me. "Cinnabar's stooge is a singer? Bust a tune for me, errand boy."

Oh, if he only knew the penalty for challenging a fairy. I could give him a donkey's head or spell him to hump a garbage can. I'd prefer to compel him to run naked down the middle of Hollywood Boulevard staring at his crotch and screaming, "*Where is my dick*?"

Aurora would never forgive me for spelling the fucker, even if she entertains negative thoughts toward Demetrius. Her kind heart has no room for such retribution.

She clicks her tongue. "Rude, Demie."

The ass in question whips his gaze between Aurora and me. She threads an arm around his, tugging him away. "I've got to get to the theater. Let's go."

The useless sack of moldy dandelion petals attempts to flash me a warning look that wouldn't frighten a drunken ladybug. I clench my fists for Aurora's sake to keep from treating Demie-poo to what the mortal's call a middle finger salute. Passivity is not in my nature. Instead of relieving him of his penis altogether, which is my first choice, I shrink his underwear three sizes and thoroughly enjoy his ass wiggle as he attempts to alleviate the sudden pinch.

Aurora snags her satchel, beelining it for the stairs as Demetrius catches up with her. When he grabs the railing with one hand and attempts to dig denim out of his ass crack with the other, she turns to me and mouths, *See you tomorrow.*

I blow her a kiss and call out, "Break a leg tonight, Rora."

Demie's angry stingbeetle face intensifies hearing her

nickname on my lips. I worry he's going to give her hell. I should follow to ensure the worthless sack of bones keeps his anger in check.

"Thanks, coach."

Nope, I'm going to let Aurora handle this her way, but a little invisible assist can't hurt. Demetrius yelps as I decrease his underthings and jeans a bit more for good measure. His jerky movements make the limping dryad look like a ballerina.

Aurora gives him a quizzical side-eye as he hurries down the steps. When he's gained a slight lead, she blows a kiss of her own in my direction.

Oooo, game on, Demetrius. Your clenched balls will never know what hit them when I steal Aurora away.

I shift for lumen travel and head for a fairy door but skitter to a stop the moment I catch my reflection in the window. My lumen light shines a pulsing peony color. Snapping back into human form, I stare down at my body.

"No, no, not so."

A corona of deep pink flickers around me. This cannot be. How in the multitudinous depths of nature does my lumen light emit the color of being struck love-blind?

With a growl to shake every bottle behind the bar, I charge through Stalk's arch, down the hallway, and through my private petiole door into the night. Beneath the uppermost twist of the green metallic beanstalk, I crash land on my favorite thinking leaf.

"Yew sludge," I curse, as I rub the side of my forehead that collided with the steel surface. A bruise is inevitable unless I get to the jar of honeysuckle sap in my bower before skin purples.

Immediately, the substance of the leaf shudders, melting from its metal form into its hidden organic nature. It unfurls a new leaflet that contracts around my body, wrapping me in a cozy green blanket. The tip caresses my skin at our point of impact like a gentle kiss. I'm rocked with slight undulations as if I'm an injured child. I pat the waxy-coated surface of my sparkly green companion.

"Not your fault, dear friend," I say, tapping a finger to the slight bump rising beneath a twist of hair. "I gave you no warning of my approach." Satisfied, the leaf gives me a final reassuring squeeze then lazily stretches to its gargantuan length, offering a straight and steady path across its expanse.,

My coterie enjoys a symbiotic bond with flora, but my attachment to the Emerald Spire is deeper. I am father and protector to stalk, stem, and leaf. My botanical progeny's affection is a welcome reminder of my true purpose...the keeper of this magnificent creation. That responsibility must come above royal schemes or personal indulgences, especially where a mortal is concerned.

Shuffling to the western tip of my favorite perch, I slump onto my bum and swing both legs over the edge to calm down. The energy of the living stalk beneath me gives me strength. My chest swells with pride. I created this beauty with nothing more than a slight magic assist from half a spell stone.

Miles and miles away, my fairy sight allows me to watch the frothy waves of the sea beat their rhythm onto shore then back out to the salty depths. I envy the Brineborn Coterie their oceanic lullaby, but I'd never trade the forest's song through limb and leaf of my homeland.

The cacophony of Hollywood Boulevard unfolds beneath me. I'm morbidly fascinated by the way the humans jockey for position in their cars, playing a colossal game of tag and dodge as traffic lights define the rules. I can't imagine the suffocation of being confined in one of their vehicles.

I'd like to ask Aurora about it.

Aurora.

Rora.

A hum races across my skin. Holding my arms before me, I can still detect the faint glimmer of pulsing peony luminosity. This cannot be. Surely, one of my kind tainted me with the glow as a prank. I am no sentimental lover who wears a lumen color signifying one blinded by love. Lovers give. I prefer to take. True, I am a lover of the body but never of the heart. The cursed pink love-blind shade signifies a heart state I've never before succumbed to.

"Aurora," I say her name carefully while studying my forearms. Streaks of vibrant peony pink light flare around me like escaped moonbeams.

I scan the leaf for the jokesters who've charmed me to appear the heartsick fool. Is this payback from Carnelian the Cobbler for overturning his wares? A darker thought plays through my mind.

Citrine.

For decades, I've shunned the litany of betrothals my mother attempted to foist on me.

Presently, I remain a man alone, master of his heart. Such independence does not preclude Citrine's delight in tormenting my emotions with her trickery. The queen is the likely architect of my love-blind glow. I picture my mother and her ladies using the reflecting pond in the royal bower to watch hapless Tek's lumen light shine lovestruck over a mortal.

I stand, applaud, and bow. "The game ends, my queen, and victory is mine."

Searching the broad expanse of the leaf, I wait for a throng of tittering fairies to appear and mock me. The air remains still. Not a breeze. Not a hint of fairy presence.

So much for the easy answer. The quandary of the pulsing peony remains. If not inflicted upon me by another...

No.

I shake my head violently. Tight spiral strands whip and sting my face.

There is always peril for mortals who fall for fairies. We toy with humans as our playthings. They are targets to use for our convenience, such as the magic mortals acting as our conduit between our realm and theirs. I have enjoyed humans for bed sport or a laugh, nothing more. It is unthinkable for an inferior human, even one as enticing as Aurora, to steal a fairy's deep love.

Flash.

The mere thought of her intensifies my vexatious pink radiance. Is it her connection to the Pristine Forest activating my love-blind color? I should regret leading her there, but I don't. Aurora raised the magic of the wood when she neither ran nor showed fear. The awakening was not my doing. What about this woman speaks to my world?

What about this woman speaks to me?

Screams from below are a welcome distraction. I lie on my stomach to study the twists and the curvature of the Spire. A looping roller coaster spits the riders far from the comfort of the main stalk as it chugs to a death-defying height before spiraling downward at a speed to scramble human senses. I suppose it's the closest they ever get to flight. A different set of shrieks emanates from a meandering tendril of the Spire that stretches far to the south. The more daring of the mortals leap off its end, plummeting toward the earth until a springy rope line yanks the daredevils back up to the leafy haven. I tip my hat to them. Foolish bravery is better than no bravery at all.

Again, my thoughts seek Aurora. She possesses a different brand of bravery reaching for a goal with such a small chance at success. Helping her fills me with unexpected pleasure. I wish she'd assert herself where Demetrius is concerned. Her kind nature is both an asset and an annoyance.

I splay my fingers over my heart as my unwelcome pink glow continues to plague me. Tek Goodfellow shuns love, but I have seen it make worthless things beautiful like the way fairy children sing to the weeds until they burst into enchanted blooms. I once had the love a young child feels for his parents before disillusion trampled it to dust.

Maybe I cannot love.

Flash.

"Oh, shut up." I wave a hand to erase the unthinkable pink luminescent infecting my skin. Love cannot be what pulls me toward Aurora. Desire, curiosity, admiration, and a certain protectiveness pool in my emotions. Those I acknowledge.

Unforgiving tension grips my heart with the strength of a taproot boring deep into soil. What does Aurora's heart tell her about me? She seeks my company as coach and employs me to help her uncover the whereabouts of the Pristine Forest. Is there true attraction or simply convenience between us?

I finger the stones in my pocket. I could easily spell her to fall for me with the *Fire Melon's* attraction spell and keep her for as long as she held my interest. I'd end this foolish game of mortal seduction I've charged myself with and control our tryst instead of being tortured by fickle wonderings about my feelings. In doing so, fate would turn me tyrant, stealing Aurora's emotions to sate my desires.

The notion of coercing Aurora is distasteful. Odd. Why should I be concerned over her approval, her interest?

But I am.

A craving for Aurora to want me without magical encouragement pulses through me again. My fingers twitch with memories of slipping down her hips and brushing the sweet lower curve of her breasts. I relish the way we fit together, the nearness of my body teasing passion from hers while she sang. That sumptuous voice alone draws me near to madness.

Ah, there it is.

I caper across the leaf as sense returns. The pulsing peony blush must be a lingering signal of lust unsated. There are no errant seeds of love in my gut for a mortal. She is but pleasant sport with the added benefit that consorting with Aurora promises to enrage my mother. Yes, satisfying thoughts indeed. I choose to accept these tidbits as plausible proof to believe I am not lovestruck.

I skid to a stop as truth and the night's oncoming chill sap my celebration.

Except...every explanation falls short.

Lust is easy. What I wish from Aurora is not. My longing for her acceptance is of the mind not the eyes.

Has bothersome Cupid's arrow indeed painted me love-blind?

Prickly pear stew, what am I to do?

11

THIEF OF LOVE

AURORA

I RETRIEVE THE SUPER-CHILLED GLASS FROM THE FREEZER IN THE storeroom behind the bar, hold it up to the light, and jiggle.

"Perfect."

The miniature gummy sculpture of the Emerald Spire is seated firmly in the center of a frozen bed of the golden berries Mr. Cinnabar imports from South America. I carefully walk the hurricane glass to the counter and scoot it far from the edge. After adding fizzy rosemary lemon tonic to the tumbler with pre-measured vodka, I pour the mixture into the glass.

I clap my hands as tiny white flecks bubble up from the icy fruit through the clear liquid and swirl around the tiny beanstalk.

I've made it snow in Hollywood.

At least in the cocktail. I feel it in my bones this will be one of our biggest hits. Who doesn't want to sip winter in the middle of a sweltering Los Angeles summer? I need to order a boatload of berries and mini-Spires.

I catch my reflection in the glass and groan at the dark smears beneath my eyes. Not an attractive portrait of a perky cocktail magician.

Every time I nearly drifted off last night, stressors dug another notch in my spine. I hyper-focused on the bad blood between Tek and Demie with a chaser of dread over the possibility Riker will continue to pester me if he manages to keep his job at the Hollywood Boulevard Theater.

I've given him undeserved grace and not called Rand to get Riker fired.

Yet.

If the jerk shows his face again to mess with me, he's toast.

"Well, looky looky. I never thought your ridiculous idea would work," says Demie, bending to stare into the effervescing cocktail.

I purse my lips. "Thanks for the vote of confidence."

"What are you going to call it?" he asks, oblivious to my frustration with him. Demie flicks the glass hard enough to slosh liquid onto the counter. The candy Spire lists at a precarious angle.

"Damn it, Demetrius. Give me some space." I snatch the glass away and try to reseat the beanstalk. I want to tell him to fuck off but won't risk Ms. Citrine or Mr. Cinnabar catching me sniping at him. After a deep breath, I reengage. "I was toying with Frostywood."

The silver-white bubbles are a delicate reminder of the beautiful mystery forest Tek and I are going to hunt for.

Demie scoffs. "That's as cheesy as a mall Santa." He straightens his tie, tucking the end behind the buttons of his vest. "I don't know why we need to suit up before opening."

I busy myself at the tablet embedded in the countertop, checking inventory and orders to keep from scowling at him. "It's called being professional."

He starts assembling ingredients to work on his own cocktails, plopping each down harder than necessary on the polished granite surface.

"Chill, Demie. You're going to break something. What's up with you?" I immediately wish I hadn't asked. No doubt it's Tek's attention to me that's put him off. He's got a right to be upset.

He kicks the low glass-front fridge. "And I suppose it's professional for you to grope Cinnabar's servant in the club after hours?"

I catch myself before I snap at him. "I told you Tek is coaching me for an audition, and he's Mr. Cinnabar and Ms. Citrine's executive assistant, not a servant." My cheeks flare with the heat of remembering my body's response to Tek's coaching style.

Demie snorts. "Executive incompetent."

I stalk closer to him, anger almost winning out over my attempt at seeing the situation through his eyes. "Demetrius, you're right. We have a problem."

"The problem, Aurora, is my girlfriend making goo-goo eyes at another dude in a dark club."

I almost do it. Breakup words fizz on the tip of my tongue. The way he dismissively spits *girlfriend* labels me possession, not partner. As I storm around the bar to put a barrier between us, I don't know if I'm more pissed at him or myself. Ending my soured relationship at work is not the right way to handle cutting him loose, especially when I'm not sure how bad his reaction is going to be. That's a conversation for a place our bosses won't stumble into the potentially ugly moment and think less of me.

Demie follows me. "Your problem, Aurora, is grabbing a taste of a flighty imbecile instead of being faithful to a man of substance." He pounds a fist to his chest.

I face off with him. "Are you going to listen to anything I say?" Damn my face for becoming a flashing billboard of guilt as I remember coming undone at Tek's touch last night and the unexpected kiss he dotted on my lips.

With horrible timing, Tek chooses that moment to stride around the corner from the offices. I've never seen such a serious expression on his face. Oh, God, he heads straight for Demie.

"Hey you, man of substance, did you ever consider Aurora

might prefer a sweet, sun-toasted delicacy." Tek fans a hand down his body. "To your pallid self-importance?"

Shit, he heard our argument.

Demetrius shakes a fist at Tek. "Who the fuck do you think you are?"

I slip between them as the walkie clipped to Demie's belt crackles to life.

"*Demetrius, you there*?"

Never taking his hate-filled stare from Tek, he snaps the walkie to his mouth. "Here."

I flash Tek a look I hope says *back off and let me handle this.*

"*Delivery at the loading dock. Need you or Aurora to sign off.*"

"On my way," he says, jamming a finger at Tek's face. "You'd better not be here when I get back, punk."

Tek opens his mouth, and I shake my head. He gets the message and keeps silent even though he refuses to break eye contact with Demetrius's nasty look before the latter heads out of the club.

I sink into a chair. "He won't let this alone."

Tek crouches in front of me, hands on my knees. "Then cut him loose. Rora, you do not deserve to be treated with so little regard. Do you seriously not believe that?"

I set hands on his shoulders, prepared to shove, but abandon the urge. "You're only seeing his bad side. I swear he does have a good one. I'll regret it if I don't let him down easy." I drop my head back and then right it. "Don't you think I owe him that?"

Tek gently takes my face in his hands. "No, I don't. Not after I've seen the way he treats you. You're allowing him to mess with your mind, your emotions. He's playing on your guilt. Classic trick to keep you under his thumb."

I slump in the chair. "You're right. I've gotta end it. Just not here. I don't want to make a bigger scene than we already have." I dart a look toward the hallway to Mr. Cinnabar's office and pray my fight with Demie wasn't loud enough for the boss to hear.

"Then let me make a scene." He laughs at the baffled look on my face. "Hear me out, Rora." The sweet way he speaks my nickname gives me a little thrill. Tek takes my hands in his. "He already caught us together last night. The groundwork is set. From his nasty boy tone, I guarantee Demie-poo assumes you're cheating on him. Let's run with it."

I start to protest when a silent purr rumbles through my body, reliving Tek's heat pressing into me and the way I responded. "Damn it. The coaching...the way I let you get close and how I felt —" I drop my face into my hands. "I disrespected him. I'd already cut emotional ties with him, but he doesn't know that."

He points at me. "You're making yourself the bad girl when he's the one treating you horribly."

I clasp a hand to my chest as if to trap my swirling emotions. Tek is right. I am guilt driven. I'd rather be the one to take on misery than dole it out. "I've spent my life getting hurt, Tek. I know how that can cut a person up. Hurting someone else is painful for me. Even when they're being an ass."

"Answer me this. Do you ever want Demetrius to kiss you again, to touch you?"

A surprising sense of revulsion overtakes me as my last intimacy fail with Demie flashes through my mind. "No."

"Are you ready to be free of him?"

I am. There's nothing left for Demie in my heart but an afterimage of affection and echoes of lingering obligation because he didn't hold my street kid past against me. I gave him power by never asserting my wants and letting him dictate our relationship. I'm as much to blame for the mess we're in as he is.

I look Tek in the eye. "I mistook lack of personality for sweetness. It's on me for letting it continue this long." A lump wedges in my throat. "All for a taste of stability in my unstable world."

"Then let me help." He clears his throat. "What if we tell Demetrius we'd like to see each other beyond our coaching sessions?" Tek rests his palms on the sides of my neck and strokes my jaw with his thumbs. His touch is warm, soothing.

"Lying is the coward's way out, Tek."

His mouth quirks into a smile. "It would not be a lie if we both choose the declaration to be true."

I take a step away from him. "I appreciate you proposing this to help me break away from Demie."

Tek's expression is surprisingly earnest. "You mistake my purpose. It is a selfish one to claim more of your attention."

We gaze at each other, and I have no doubt he's telling the truth. Is this what I want? Instead of agreeing right away, I rake a hand through my hair. "Standing up to Demetrius is long overdue. I am sick of being a pushover."

He closes the distance between us. "Would a pushover refuse to take shit from Cinnabar? That gumption brought you to Stalk."

I stood up to Riker as well.

Do I choose to explore something with Tek? Claiming an interest in him puts a definite end to things with Demie. He'll be furious. I just pray he won't turn Stalk into our battlefield. The anticipation on Tek's face as he waits for my answer boosts my courage. He's helping me detonate the Demetrius bomb. "Jumping right from Demie to you is not a good look."

"Then not a jump, but a small skip. Think of us as a trial. I'm a new set of clothing you'd like to try on."

I cock my head to the side. "Even if I can't afford it?"

"My price will be nothing more than the pleasure of your company."

I study the floor to avoid his eager gaze and think. Tek is certainly making me a generous offer. My lie would be to deny my interest in him. I'm not committing to commitment, just a tentative step.

Tek raises my chin with a gentle touch. "If you dare our unmarked path, alone you shan't face Demie's wrath."

The earnest look on his face stirs a gut feeling that Tek isn't afraid to navigate the fallout with me.

I close my eyes for a beat, gathering courage to cross a hazy line of truth. Maybe Tek's confidence will rub off on me. "This isn't my proudest moment, Tek, but I'm onboard with getting to know you better." My next breath feels weighed down by rocks. "The reality is that I've let Demie become a thorn stuck in too deep to remove gracefully." As I speak the words aloud, my belief in them grows even stronger.

Raising a finger, I look Tek dead in the eye. "No big expectations. Promise. We're just testing the waters." Am I trying to convince him or myself?

Tek's tongue peeks out to moisten his lips, and for a moment, I think he's going to kiss me.

I lay a hand on his chest to keep him at bay. It's not him alone I don't trust. "Let me break the news, and you back me up."

"Atta, girl," says Tek. "Courage suits you."

I grin. "I'm working on it."

A jumble of voices sounds from the stockroom behind the bar. Demie's bitching rises above the others as he orders the delivery crew around.

I straighten my vest and check my work bun for stray hairs. "Here we go."

To my surprise, Tek moves in behind me and rests his hands on my hips. I swat him away.

"Too much?" He laughs.

"Obviously." I step away. "Don't make this any harder than necessary."

Tek waggles a finger at me. "I see you have no trouble being bossy or standing up to me."

I study his face. "You're right." I wonder why. Is it Tek's direct, no-filters approach to a situation? I don't feel the need to please the way I do with Demetrius. With Tek, there are no qualms about speaking my mind.

"Don't you have somewhere else to be?" says Demie, targeting Tek with his distaste as he storms out of the stockroom. He tries to grasp my hand. "Let's go to lunch, Aurora."

This is it. My moment is here. Either I take the leap onto a different path, or chicken out and prolong my dead-end relationship with Demetrius.

"Demie, there are a few things I need to share with you."

His face brightens. Damn it. I'm blowing my attempt at the breakup.

"New cocktail? Wow, you're on fire today." He snaps his fingers. "Oooo, fire. Drinkable flames." His gaze drifts to a nebulous region above my right ear as he ponders flammable cocktails.

I swallow hard. "I'm going to audition for the *Saturday's Star* spot to be one of Stalk's opening night warm-up singers."

Confusion pinches Demie's features for a moment before he waves a dismissive hand at me. "That's aiming ridiculously high."

His condescension gives me courage. "No, it's not." Out of the corner of my eye, I catch Tek's smirk.

"I agree with her," says Tek, stepping next to me. I silently will him not to touch. "It's why I'm coaching her."

Demie, the bastard, actually laughs. "You buy his line, Aurora?" He flaps a hand at Tek. "He's making a move on you."

Almost without thinking, I'm the one who gets physical and grabs Tek's hand. "Not that you'd ever bother to ask, but Tek is quite an amazing singer. With his help, my performance is already at a whole new level."

Demie's stare locks on our hands. I don't look at Tek, afraid he's flaunting an incendiary expression of victory.

"Okay, he's your *la la la* buddy." Demetrius's voice drips with disgust as he sings three sour notes. "Got it. Let's go eat."

"Tek and I made a strong connection through our music—"

He cuts me off, his face flushing redder. "Aurora, what's going on?"

I pull away from Tek and lay a hand on Demetrius's arm.

"Things haven't been okay with us for a while. I've been trying to tell you we should cool it, but you don't listen."

Demie jerks his arm away so fast it bends my wrist painfully. His hands clench into fists. "You're shitting me. Are you seriously breaking up with me for this clown?"

Tek steps between us and looks down at Demetrius. I grab my wrist and stare. It never registered before that Tek is a head taller than Demie. He's also struck me as slender, not the guy currently flashing no-nonsense biceps.

"We're having an adult discussion here," says Tek. "Let the lady finish."

I move to the side and face Demetrius without Tek between us. "It isn't fair for me to pretend to be invested in our relationship anymore when—"

"You're giving up," says Demie.

"I'm sorry. This is overdue. I should have broken things off before—"

"You fucked another dude." Demie punches the closest padded chair back.

Tek pivots again to block any move Demetrius might try. "Why am I not surprised you frame it cheaply? Rora and I have discovered a shared attraction we wish to pursue. She deserves more than a bully-boy."

I wish Tek had left off the last snark. I grasp my hands and squeeze to fight off tears. "Demetrius, we're laying everything out in the open." My eyes plead with him to accept the situation. "I'm sorry. I really am."

Demie responds in a venomous tone. "The lowlife has done a number on you."

I'm not surprised this is how he sees the situation. I've brought this on myself by avoiding rather than facing our flawed relationship.

Tek's shoulders tense as he pulls an arm back. Oh hell, he's going to punch Demetrius. We'll all get fired. I step up to the pair.

"Stop, Demetrius. I'm sorry but this is the way it is. I'm going to see where things go with Tek. I know it sucks we all work together, but that's reality."

Demie backs away and presses fingers to the corners of his eyes. "You could have had the decency to humiliate me in private."

He's right. I shouldn't have given in to Tek's suggestion so easily, but if I hadn't, would I have found the courage to walk away on my own? I made Demetrius cry. I'm a horrible person.

A sob joins the waterworks. Behind me, Tek makes an unflattering noise. Thankfully, Demie misses it.

"Please, Aurora. Don't do this. I love you. Shit, I wouldn't be crying like a weak ass if I didn't." He turns away to wipe his face on a sleeve.

Tek stage-whispers in my ear fully intending for Demie to hear. "Next, he's going to tell you tears don't lie."

Demie glares flaming arrows at Tek. "You're a thief, errand boy."

To my shock, Tek reverses his retreat and strides right up to Demetrius, clamping a hand on his shoulder. "The course of love never runs smooth, my man."

Demie shrugs him off then reaches for me. "Please, Aurora. Come with me. Let's work this out."

"No, Demie. I'm sorry—so very sorry." My throat tightens. I fight the impulse to hug and comfort him.

As if sensing the weakening of my resolve, Tek threads an arm around my back, pulling me to his side.

Demetrius clenches his jaw, gives one curt shake of his head, and pounds out of Stalk. The percussive clip of his work shoes echoes on the marble stairs. I stare at Stalk's silver and glass arch, fully expecting him to surge back into the club to continue fighting. It's pathetic, but if Tek wasn't backing me up, I might run after Demie. I hate the burn of conflict and guilt tumbling in my stomach. Worse is the ice bath of truth—I'm alone again.

I appreciate that Tek helped me take the final leap, but was this truly the best way to go about it? Does is make me heartless to be drawn to another so soon?

This what I wanted, independence and a non-judgmental path to my dream. The deeper dream of being loved hasn't disappeared. Demetrius offered that possibility at first. Maybe that's why it's been so hard to let go. It's tough to face the reality that I wanted more than he is capable of giving. God, what if I'm making the same mistake with Tek?

The soft pad of Tek's thumb swipes away tears I wasn't aware had fallen. "Shh," he whispers and takes me in his arms. I tuck my head against his chest while clutching handfuls of his green button-down shirt and weep. His soothing back rubs are as soft as the brush of kitten fur against a cheek.

I gulp a breath. "W...why does doing what I need feel worse than the alternative?"

Tek's lips nestle in my hair. "You want to give the world nothing but sunbeams and birdsong. It's a beautiful wish from a generous but delicate heart."

I pull back to meet his gaze. "Too delicate. It's easier to be the one to make everyone else happy instead of grabbing a piece of it for myself."

I'm still in Tek's arms. He covers my balled-up hands and tucks them under his chin. "You handled that well."

"Did I?"

He chuckles. "Answer the question for yourself."

I sink teeth into my bottom lip. "I suppose I did."

The corners of his eyes crinkle as his smile grows. "Our Demie did cry when she bade him goodbye."

His good humor is contagious, and my newfound freedom a heady rush. The corners of my lips rise. "Though despair she did feel, before her a sweet suitor did kneel."

Tek lays my hands over his heart. "Alas, dear Tek, stuck out his neck and offered a kiss that may go amiss."

He leans forward, eyes glued to my mouth. I press two fingers against his lips. "Pushy, aren't you?"

Tek mumbles against my fingers. "Shall we not seal our beginning with a kiss?"

If the time comes when kissing Tek feels right, I doubt I'll have trouble being convinced. Based on our coaching session, I suspect our PDA will be toe-curling.

Tek settles for grabbing my wrist and kissing my fingers before he backs off.

New worry causes pinpoints of moisture to settle along my hairline. "What are Mr. Cinnabar and Ms. Citrine going to think about us?" I start nervously pacing between tables. "They knew Demie and I were already together when they hired us." I press the heels of my hands to my eyes but immediately remove them before I smudge mascara any worse than I probably already have. The black smudges on my skin prove the damage is done. "What if they fire me? Or fire you?" My breathing comes rapidly and I grab a chair for support. "We didn't think everything through, Tek."

He gives a humorless laugh. "I guarantee I am un-fireable."

"But I'm not."

Tek grabs my shoulders. "Aurora, they aren't going to care. Believe me."

His stare is intense, but earnest. I believe him.

"You might call the bosses hopeless romantics. They may already be shipping us."

The thought of Mr. Cinnabar and Ms. Citrine wasting a single thought on my love life is so ludicrous I snort. "Shipping us? Is that even a thing anymore?"

"Ah, there's my sunbeam and birdsong," says Tek, dotting a kiss to each of my cheeks as his hands tease my arms.

"Are you kissing mascara stains?"

I swear he doesn't seem as tall as he looked facing off with Demetrius. In fact, his height is a perfect complement to mine.

Those poufy pink lips of his are in easy reach without rising on my toes.

Tek fans his fingers in front of my face, and I swear I feel a little puff of heat. "Not a drop out of place. You are your beautiful self."

I stare at my smudge-free hands and then back at him. There's a loaded moment between us, and Hollywood help me, I almost press my lips to his. Good sense prevails, and I nod to the bar.

"Back to work. Heaven knows what a mess Demetrius made of unloading the shipment." An unexpected wave of relief relaxes muscles I hadn't realized have been locked up for months.

I broke up with Demetrius. It's done.

As I step away, Tek grabs my hand. "What shall we do tonight? Coaching? A hunt for your fantasy forest?"

Excitement fizzles through my chest at the thought of Tek's coaching techniques. "Let me get through the rest of the day."

"On and on you go," he says with a merry lilt. "I'll check in later." Then, with an odd little salute, he practically dances out of the club.

I giggle at his antics, but as I turn toward the bar where Demetrius and I spent hours creating fantastical cocktails together, my step falters.

For a woman who just dumped a guy I'd attempted to convince myself I was in love with, I'm awfully happy. Relief is one thing, but here I am on a giddy high about meeting up with another man hours after I hurt someone's heart. I grip the edge of the nearest table hard enough to snap a fingernail.

Maybe I really am a horrible person.

12

MEADOW MELODY

TEK

THE BLARING SOUNDS FROM THE THREE-STORY, STATE-OF-THE-ART arcade surrounding us are deafening. How the mortals could call this den of clang and caterwaul amusement escapes my understanding. Aurora drags me by the sleeve from the melee over to the central elevator.

It's the third time this week we've traipsed through dozens of floors visiting the Spire's test runs of businesses and attractions. She jokingly calls our jaunts "*getting to know you*" dates. I call them torture, not because I don't crave her company, but because contact outside our few clandestine coaching meetups has been limited to hand-holding or the subtle brushing of shoulders.

My solace has been after-hours coaching sessions where I am permitted to stroke her soft skin and run my fingers through the endless waves of her yellow hair to coax raspy, voluptuous notes from her lips. Once she's recorded her audition video, the frequency of my mentor services may no longer be required.

But will my company be just as welcome?

As much as I yearn to prolong these opportunities to feel the warmth of her skin and hear each breathy sigh, we can't ignore the video deadline galloping toward us.

My aching balls from our glacial slog at forging a deeper connection are a constant reminder I want more from Aurora than gratitude. I am bound by my promise of no expectations. Attempting to accelerate the pace she sets may lose me the prize.

"I hoped there might be a secret door to the forest in here," she hollers over the riot. "Don't stories say that magic portals always hide in plain sight? In the back of wardrobes or at the center of mushroom rings?"

"How can the door be in this madhouse if you discovered the forest walking straight off the elevator?" I plaster a look of complete innocence on my face. There's the faintest sting of guilt as I lead her on a merry chase up and down the Spire to seek a place she only discovered as a result of my jest. I'd love to satisfy her desire and possibly earn a kiss of gratitude, but returning to explore the Pristine Forest risks a more severe penalty from the royals. I rattle the spell stones in my pocket. I must not give the king and queen cause to force another treasure from my keeping.

The high-speed elevator arrives and its curved glass door slips aside to admit us. Aurora stares at it dubiously. "I hate riding this thing. If I wasn't late getting to work..."

If we're talking ifs...if only I could take her in my arms and fly up past the circuitous bends and tangles of the Spire to its pinnacle. Oh, how the view alone would enchant her.

I slide a hand around the small of her back. "Three hours before your shift starts is late?"

She freezes for the briefest of moments, the same way she's been doing the last few days whenever I attempt to touch her romantically outside of coaching time. Aurora neither repels nor encourages my touch, yet there is a distraction about her I cannot crack. I fret the fire that kindled between us has been banked and not by me.

Instead of loosening my tether to the woman, her imposed distance tempts me to accelerate the chase.

I decide on an action to intrigue her that I most certainly will regret, especially if I'm caught. Taking her hand, I wink. "I've got an idea." Instead of hopping in the express elevator, I lead her to one of the active auxiliary elevators.

She eyes me suspiciously. "I need to get to Stalk."

I slip my fingers between hers. "Stalk will wait. I have discovered the perfect place to record your video."

She hesitates. "What now?"

"Call it a dress rehearsal."

Tugging her into the elevator, I murmur a false request into the controls.

The car jolts, and Aurora gives a little squeak. "Where are you taking me?"

I flash an enticing smile that's lured many a would-be lover to my bower.

"Tek?" To my delight, she moves closer to me. Ah, do I sense the beginning of a thaw?

I take advantage of proximity to claim her other hand and draw her body nearer. "I did some snooping around on my own."

Aurora's brows wing up. "And you didn't tell me?"

"When I found no clues to further our hunt, I hated to disappoint you. Luckily, what I found may bring your smile back."

A chagrined expression rests upon her lovely face. "I'm sorry, Tek. I've been a total downer lately. Why would you want to invest time on such a mess?"

I tuck our joined hands against the hollow of my throat. "No, no, not so. Don't apologize. Your angst over the weeping starling adds color to your song."

"The who?"

"Demetrius." I spin her around as if we're dancing. "Do you know starlings are the most annoying of birds? They possess a natural ability to irritate."

Aurora's gaiety appears with a delightful laugh. I haven't heard the merry sound in days. Bubbles jig through my blood. Suddenly she claps both hands over her mouth. Her words are muffled behind them. "I'm awful for laughing when I caused Demie pain."

Any doubts about the audacity of what I plan for her vanish as the key behind Aurora's distance and dour moods comes clear. Misplaced guilt over blubbering Demetrius is what shadows her sunny nature.

The elevator jolts to a stop. I pray the corner of her vision doesn't notice the subtle shadow of a carved wooden door superimposed over the brushed metallic surface. I need her to think the elevator delivers us to a mortal-trod location in the Spire. Reaching out with my magic, I turn the knob she cannot see and step aside.

As I hoped, Aurora gasps at the scene before her. As well she should. The Meadow of Mirth is stunning as are most vistas in my realm. I've grown lax in my appreciation of this dimension's lighthearted beauty. Surrounding us, the grove of copperbark elm emits the faintest glint from the metallic core hidden beneath the outer layer of sienna wood on their trunks. Each blade of sweetgrass melts from hues of night-forest black at its base before fading through a parade of lighter shades of green up to tips kissed with a flaxen splash. The effect is a carpet of emerald silk, rippling in a nearly imperceptible breeze.

Seeing the shining wonder in Aurora's eyes gratifies me. I took a chance that with the tiniest push of my magic, the same ability that allowed her to see the Pristine Forest might reveal this venue hiding alongside the mortal veneer of the Spire. Most humans, unless granted the temporary ability to enjoy our realm, only perceive a wall of cloud if they happen to stumble near our barriers. They wander back to their reality with no memory of their trespass. I barely touch Aurora's perceptions, yet she easily glimpses parts of my world. Whatever allows this does not extend to full sight of fairy countenance or she would recoil at the unmasked visions of my parents and the other fairies surrounding them. I can no longer deny there is some mystery at play here with my alluring friend that I do not understand.

"I didn't see a park or meadow in the directory. Where are we?"

"I believe the company leasing this space is trying to keep it under wraps. Probably for fear of copycats before they complete construction. Cinnabar got wind of the project and mentioned it to me as an investment opportunity he was considering."

"So..." She gestures to the tree line. "...an indoor wood? A park?"

"Picnic spots intended to mimic Griffith Park. The joy of eating out of doors without bugs. We're in one of the finished sections." I'm such a smooth liar. Given I created the Spire, I suppose I could call myself President of the Tek Landscaping and Illusions Company.

"Griffith Park is one of my favorite places."

Aurora flies from the elevator. I hold my breath, bracing for signs we've been discovered as her bright blue slipper shoes touch meadow grass.

Nothing happens. No shaking of the ground beneath us to signal displeasure from the royals or guards.

Relief turns my bones from stone to softer stuff. My gamble works. The combination of tossing a thin sheath of magic around Aurora and sneaking into a remote corner of the Arborborn Coterie's realm does not set off fairy warnings of mortal intrusion. It is fortuitous that royal bowers and courts are a far-flung distance from where we stand.

My beautiful lady kicks off her shoes, flings her arms wide, and twirls under the fairy sun. A pair of iridescent, raspberry-colored finches dart in for a closer look. I waft a flare of magic to encourage the birdies back into the trees. The unnatural vibrancy of their feathers might raise questions from Aurora I must not answer. The flighty duo sends scolding chirps my way.

Aurora lets out a melodic, "Ahh."

The strap of her delightfully clingy sundress falls from one shoulder as she stops her dance, swaying to catch her balance. I'm at her side in an instant and brazenly lift her into my arms. "I think a few more spins will do it." As I circle with Aurora cradled against my chest, she drops her head back and squeals. On impulse, I press my lips to her shoulder and kiss her blushing apricot skin. She lifts her head then, and I prepare to be admonished. Instead, she delivers her own quick kiss to the side of my neck, and I lose my footing. We tumble onto grass as soft as a pile of down, both laughing with childish delight.

"Dizzy—head rush," she says, laying palms to her temples.

"Given the sparkle in your eyes, I assume you enjoy this state?"

Her lips curve down. "There hasn't been enough time in my life for twirling."

I jump in before she shifts back into her maudlin mood of the past week. "Shall I tick off your love of twirling as one of the three new things I'll learn about you today?" I'm eager to continue our ongoing game of trading snippets about ourselves. So far, we've shared past misadventures, as well as semi-personal dribs and drabs such as our mutual only child status. The topic of birthdays surfaced early, her age being twenty-five and mine a lie. I doubt she'd be anything but shocked I've recently passed the milestone age of double eights, eighty-eight. I used a portion of my true age and claimed to be twenty-eight.

"I'll allow it. Now, your turn."

There's always a nervous stitch in my sternum when she asks me questions about my life. I have scant details to share that fit the framework of a mortal existence. "I'm a disappointment to my parents." Concern crinkles the skin near her eyes as I continue. "They expect more from me than the life I live."

"I think it's pretty impressive you're an executive assistant to the two big-wigs responsible for Stalk." She sets a hand on my knee.

I lay a hand upon hers. "If you wish it, I shall be impressed with myself."

Her laugh is explosive. "That's not a big stretch. You're the most self-assured person I've ever met."

I shake my head to set dangling strands of my hair dancing. "And you like that part of me?"

She contemplates the puffs of clouds above us. "I envy it. It must be kinda great not to always worry you might hurt or offend someone." Before I can jump in with any encouragement, her gaze is back on me. "Okay, Tek. You know my passion…"

Aurora elongates the word just enough to stir my constant companion of a pulsing peony glow. Thank nature, she lacks fairy sight or I'd come off like a blushing maiden in her presence.

"…is singing, but I don't know yours." She continues before I answer. "I'm not talking career ambition. What makes your heart beat so incredibly fast you worry it may wear itself out?"

We stare into each other's eyes as if answers hide within them.

You, Aurora, you.

I blurt different words to mask what my lively heart is shouting. "Gardening." Surprise blooms across her features as I stumble on. "Botany. Plants. Trees. Flowers."

She gazes at me with interest. "That's really cool." Her arm sweeps the meadow. "It's why you're drawn to places like this." Rora turns her palm up to twine her fingers through mine. "It brings you peace, doesn't it?"

I want to stare at the mingling of her creamy peach and my burnt ochre skin. We are light and dark in balance together. My breath catches. Like my parents, shadow and spark, an incendiary combination.

"Tek?"

I look up realizing my thoughts have pulled me far from the moment. "Peace. Yes. I am most at peace among natural things, simple things."

"I can tell. You're always zipping around." Her thumb strokes the back of my hand. "But here, you're calmer."

I inhale deeply, allowing the scents of grass, bark, and bloom to fill my senses. "Believe it or not, I often crave the quiet hum of solitude."

Aurora shakes our joined hands. "There's a special bench in Griffith Park I go to early in the morning to write songs." She gives me a shy smile. "We could take in a sunrise together."

Sadness coats my spirit. If only I could share the desire to return to my homeland and greet the sun, moon, stars, night breeze...

Pangs of longing steal my breath, but I have angered my king and queen enough of late. There is no valid reason other than my selfish whim to reveal my truth to Rora. "I'm not a morning person."

"There." She beams at me. "I've learned another thing." Aurora settles onto her back, reclaiming her hand to link it with her other that rests on her stomach. "For now, I'll settle with sneaking into this place together." She sighs. "Once it opens, I'm sure it'll be crawling with people. It's too beautiful to be left alone."

Insanity burrows into my thoughts. How I'd love to bring Aurora into my realm for more than a sneak peek at the Pristine Forest or stingy moments in a remote fairy meadow.

I pluck a red sugar daisy with tangerine tips from the grass and tickle it over her still bare shoulder. "I enjoy this more relaxed version of you as well."

She rolls onto her side to face me. The scoop of her neckline treats me to the swell of her breasts. Catching my glance, she attempts to cover herself, but I stop her. "You've no need to hide from me. I already imagine sampling the delights of your body."

Aurora gives me a playful slap. "You wish."

"I do wish." Trailing a finger across her collarbone, I pause along the top of the cleft between her breasts. "Here's my third fact of the day. I am an excellent lover. Feel free to take advantage."

"You are a giver, aren't you, Tek?"

Words more breath than voice and her hooded gaze embolden

me. I scoot a little closer. "And a taker. Isn't that what lovemaking is? Give and take?"

She licks her lips then presses them together as if she's decided to hang a *Do Not Enter* sign on her body. It's a contradiction to the smolder in her eyes. Ah, a mortal in conflict always has a vulnerability. I just need to find the way in.

Her chest heaves as she takes a deep breath. I want to slip the other strap off her shoulder and lower the dress to taste...

"I wouldn't know." She sits up, drawing her knees to her chest.

Her words snap me out of my lusty haze. Oh, nature's promise. Did the puny-dick Demetrius not partake of this beauty's bounty? I sit as well and cock my head to the side. "You're a virgin?"

Aurora snorts. "Hardly."

"But you have not enjoyed skilled lovers?"

She drops her forehead onto her knees. "Are we really going to talk about this?"

"Isn't it a topic couples desiring to move forward discuss?"

Aurora turns her head to look at me and takes a fortifying breath. "I've got enough guilt over stabbing Demie through the heart. Outing his, ah—performance on top of that seems even worse. I don't expect you to share your sexual history with me."

What an odd bit to withhold. "I've enjoyed both men and women."

"Adventurous," she says, hesitating for a moment. "Just guys for me."

I am perplexed. "Then how do you know which you prefer...if not both, without sampling diverse pleasures?"

She fidgets a little. "I guess sampling, as you put it, is the way to settle things for some people." Her shoulders lift in a sweet shrug. "Since we're oversharing, I've only ever been sexually attracted to men."

I lie back on the grass, pluck a few tiny blades, and blow them into the air. "I do not share your preference. To me, women alone bring magnificence beyond basic satisfaction to sexual encounters."

"So, we're both straight." She chuckles and stretches her legs, allowing a crack in her cocoon of self-protection. "Definitely information a couple should share with one another." Aurora's face flushes an enchanting shade of dawn. "Have you fallen in love with any of your..." She tilts her head to one side. "...encounters?"

I pause for a moment, searching my history of bedsport. "Fleeting affection, but not for any notable span of time. Certainly, none fell in love with me."

"How sad."

"I'm a challenge." I capture her gaze. "Did you feel this for Demetrius?"

A wistful expression brings a shadow of melancholy across her loveliness. "It would have made sense, but no."

I give her leg a playful squeeze. Her skin is smooth and warm. My naughty fingers itch to slide up under her dress. "Ah, we get to it at last. Your investment was weak, and he is a terrible lover. Proof any guilt over dumping him is misplaced. Especially when you've found a handsome and sexually gifted new beau." At that, I take a chance and allow my hand to travel above her knee. Her succulent skin begs for a nip of my teeth.

Aurora wiggles away from me. "Truth. Demie was shit in bed."

I leap to my feet and break into the first steps of a jig before settling back next to her. "I knew it. Tell all."

"Oh, what the hell. In his defense, he had no experience. He approached the process like he was following directions on furniture assembly. Insert tab D into slot V."

My dick rumbles at the thought of inserting my tab D into her slot V.

"I had previous experience so the next time we, ah, were intimate, I tried to seduce him."

I flip over onto my stomach to hide my cock's particular interest in her narration. "What does sweet and kind Aurora consider seduction?"

She shoots me a sarcastic glare.

I'll pluck information out of her even if I need to straddle her delicious body until she confesses all. Maybe I'll straddle her for the pure pleasure of it alone. I wonder if we have reached such a juncture in our coupling or if she'd push me off. "I think if you explain, we may be able to use such knowledge in your performance."

Aurora blushes as peony pink as the sheen I've been wearing since the night it first appeared. "There was some dancing…and stripping."

"Excellent methodology. Go on." I swallow hard and force a look of clinical disinterest while wriggling into a position where I'm not painfully mashing my fully aroused dick against the ground.

"Then a little grinding, which finally got him hard even though he was a freakin' statue, expecting me to do all the work."

"Uh-huh." Picturing the expert naked grinding I could treat Aurora to nearly sends me over the edge. I twist my mouth, attempting to appear introspective while my bulge pulses a tortuous rhythm. "We can work with those moves."

"The rest is embarrassing."

"Let your objective coach decide. I'll never share this with another soul if that's what worries you." Poor Aurora. She's kept much bottled inside. I hate the thought she finds fault in herself for Demetrius's sexual buffoonery. Fighting the urge to editorialize, I allow her to continue since confession seems to afford relief from her simmering emotional turmoil.

Aurora closes her eyes as if it will be easier to finish if she's not looking at me. "I encouraged him to feel how ready I was for him, but his touch was as sexy as a dead fish."

Oh, how I'd swim through her liquid tide with stroke after stroke of my fingers. Demetrius sinks below my already stale opinion of him. What man could revel in the satiny slickness between this woman's legs and not fall to his knees and worship her? Rancid coralberries, his sexual ineptitude is tantamount to misery purposefully inflicted. My darling Aurora deserves infinitely more from a lover.

"Okay, then I basically shoved him onto the bed to get it over with. He came before I finished rolling the condom on. The end." She hides her face with her hands.

"And he's been a dick to you ever since?"

She separates her fingers enough to see my face. "We tried again, or I should say, I tried again. I suggested massages, less aggressive foreplay, even porn, but Demetrius accused me of putting too much pressure on him."

Thank the glimmer of starshine I've never had to suffer such a farcical carnal encounter. "What did you do?"

"I suggested we take sex off the menu for a while." She deflates at the memory. "I needed a break from his drama."

"Let me guess, the idiot cried."

"Yup, and with the waterworks came begging, but he still refused to discuss, ah...technique. I finally gave in." A fluttery stutter colors her sigh. "Big mistake." She lowers her gaze to the grass. "It's mortifying when the person you're in a relationship with doesn't find you attractive enough to get it up then blames you."

I'm so angry, every last drop of lust leaks away. "And you hadn't left him because you blame yourself for his sexual shortcomings?"

She nods, and a single tear drops from her chin. I burn to make love to her right here in the meadow to show her she is the most desirable woman, mortal or fairy, I've ever known. Then while she's basking in the afterglow of what a woman should feel after a man celebrates her body and soul, I want to excuse myself to drag Demetrius to the highest pinnacle of Stalk and fling him over the edge.

I stand and offer a hand to pull Aurora up. This time I do not hesitate to fit my body to hers, willing my heat to burn away any remnants of Demie's poison. "Aurora Herman, you..."

I yank both her straps back down until the front scoop of her dress rests just above her nipples. "...are..."

Reaching behind her head, I destroy the bun, allowing her golden locks to cascade freely. "...the..."

I fan thick blond strands across her bare shoulders. "...most luscious..."

My hips thrust into hers. "...lady..."

I capture her face in my hands and guide her lips to mine. "...in the entire fucking world."

My mouth covers hers to deliver a kiss leaving no room for any doubt she makes the ground shake for me. My teeth gently bite her plump, rosy bottom lip. I intend to wipe away any notion she isn't every man's sweet dream. I hold my breath anticipating the slap I deserve for taking advantage of her moment of weakness. Before I can disconnect, her hands grip my ass, yanking me against her. I've barely processed the move when her tongue strokes mine, dripping with permission to devour.

I grab her thigh and lift her leg around my hip to send the scorching waves of heat flowing from her sex across my throbbing cock. Strands of my wild hair tangle with hers as I worship every inch of her delectable mouth. When she sucks hard, pulling me in deeper, I moan and rock against her. My pulsing dick screams to magic every stitch of clothing off us both. What I'd give to bury my staff balls-deep inside my sweet Aurora.

"Tek," she murmurs in a rough voice so laden with need, I'm blind to everything but the flashes of pulsing peony surrounding us.

I freeze.

Pulsing peony.

Realization squeezes my chest. The colorful shimmer I wear does not lie. I'm not the victim of a jest or prank. My lumen light radiates truth.

I am indeed love-blind.

What began as lust and challenge born, I see with altered sight. Restrain falls tattered beneath pulsing peony light.

Aurora ceases to be a simple challenge for my riddling wiles to conquer. This mortal woman punctured my veneer of mischief and misdeed to wrap around my heart.

Her body tenses. "Tek, are you okay?"

It's imperative I control my yearning for her before I'm fully consumed and can't restrain from proving to her right here in the meadow that love-play can be a beautiful experience. Especially when she's vulnerable after gifting me with her private fears and doubts.

I fight the urge to jump backwards and do something ridiculous like profess my love.

No, no, not so—not love.

Such a declaration is unfair to Aurora. She is newly healed from the ruination of her bond with Demetrius. I would saddle her with a burden, a secret she must bear in silence. To what purpose other than my own selfish heart would I subject her to this? Any lasting future between us is in truth as fleeting as a fickle fairy's promise. I shall tuck my desire deep within the brambles of my yearning and not allow this to go beyond lust play. This Tek will not be another bruise blemishing her goodness. It is best to practice restraint in this moment and only allow my advances to proceed far enough that I may claim this seduction was to awaken a lusty Aurora for her video, not seek a balm for my lovelorn heart.

Weak Tek.

How will I play the gentleman and hold back when my need for her roars like a beast in dire need? Instead of the respectful retreat I counseled myself to pursue, I release her leg so my hands are free to roam up her sides.

I want you, Aurora.

My fingers close around her breasts. Their heavy fullness and inviting peaks are my undoing. I knead her in a gentle rhythm until I'm rewarded with a throaty moan. Easing her shoulders back, my tongue travels in a languid lick down her throat then lower until I savor the salty tang glistening between her perfect tits. When she begins to quiver, I pull her mouth to mine and growl against her lips. Her eyes are wild and feverish.

Stop, Tek. Stop.

I have come to the divide I must not cross. My mind finally outpaces my lust as I force words to justify my carnal advances with my intention. “Now, we record the video. Your phone?”

Still tethered to her own lusty haze, she nods at the chunky fabric bag on the grass. Keeping her pinned to my side, I reach into the outer pocket and snatch her cell.

I slide my hands around and squeeze her ass. “Sing your lust, my darling Aurora.” I walk her backwards until we’re in the shadow of the trees. Unsated lust heats my blood to a degree that will surely melt the very vessels that carry it through my body.

With a ragged tone to match my ragged restraint, I chant, “Voice and body, ache and burn, as torch song now shall take its turn.”

As desire threatens to drop me to my knees, I ease her next to the smooth trunk and twist her hips to face it. I adjust her hands against the bark as if she’s caressing a lover. Oh, to be the object of such ministrations. Amidst her rapid blinks, I arrange the straps of her dress and bra until they drip off those delicately rounded shoulders. Her neckline settles at an almost indecently low level on her breasts. For a final touch, I muss her brilliant yellow hair.

Stepping away, I lift the phone and frame the shot. With a tiny assist from my magic, I coax a single beam of sunlight to settle around her.

“Make love to me with your song.” I cannot bear forgoing yet another taste of this exquisite woman and stalk closer, kissing her until Rora’s lips swell and tremble against mine before reluctantly assuming my duties as cameraman. Her sultry look is tantalizingly on point. My Aurora is every bit the forest nymph seeking a victim to seduce.

I am ever that victim.

Growling my direction, I break the silence of the meadow. “Force me to beg, you perfect, perfect beauty.”

And she does.
Nature, help me, she does.

13

SUNSTONE

TEK

I CHECK THE *PEARL TEAR'S* SPELL AROUND THE MAGIC MORTAL'S TABLE. The power remains true. It will stand tonight during what Cinnabar dubs a *soft opening* when a handful of investors gather for a preview of the club. Gothel and his witches insisted they be in attendance. Thanks to my magic, they will be invisible to all but the keenest of fairy eyes.

A foul mood as thick as the cloaking spell surrounds me. In night after night of spying, I've learned nothing more about the Dark Vinyl Artists' plan to betray us.

My gaze wanders to the stage, lightening my spirit as I imagine Aurora's sultry torch song. The simple thought stirs a longing in my belly alongside the mountain of frustration where she is concerned. I've deftly assisted Aurora in shedding her Demetrius coat and teasing the possibility of something more between us, but our near-tryst in the meadow came too close to me losing myself to her. Self-preservation to guard my own heart from that which must not be, as well as true caring for her, led me to let her believe our foreplay was nothing more than stoking lust for the video.

I grunt. Aurora apologized for taking things too far too fast, and I allowed her to accept blame.

Disgraceful Tek.

We safely remain as potential amours and play our parts well, given the noxious glances Demie-poo aims in my direction. Oddly enough, this tentative pace, while frustrating, has been interesting in a way I've never experienced with a woman before. It is a maddening type of addiction that keeps me in check even as my resolve to be more to her than a man who cries her name at the pinnacle of lovemaking increases.

Love-blind Tek.

"Playing at patience claws Tek's tortured heart. What measure shall end two souls yet apart?"

A nobbly buzz in my stomach solves my self-imposed riddle. I press palms against glass. No *measure* separates us physically. Aurora's actions in the meadow made it clear she'd welcome me into her bed.

If I'm honest with myself, which I make it a practice not to be, more than one creeping shadow of fear kept me from giving in to my desires as I held Aurora in my arms. My parents are vengeful and unforgiving. If they suspect Aurora is more than just a libidinous distraction, they may harm her. I am not so much love-blind as I am love-affrighted of those consequences. Then there is the promise I made to myself to avoid love at all costs lest it devolve into the enmity that exists between the king and queen. I'd rather pluck an eye out than subject sweet Rora to the decay of love.

When did I become noble? My hands smear down the glass.

"Back in the meadow when you were forced to accept the boundary of lust into love had been crossed, you foolish fairy."

The practice of fairy acquisition is simple. We lure, entice, and then discard humans. It is our way. Never do we open our hearts to the impossible.

That way courts disaster.

Scrambled voices like the low rumble of mechanicals invade

my pathetic introspection. It's the Dark Vinyl Artists slithering their way to courtside seats before Cinnabar throws the doors wide for tonight's soft opening of the club. My eyes flash to a less-muffled hubbub coming up the grand marble staircase, signaling the pre-game briefing of the staff has ended.

Stalk is poised to come alive for the first time.

Aurora is first through the arch. My breath catches as she almost collides with the perky blonde number, Brandy Winter, Rubata Lear's shapeshifting doppelganger. Demetrius distracts Aurora just as the two women are about to brush shoulders. The pinched look on Rora's face tells me the bastard is spewing unpleasantries in her ear.

I'm so fixed on the pair I fail to notice the queen slinking up behind me. "Tell me, Tek. What do you know of our pretty little cocktail magician?"

"Now I am bidden to spy on your staff as well as the magic mortals, Your Majesty?"

Citrine clucks. "You waste plenty of time around Stalk doing Cinnabar's bidding. I assume you're familiar with the help."

I dislike the way the queen's gaze fixes on Aurora. "I confirm the male cocktail magician, Demetrius, is a donkey's ass."

"He is not my concern. I sense the mortal woman, Aurora, who you allowed to venture into my Pristine Forest, is more than she seems. Would you agree, Tek Goodfellow?"

My insides curdle. What can she mean? How much does Citrine know about Rora and me? Was I wrong, and our visit to the meadow did not escape royal attention?

The queen taps a long, silver-tipped fingernail against her chin. She aims a piercing gaze at me when I fail to answer then continues. "I finished reviewing the final batch of audition videos *Saturday's Star* sent over, and it seems our gifted cocktail magician is quite the accomplished singer."

Thank the Spire, that's Citrine evaluation of Aurora being more. I stuff down pride at the queen's praise for my lovely companion and reply. "The saying goes that the roots of creativity extend in many directions. Since the woman is indeed a whiz at creating unique cocktails does not her possession of vocal talent follow the adage?"

Citrine continues to assess Aurora. "Yes, creatives are creatives. I wonder..." She strolls toward the bar lost in her musings.

It's rarely a fortuitous outcome for a human to garner the queen's notice. "Wonder what?" For all the attention my mother affords me, I am no more notable than the upholstered high-backed bar seats.

I calm my breathing. This could be a good omen. If Citrine is complimenting Rora's video, my girl does indeed have a shot at her dream.

The queen's buttercup evening gown swishes against the floor as she approaches a totally preoccupied Aurora. "You've been keeping secrets," she purrs as she meanders round the bar to settle next to her target.

I trail her, stationing myself nearby, coiled to intervene if necessary.

Rora's head pops up from her duties. She is shaken by Citrine's proximity. "Pardon?"

My mother drapes an arm across the cocktail magician's shoulder. "Cinnabar didn't mention he'd hired a linnetgale."

I sink my teeth into my lower lip at the queen's slipup. Linnetgales are fairy birds. Ones whose song is said to spin the darkest spirit into gossamer.

The royal covers quickly. "I'm referring to your rather alluring audition tape."

Rora flushes as crimson as a linnetgale's breast. "Yeah, I mean yes, ma'am. I never mentioned it since I didn't think it was appropriate to mix the *Saturday's Star* contest with work. It felt like cheating."

Citrine's tinkly laugh floats across the bar as she fingers a stray wisp of hair that's escaped from Aurora's bun.

Spindlewood! The queen is flirting with my woman. I silently curse the waves of seduction flowing through the video that were supposed to work in Rora's favor. I'm the dimwit who didn't foresee Citrine being titillated as much as I was by the performance.

"Nonsense. Talent is talent, my dear. It never hurts to have an inside track, especially here in Hollywood with its bloodthirsty competition." Citrine tilts her head slightly and purses her lips. "There is a problem though."

The color drains from Rora's blush. "Does the contest break a conflict-of-interest rule?"

"No, no. The problem is mine. I need to experience your performance in person before I decide if you'll make it into my top recommendations."

Blood rushes to my face with such a surge, I'm surprised I don't combust. I'm about to insert myself in their conversation when Citrine beats me to the punch.

"It happens we've only booked one act to perform tonight for the soft opening. What do you say to closing the evening with your song once they've finished their set? Allow me a closer look at your talent."

"But...I...cocktails..." Aurora sputters.

"You over there," says the queen, pointing a finger at Demetrius who hovers nearby. "Can you handle the specialty cocktails on your own for a few while our darling Aurora here favors us with a song?"

The ass is as tongue-tied as Rora and just nods.

"It's done then." Citrine trails a finger along the underside of Aurora's chin. "Let's see how brightly you shine, my dearest."

Cinnabar appears next to her and claps his hands. The sound reverberates off the glass walls. The maître-d, hostesses, waitstaff, the two cocktail magicians, and their bar assistants turn toward the sound.

"And so it begins, my friends. The elevator approaches with our first guests. Let us bring Stalk to life," announces the king.

As everyone scurries into place, my parents linger at the end of the bar, heads together in a heated discussion.

Demetrius doesn't temper his volume. "I see your fuck buddy scored you an in with the boss lady."

I would expend so little effort to send the bastard's head crashing into the granite counter.

Rora snaps at him. "Keep your voice down."

Too late. The queen's sidelong stare is riveted on her.

Demetrius shifts his malevolence to me. "Watch out, errand boy. Aurora's just playing you for the connection to Ms. Citrine the way she played me to pull her out of the gutter."

I should pepper his vituperous tongue with pox. Citrine's glare shifts focus to me, sending a sharp pain through my temples. A summons brews in her eyes. Before she has a chance to crook a dreaded finger my way, the first wave of guests reaches the arch, granting me a temporary reprieve. Everyone springs into action.

En route to take my place in the vicinity of the magic mortals table to siphon off any information, I slide along the bar until I'm directly in front of Aurora. "Ignore him. I'm here for you." Since rotten Demetrius outed us to the room with his toxic barb, there's no point in hiding our brewing relationship. I reach my hand over the bar. She grasps it and squeezes. If the counter wasn't between us, I'd be able to drop a kiss on her knuckles. As it is, a squeeze will have to do. Her eyes are dewy as she sends me a grateful look that tempts me to fall to my knees and confess the meaning of my pulsing peony lumen light. Rora saves me the mortification by turning to her bar duties.

I manage to avoid the queen while she and Cinnabar make the rounds. Aurora's cocktail creations are a hit. She's a blur behind the bar zipping between blenders, bottles, and the fridge to keep up with the orders. Luckily, sulky Demetrius is too busy to be a scoundrel.

A shudder in the masking shield rips my attention from the bar over to the Dark Vinyl Artists' table. For a gut-clenching moment, I fear the magic of the spell stone is weakening, but the disturbance is Rubata, aka Brandy Winter, and a man I assume to be Claude making their way across the boundary to the shadows of the hallway. The Lear Witch has indeed disguised her partner with copper tresses down his back and copious makeup, enough to ready him for a fairy masque. They'll make their entrance from near Stalk's arch, posing as non-magical talent.

Citrine announces the duo as Brandy Winter and Clive Summer with regal flair as they take center stage.

The magic mortals listen to the performance of their witch and stooge from beneath the guise of an empty table, not saying anything of substance. I wonder if my presence has been sensed, most likely by the enchantress, since they seem especially guarded tonight.

"They truly are quite ghastly," says a voice behind me. The queen breaches the solitude of my post. "Shrieking crows in a tin can."

I search the patrons. Many are smiling at the singers and moving to the rhythm of their song. "Perhaps to our discerning ears. The guests approve."

"Of course they do. Their kind has no taste." Claude hits a particularly offensive note. "The woman may be passable, but the male...excruciating. Mixing sugar with grit does not make it edible." She huffs a breath.

I let the comment lie, hoping the queen moves on. Instead, she sidles closer. Warm breath wafts across the tip of my ear. "You've been keeping secrets, Tek Goodfellow."

Ah, here it is. The reason she deigns to speak to me. I will not take the bait. Let her try to pick the lock of my mysteries.

Citrine rakes a fingernail across my cheek. Ah, a mother's gentle caress with the potential to draw blood. An apt illustration of our relationship.

Still, I remain silent, willing myself to breathe easy and mask the dread swimming through me like minnows in a still pond. Which of my many secrets is she about to prick with her needle?

"Follow me, miscreant."

She saunters through the arch, staying close enough to appear as if she's waiting to greet latecomers. This should prove to be a jolly chat. I join her, keeping well out of fingernail range.

"Come closer."

I obey, and she nods to the cell phone cradled in her palm. "Did you think I wouldn't notice, you disobedient cur?" she hisses.

Playing on her screen is the audition video we shot in the Meadow of Mirth. As Citrine zooms in on a bright splash of color in the picture, I teeter from the visual blow. Perched on the branch above where Aurora's fingers stroke the trunk is a damned raspberry finch. In the queen's zoomed image, streaks as bright as a copper penny blare through grooves in the bark to reveal the fairy tree.

Reckless Tek.

I was so enamored with Aurora's song, glaring details identifying the fairy realm skipped my lust turned love-hazed notice. I'd assumed it would appear the video was shot among the trees of Griffith Park where mortals are free to roam.

I am love-blind indeed, and laxity in judgment will be my undoing.

"You have been chastised once over forbidden transgressions with that human. Your never-ending habit of shirking the vital rule to mask our realm is reprehensible and perilous."

I bite my tongue before commenting how easily Aurora perceived the forest and then the meadow with the barest trace of my intervention.

The air boils around us as Citrine's anger intensifies.

"And now you dare to become carnal with your mortal as well? You are as deceitful as your arrogant sire."

My voice is low. "My queen, my knot with Aurora is more than a mere dalliance."

Citrine hisses as I speak the word *knot*. She grabs my chin, and I open my lumen light, allowing her to see the pulsing peony sheen clinging to me.

"You dare to claim a *knot*?" Her nail scrapes the tender flesh of my neck as she releases me. "It is detestable for royal blood, no matter how abhorrent its bearer, to bind themselves in a sacred knot with a human."

I have no other recourse but to admit deep love for Rora by claiming we are knotted. Stating a fairy bond is my only weapon to protect her from any in my coterie who intend harm. Fairy knots surpass lust and budding steadfast affection into the sanctum of oath and vow. This profession of an authentic and mutual promise is a sacred commodity to my kind. The color of my lumen light proves this truth to my queen just as it has to me.

I am indisputably in unlikely love...with Aurora.

Thank every turn of the seasons, the truth of whether or not Rora returns my love is hidden from my mother. As powerful as Citrine is, she cannot read a human heart.

The king will take my side in this standoff, and my mother knows it. She will not yet act against me. There is time to warn Aurora of my declaration to the queen, if only it were but one of the revelations I must share. My love knows not what I am. Explaining the concept of a fairy knot is the least of the confessions looming before me.

My deep pink glow reflects in the queen's limoncello eyes, darkening their shade. Citrine looks poised to snap my neck. "Emotional gluttony. I should expect no less, you living travesty of Cinnabar's seed."

I refuse to stay mute as she attempts to flatten me with her scorn. I detest the way she considers Aurora a weed in my garden. "Do we choose love or does it capture us? I do not willfully pursue a human out of defiance or disobedience. It is nature's will."

"Bah. It is your defiance that endangers the secrecy of our realm. Twice you expose our presence to her." Murder colors her stare. "Know this, consequence for your conceit will fall not only on you, but your mortal plaything as well."

War rages between head and heart. Do I reveal how little of my influence Aurora requires to see our dimension? What does Citrine know of this rare trait in a human? Does that put Rora in greater or less danger from the queen?

A couple decked out in tux and gown approach the top of the marble staircase. Citrine dons a radiant smile to greet them. She delivers a furious parting whisper before approaching the latecomers. "Return to you duty, Tek Goodfellow. We are not finished."

I force my legs to carry me to my spy nest since they've adopted the consistency of pepperfruit jelly. I've no sooner supported myself against the black marbled wall when applause fills the club.

Queen Citrine joins Claude the clod and Brandy/Rubata onstage, interrupting their set to offer praise that surely burns her tongue. They're given the boot or in Citrine's case, the dagger-like heel of her unapologetically ostentatious crystal stilettos that push the boundary of hiding a fairy in plain sight. The two exit, offput their performance has been curtailed.

At her next words, my lungs refuse to fill.

"We have a special treat for you all tonight."

I dash to the bar in time to see Aurora emerging from the storeroom door. My breath catches as the soft lights from the bar illuminate a beauty. Her voluminous yellow hair tumbles down her back in curling waves. She's wearing a saffron shift dress with red embroidery around the scooped neckline and waist. It flatters her curves enough to send a flare of jealousy surging up my middle. Nature, help me, her lips have burst into bloom and are as red as the stitching on her dress.

I burn for her.

My body vibrates with urgency to leap over the bar and fly her to the safety of my bower. I meet her before she rounds the end of the counter to take the stage. I wrap my arms around my woman, dangling my hands above the delectable upper curve of her fine bottom, and pull her close.

"Tek," she breathes, half in surprise, half in protest. "I'm about to go on."

My mind is racing faster than a lumen travel game of tag. I brush lips to her ear. "Dearest darling, I speak true. True words of love we now must coo. Convince the room our knot is strong. I shall explain the *why* ere long."

She buries her nose in my loopy strands to return a whisper. "What the hell is a knot, and why are you rhyming a hundred miles an hour?"

Isn't she listening? I just said I'd tell her soon. I try to speak plainly but utterly fail. "Trust in me, you soon will see. A game's alive, and so we dive." My lips linger at one corner of her mouth then the other. Smearing Rora's screaming red lipstick before she sings will not earn me favor.

Aurora leans her head on my shoulder. "I trust you, Tek."

The sweet gesture temporarily waylays my mania. "Sing for me alone, Rora."

Citrine announces Aurora's name from the stage. My darling straightens, checking her dress and hair. Meeting my gaze before her big entrance, she murmurs, "I always do."

Fire blazes in my chest at her words. One I wish will rage on and on. It's been ignorant folly not to boldly act on our mutual affections. Restraint did not protect her. The battle to resist the message of my pulsing peony lumen now bears the markings of a tragic misstep for us both.

Aurora approaches the stage with the sultry gait of a temptress as we've practiced in our sessions. I'm too nervous to be turned on. She purrs her opening notes and the *ting* of utensils against china stills. The song is a spell she casts over every soul as the turntable slowly journeys round and round, taking every ear, heart, and groin in the room prisoner.

I miss the queen's approach as I'm sure she intended. She is not immune to Aurora's musical magic.

"This woman is a sunstone, Tek Goodfellow. Look how her light chases the dark. She is no common human."

My fairy sight allows me to see what Citrine has discovered. Delicate beams of honey-colored light stream from Aurora's chest to bathe the room in golden splendor. She is sunlight in the darkened club, a sunstone to be sure. How have I not noticed before? What does it mean?

Stupid, love-blind Tek.

My senses have been ruled by lust and longing. I did not look past Aurora's mortal charms, which were enough to thrust me into a smitten spiral, to discover my love's true light. How irksome the queen uncovered my darling's secret treasure before I did.

Citrine's vicious purr vibrates against my ear. "A mortal possessing crystal qualities is too good for your tektite core. Aurora and her petals are better suited for my royal garden than your threadbare knot. Chalcedony nurtures while Galena brings harmony. Peridot erases my burdens, and saucy Tourmaline fuels the physical pleasures of my ladies. This mortal sunstone of yours will enrich the gifts of my beloved favorites with the shine of her inner goodness." She chuckles. "An attribute we do not practice in abundance."

I force an encouraging smile as Aurora's revolution allows her gaze to fall to mine. Her sensuous song continues to captivate. My body tenses, prepared to claim her the moment she leaves the stage.

Citrine will not touch her.

The queen dances her fingers across my shoulder in celebration of her perceived conquest. "I am not heartless, Tek Goodfellow, nor impatient. Finish your love-play with the mortal then dissolve your knot. Once she is free of you, I will claim her as one of my favorites. Consider it fresh punishment for knotting with a mortal." Her hungry expression captures Aurora. "She will be resplendent in chiffon the color of honey, draped in amberglass gems."

"Ah, I see. Thievery of a human is an acceptable offense, but you decry my knot with her an outrage."

Citrine incinerates me with a glare. "Precisely."

The torch song ends and robust applause reverberates off every steel, glass, and marble surface. Patrons stand at their table. Some blow kisses. Possessiveness explodes through me like fast-acting poison. As Aurora takes her final bow, I charge the turntable, reaching a hand to guide her down.

I must protect her from my mother. Prove to the queen I have no intention of letting Aurora go. I consume my love's intoxicating red lips. This time our kiss is not designed to ignite sensuality in Aurora as were the touch of my lips upon her skin before she sang. It is to steal her passion for myself and give her mine in return. With a selfish moan, I take all I want before she can retreat.

She does not retreat.

Our kiss deepens as if we were back in the meadow with no one watching. Her hands clutch at my hair to draw me closer as she seals her mouth to mine. Our bodies fuse, and I thrust my tongue, roughly lashing the length of hers. Can she tell I am changed? No longer a seducer but a true victim of love.

A strong hand claps my shoulder, and we break the kiss. Cinnabar gives a hardy chuckle, then proclaims in his booming bass. "I believe you are the envy of everyone in this room, young man."

The crowd rewards his comment with laughter as Aurora ducks her head, embarrassed.

"However, I'm afraid our lovely and talented cocktail magician is still on duty." The king offers her his arm and escorts her to the bar, but not before he flashes a glance toward the magic mortal's table.

I muster the look of a thief caught in the act and slink back into the shadows. It's torture not to stay at Aurora's side with the queen on the prowl. I shall cling to hope that Citrine's intention remains to allow me a measure of time before she steals my love away.

My body thrums and sizzles with the need to fly from here with Aurora. Instead, I'm shackled to the magic mortals who will spew their vapid chatter and give me nothing of value to report to my monarchs. Moments tick by as I attempt to slow my raging thoughts enough to focus on the sorcerer and his witches. It's Gothel's voice that breaks through my muddled awareness.

The sorcerer catches himself before he smacks the table. "The last torch singer is exactly the model we've been looking for both vocally and..." The salacious way he licks his lips disgusts me. The thought of anyone lusting after Aurora triggers my most dangerous instincts.

"I agree," hums the sea witch. "Her range is quite accomplished, and she possesses a mature presence our Golden Harp is sorely lacking."

The enchantress, Tressa, shakes her head and snowflakes swirl inside their private bubble. "Have you lost your minds? We can't risk adding another inane mortal to the group. Claude is bad enough." She lifts her bosom. "I can teach our girl how to stick her tits out when she sings. Baby girl isn't used to having a rack."

Sulaa glowers. "I'm referring to her musical education, not teaching her how to be a slut. Let's be frank, Tressa. You don't have the patience to act as tutor. Your whims are dangerous. The poor child is still adjusting to your overenthusiastic aging spell."

I am a decidedly quick-witted fellow but teasing out the jumble of their meaning takes several ticks to decipher. My breath catches the moment clarity sinks in. These horrors want Aurora under their power. This is every bit as unthinkable as allowing Citrine to coerce my darling into her harem.

Tressa crosses her arms. "Fine, but I reserve the right to critique anything the Aurora chick teaches Maisie."

Maisie?

Is she yet another player in their twisted theatrical?

Gothel's hands begin to glow, matching the glower on his face. "Quiet, Tressa. Don't speak the Golden Harp's name."

The enchantress shakes her curls as she waves her hands, raising her voice. "Hello, guests of Stalk." She wears a smug grin when no one spares a glance her way. "See, you're paranoid."

Gothel takes in his surroundings with a cautious scan. "Refrain from testing the fairy's limitations."

Limitations!

I raise a hand to deliver a sting to the magician for the insult. No, no, not so. I must swallow the sting so as not to give myself away, especially now that my Aurora is in peril.

There is news to be reported. The Golden Harp has a name—Maisie, and it seems she's vital to the Dark Vinyl Artists' plots. From the intentions I'm getting from the vile trio, their plans for the Harp require a music master. They will seek to acquire one for their cabal. I must give the royals this information, but their specific desire for Aurora, I will omit.

The enchantress waves a dismissive hand. "Unknot your panties, Grant."

Sulaa runs a finger up inside Gothel's cuff. His fire disappears as the kelp-loving witch speaks. "Since the singer is already in the fairy's employ, perhaps they'll enchant her to serve us as well."

I fight my need to burst their comfy obfuscation dome and deliver a magical shock to stop four fiendish hearts. My gaze falls to Rora, who works at a frenzied pace behind the bar. I will protect her from every ill intention slithering toward her, be they from fairy or fiend.

Gothel grins. The teeth of a beast are never a welcome sight. "We will congratulate the king and queen's talent at finding so gifted a singer. Flattery always makes an opponent more malleable—the exact state we require to best them."

Keep talking villain. Speak more of your fantasy to overcome the Arborborn Coterie so the royals will have cause to act against you. Revealing their plot may be the remedy to keep Aurora from their grasp.

The sorcerer refills the wine goblets. "Stalk's gala is close. On that glorious night, we will finally take back what has been stolen from us." He rubs his hands together then lifts his glass of blood red wine. "Revenge and triumph with a single stroke. A toast to Zeli, Justin Time, and the tedious Santino Fedele. May they rot alongside Midas Lear and any loyal to the old bastard."

Sulaa clinks with him. "Now toast to the rancid magic wielder Prospero Tempesta, the buffoon Rai Cloud, and my traitorous daughter, Azure."

Tressa adds her glass to theirs. "To Benedict Boyd and his mangy harpy, Beatrice Sharpe. She will once again embrace the beast she's meant to be."

Gothel scrutinizes what he perceives as their bubble of protection. Satisfied, he raises his wine above the rest and speaks in low tones. "And finally, a toast to our Brineborn allies."

No, no, not so. I recoil at this proof they are allied to the base Brineborn, robbers of home and hearth. Soul sworn enemies to the Arborborn.

"Drink up, ladies. It's time we melt into the shadows before tonight's exodus begins," says Gothel then drains his glass.

My heart thuds.

Curse the wicked, wicked, wicked Brineborn.

Curse the malevolent Dark Vinyl Artists.

I back away from the *Pearl Tear's* shroud. Impossible. How did these magic mortals align with our greatest enemies without Cinnabar or Citrine sensing the conspiracy? I fear fairy cockiness and the distraction of Stalk blinds the royals to the vile danger surrounding them.

My night is indeed laced with terror and layer upon layer of treachery. The majesties must be made aware of this peril before the trap can be sprung. The magic mortals spoke of Stalk's opening as their night to conquer. Mere days to prepare for battle.

I weave a circuitous path between tables, forcing my progress to stay within slothful human speed. It may be a breach of loyalty, but my heart insists I must ensure Aurora's safety first. My travels carry me to the bar. Thankfully, they're winding down for the evening.

I lay a hand on Rora's arm. Her face lights. I gently grasp her elbow and pull her close. Before I can whisper into the delicate curve of her perfect ear, a beefy hand swallows my shoulder.

"Mr. Goodfellow," says Cinnabar with shadows swirling in his midnight eyes. "Please return to your duties."

I spin toward my king and flick a gesture at the magic mortals. "Something has come up, sir, that I am keen to discuss."

Cinnabar narrows his glare.

"Sir, I believe Ms. Citrine would also appreciate being informed of my news."

His gaze snaps to the queen. Sensing his attention, she slowly lowers her chin, glancing through lashes to meet his stare. Hand still on my shoulder, he pivots me to face her. I flare my eyes, knowing their golden sunburst will telegraph warning. She hastens in our direction.

"My office," says Cinnabar in a tone below mortal hearing.

He gives me a gentle shove, but I circle back to Aurora. "Do not stay tonight. Leave as soon as you are able."

The disappointment in her eyes grinds my heart. "But I thought we could go for a drink."

I spell my voice for her ear alone. "I will explain, but please get out of here fast when your shift is finished. Trust me."

As I turn to join the royals, I hear fucking Demetrius's bitter laugh behind me. "You couldn't even hang on to Cinnabar's shitiot lackey, huh, street trash? You had no idea how good you had it with me."

I swear I hear her heart bruise as I follow the royals.

As soon as the door closes behind us, they both whirl on me.

Citrine is fuming. "What have you done?"

Cinnabar stands shoulder to shoulder with her. "On this of all nights when everything we've planned is ripening before us, you choose to roust us from merriment."

I may be foolish, but I am not a fool. My snippy tone must be tempered. This is potentially catastrophic news, but the queen's eye on Aurora provokes genuine anger in my breast.

"Speak, bitter fly," roars Citrine.

I manage to meet her gaze with stoic calm and answer. "The Dark Vinyl Artists admitted alignment with the Brineborn Coterie."

My father's dusky skin pales, and my mother's hand clasps the base of her throat.

Adopting the regal stance of a prince that I regularly avoid, I continue. "I know nothing of how this came to be, just that the connection exists. I've brought you the news freshly flown from foul lips. They spoke of triumph and revenge set to be enacted at Stalk's true grand opening. They named many investors on your guest list as the targets of deadly action."

"And you fled without hearing them out," says Citrine.

"They were preparing to leave. I thought it vital to swiftly convey news of the Brineborn's association."

Cinnabar thunders around the room. His skin alive with spinning black spirals. When his path takes him behind the desk, he stops, leaning on his hands to stare at the queen. "It is imperative we speak to Brineborn King Cavancite and Queen Aventurine."

Citrine does not move but wrinkles her nose. "They reek of spoiled fish belly. Isn't it enough the Emerald Spire must suffer the stench of Sulaa Kylock's filthy aquariums?"

The room quakes underfoot from Cinnabar's rage. "The sea witch, of course. There lies the connection," he roars. "We've been blind."

The queen drops into a chair. "Curse this human realm for spawning our complacency."

I look back and forth between my parents. "What am I missing?"

Citrine flies at me to knock a knuckle against my forehead. "Is there nothing of royal intelligence in your head, Prince?"

I'm so stunned she called me *Prince* it takes a moment for my reason to click into place. She sees the truth dawn on me and clicks her tongue.

"The Brineborn and the sea witch, both beasts of the tide, are aligned," I mutter.

Citrine ignores my moment of revelation and walks straight up to Cinnabar. "We must concoct a bargain strong enough to break whatever contract that sodden coterie has agreed to with the witch."

The king nods. "Tek Goodfellow, gather the council of warriors to the throne room."

I bow and leave the regal pair.

Nature willing, tonight's revelation concerning our rival coterie will distract the queen from her fixation on Aurora. I step through the door and brighten to lumen form but immediately lose my light and stumble onto human legs as the still lurking danger batters me.

A greater challenge is upon me. I must destroy the magic mortals' foul interest in my Rora.

14

LURE

AURORA

Ms. Citrine's intense attention of a kiss on the lips and laying a hand on the base of my throat after my performance threw me. I hope my startled reaction didn't offend her.

The weirdest part was when she called me "sunstone" and checked the palm of the hand she'd touched me with. It must have been a trick of the light, but for an instant, I swear I saw a faint lemony sheen covering her skin.

"Be happy Stalk's talent coordinator liked you," I say to my reflection in the door of the fridge as I put containers of puree away.

Talent.

I savor the way the term rolls around on my tongue. I believe my performance touched her and pray I made enough of an impression to put me in striking distance of the opening night warmup spot.

I raise a finger to my lips, not recalling Ms. Citrine's peck, but the far more sumptuous kiss with the kooky and undeniably sexy

Tek. I shake the memory of his kiss from my finger. The same Tek who blew me off and disappeared while we closed Stalk.

There's no denying something deeper sparked between us in that secret meadow. I've tried to play it casual with him, but I don't believe our roll in the grass was just for the video. Our kiss tonight echoed the intensity of that day. Even though we've only known each other a few weeks, I feel a stronger connection to him than I ever did with Demie. Tek and I actually talk. He's been more generous and supportive than anyone in my life apart from Rand Diggs. Two men who turned my life around.

Dammit. I'm starting to cry. I lean on the counter and hang my head. My hair dangles in thick wavy hunks. I wanted to celebrate with Tek tonight. It hurts more than I expected that he basically ordered me to leave on my own then disappeared.

I'm able to sniff away the tears before they become ridiculous. Stubbornness gives me a rush of purpose. Forget Tek's bossy edict. I can trust him without giving him carte blanche in deciding what I should do with my life. I'm done being ordered around. Demie felt it was his right. A right I allowed him, acting compliant to maintain harmony between us.

I'm not going to play a submissive role with Tek. I want an explanation of why he's being so elusive.

I do one more visual sweep of the bar. It's ready for the cleaning crew. Striding onto the stage, I put hands on my hips. "Okay, Mr. Tek Goodfellow. Where are you?"

The club and storeroom are deserted. No Tek. Slipping down the service stairs, I check wardrobe and peek into the offices of lesser club personnel. All empty. Wandering back up to the club, a less than attractive thought hits me.

After his PDA at the club, my mind says we're a couple. Is it the same for him? We've been casually dating but we've never declared exclusivity. Shit, is he seeing someone else? Did Tek have plans with her tonight and didn't want to rub my nose in it?

But why would he kiss me like that if his heart might belong to another?

I grab fistfuls of my skirt. "Are you a naïve fool, Aurora Herman?"

Slowly my hands relax. We're not committed, but Tek is so damn blunt, I can't believe he'd fail to mention he's dating others.

Or would he?

I know plenty about Tek, but do I really know him?

An ongoing topic of Rand's fatherly chats when he learned I dreamt of being a singer was to stay ever aware of the plasticity of this town. Hollywood is not the land of straightforwardness. It's a hive of deals and competition. A place where insincerity and coldness can break a spirit that's not shored up.

But it can also be the place where a girl who was thrust into a heartless world has a chance to reach for moonbeams. Look at Robo Robbie and Justin Time. They were no better off than me once, and now they rule the blue neon tower of a major record label. Sometimes it's not how much you give, but how hard you refuse to give up.

I'm not ready to give up on Tek. I need to share my thoughts about us with him. My mind is not going to stop torturing me with doubts until I talk to him.

I haven't had a reason to venture into the hallway behind Stalk since the day of my job interview in Mr. Cinnabar's office. Since Ms. Citrine's office is next to his, I imagine Tek spends much of his time bopping between his two bosses like a tennis ball. Maybe, just maybe, he's still here at work.

I stroll through Stalk's silver filigreed arch and glance down the darkened hallway. From the space under a door, halfway to the bosses' offices, a faint blue glow shot through with foamy white streaks, spills onto the carpet then retreats. It gives the illusion of a wave rolling onshore and receding back to the sea. As I watch, the tide of light continues, each time coming farther into the hall.

By showing me the meadow, Tek proved my suspicion the

Emerald Spire is full of secrets. Another might lie behind this door. My gaze locks on the fanciful waves as they draw me in. I wish Tek were here to explore with me. Good sense warns me to wait for him before I go any farther into the off-limits hallway, but curiosity about the watery light wins out.

Where's the harm in a couple more steps?

The tiny tide stretches farther along the carpet to meet the toe of my gray work slip-ons, bathing them in sapphire light. My first instinct is to bolt, then I remember the mystery forest. Nothing hurt me there.

Before I realize how far I've moved, I'm directly in front of the door. I rest my palm on the surface. Deep ocean blue light climbs up from the carpet to surround my fingers. A cool but not unpleasant chill passes over my skin. I quickly remove my hand from the door, and strings of blue light come away with me. I press and pull several times to watch these luminous threads play with me.

A tentative push opens the door a crack. I stumble backward when sprays of light tumble over my body. Gentle pressure drags me toward the opening like a retreating tide. I poke the light to convince myself it's not real water.

No wetness. No substance. But still, the sensation of cool splatters tickles my face. How can an illuminated current do that?

Do I dare to keep exploring?

I glance down the hallway. Nothing but total stillness greets me. What would it hurt to follow this strange beckoning glow? Time on the streets honed my sense of danger, but no alarm bells ring in my gut.

Why not snoop a bit? It'll be fun to show Tek this strange phenomenon. He treated me to a secret meadow. I'll reciprocate with this odd beachy light.

I open the door enough to squeeze through then pull shut it behind me. Slowly I turn to take in the space.

I'm in a small room no more than ten feet square. There's water on three sides held back with thick glass. A staircase opposite the door cuts through the towering glass walls. Driftwood handrails flank steps bordered with purple, cerulean, and tangerine coral. The place has the vibe of an aquarium walk-through tunnel. Undulating ripples of light flash through the tank's wavering sea blue water.

This feels like the foyer of a private sea-themed suite. I shouldn't be here. To my right, a shadow catches my attention and I tap on the glass. An evil-looking, ugly-ass fish thing with an open mouth filled with craggy pointed teeth shoots out of the shadows to ram the glass near my shoulder. The tiny room amplifies my scream.

I lunge for the door. There's no knob on its smooth driftwood surface. I pull, push, and kick at it but it doesn't budge. The horrible sea monster keeps banging at the glass. I'm terrified the wall is going to crack and drown me while the monstrosity eats me for a late-night snack.

I call for help, but I'm screaming into a void.

On the killer fish's next pass, it drives one of its teeth into its own flesh and a ribbon of blood snakes through the water. Seconds later, sinister shadows surround me as other aquatic nightmares close in on the wounded. I can't escape to Stalk, but I'm sure as hell not going to stay here and see what other horrors exist in this macabre fishbowl.

I dash up ten steps of the coral staircase and collapse onto the eleventh. Covering my ears, squeezing my eyes shut, and humming partially block out the thrashes and thumps below me.

When the melee quiets, I open my eyes to find a watery reflection playing across the coral-textured wall beside me. The glow is the same color as the sapphire wave that first caught my attention under the door. I can't identify the source, but it's the only light in here since I stupidly left my tote bag with my phone behind to go hunting for Tek.

I hunch on the step, trying to figure out what to do. There's no choice but to stay here until morning when staff will be outside this freaky place to hear me yelling. Worst case, when I don't show for my shift, Tek or even Demie will come looking for me.

I shudder, murmuring to break the ominous silence. "You better hope that whoever is responsible for this watery hellscape won't find you first and turn you into fish food for breaking in."

I whip around to face the darkness farther up the staircase when I swear I hear the low chuckle of a sultry female voice. A faint bluish bubble the size of my fist blinks in and out of view.

Holding my breath, I wait for more. No voice. No bubble.

I exhale, shifting into positive self-talk. "You're freaked out. Breathe, Aurora."

I drop my nose to my knees and attempt to clear my brain. My options grow grim. Stay on the coral steps and be discovered or go down and rile those creatures. Maybe if I climb higher, I'll find a way out or at least a better place.

"Ah…ror…ah."

I brace a hand on the rail and stand. Like the mysterious forest, a voice teases the edge of my perception.

Step by tenuous step, I climb and the bubble reappears, blipping in and out of sight. I follow but find no escape.

I halt. The blue orb bobs in the air ahead as if inviting me to continue. The same strange tug that led me into the aquarium room lures me higher on the stairs. Peace not panic overtakes me as I trail after my strange guide.

Floating down the stairway, a new sound greets me, a woman singing. There are no words to her song, only notes chasing one another up and down a scale. It's beautiful.

Squinting into the darkness, I see a single strand of gold light ahead curling gracefully through the dimness. My mind fuzzes as I move trancelike toward the singer and the luminous thread.

There's a stitch between my ribs. When I cover it with my hands, a faint ray like yellow sunlight as thin as the stem of a baby rose flows from my chest to meet the golden thread. They twine together, pulling me to an ornate, gilded door. In its center is the carving of a harp.

Golden light and the sweet song flow through a keyhole in the door. A phantom voice purrs in my ear. "Your breath is the key, Aurora."

I'm overcome with longing to sigh into the keyhole and meet the singer beyond. I open my lips, drinking in her delicate song. Bending so my mouth is even with the opening, I prepare to add my breath to the golden light and send it through the keyhole.

"Aurora," calls a loud and semi-panicked voice from below.

Tek.

I startle and stand. Tek's cry clears my brain fog. Light disappears, leaving me in pitch blackness. I lean a hand against the wall to steady myself.

"Aurora, where are you?" His voice is closer.

Sweet relief rushes through me. "Here, Tek."

"Stay where you are. I'm coming."

Tek is at my side in an instant. As soon as his arms go around me, I swear I see a faint pinkish glow surrounding him. His grip is so uncomfortably tight, the rosy tint is probably from blood rushing to my head.

"Sweetheart, we need to leave."

Tek lifts me. The momentum of descending gives me a nauseating sense I'm about to fall face-first onto the staircase. My feet don't touch the steps as we barrel back to the bizarre antechamber of fish and through the driftwood door.

Once we're in the hallway, Tek kicks the door with his foot, slamming it shut. He still has me plastered to his body.

"Put me down, Tek."

Dim light from wall sconces is enough to see his face—an extremely wide-eyed, agitated face. He gives a nervous shake of his head and loosens his grip. I don't get the chance to ask how he found me or offer an explanation about that strange place before he's snatched my hand to lead me to Stalk at a run.

As soon as we're through the main arch, he throws a desperate glance at the table closest to the bar. Whatever he sees, calms him. Well, calm is too strong a word. He downgrades from a hurricane to a rainstorm, but he's still distraught. He darts behind the bar and grabs my stuff. I've barely caught my breath before he's dragging me out of the club to the grand staircase.

"Tek, slow down. Why are you freaked out?"

He gestures wildly with the hand that isn't crushing mine. "Off we go to flee the foe. Danger will find you, and then they will bind you."

I plant my feet on the step and refuse to budge. "Stop. This is no time for your riddles and rhymes. How did you find me?"

"Please, Aurora." He tugs hard enough to force me down the stairs. "I'll tell. I'll tell. When once again we safely dwell."

He's so determined, I give up and let him guide us to the high-speed elevator. The door is already open and waiting. We dash inside and he hits the express button to the bottom. Once the curved door slides shut, he pulls me into his arms. Tek shakes so badly, I pat his back attempting to comfort him into coherence. I give him less than ten heartbeats before holding him at arm's length.

"Spill. What do you know about that pond of horrors behind the mystery door?"

Tek looks stricken. He tugs at his hair and paces around the elevator.

"Tek." I grab his sleeve and yank him to face me. "Look at me. You're obviously hiding something. Once I went inside the freaky aquarium, I was trapped. How did you get in?"

He grips my wrists. His eyes dance in a wild roll unable to settle. "There's so much, so much, so much. If I tell, it may not go well."

"If you don't tell, I guarantee it will not go well." I grab his wrists, and we cling to one another.

Suddenly he crumples onto his ass, chest heaving with ragged breaths. I sink down next to him and kiss him hard. I'll bruise those lips into a confession. He pulls me onto his lap, hands weaving through my hair, his tongue stroking my upper lip, but I don't allow the kiss to deepen. Instead, I pat, okay, gently slap his cheek. My surprise onslaught of kiss and smack derails his frantic spiral, and a steadier, although still skittish, gaze meets mine.

Moving my hands to the sides of his face, I stroke the soft skin under his eyes with my thumbs. "It's okay, Tek. Whatever is going on, we're in this together." I realize I'm not just trying to pry words from him. I mean it. This unpredictable, goofy, intense man has burrowed into my heart. He's become the main reason I look forward to going to the Emerald Spire. Our safaris to find the mysterious forest or easily chatting over chili cheese fries bring out a relaxed joy I've never felt with anyone before. The hot coaching sessions and his help with my leap to break free from Demie make my life easier. Tek encourages me to believe in myself like I haven't in...well ever.

He awakens a confidence in my dreams I didn't believe myself capable of.

And tonight—when I felt trapped and alone in bizarro water world on the stairway, it was Tek I longed for.

It was Tek who came for me.

He stares at me without blinking. "Together?"

I smile at his eager expression. "Yes, coach. Together. You and me exclusive. I want something real and lasting with you." When Tek doesn't answer, I pull one of his corkscrew strands. "My turn to coach you. Say, 'Yes, Aurora. I want that too.'"

In a flash, he pulls us to our feet. Tek crushes his body to mine and drops long slow kisses down my neck. "Yes, Aurora. I want that too."

I melt into him, burning for those lips to capture mine. Instead, Tek jumps backward away from me.

"No, no, not so." He tears at his hair until a riot of strands sprouts in every direction. "We cannot do this until you know every one of my truths." His expression is so pathetically sad, I want to fold him back in my arms.

The silky female voice of the elevator interrupts.

"Five minutes to your destination."

I cross my arms to keep from touching him. "You heard the lady. You've got five minutes to explain everything."

He wobbles his head, gaze darting around the elevator, landing on nothing. "Where to start? Where to start?"

The man needs a sedative.

"Do not trust Citrine."

I gape at him. "What?" I flash on her overly familiar fussing after I sang. Tek's warning suggests ominous intent to what I assumed was just her quirk. "Why not? She was very complimentary after my song."

"She wants you."

I drop my arms and stare at him. "Wants me?" A little flutter of heat rises in my chest. "For the warmup spot? Isn't that what we've been working toward?"

"No, no, not so. She wants to acquire you…enlist you…entrap you."

The seriousness of his voice and expression is proof enough he's not teasing. "I don't understand."

"Citrine wants you as one of her ladies."

"Her ladies?" I think of the collection of runway model assistants who constantly flutter around her.

He grabs my hand. "She is not the only one to fear. The magic mortals want you too."

"Do you hear yourself? You're speaking gibberish. What the hell is a magic mortal?" A creepy crawly sensation of fear trickles through me.

"Grant Gothel, the fire-wielder, do you know of him?"

"Of course, the horrible man who used to own Rampion Records who attacked Justin Time and kept Zeli as his personal pet." I shudder. "I can't fathom being that controlled. He died in a prison fire." I huff. "Poetic justice, I suppose."

"He is alive. The sorcerer has aligned himself with three witches and named themselves the Dark Vinyl Artists. They dwell here in the Spire."

I back away from Tek's rantings. This is crazy talk. Sorcerers. Witches. Yes, I've heard of the Dark Vinyl Artists. They're a hotshot European company. Brandy and Claude, the duet who sang before me, are repped by that up-and-coming label. The DVA, as they call themselves, are gaining momentum in the Hollywood market, poised to compete with the big four music giants—Rampion Records, Golden Pipes, Tempest Tunes, and Caliwood Inc.

"How do you know? Did Mr. Cinnabar tell you?" When Tek moves a step closer, I hold up a hand. "Stop raving and explain."

"Close your eyes. I cannot say the next as you look at me. It will be the glue that brings the disparate parts together, and you may choose never to look on me again."

"I'm not going to close my eyes."

"Then I will close mine." He does. Long golden-tipped lashes dust his dark creamy cheekbones. "The forest we've been hunting and the meadow are not of your realm. Your human realm. They are part of a fairy realm. My fairy realm."

Fairy realm.

I grasp the handrail of the elevator to keep from keeling over.

"I am what you humans call fairy. Magic folk."

You humans.

Tek dips his head and gazes at me through barely open eyes. I stare at Tek and begin to string pieces together—the perfect rounded cut of his jaw, his flawless skin, those strange deep rust brown eyes with their golden flair, the frenetic way he moves, his odd phrase shifts between casual and formal, his bizarre changes in height. I chalked it up to cute and quirky or my imagination. It is blatantly apparent now as he speaks, the man in front of me is far afield from any person I've known.

"I tell you now, Rora, because you are in great danger from Citrine, the queen of my people, and the magic mortals who watch you from behind a veil of my making. Two enemies who would steal your freedom for their own purposes."

"Ms. Citrine is a fairy queen?"

He nods. "And Cinnabar, her king."

I pinch the bridge of my nose as an overload headache hits. "This is absolute insanity, Tek."

"Can you, do you believe me, my darling Aurora?" He reaches for me, and I bat his hands away.

"What proof do I have you're not a lunatic trying to mess with my mind?"

A tiny pop rattles my inner ear, and Tek disappears. In his place is a baseball-sized, sizzling pink light floating in the middle of the elevator. The ball flits in a circle around the car for a hot second before it literally melts like an overheated scoop of ice cream back into Tek.

He holds both hands out to me. "My change is no mortal feat."

That's the clearest statement he's made all night. Do I dare believe what's right in front of me? His transformation was no trick. It was...otherworldly.

Well, shit.

No other rational explanation comes to mind, so I go with the irrational. I'm trapped in a speeding cylinder with someone clearly not human.

Keep it together, Aurora.

I narrow my gaze at him and swallow hard. This is Tek. He's babbling about protecting me, not harming me. I need him to keep talking to make sense of this. "For the sake of argument, let's go with—you are a fairy." I grunt. Did I really just voice such a ridiculous assumption? "Did you use tricks or enchant me to fall for you?"

He clasps his hands and shakes his head. "No more than you used trickery for me to fall for you. Fate has the power to trump fairy magic." Tek opens his arms, inviting me in. "I am love-blind for you dearest, Aurora, and happy to be so. It is why my lumen light is a pulsing peony."

Love-blind? Lumen light? The parallel reality Tek presents shatters everything I know to be true. This man I'm falling for is not a man at all. Witches and queens are after me? I've walked in the realm of fairies and had no idea?

A whimsical optimist would believe it all, but I'm terrified to believe any of it. My breathing shallows. This free-falling prison threatens to suffocate me.

Tek practically vibrates. "Aurora. Rora. Speak. Ask. Do not fear, my heart. I am love-blind, wholly devoted to you and pledge to keep you from harm."

I don't know if my heart or mind screams louder. I'm no one. Nothing. It's impossible mystical enemies penciled me on their to-do list. My heart tries to shout over the objections in my mind. Tek and what I feel for him are not imagined. What the hell do I do with that?

"*You have arrived at Hollywood Boulevard*."

The door whispers open, and I bolt from the elevator. Tek tries to hurry after me. I whip around to face him. "Please, give me space."

If I walk out on Tek, he'll see it as a rejection. Right now, I can't deal with his intensity while confusion and fear tumble through me like battling beasts. Despite the pleas of my heart not to leave him, for something as huge as what he's just revealed, I can't bow to my tendency to make someone else happy. I need to absorb this bizarre newsflash alone and away from him.

Tek protests with earsplitting volume. "I am sorry my truth was given with too much haste, but it is still truth."

His truth is too much. "I can't process any of this with you shouting in my face. Please go."

He stills, reining himself in. The sadness on his face almost breaks me as he backs into the elevator and allows it to carry him away.

Immediately regret squeezes my ribs. What have I done? How can I hope to navigate Tek's bombshells without him?

I should trust my instinct, go home, and unpack the weird, but is that the right instinct? I stare up at moonlight glinting off the Emerald Spire's green steel. The farther the elevator takes Tek from me, the greater my need to call him back. I huff. Is this a true feeling or a fairy lure?

I press fingertips to my eyelids. Whatever it is, I can't force myself to leave the place where Tek is.

"You're losing your mind, Aurora." Or am I just beginning to understand it?

I know where to go in the Spire to wipe my mind clear of all its spinning thoughts so I can reset my reality through the lens of everything Tek just dumped on me.

The Cloud Smasher.

The ride is a terrifying roller coaster whose track curls and dips around the middle of the Spire then mimics flinging riders into the sky before returning them to the safety of the beanstalk. Thank goodness the ride and the club situated next to it are open all night. I make my way over to one of the side elevators and request to be taken to the coaster's floor. In the space of a single heartbeat, regret crowds into the car with me.

I want to rewind and not have sent Tek away. Why didn't I wait for that first shock wave to pass and insist he walk me through details of the fairy entanglement I've fallen into? I fled when I should have taken a breath.

I'm taking one now.

How many hearts have regretted letting a lover walk away? Leaving Tek behind breaks something vital inside me.

Is that what he means by being love-blind? Am I love-blind too?

My hands shake. Reality doesn't matter anymore. Whatever Tek claims to be doesn't overpower the fact I want him in my life.

The virtual confetti explosion of revelations he unleashed in the elevator begins to settle. I just told Tek I want to be with him and then left him behind. He's invested in me without a single ask in return. I feel lighter, less burdened, dare I say hopeful in his presence. For me, what he gives me should be reason enough not to run away.

I need Tek. When I pull my phone from a pocket and call him, the damn fairy doesn't pick up. Suddenly, I burst into crazy laughter.

The damn fairy.

Hollywood, help me, I believe the man. How can I not? He turned into a fucking ball of pink light. Tek's truth settles inside me —a riddle solved. His oddness, I guess I can now call a supernatural quality, is kind of wonderful. If Grant Gothel is a sorcerer, why can't Tek Goodfellow be a fairy? He claims Mr. Cinnabar and Ms. Citrine are fairies as well. Those two are very strange people, graceful with subtle shading of otherness that's hard to define. I suppose it's a challenge being a magical being, trying to fit in with us bland mortals.

I type a message to Tek.

Sorry I blew you off. Temporary insanity. I have questions. Heading for the Cloud Smasher. Meet me there?

Thank the most high-end bottle of whisky at Stalk, fairies use cell phones. I stare at my screen the whole time I ride the elevator back up. When it drops me off, the floor vibrates beneath my feet in time with the music blasting out of the Coaster Club, the bar next to the ride. Showing my employee ID to the operator, I push through the turnstile to join the front of the line. Free admission to the Cloud Smasher is a nice perk of working at Stalk.

I check my phone again. Nothing from the damn fairy. My damn fairy. I blow the air from my lungs. My life has been anything but predictable. Falling for Tek fits right in.

Once I get to the head of the line, I let a couple of groups go in front of me, hoping Tek will answer. I deserve his silence after the man spilled his guts, and my knee-jerk reaction was to push him away. I want a do-over. I'm tempted to go straight back to Stalk and see if he's there, pouting with a drink in his hand. Do fairies drink human liquor? Ha, look at me totally buying into Tek's literal fairy tale.

Dammit, if it means keeping him in my life, I'm willing to take the leap. Isn't living a creative life accepting the possibility of dreams? Aren't dreams a form of altered reality?

What have I got to lose?

My chest tightens. Tek is who I'd lose. I may be nuts, but I want to take his hand and see where his truth leads us. My eyes burn as tears conspire to break free. Did I ruin us before we had a real chance to begin?

The ride attendant in shiny sky-blue coveralls dotted with clouds motions me to the front car. As I step forward, a hand fits on the small of my back and breath smelling of sweet meadow grass brushes my cheek.

Tek.

I spin and throw myself into his arms. My heart joyously triumphs over any fragment of doubt. This is right. So right.

He grins that grin I've come to crave then brushes his lips against the curve of my ear. "Wanna smash some real clouds?"

15

BREAK OF DAY

TEK

For one beautiful moment, I stop dwelling on the dangers closing in around Aurora and enjoy the stillness in our embrace.

"You came," she whispers. "I was afraid you wouldn't."

I bury my nose in the thick pillow of her hair. "Silly mortal. Did I not confess I am love-blind for you? You have me in your thrall."

Her fingers bore into my ribs. "Tek, you freaked me the fuck out. I'm sorry I ditched you before I allowed everything to sink in."

I breathe against her skin. "Forgive me. I was none too delicate with my word flurry."

She grasps my chin so we are eye to eye. "This love-blind thing, is it real or a fairy trick?"

I dot a kiss on her ear. "Oh, my sweet Rora, a trick? No, no, not so."

The ride operator clears his throat. "Are you two gonna ride or what?"

I swing Aurora to my side. "We changed our minds." We step out of line. The people behind us eagerly hop into the sleek silver and blue car.

"Tek, there are questions I should have asked before I shoved you out the door so heartlessly."

I raise her chin with a finger and brush my lips against hers, speaking softly. "Kisses first and clouds behind, a wondrous sight your eyes will find. Above it, every star we'll tour, and answers all will soon be yours."

I've kissed Aurora to convince Demie and the royals we're a couple. I've kissed her to tempt and coax a sexy performance out of her. I've kissed her because I was driven to seal myself to her goodness.

This kiss is different.

I kiss her because she turns my blood into a honeyed river. I kiss her because Citrine was right, and Aurora's sunstone light is bright enough to overcome any shadow. I kiss her not because I am love-blind, but because in spite of forces both fairy and human that will oppose our bond, I truly love this woman with passion newly awakened in my soul. I pour every drop of my light into a slow, absolutely genuine kiss driven not from lust or show, but my heart alone.

Rora responds by tickling her hands around my side, learning the shape of me until her fingers dig into the muscles of my back. I sigh against her mouth.

Lucky Tek.

I keep a tender grip on her waist, vanishing into carefree brushes of tongues that steal lazy tastes. We kiss as if forever is ours.

Without breaking the kiss, I maneuver us into a dim nook next to the Coaster Club with tin walls stamped in a cloud pattern. Reluctantly, I pull away, reeling from delicious lightheadedness. "Darling dear, are you ready to fly?"

Her eyebrows tick up under fluffy bangs. "On the Cloud Smasher?"

"No, truly fly." Scooping her into my arms, I flick into lumen form. She's even more breathtaking within my light, my now deep claret-colored light. Gone is the pulsing peony of blinded love. Tek Goodfellow, player of pranks, master of mischief, has fallen into clear-sighted love with his sunstone.

Nature blessed Tek.

I launch us as no more than a flicker of light to mortal eyes above the line of Cloud Smasher cars and into the night. Aurora has a death grip around my neck; her head burrowed under my chin.

"Never fear, dear heart so brave..." For once, my riddler stalls. Perhaps this isn't the moment for riddling.

Tentatively, Aurora eases out of her cocoon not to enjoy the vista I've laid before her, but to treat me to an adoring smile. "My fairy Tek now must behave."

It is strange to find what I never knew I sought, a woman who revels in riddles and not only tolerates my rhyming habit but finishes my phrases.

Keeping one arm snugly around Aurora, I grin. "You're flying."

"You're flying," she corrects. "I'm trying not to faint."

"We're flying." I dot her forehead with a kiss. "Think of me as your personal cloud smasher."

Rora screams as I soar above Hollywood Boulevard and punch into the billowy line of clouds drifting over the city. Shifting to my back, I pull her on top of me. Our fleecy carriage bobs along on a river hidden by the night.

I've always loved to linger inside a cloud. It's a place where mist is monarch, shutting out the rest of the world. The mind is free to create its own images and dreams with no interference from any space beyond its limits. Within a cloud, anything is possible.

My lumen light tints our fluffy host with my freshly minted claret glow.

Aurora relaxes. I marvel at her acceptance of wonder. "It's so quiet."

To my surprise, she begins to sing. Soothing vibrations pass from her chest to mine. It is not the sizzling torch song I'm used to, but a gentle song of daydreams. As much as I love what her song of heartbreak and yearning does to me, I am awed by the simplicity of this brighter shade in Aurora's spirit. It suits her.

"Deep in a cloud the world falls away.
Dreaming and wishing both come out to play.
Lighter than air, the dance of a soul,
Careless of happenings in places below.

Paint me with mist from morning to night,
Blooming enchantments away from all sight,
Let skeptics dwell on so blindly beneath,
Celestial fire burns wild in sky's sheath.

Allow me to linger in bedding so soft,
Never recall me from kingdom's aloft.
Lightness of spirit its magic does shower,
Up in these heavens, the cloud is my bower."

The light of Aurora's sunstone heart mingles with my lumen light to turn the mist surrounding us into a swirling gale of pastel ginger. I hum a counterpoint to her melody. When we finish, she rests her head on my chest. She allows herself to just be. What a remarkable being has come into my life.

"That is one of the first songs I ever wrote. I'm enchanted by clouds. They deserve thousands of songs."

I stroke her hair. "Kudos for the Tek Goodfellow-level rhyming in your cloud song."

She nuzzles closer. "What is it with fairies and rhyming?"

"We fancy the challenge of fitting words together as is the way of rhymes, chants, and songs. To be chipper, merry. In long lives, having instant entertainment at your fingertips is always a pleasant distraction."

Aurora arches ever so slightly to look into my eyes. "Can you fly us all the way to the stars, Tek?"

"Literally or…" I give her bottom a playful squeeze. "… metaphorically?"

She wiggles against me. "You're not very subtle with your metaphoric reactions. It's certainly no secret how much I turn you on when I sing a certain song."

Her friction achieves its purpose, and I literally begin to rise at the sexy invitation.

Aurora nips the side of my jaw. "For the record, turning you on does the same to me." A kiss covers the spot she bit. "I was beginning to worry I'd never have that effect on anyone."

"Worry no more, my sweet." Quickly, I dial us back to vertical. "I approve of the activity your attentions suggest, but love-play is the one distraction sure to punch serious holes in the safety of lumen travel."

"Lumen travel?"

"The way fairies fly as light."

Rora stares at her arm. "Am I light?"

I nuzzle her neck. "Yes and no. It is just so."

"That's not an explanation, Tek."

I chuckle at the annoyed tilt of her brow. "I've drawn you into my lumen. When we dwell within it together, we see one another as body, not light."

"I'm going to pretend to understand." Rora shivers. "I've always wanted to play in the clouds, but I ignored the reality of lingering in cold, foggy soup."

Thoughtless Tek.

She is not fairy. Aurora will be affected by the cold. I gather my sunstone closer and shoot out the top of the cloud, flying as high as I dare to treat her to the brilliant pinpoints splattered across the Hollywood sky.

"Before we return, my darling, it is only right to formally introduce you to the stars."

Her gaze travels slowly across the radiance-peppered dome above us, mouth hanging open. “Wow. They truly do twinkle.” Her shivers grow stronger.

Oh, the delights I’ve yet to show her, but I must quicken my pace. “Pick one.”

Adorable confusion pinches her features. “Pick one what?”

I chuckle and pull her closer, bathing her in my body heat to forestall our return to the Spire a little longer. “A star. Choose one that calls to you and show me.”

“Why?”

“Always questions, my sweetest. I wish to give you a gift, but first you must pick a favorite star.”

She gives me a quizzical human side-eye before searching the cosmos. A corner of her lip curls as her finger targets a smallish star nearly hidden by the brightness of its near neighbor. “That one.”

A sense of dread travels through my body. Aurora chooses the Harp Star. I pray this is a coincidence, not portent. Did her sojourn into the radius of the sea witch’s dwelling begin to craft a tether between my love and the Golden Harp?

I will examine fear soon. Now, I keep to my purpose of dazzling Aurora. Wrapping my hand around her finger to hold it in place, I kiss the corner of one eye and then the other. “Now close your eyes.”

Aurora squints.

“All the way.”

One eye opens wider with a skeptical glare before she huffs and closes both. I gaze at the star and send my request.

The Harp Star begins to pulse daintily, increasing in vibrancy before squeezing a pearly drop from the depths of its fiery splendor.

“Look now.”

She watches breathlessly as the ivory bead drips through the blackness, leaving a luminous trail between its mother star and Rora. She gasps when the once molten pearl now cooled by the night sky, alights on her fingertip. The celestial gift mimics the flare of starshine before evaporating into a puff of mist.

She stares at the faint shimmer left behind on her fingertip.

"I shall now call you Aurora, star-friend," I say, pressing my lips to her hair.

"That was..." she says, her gaze never leaving the fading light on her skin. "Extraordinary."

"Now look over the top of the highest peak." I rotate us and point above the wondrous hills of my tainted ancestral land.

Aurora follows my gaze and gasps as one-by-one clusters of new stars wink into existence over the dark silhouette. "There are more than I've ever seen. Where did they come from?"

"Mortals are only equipped to observe a limited starfield." We change direction again until we face the sea. "See there."

A long band of glittering starlight comes alive like the first licks of flame in a bonfire above the barely visible horizon where a midnight blue sea scrapes onyx sky.

"Star-friends too are able to watch each layer of dazzling beauties greet each newly forged night."

"Oh, Tek. Can we go closer? I want to fly over the water."

It's my turn to shake. "No, no, not so. That is territory I will not enter."

"Not a fan of the ocean?" she says in jest. "Do I need to teach you how to swim?"

I can't answer her teasing mood in kind. I've shared beauties of my world; she should know there is also darkness. It will raise her caution, a necessary evil. "I am of the Arborborn Coterie of fairies who now dwell in the Emerald Spire, but it is not our homeland. The hills and area you call Griffith Park is our true realm."

Nodding toward the shoreline, I continue. "On beach and over sea live the Brineborn Coterie, our enemies. It was they who attacked us, unleashing a tempest of salt over our kingdom to spoil our blessed home. We were forced to flee, to scatter and seek refuge within the confusion of Hollywood."

Her face is ashen, forgetting the recent beauty of the starscape. "That's despicable. Was it a land grab?"

I shake my head. "No fairy can survive on salted land. Their's was revenge inflicted after my king and queen could not fulfill a marriage pact promising to join the two coteries in a truce, albeit a fractious one."

"Who was supposed to get married?"

Do I reveal the whole of my identity? How much fairy caprice can the human mind withstand in one night? I will tiptoe to the truth, testing her receptiveness as I go. "It was the prince of our coterie who refused to honor the bargain."

"Well, good for him. Arranged marriages are ridiculous. How are people..." She hesitates. "...or fairies supposed to find happiness if they don't love the person they marry?"

I feel the earth turn and the stars look down on us from a new perspective. Her question gives me the courage to poke on a little more. "Do you not think the prince a selfish bastard to incite the disaster that followed?"

She studies my face. "Did you know that evil sea fairies were going to trash your home?"

My back stiffens. "Of course not. What villain would condemn his kingdom to the disgrace and agony the Arborborn endure due to his act of disloyalty?"

Aurora is as still as a fixed star, and I realize my error. She did not ask about a nebulous prince. Not, did *he* know, did *you* know...

She stares deep into my eyes that hold traits from both my royal parents. "You're the prince."

A statement, not a question. I press my lips together and drop my chin to prepare for her disgust before I meet her gaze. "I am he, Prince Tektite Goodfellow of the Arborborn Coterie, sole offspring of their most honored majesties King Cinnabar and Queen Citrine."

To my surprise, she snaps her fingers. "I knew those two had a thing for each other."

The force of my laugh releases billows of foggy steam. "I've just admitted to being a non-human prince, and you're more concerned with the sexual tension between my parents?" I lay a hand on her cheek. "You are a strange and remarkable woman."

"Don't give me too much credit. I am an overwhelmed, *trying to make sense of this* woman." Something catches her eye above my shoulder and her mouth drops open.

Protectiveness clicks in. I spin, smiling when I see what took her breath away.

"Tek, the sky is leaking stars," she whispers.

I fly around behind her to cradle her against my chest. Off in the distance, a shower of dancing lights cascades out of the blackness to sprinkle over distant mountaintops like sugar on a confection.

"It is star drizzle," I sigh against her neck. "One of the great beauties human eyes are too dull to see." I brush her voluminous hair aside and kiss my own star drizzle across her skin. "So, star-friend, do you admit there are advantages to lumen traveling with a prince?"

Aurora presses her finger still glowing with the Harp Star's approval to her lips. "You've invited me inside a miracle, Tek."

My smart-ass side nearly pipes up with *you're welcome*, but it is quickly overcome by my enchantment with this being who is surely hewn from starlight itself. Bewitching a fairy is no easy business.

A more violent shudder courses through Aurora's body. I need to take her home before her skin turns as blue as the distant stars.

"Say goodbye...for now. I promise to bring you back as often as you wish. Perhaps in warmer dress."

"Goodnight, stars...my friends," Rora whispers with such innocence, I fall more madly in love.

Within my lumen light, we swoop low over Hollywood Boulevard and rise again to fly over the huge, illuminated letters braced on the roof of Hotel Caliwood. A trysting couple glances up at our flash of light from their open-air rooftop bedroom suite as I speed us away. For the flight's finale, I circle the glowing blue neon record stack of the Rampion Tower.

Aurora giggles with delight at every dip and twirl. "Who needs a magic carpet when they've got a fairy prince as a boyfriend?" she says and kisses my cheek.

This woman belongs in the sky.

"I've much more to show you, my beauty."

She steals a kiss but pulls back abruptly. "Sorry. Didn't mean to distract you."

"I can handle a kiss." Pulling her in even tighter, I dive into her warm, damp mouth. When all my senses race to her like water spilling from a pitcher and we drop suddenly, I break off the kiss. Apparently, I cannot handle the overwhelming ecstasy of kissing my sunstone and still lumen travel safely.

As we approach the Emerald Spire, she inhales sharply. "Tek, do you see that? Is the Emerald Spire glittering?"

I puff with pride. She sees the glow of the delicate gilded, fairy-silk net I've cast over the Spire. The true glimmer of my realm. Does she see it because she's within my lumen light, or as I am beginning to suspect, is gifted sight part of my darling sunstone's yet undiscovered magic? I intend to delight in unearthing her secrets.

Surging upwards with enough speed to make Aurora squeal, I head for my private leaf at the top of the Spire. This time my landing and transition to human form are graceful without bruising anything.

Sensing the presence of a human on its surface, my botanical friend remains in its metallic form. Since I've drenched Aurora in a cloudburst of new truths already tonight, and there are still more unpleasantries to come, I decide to keep the leaf's secrets for now.

She clings to me as the night wind nudges her. "There's no railing. Here's a disaster waiting to happen. What shitiot thought this attraction was a good idea even if the view is..." My brave girl takes a few steps toward the leaf's tip as her voice trails off. She shakes her head as she takes in the city and the faraway ocean. "Life-changing. Like everything else about tonight." Aurora turns in a slow circle, soaking in the same sights that always reset me then settles her gaze on me.

When a burst of screams from the Cloud Buster below us cracks through the air, she scampers over to me, grabbing a handful of my shirt.

I pat her back. "You allow me to whisk you into the air as if you were born to it, but human hubbub sends terror through your bones?"

Other terrors of the night return to haunt me. It is time my Rora understands the depth of her danger. Guilt seizes my gut. I am indeed the selfish prince who doomed a kingdom. I should be dissuading Aurora from becoming more deeply involved with me, not giving in to my obsession with her. Her life is fraught with enough peril.

She releases me and heads to the petiole where I transported her things and pulls a mauve sweater from her satchel. The color contrasts with her honey blond hair while brightening her lips and the blush of her cheeks. I'm pleased when she returns to the safety of my arms. I wait for fresh panic to seize her, but it does not come.

"So Tek is short for Tektite. It's very exotic."

As usual, her question is unpredictable. "Everyone in our coterie is named for the crystal encasing their heart."

Aurora grasps her chest. "Ms. Citrine, uh, Queen Citrine called me her sunstone. Do humans have crystal around their hearts and we just can't see it?"

"I did not think so before I met you."

"But you don't know for sure?"

I lead her to the vein of the leaf robust enough to serve as a bench of sorts. "You are a mystery to me in many ways, sweet one." I lift my gaze to the sky. My fairy sight detects the subtle shift from onyx to indigo. Dawn will be upon us soon.

Rora chatters like a jay. "Why do you look the same age as your parents? Do fairy babies pop out fully grown?" She clutches her stomach as if she already carries the product of my fairy seed inside her. Oh, to dream of such a miracle with Aurora.

Impractical Tek.

"Nature's light, no." She eyes me with a slash of contempt, as I snort my answer through a laugh. "Forgive me, darling one, for making light of your question."

I'm relieved when her eyes brighten and her features relax.

"We are infant, child, then adolescent much like humans. When we come of age, our appearance settles until we choose to drink the spirit of fairy elders and fade into the realm of wisdom."

"That sounds deep." Aurora ponders and then continues to muse over her new insights. "But if your parents' hearts are inside citrine and cinnabar casings, how did they have a tektite son?"

I don't want to squelch her curiosity over fairy genetics, but I need to get down to hard truths concerning her safety. "Individual crystals occur once in a coterie. I inherited light from my mother who carries the power of flame, and darkness from my father who rules the shadows, but my crystal essence is unique to my nature."

A gentle smile graces her lips as she takes my hands. "To me, you are all light."

I bobble my head. "Many would disagree, including the king and queen. I am their disappointment." I stop. This is not a subject to delve into at present. "We need to discuss what occurred earlier when you were trapped on the wicked stair."

Her fingers quiver where they lace between mine. "Do I want to know?"

I squeeze. "It is imperative. We must scheme to keep you safe."

"Don't worry. I'm never going near that freaky door again."

I put an arm around her to nest her against my side. "It may not be your choice. The staircase and the foul caged water beasts are the domain of the sea witch. You would not have been able to gain access through the door of your own free will."

She rests her head on my shoulder. "Was it magic that sucked me in?"

"Dark and tainted, but sadly, yes. You are vulnerable to the whims of magic mortals and my kind."

She lifts her head to face me. "I heard singing." She winces. "A streak of light poured out of a keyhole. It whispered to me."

My breathing speeds up. I swallow the frantic rhyme attempting to bubble from my mouth. "What did it say?"

She licks her lips, strain pinching her face as she struggles to remember. "Something odd about my breath opening the door. It's fuzzy." Her focus on me sharpens. "Do you know who was singing in there?"

Do I dodge or tell? I want Aurora to comprehend the seriousness of her predicament, but I don't want her to dissolve into debilitating fear. "I have never seen the singer, but I do know of her. She is called the Golden Harp and the very reason the magic mortals want you under their control. Like everyone else in the club, they were affected by your performance. They believe you have musical gifts to teach the Harp." I clutch her upper arms. "You must under no circumstances go near that door and the sea witch's lure. Swear to me, Aurora."

Her eyes flare. "Is the Golden Harp singer under their control against her will?"

My shoulders sag from the weight of my ignorance. "I do not know."

She looks to the stars, considering my answer for a moment before her attention flies to me. "Tell me the truth, Tek. Does your magic mess with my free will?"

I drop to a knee before her. "I give you my heart-sworn pledge, I shall never use enchantments or any other fairy coercion against you without your permission. I am your servant, Aurora."

The worry lines across her forehead disappear, and she beams at me. "Wow, a prince kneeling to me. Talk about making a girl feel special."

The fresh-born orchid sky provides a perfect backdrop to her beauty. I rise and pull her to her feet, pointing her toward daybreak. "You are my dawn, Aurora, as your name decrees. See the sky change and the world begin to wake for you."

The dawn light in my arms shifts, and we embrace with the silent promise this new day is our new beginning as well. She giggles, pressing her face into my shoulder. "Don't laugh, but when I was growing up and life went to shit, my daydreams kicked into serious *rescue the princess* mode. I'm fully aware how sappy and devoid of agency that sounds."

I rest my head against hers. "I'm happy to honor such daydreams. I, too, have wished for rescue from my reality. In this we are matched." I lose another piece of my heart to Aurora.

She pulls away until her gaze falls to my mouth. "Then kiss me as the sun rises, my prince."

I press a finger to her lips. "First, give me your solemn vow you will not be in Stalk, or anywhere in the Spire alone from now on. I give you my vow I will be by your side at every turn unless my king and queen insist on sending me on royal business." I fix my attention on the lightening sky and exhale slowly. "I owe them my loyalty as son and subject."

She kisses my finger and removes it from her lips to speak. "I promise, but what if your mother puts the moves on me when you're not there?"

I run my hands through her bountiful, silky tresses. "The queen does not dare touch you as long as I declare we remain knotted. This she has already agreed to."

"Knotted?" She nudges me away just a bit and narrows her eyes. "You said something before about people believing our knot is strong. Which means...?" She spins her hand, a request for me to continue.

"My love-blind pulsing peony lumen light has transformed into a claret glow. This is proof of my unquestionable devotion to you. I am yours, Aurora." Gently gripping her hips, I reverse the distance she put between us. "If you return this intensity of feeling, it weaves our spirits into a knot, a bond of mutual intention to inform my folk you are mine..."

I falter at the surprise animating her features. "...for now." I'm strangely nervous speaking of the knot. Is it fair to rush her into a deep romantic entanglement? "If indeed it is a truth we share."

Her eyes lighten with the rising sun as her expression softens. "You want me to commit to this knot?"

There's a quiver in my voice as I ask, "Can you be mine, Aurora of the dawn?"

There is no sign of mirth in her expression as she gazes at me with strength of will. Behind her, a blushing sky bleeds shades of primrose and fire to meet the sparse collection of clouds.

The boldness in her tone is as brilliant as the waking day. "I am yours, Prince Tektite Goodfellow of the Arborborn Coterie...for now." She snatches handfuls of my hair, urging my lips to hers. "Now, kiss me before we lose the dawn."

I smile against her inviting mouth and obey.

16

SUCH SCHEMES

TEK

IT'S TORMENT TO WATCH THE CAR DRIVE AWAY WITH MY SUNSTONE. Every muscle twists tighter than the braided honey bread my folk eat on the solstice with the urge to steal Aurora away to my bower where I can keep watch over her. She insisted it was best she return to her home after the befuddlements of the night to do what she termed *recharging* and *recentering*. Being her dutiful Tek, I only raised a moderate fuss.

I grind a knuckle against my chest where constant fear will hum until I am assured my love is safe. I flick into lumen form and start up the Spire, spinning around offshoots and leaves in my version of Rora's *recharging*. The early morning sun intertwines with my gossamer protection shroud, setting the beanstalk aglow like a lovely gold-tinted emerald.

I must find time today to nurture my creation. I sense its longing for my fortifications and send beams of reassurance from its base to its lofty heights. After I tell Aurora the full tale of the limping dryad and the spell stones, I'll bring her with me on my delightful gardening chores. I want her to love the Spire as I do, and to watch the way it thrives under my care.

When I soar toward a fairy door halfway up the beanstalk, a bright blue lumen light melds with mine, halting me mid-flight.

"Oh, Tek. Shall I weep your light has turned claret and not for me?" teases Chalcedony.

I float beside her within our mingled lumens. "Weep away, fairy maid."

She pouts. "Do not tell me it is that temptress Tourmaline who's finally stolen your heart."

I crinkle my lip. "Don't be coy. No doubt our queen, your mistress, told you of my attachment to the human."

She taps her lip. "Ah, yes. I do remember a passing mention of your folly."

"I'm tired, Chalcedony, and my bower beckons." When I try to separate my lumen from hers, she holds tight to our connection.

"Alas, a lonely bower mine shall be without you." She flashes a pretty pout. "The king insists you take up your position in Stalk near the magic mortals at once."

I groan. "Spindlewood blight. What will it take to earn a few moments of rest?"

Chalcedony smirks. "I've never known you to lack energy." She flicks a thin corkscrew of my hair.

I return the expression. "I'll take that as a compliment instead of a barb."

Her lips smack the air as she flits away.

Blasted magic mortals. Why can't they keep to their late-night routine? Worrisome thoughts increase my speed to the club. It was reliance on their nocturnal pattern that lulled us into a sense of security. We've been duped into believing the Dark Vinyl Artists use daylight hours for seclusion. It is clear now the foul quartet met clandestinely with the Brineborn Coterie as the sun shone over the waves.

Any fatigue in my bones snaps into heightened awareness. I

cannot miss the smallest snippet of their scheming, especially if it involves Aurora.

Rumbles of dissent from the villains spill from their table through Stalk's entrance arch. I ease into position just outside the *Pearl Tear's* shield.

The sea witch leans an arm on the table to glower at the enchantress. "Cut the whining, Tressa. How was I supposed to know Cinnabar's little fairy prick could get through the door to my suite and interfere with the lure spell?"

Tressa wrinkles her nose. "If you'd spend more time strengthening your powers in that algae-ridden tank of terrors, Sulaa, instead of servicing Gothel, your magic wouldn't be so flaky."

The sorcerer sits with closed lids, one hand playing across the sea witch's thigh under the table as he waits for the two adversaries to finish their sniping.

I do love the tang of sexual tension.

"Just 'cause you're not getting any, Tressa," says the Lear witch, blowing on her fingernails. "Doesn't mean you have to be nasty." She waves a hand. "I'm willing to share Claude."

Tressa fires back. "If I want a taste of your dolt, I'll take him."

Rubata's expression turns feline. "He enjoys a saucy spanking. Are you into the rough stuff, Miss Priss?"

Gothel smacks his palms on the table. "Enough, damn it. We need to get back on track." He turns to the sea witch. "Sulaa, did Aurora get inside the Golden Harp's rooms?"

Sulaa preens and tosses her head. "No. That bothersome fairy gnat stole her away before she breathed into the keyhole."

"I told you it was too soon to try the lure spell," says Tressa, wearing the pinchy-face of the disgusted. "You were too determined to show off."

My stomach drops. These vandals are set on entrapping my darling.

"I instructed Sulaa to summon the woman," says Gothel through gritted teeth. "Time grows thin before we enact our revenge at Stalk's opening night gala. All else must be in place, including the Harp's new musical tutor." He aims his perpetual glare on Rubata. "Where is the RSVP list you were charged to acquire ensuring our targets will be at the gala?"

The Lear witch adjusts her breasts, presenting a greater percentage of skin above her neckline then pulls a folded piece of paper from her cleavage. "Here's the printout I lifted from Cinnabar's desk."

Gothel smooths the paper, scans it, then frowns and lights it on fire with a flaming fingertip. "Stale information. This is from two days ago. I must have updates at least twice a day between now and the gala." Charred cinders scatter across the granite tabletop.

Rubata shrugs. "Ugh. Shifting into Cinnabar stretches my skin. It takes hours for everything to settle back."

My eyes snap wide. The king smote enemies for lesser crimes than stealing his form. Taking on the guise of a royal is unthinkable. These mortals demonstrate sheer ignorance of the fairy wrath they tempt.

Gothel pushes fingers into the corners of his eyes as he answers with a bite in his tone. "Any targets escaping our net will be a viable threat to our future."

"I get it, Grant." Rubata waves her arms. "Kill them all."

"You are so crass," scolds the enchantress.

Fiends, thieves, and murderers. This quartet is truly a cadre of nature's horrors.

Gothel stands and stalks around the table. "There must be no flaw in your assigned tasks." His gaze lands on the enchantress. "You guarantee none of the guests will recall seeing our targets present at the gala?"

"Relax," she says, waving a dismissive hand as she nods to Stalk's grand entrance. "It's a breeze to alter non-magic human brains." The enchantress nibbles on a fingernail. "No one in the room will have a clue our special friends ever stepped foot in the place."

Gothel narrows his gaze. "And what of photographs? Reporters?"

Tressa giggles. "The ghosts will be on duty to blur any pictures of our soon-to-be-disposed-of adversaries."

Her tiny bow lips stretch into a smirk. "My spirit patrol will whip through mortals, stripping their memories." She shimmies her shoulders. "A little fright—a lot of forget."

Gothel grips the back of his seat and leans in. "No one is to be permanently damaged apart from those we execute." He shifts his gaze to the sea witch. "Sulaa? What have you concocted to explain the death of Rai Cloud and Azure to the gossip-mongering press?"

She fingers her trident necklace. "Such a pity the pretty little speedboat they raced across the channel on their way to the gala was..." There's a loud crack in the air as she claps her hands together. "...lost to the depths in a sudden squall. The sea can be so unforgiving."

Gothel continues to stare. "And the selkie sorcerer, Prospero Tempesta?"

Sulaa licks her lips. "His appetite for pufferfish will be the culprit of my former lover's demise."

Tressa crosses her arms. "What's your story, Rubata? How will you report dear old Daddy Midas and your sister Chorda's sad endings?"

Rubata Lear clicks her tongue against her top teeth. "Private planes are so unsafe, especially when they crash in the dense wilderness like the one near Daddy's mountain hideaway. They'll never find the wreckage."

I can barely continue to listen. It's luck I haven't eaten in hours or my stomach would empty its contents all over the magic mortals' *Pearl Tear* canopy.

Killing father, sisters, daughters... There are schemes and there are evils.

Rubata jabs a finger at the enchantress. "Your turn, Tressa, spill the tea on the tragic demise of the Hotel Caliwood bunch—Beatrice, Benedict, and Leonato."

The enchantress's tittering laugh makes my teeth throb. "If you ever paid attention to anything but your tits, Rubata, you'd remember Leonato isn't an issue. Our magic still controls him." Tressa's smile turns feral. "The harpy Beatrice will return permanently to her beast form. No loopholes this time. She pulled a vanishing act once. No one will be surprised when she does it again. Benedict's cover story is a snap. With his previous bad boy record of excesses on tour, drugs and a missing rocker—" She flicks her wrist. "A tale as old as time."

When Tressa walks her fingers up Gothel's arm, iridescent disks on the sea witch's shoulders swirl with hues of aqua and a menacing dark lavender.

"So, boss man," says Tressa, tilting her head. "What about your precious Zeli and that piece of work Justin Time who bested you? What little yarn will you weave about their ultimate curtain call?"

Gothel's eyes gleam with an unearthly glow more demon than sorcerer. Waves of heat rise from his fingertips. "Don't you concern yourself with my details."

"No fair," whines Rubata.

Gothel moves behind her, laying hands on her shoulders and leaning close to her ear. "Fairness is and never has been how I operate, my dear shapeshifting witch."

Rubata flinches in pain at his none-too-gentle touch. The thinnest wisp of smoke rises from her skin.

Sulaa taps an overlong fingernail on the table. Her trident necklace glows with a sickly green corona. "And you trust the Brineborn to support us?"

Gothel pours into his chair, pushing away from the table and crossing his ankles, the picture of nonchalance. "I trust no one. Not even you, my fine witches. It's why I shall never be diminished again."

Sulaa wears an admiring smile. "And woe be to the idiots who trust you."

"Exactly." He aims a smoky gaze at her. "The Brineborn will drive the Arborborn fairies from the Emerald Spire." His expression curdles. "All except that capricious twerp, Tek." Gothel steeples his fingers. "Apparently, he's the key to maintaining the health of the fairy dimension within the beanstalk our oceanic allies wish to lay claim to."

The tender skin sketching the path of my missing wings burns. My duty is to protect the Spire for my people, certainly not the cursed Brineborn or these magic aberrations.

Tressa swirls a finger, sending a delicate transparent frost spiral into the air. "Why would the twerp agree to stay?"

Gothel shows teeth. I'm surprised they're not chiseled into demonic points. "Who says we'll ask?" His expression shifts to boredom. "The Brineborn will subdue and manage him."

The plans of these nasty, nasty nasties spin me into a mental cyclone. How dare they assume I am weak enough to be trapped by the Brineborn? This is beyond my capacity to bear. I blaze away from Stalk and burst into Cinnabar's office.

His head whips up. As soon as he senses my state of utter distress, he's up and around his desk in an instant, gripping my arms. "Speak, Tek."

"You must come with me, Highness. The magic mortals bring the onslaught of doom to the Emerald Spire in their dealings with the Brineborn." In a single breath at a speed no human could process, I parrot to him what I've learned of their intention.

He nods, and we return together, unseen by the unholy congress.

Gothel lords over the group. "The full rebirth of Opus will be untouchable. The Brineborn agreed to enchant couples to produce children with musical gifts then dispose of parents once the child is born. Our hands will be clean. We'll raise and train the young ones here in the Emerald Spire as we once did on Rampion Ranch. It's shameful our current sparse Opus crop is subjected to Tressa's ghost overseers in those filthy abandoned basements of Hotel Caliwood. This time we will be untouchable. Our partnership with the devious Brineborn will nurture an endless river of future stars for Dark Vinyl Artists."

Cinnabar and I exchange a horrified look. Rage swiftly overtakes his surprise. Charcoal spirals cover his arms, neck, and face. "These villains and their plots must not prevail."

"What will you do, Your Majesty?"

Pain consumes his features. "We must treat with the Brineborn against the magic mortals and best whatever these serpents promised the eel eaters." He spears me with a look. No doubt my rejection of a betrothal with their princess, the slight that brought about the great salting, smolders in his memory.

A muscle ticks painfully in my jaw. "Such foul plans we must allay. What bauble can be put in play?" I swallow to prevent a deeper fall into panicked rhyme. "At best, from what these nightmare's speak, the Brineborn wish to oust us from the Emerald Spire. I fear, at worst, our very extinction is the coveted prize."

Rare sympathy shines in my father's eyes. "Fly away from here, Tek Goodfellow. Responsibility now falls upon me. I relieve you to prevent pollution of your spirit from exposure to these poisonous plots."

I can't leave. They may yet speak of a scheme to steal my love. I shake my body and slowly drink in new air. "I will remain on duty as is my penance."

Cinnabar studies me. "So be it. I must seek the queen." Reflections of shadows streaked with black lightning flare against glass as the king vanishes.

With trepidation, I return my attention to the magic mortals. They speak in low tones adding strokes to the details of their treachery until her name is once again upon their lips.

Aurora.

The enchantress is charged with the next lure to unite my

sunstone with their Golden Harp. There is no elaboration on her scheme before the magic mortals leave the club to return to their private lairs hidden within my beloved Emerald Spire.

Seething resentment that my parents aligned themselves with these abominations nearly chokes me. The despicables would steal my Aurora. I must protect her. The king and queen will not waste effort on a human they see as my transient plaything. Do my parents even remember the true taste of love?

Love.

Love is one power I hold in my pocket. I roll the spell stones in my hand, pluck the *Claret Blood* pebble apart from the rest, and hold it up to the light. Its polished surface matches the color of my lumen glow. My knot with Rora will be perceived as fleeting and flimsy in the eyes of the fairies. Since we have acknowledged our bond, unleashing the power of the *Claret Blood* stone would surpass our knot and permanently seal her to me. The spell stone cannot create love where it does not exist, but I have to believe the spark of such feelings flow freely between my sunstone and me. The king and queen would be honor bound to acknowledge our union and take my chosen mate under their protection.

The stone grows warm between my fingers, and I quickly shove it out of sight. Enacting a magical union would rob Aurora of any power to leave me. I can't stomach the thought of nullifying her free will. I swore I would refrain from using fairy charm or magic on her. Many consider my word untrustworthy, but my promise to her goes beyond an agreement. In my heart, it is a blood oath.

I am the prince of mischief, but I will not break my vow to the woman I love. For if I did, I might lose Aurora's heart. She may be a human who my people perceive is of no value, but I revere her as the rarest of nature's blessings.

I will find a way to save my sunstone.

17

SWEET SECRETS

AURORA

Meeting Tek at Stalk is a bad idea. I'm stressing over the potential awkwardness of running into Ms. Citrine—*Queen* Citrine.

The deadline to be notified if I won the *Saturday's Star* gig for Stalk's opening passed, and I never heard a peep from Ms. Citrine or the show. I honestly thought I'd wowed her when I sang the other night. Tek's warnings about the queen's interest in me lurk in my mind. Did that kill my chance at the contest?

No point dwelling since there's not a damn thing to be done. Unfortunately, I'm a dweller.

I admonish myself. "Positivity is free, Aurora."

I'll keep singing on the sidewalk in front of the theater. Another chance will come.

I hope.

Tears sting my eyes. I believed I had a shot at *Saturday's Star*.

My thoughts stray to Robo Robbie and his offer of an introduction to Zeli and Justin.

"Not yet."

If I couldn't cut it for *Saturday's Star*, I'm definitely not ready for the top brass of Rampion Records.

There's too much time to think during this damn elevator ride. A sharper cut slices through my waning confidence. Will Tek be disappointed in me?

"Stop it."

My focus now must be on a stellar performance as a cocktail magician.

Mr. Cinnabar... "Ach." ...*King* Cinnabar promised to hire a few more barbacks for Demie and me to train so we'll be able to take time off if we need it. I don't mind working. Crafting new cocktails energizes me. It's a creative endeavor like singing and songwriting. My spirit would shrivel without an outlet to invent and express the mishmash of thoughts and emotions constantly swirling in my brain.

I compulsively play with my over-fluffed bangs. "Ouch." A stray hair catches on a broken fingernail, giving my scalp a little sting. I chew off the jagged bit of nail as my tension level continues to rise nearly as fast as this god-awful elevator.

So—many—questions.

Are Tek's royal fairy parents aware I know their truth?

Could falling in love mean the same to a fairy as it does to me?

Every story I've ever heard of Tek's kind paints the creatures as unabashedly promiscuous. Am I Tek's flavor of the month because that's just the way fairy romance works? I grunt a laugh. The stories also describe fairies as teeny with fancy fluttery wings. Tek is a handsome, fully formed man. His level of smitten appeared to equal mine when we were on his private leafy perch. The guy kneeled in front of me with his sincere pledge of a fairy knot.

Which I agreed to.

It felt so right. Holy Hollywood, am I falling in love with him?

I've never fallen in love. I've just dreamt of the possibility like one would wish upon a star. First with Riker for a hot second before I understood our connection was purely physical, and then with Demetrius because he represented the possibility of a more solid future.

How fast can you fall in love?

No matter what's right or wrong or too fast or not fast enough, I think I want to be in love with Tek.

Has it already happened? Logically—no, but illogically...I might be.

There are a billion reasons why daring to love him scares me shitless. Wildly, the first is not just because he's a fairy. Tek is a freakin' fairy prince.

The survival voice in my head clears its throat, reminding me a musical career is the priority. Demie sucked so much of my time with his neediness, I've neglected songwriting, auditions, rehearsing, and making more contacts in the music business. Tek gets credit for getting me to a level where at least *Saturday's Star* didn't hit an auto-reply NO when I submitted my video.

Oh, how I wish they'd called me.

Tek's coaching made me confident enough to sing that night at Stalk to at least try to impress Ms. Citrine.

Oh, hell. Am I into Tek because I feel like I owe him?

I grip the handrail of the elevator. I consider how easy and entertaining Tek is to be with. I love his unpredictability. I crave the passion he doesn't hide for me. Coach, man who makes my heart go crazy, partner in my obsessive search for the hidden forest, protector. Those are what Tek is to me—all things to love about him.

I don't owe Tek.

I don't need Tek.

I want Tek.

I fiddle with the flouncy front of my summer dress and pull the elastic neckline a little bit lower. I am ready to drive our saucy preambles past preludes and into the full deal. Whether he loves me according to my human terms or I'm capable of loving him or whatever the hell we're getting ourselves into...I want all of him. And dammit, I'm going to have him tonight.

The elevator glides to a stop, and I freeze.

It can't be.

My heart races at the vision on the other side of the glass door.

Silver. Diamond light. Glittering trees.

I press a hand over my mouth as the door swishes open.

Stepping out of the elevator, I cross the emerald circle to gape at the incredible forest Tek and I have been searching for. Instead of shadows, a thousand tiny silver lights twinkle like fallen stars nesting among the trees. The path of diamonds trapped under glass is aglow, radiating streaks like rainbow light through a prism.

None of that splendor compares to the grand sight stepping from behind a tree.

Tek is a character from a storybook in his forest green, sleeveless, belted tunic covered in gold leaves from a dozen varieties of trees. He wears loose brown trousers a shade or two darker than his gingerbread skin. Around his head is a wreath of orchid, periwinkle, and white flowers woven together with tiny leaves, each no larger than my thumbnail. One larger purplish petal droops over the bare expanse of his forehead, revealed by his cascade of corkscrew braids flopping to the left. The golden yellow tips of those untamed strands shine as brightly as the lights in the trees. He exudes an aura of wildness, as if the forest itself created this beautiful man.

Tek walks toward me and bows. "Welcome back to the Pristine Forest, Aurora."

"Splendid." I'm not simply referring to the forest.

It takes me a moment to reconcile this vision with the Tek I know. "You stinker," I say and swat his shoulder. "You knew where the forest was the whole time. Thanks for the wild goose chase."

"Hunting with you was time well spent, my sweet Aurora." He lays a finger on his plump, dusty-pink bottom lip and gives me a toothy smile.

I lick my lips and run my gaze over his body, taking time to enjoy the hints of lean muscles on his forearms and biceps. "You prince up real nice."

He returns the favor, stalling at the low-cut neckline of my flowery print dress. It's kind of perfect we've both chosen nature motifs for tonight. I don't have the heart to admit my chance at *Saturday's Star* died and he doesn't need to squander any more time coaching me.

"Why are we meeting here instead of Stalk?"

Tek chuckles and threads his arm through mine. "I promised you we'd find the forest, and I've kept my word. Now we must be off."

I don't budge. "I want to explore." My attempt to drag him onto the path is fruitless.

"This is the queen's woods. I will not risk going any farther into her territory."

I'm annoyed as hell but remind myself I'm involved with a fairy who comes with a set of rules I don't pretend to understand. "Fine." Disappointed, I head for the elevator but then turn back to Tek. "How did I ever find this forest in the first place if it's fairy territory?"

Little splotches of pink burst across Tek's cheeks. "Um, I brought you here. You intrigued me. Apart from my curiosity about what a mortal's reaction to the royal woods might be, your presence would irritate my mother."

I arch a brow. "I intrigued you? You've been spying on me?"

Tek has the good sense to rock a smidge of embarrassment. "If you must call appreciating your work from afar spying."

Banishing judgment from my tone, I ask, "You stopped the elevator on this magical floor to see what I'd do with the added bonus of pissing off your mom?"

"Guilty. More to the point, I wondered how much you'd be privy to with the tiniest drop of my magic. Truthfully, I didn't expect you to be able to see the forest in detail. It's meant to be shielded from humans. I saw fascination reflected in your eyes and knew the wood was clear to you." He gives a nervous titter. "I was even more surprised you could hear me."

My stomach tightens. "Then I'm not crazy. Those bird chirpy sounds were words."

Tek stares upward, drawing a breath, and then mimics the trilling voices I heard that night. "*We'll be waiting, Aurora.*"

I pinch his forearm. "Tek Goodfellow, Prince of the Arborborn Coterie—you lured me then toyed with me."

I'm gratified by his chagrined expression. "If it's any consolation, I am being punished for it."

My anger fizzles. "Oh no. Punished?"

He gently seizes my upper arms. "Do not be upset. Punishment has turned to fortune. I was bade...ah...ordered by the king and queen to spy on the magic mortals."

I can't help but smile at the way he's trying to speak less formally to me. "I know what bade means, Tek."

He draws me closer. "In a twisted turn of fate, it is a boon I allowed you to trespass here and thus was punished. If I hadn't heard the putrid plots of the sorcerer and his witches, I'd be blind to the danger you're in." When a low murmur sounds from deep in the forest, Tek spins as rapidly as a tornado set to drop from the clouds. He slips an arm under my knees, lifting me against his chest where more hidden muscles lie. "On and on we go."

I retain enough forethought to reach down for the strap of my tote before he launches off the ground. "Go whe—"

Tek is his own roller coaster bathed in the wine-colored glimmer he calls his lumen light as we speed through the outskirts of the forest on a collision course with a bunch of trees. I bury my head against his collarbone as we punch through the wall of wind blowing in our faces. Once the air settles, he slows, chest heaving.

I dare to peek. My breath catches at the sight. There is a vast field of grass stretching before us, but not like any grass I've ever seen. Its color shifts in a slow fade from one shade of green to another, never repeating the same hue. It's hypnotizing.

"The grass is moving. It's alive."

We hover above the field. "All grass is alive, ever changing, ever growing. Maybe you just haven't looked closely enough."

I shake my head. "Magic grass. A hidden forest."

"Don't forget the meadow," Tek adds.

I squeeze the back of his neck, soft hairs tickling my fingers. "The meadow? That wasn't a...a...people-made picnic attraction?"

"No, no, not so. We were in a remote meadow of my kingdom."

"Tek," I say, steadying my voice. "Why do I see fairy places?"

He sets me down and his lumen light fades. Oh, my sanity, I was traveling in a ball of light again, and I didn't even register the shift. Tek's arms wrap around me. We're practically nose-to-nose as if he shrank to match my height.

"I don't know why you were able to see my world before. You see it now because we accepted the knot between us." He rubs his lips together. "When you sang at Stalk the other night, there was a glow, from here." Tek lays a gentle hand over my heart. "As if light reflected off a sunstone."

I grasp his hand. I swear I saw light streaming out of my body in that creepy stairwell, but I was not myself. Even now, I can't separate what was real in the shadows from unreal. Could this mean...?

I squeeze his fingers tighter. "Are you saying I'm a fairy?"

"No, no, not so." He wiggles his head. "That would make our situation so so so easy." He kisses my temple with each *so*. "But you possess a quality that thins the boundary between my realm and yours. I do not understand it. I suspect the queen does. It fuels her desire to acquire you."

"Will you ask her what my mysterious quality is?"

He wobbles his head as if he's trying to spill my question from his mind. "You should be inquiring how I plan to prevent the queen's eye on you."

A frisson of fear bubbles inside me. I have no desire to be on a fairy queen's wish list. "Point taken."

"I will dig into your sunstone light after I am positive you are safe from both Citrine and the magic mortals. Not until. Do not ask it of me."

Tek is genuinely freaked so I don't pursue the issue. My gaze drifts over his shoulder. Past the far end of the field, I catch sight of a line of thatched roofs. This fairy world is a page from a calendar of quaint, old-fashioned country towns. I point to the row of brightly painted, cottage-style buildings. "Tek, do you live in that cute little village?"

His eyes mimic the wobble of his head, and I hold back a laugh. He looks like a cartoon. "A village it is, but not where I rest. O'er woodland and meadow my bower does nest."

My sweet Tek rhymes when he's nervous. I know the perfect way to calm him. "To your home take me now, so that I might see, where Tek lays his head in sweet revery."

He flashes me a grateful smile. "I am a wise fairy indeed to court the love of an exceptional rhyming mortal such as you, dearest Aurora." His lips brush mine as the grass beneath our feet smoothly shifts through its never-ending palette of greens.

The kiss is brief but holds the promise of more to come. He quickly scans the field as if he doesn't want us to be discovered.

"Tek, what's got you jittery?"

"There are always eyes about that shouldn't be focused on you. Let's fly."

"Am I not safe here?"

He dots my eyelids one at a time with soft full lips. "You are always safe with me, Rora."

Once again, I'm in his arms, a position I've grown quite fond of. I do feel safe with him. Safer than any time in memory other than vague, long-ago flashes of my parents so faint they lack specific wheres or whens.

We skirt over the charming field and into another small wood.

It reminds me of a botanical garden showing off every possible species of tree from oak, pine, and willow to birch and many I can't name. No two trees match. Each sprouts from a bed of ferns at their base more feather than plant. My skirt billows around us, the reds and russets of the fabric glowing in deeper shades within Tek's claret lumen.

Bursting through the trees, we land in a perfectly round clearing. Tek sets me on my feet amidst towering foliage. The circle of trees ringing the space block anything beyond. Their perfectly straight trunks remind me of old-fashioned stockade fences, but these are not stripped of branches. They are lush and gorgeous. Overbright green leaves bear clusters of thin crimson stalks like tiny tentacles. Topping each is a cap resembling a single blueberry. The sweet smell of a root beer float permeates the air. Beneath us is a carpet of dark green moss that looks soft enough to cuddle into and dream sweet dreams.

Tek holds my hand and swings our arms. "Welcome to the Sassafras Glen."

I pull out of his grasp and walk over to sniff a bright leaf with its odd adornments—definitely root beer. Bending into a crouch, I brush my fingers over the moss. It's as soft as the cashmere scarf Demie had given me soon after we started dating. Everything about the place, from its sugary smell to the vibrant colors, enchants me. Standing to face Tek, I lock my hands to my hips and keep up the pretense of our meeting. "This is a rather unusual coaching location."

I'm about to confess my failure in the *Saturday's Star* contest until Tek dances over to me with springy steps and replaces my hands with his to grasp my hips. Slowly his palms slide lower until they're against my thighs, and I choose not to ruin this moment with bad news. There will be time to tell him later.

When he presses his body to mine, my blood sizzles and my pulse dances. Tek's juicy mouth dips to claim my lower lip. He tugs slowly, maddeningly, teeth barely grazing before releasing me to trace the tip of his tongue over my top lip with delightful torture.

One warm hand cups the side of my neck. I lean into the touch. Closing my eyes, I offer my throat. "Should I add this move to my performance?" A barely perceptible moan of pleasure trickles from my lips.

Tek's cheek rests against mine as he slides his other hand around to the base of my spine, allowing one finger to trail up my back. "Perhaps. What other suggestions do you have, singer?"

"This?" I connect two notes in a sustained legato blend singing "Ah…Oh…Ah…Oh," while my hands enjoy a slow path over his trim waist, exploring his hips, and over the back of thighs that hide tight curving muscles. His hot breath riffles my hair when I stall my explorations on the lower curve of his ass.

There's a flick of tongue against my ear before Tek's husky voice purrs. "My work is done here. You," he says, as a wandering finger slides down my backbone to the hem of my dress.

"Are."

Warm breeze tickles my thighs as he lifts the fabric, hand disappearing beneath my dress until he crooks a finger around the elastic of my panties.

"The."

He delicately licks the side of my neck, pushing his hips harder against mine.

"Sexiest."

Now two fingers breach the confines of my green lace panties as they sneak around the front, stalling at the barrier of where our hips are locked together.

"Singer."

After snapping the elastic of my panties, Tek threads fingers into my hair at the nape of my neck. He draws my head back, not roughly, but decisively.

"Ever."

His steaming gaze sets my core on fire.

"Born."

His mouth consumes mine, tongue plunging deeper and deeper with every stroke. I long for this brand of fevered attention against my willing sex. Feeling the hard ridge beneath his tunic, I wrap a leg around his hip. To the tune of the torch song playing in my head, I work the friction between us like a frantic bow against violin strings.

The groans and growls pouring into my mouth from his play a hungry counterpoint. My fingers lose themselves in his wild hair as I continue to pull those lips hard against mine with intention to bruise.

Tek breaks away since my control is nowhere to be found. Our labored breathing heats the air around us as he grasps my elbows to guide my body away from his.

"Why are you stopping?" My face flushes with embarrassment before he can answer. Is turning each other on as far as our knot situation is allowed to go?

"Oh, no." I back away as an unnerving thought shows up uninvited. "If we keep this up, are we breaking a fairy law?" Will there be punishment if Tek makes love with me, a human?

He's careful as he moves closer, his lips curved in a lazy smile. "No law, but I prefer to welcome you into my bower for our passions instead of here, out in the open."

I glance around. "You call this out in the open? It looks pretty private to me."

He takes another step toward me. "In past times, I trusted no one would dare come so close to my home without permission." His expression turns weary. "But much is happening I'd never thought possible." One side of his lip quirks up. "I've lived long as the prince of indiscretion. I don't want to be that sort with you, my darling one." He offers his hand to me. "May I welcome you to my bower?"

His pause gives me pause and too much time to think. I hesitate.

"Tek, you're a fairy, I'm a human. Surely, fairy women must be more appealing to you."

Tek's head shakes rapidly and his deep red glow flares around him. "No, no, not so. I have never felt the stirrings of joy with any other that you move within me. It's your straightforward affection and honesty drawing me—blazing my fire of want."

His caring for me, his generosity certainly blaze my fires of want, but I'm in uncharted territory here. "If we..." My eyes fall to his lips still glistening with moisture from our kiss. "Will our knot take away my freedom?"

Tek grabs both my hands. His eyes are bright with open earnestness. "My beautiful Aurora, I give you my vow of honesty. I was love-blind for you and now call me lovesick in the best of ways. In all my years, certainly never with another fairy, have I felt the hope of a true love knot with anyone but you."

I stare at him in stunned silence. Tek puts into words the same journey that my heart has travelled to his. He's not a novelty or a safe port in a storm. I've felt an inexplicable pull toward him since he first crashed into me at Stalk.

Holding my breath, I set a hand to my chest. Is Tek the personification of that glimmer of hope for love, for belonging I never let completely die in my spirit? I search inside for the darkness warning me life might never be a place of happiness, but only one of fear and rejection. The darkness is gone, and in its place—Tek's lumen light.

I release my breath and with it, doubt.

"Rora," he pleads. "I do not wish us to lie together to prove claim over you or to paint you with a mark of protection." He rubs his lips together. "Although it may be interpreted as such by my kind." His gaze connects with mine, and the invisible tie between us suddenly feels tangible, a warm strand of silk delicately connecting my body to his.

Tek leans in until our foreheads touch. "I want, I need, I beg for your light in my life."

I fall into his arms. "Yes, Tek. My light is yours."

He lifts me off the ground and spins. "And mine is yours." Setting me down, he takes my hand. With his other he waves at a portion of his botanical stockade. The leafy wall parts to reveal a curtain of loose-hanging vines that matches the vibrant greens and gilded leaves of his tunic. Pulling it aside reveals a mini wonderland, teeming with white lights no larger than the tip of a pinky finger. They flicker on and off, adding a sparkling sheen to everything. A stream of shimmering aqua water as twinkly as the diamond path in the Pristine Forest flows between strange silver trees of a type I've never seen before.

Tek leads me over a high curved bridge that could be sculpted from the blue ice of a glacier. I expect it to be slippery, but it's easy to walk across. It's not ice at all but glass tinted by the color of the stream. On the other side is a riot of color from a thousand blossoms in shades of red, orange, yellow, blue, whites and purples—a floral rainbow. No two flowers wear the same shaped petals. I recognize poppies and honeysuckle, daisies and lilies, but most blooms are exotic and new to me. Some flutter as if caught in a gentle breeze, others spin like tops at the end of their stalks, slowing to change direction before taking off again in their flowery dance. And oh, the fragrances. There's no root beer here. The scents are sweeter, enticing not overwhelming. It's the garden equivalent of the delicious smells in a bakery.

"I present to you Tek's bower, my home." He stares expectantly into my face.

I throw my arms around his neck and kiss both his cheeks before releasing him to take in more of this paradise.

"Oh, Tek." I hug myself as I bounce on the soft, spongy moss carpet. I'm in a fairyland sure to inspire story and song. As gorgeous and charming as the Pristine Forest, the meadows, and little village are, Tek's bower surpasses them all. This is a living dream of flawless beauty.

His gleeful laugh is full of joy. I take both his hands and twirl us in a circle, conjuring our childish hearts as we banish the weight of adulthood. After a handful of dizzying revolutions, we fall side by side onto our backs.

"Cover your eyes," I tell Tek.

"Why?"

I don't answer but lay my hand over his disobedient eyes. "Let the world spin." I sink into the delightful, heady feeling of the ground beneath us continuing to go round and round even as we lie still. When my equilibrium settles, I miss the freeing sensation.

Next to me, Tek turns on his side to face me, sliding one hand over my stomach. "You alone make my world spin, Aurora."

I shift onto my side and take his face in my hands. "It is my pleasure, Your Highness." I kiss him slowly, sliding my mouth against his, our lips quickly turning slippery and eager. I tangle our legs to scoot closer, ready to pick up where we left off in his root beer float entry hall.

Tek chuckles against the kiss. "So impatient, my darling one."

I slide a hand under his tunic to enjoy the contours of his bare skin. It's smooth with countless grooves to explore. "That's one word for it."

He retrieves my wandering fingers and pulls us to sit "I've a riddle for you."

The pulse low in my belly is in no mood for riddles, but if this is fairy foreplay, I'm all in.

Tek nibbles on my fingers, gaze locked on mine. "Not floor, nor moss should lovers lie. Sweet secrets shared are better made, where soft beneath their bodies laid." When he sucks my finger into his mouth, the steady beat drops from my navel to a more intimate and thirstier area below.

Sadly, the damn riddle suggests we're not going to get down to business right here. What's soft? Kittens, silk, flowers... I look around the bower to see if there's a giant flower petal for two.

Above us there is no sky. Layers and layers of leaves and flowers provide a canopy of a thousand bouquets. Not a dark and dense ceiling at all. Bright beams find their way through the foliage in meandering paths that join the floating prickles of light to set the bower aglow with the luxury of a gentle sunshiny day.

Tek ends my wandering thoughts by sucking the next finger. The distraction is ridiculously hot. "Give up?"

I throw my leg over him to dig my heel into his nice firm bottom. Two can play at the distraction game. "Absolutely not." Could he be talking about this frothy little stream? Or the soft meadow grass where I was ready to cross a line with him before he coaxed me to make the video.

Tek's tongue slides over my palm. The wet path he leaves is nothing compared to the dampness between my legs. "Would you like a hint?"

Instead of a hint, I'd prefer him on top of me, showing me the type of teasing his body is capable of, but this prelude is too enchanting to rush.

His tongue travels across the inside of my wrist, leaving a yummy, satiny trail. "Okay," I breathe.

A low mist begins to rise around us, slowly seeping beneath our bodies. It's as delicate as fog but as warm as tepid steam. We slowly rise above the moss. Memories of our starry night in the cloud drift through my mind.

I smile. "That's an obvious hint for a fairy. The answer is a cloud."

Tek gives a satisfied chortle. "No, no, not so."

The mist lifts us higher toward the far end of his bower until we drift over a sage green hedgerow adorned with a profusion of tiny yellow and magenta flowers wearing neon-orange centers, each bloom no bigger than a butterscotch candy.

"The answer is my bed," says Tek, flashing me a look equal parts smolder and pleased with himself for confounding me.

I squeal and grab Tek as the mist disappears with a pop. We fall onto a deliciously soft surface that gives under our weight and then flings us into a low toss before once again catching us in its pleasantly squishy embrace. Delicate currents of air ripple against my body as if coaxing me to relax.

"Nice bed," I say, lounging on my side while I reach for the braided belt around his waist. There's the tiniest clasp that comes undone at my touch. "I'll bet it would feel even nicer without clothes." I grip the bottom of his tunic and lift. Using his heated stomach as my saddle, I slip his fancy fairy shirt the rest of the way off. Next, I position his hands behind his head, giving me full access to his naked upper body.

The soft glow of the little glitter sparkles adrift in the bower bathe his golden-brown skin with a summery flush. The defined muscles of his chest are evident but not ostentatious beneath my roving fingers. His skin is perfectly smooth without a single hair or blemish.

"Why do you hide this gorgeous landscape under loose clothing?"

"I don't flaunt my physique as an advertisement as is my father's way." He circles a finger on the inside of my wrist. The touch is simple yet arousing. "I prefer mine to be discovered exactly this way." He guides my hand back to his chest.

Tek is motionless as I stroke his skin except for a hitch in his breathing as I circle his puckered chestnut brown nipples with my fingertips. I can't stop petting him from waist to neck. "You're exquisitely sleek."

Tek gives a slight grunt. "If you'd prefer more texture..."

Suddenly a forest of silky dark curls, miniature versions of his headful of corkscrews, sprouts across his pecs.

I slap him. "Put those away." My cheeks burn. "Unless that's the real you. Don't give me anything but one hundred percent authentic Tek. No tricks."

The illusion vanishes, and I slither lower down his body until I perch on his thighs. His inviting length presses against my panties as I travel. Easing my dress low on my shoulders, I lean forward, treating my fairy lover to a view of the upper slope of my breasts. He licks his lips as his gaze rakes my skin. Pulling the drawstring on his blousy trousers to loosen them, I ease the waistband below his navel where I find a delicate trail to follow. "I prefer the hair, just here." With my finger, I trace the delicious feathery line lower until I lightly graze the tender tip of his rising cock.

Tek groans. I bend to circle his now exposed crown twice with my tongue before gently nipping down his length as I rid him of his trousers to expose every alluring inch of his arousal. How considerate of him not to wear anything underneath his pants.

Once he's naked before me, I take a moment to admire the whole picture, his lithe frame, the inviting subtly hidden contour of chest, stomach, thighs, and high-arched feet. Every bit of his unique strangeness appeals to me.

Tek pulls his hands from behind his head, but before he can reach for me, I cup the root of his shaft and heated balls with one hand while twirling a finger through the thatch of night black hair at his base that I can't resist petting. "And here."

"A fan of my cock's garden, are you?"

I treat him to a wicked smile and grasp his rigid stem. "Especially this particular sprout." With painstakingly slowness, I draw my hand upward, slightly twisting as I travel from his root to tip.

"Nature, take me," he gasps, and I make another round trip, savoring his girth as it thickens within my grasp. In a move so fast, I barely have time to register the change, he lifts me to my feet, steadying me by grasping my thighs under the skirt of my sundress while he kneels in front of me. His head sneaks under my skirt for a beat before he reappears to smile at me. "I very much approve of the floral lace design adorning your panties."

I grip his shoulders to keep from melting. "I thought you might with your appreciation of gardening." The trip to Flo and Edie's boho boutique on Hollywood Boulevard is paying off.

A lusty grin stretches across Tek's face as he disappears back under my skirt. I quiver anticipating the catalog of things he might do to me. The steady stream of air he gently blows upwards across my body is a complete surprise. My dress peels off and flutters over my head as if caught in a brisk wind before it floats away from Tek's bed to who cares where.

My fingers dig into his biceps as my body tingles with pleasure at the caress of his breath. The warmth has substance to it, lending an exquisitely velvety soft yet persistent pressure along my skin. He sends another gust of sultry wind up my legs, mingling with the slickness covering my sex to set off the most luxurious sizzle.

"Lean back, my darling."

I don't loosen my hold on him. "I'll fall."

"Never." He unleashes a second enticing zephyr that strokes my thighs for a moment before teasing the nerves nestled between them. I nearly come apart before he's touched me with his hands or that thick wet tongue of his.

The sensation loosens my hold on him, and I fall backwards. Instead of landing on the bed, a pair of green-gold vines instantly weaves a gauzy sling to catch me. Lounging on my back, I sigh as the impromptu hammock brings me to hover above the bed at the perfect height for Tek to prowl on hands and knees and position his swollen lips in line with my slit. He eases my legs apart, kissing and licking his way up the inside of my thigh. His twisty braids scratch over my lace panties. When I reach to bring him closer, he flashes a smile so naughty, tremors of need course through my body.

"Touch me, Tek."

He playfully shakes his head, then repeats his sensual travels up my other leg. When his tangle of braids rubs against me this time, I screech, plummeting toward the brink of release, but then he's gone again. I reach for my panties to rip them off and force the issue, but he grasps my hand to stop me.

"Not yet, my beauty."

I swivel my hand to grab his wrist. "Help me get rid of these."

Tek blows another teasing breath across me, not lessening my need for him, but stalling it. Never has a man controlled the crests of my waves so expertly. Tek keeps my want circling and circling in a whirlpool of desire without reaching completion yet not retreating either.

Tek grasps the edges of my vine sling to lower me. Once my delicate chariot deposits me back onto his bower bed, it slips away. Just as I licked my way down Tek's body, he returns the favor tasting his way from my navel to the bottom edge of my bra. I writhe beneath him, wanting to let go and wanting to hold back so this will never end. His hands splay across the green floral lace cups that match my panties. My breasts are heavy with desire and strain against the strapless band barely holding the girls in place.

"Blow it off," I beg him, arching to offer myself to his pillowy lips. "The way you did with the dress."

The naughty grin stretches wide as he treats himself to a teasing bite of one nipple and then the other through the fabric. "Hmm. It is rather hard to taste—"

I pull away and rip my bra off with a growl. Shoving him onto his ass, I climb onto his lap and pull his mouth to mine. I've never felt this ravenous for anyone. The attentions of this man, this lover, sing to my body, my heart.

He obliges with a thorough tasting of my tits as I rock against him in an increasingly desperate rhythm.

"You are nectar and spice, burning and sweetening my tongue," he moans against my skin.

His pulsing cock rubs across my dripping lace again and again to the rhythm of his greedy sucks. I'm drawing closer, closer, this time I'm going over the...

As if sensing I'm about to finally reach the finish line, Tek pushes me onto my back, withdrawing his brilliant friction to brace himself above me.

"I swear..." I pant. "If you don't drive your fabulous dick inside me right now—"

He cocks his head to the side. "You desire my seed?"

"Yes," I practically scream, until panic winds through my gut. "I want you to come, but don't you dare blast me with fairy baby-making cum." How potent is a fairy? Dammit, I should have asked for more specifics. "Do you have a condom hiding in these petals?" My gaze rakes the bower for my tote. "If you don't, I do."

Tek pets my hair. "Don't worry, my love. I will only share empty seed."

"You can shoot blanks on purpose?"

He's baffled by the phrase, but I've got no patience for a detailed explanation. "Swear to me your seed is empty, no hidden fairy baby starters." His mischievous expression does not give me a whole lot of confidence. "Tek," I warn.

He rests his hand over his heart. "I swear on my honor as a prince of the Arborborn Coterie, I will not cause your womb to blossom."

Tek may not be in great standing with his parents, but I suppose a bona fide prince's word is the most genuine promise anyone has ever given me.

I treat him to one of the sexy smiles his coaching made part of my repertoire. "Well then." I close my hand around his finely sculpted dick. It's grown even thicker with our playing. If I wasn't as wet as the bubbling brook of his bower, I'd be more nervous than ravenous.

He cups my sex over my panties. "So ripe. So ready."

"That's—what—I'm—saying!"

Mercifully, he slides his hands to my hips inside the lace and finally rids me of panties. I draw my knees up inviting him to indulge. I'll take any wicked means he offers to shove me off this ledge of wanting into blissful release. His hot mouth or pulsing cock is equally welcome as long as he gets on with it.

"How ripe, I wonder?" He croons as he lowers himself until his tongue laps at the deluge between my thighs. The whirlpool of my lust he's revved higher and higher threatens to drown me.

When he raises his head to meet my gaze, the look alone almost does me in. "My Aurora, you flow with beads of sweetfire." Tek licks his lips. "My lips and tongue burn." He dives back between my thighs. Hands grab my ass to bring my body tight against his gorgeous tongue that curls relentlessly around the center of my pleasure harder and harder until finally there's no chance of retreat. He consumes me. I scream and buck against his mouth with my climax.

Tek slows his ministrations and delicately drinks in my release with sighs of delight that continue to draw pleasure from my core. He summons one crashing orgasm after another from me, setting my body aflame until I'm almost too weak to ride out another.

"How do you make me..." Breath doesn't come easily enough for me to finish a sentence. "...so many times. I never..."

My prince's hands roam my back while he eases me to sit until we face one another. With his pinkie, he captures a tiny dot sparkling at the corner of his lips. Holding it for me to see, he whispers with awe. "Your beads of pleasure are as perfect as dewdrops that linger after a lover's moon. See how your nectar shines?"

His lumen light sets the droplet aglow—a pearl dyed the color of claret wine. I've never considered the evidence of my lust to be beautiful. Through Tek's awe, I experience the wonder of what he inspires my body to give in the throes of pleasure. Watching him dab the tip of his tongue against my nectar, I nearly come again.

My body objects. I'm jelly as I semi-collapse against him. Tek gathers me onto his lap. His thickness throbs against my thigh. I've been greedy, allowing him to stoke my lust over and over to the point where I've become a rag doll.

"Indelicate Tek," he admonishes himself as he rubs my back. "Forgive me, Rora. I am not versed in the sexual stamina of humans. Have I spilled too much of your wine?"

As exhausted as I am, I can't help but giggle at what must be the fairy phrase for *banged you senseless*.

Tek traces a breezy line of kisses across my cheeks and the bridge of my nose as he carefully settles me onto my back. "Relax. I will restore you."

If he means to take his turn right now, I'm afraid I'll only be as responsive as a wilted daisy. Tek deserves more. I want to reciprocate as an active and appreciative lover. He coaxed otherworldly storms of desire from my body. This man turns my life into a love song.

Before I have a moment to confess this to him, he disappears.

By the time I find the strength to prop myself up, he's back by my side. Cradled in his hands is a peachy-pink flower the size of a baseball with a rounded bottom out of which sprouts long leaves that taper to form a scallop pattern around the rim.

"I promised I would never use magic on you without your permission. If you drink the ambrosia of a blushfruit flower, it will awaken your spent body. Nothing more. No lasting effects."

The thought alone of having enough energy to treat Tek to even a speck of the ecstasy he's showered on me is the only convincing I need. Sitting up next to him, I cover his hands with mine and tip the edge of the blushfruit flower cup to my lips. Sugary liquid with the tiniest bit of fizz trickles down my throat as his other hand draws loops and curves against my lower back. Stories of heroes sipping supernatural beverages flutter through my mind. If those mythical drinks were anything like this deliciousness, they deserve to be celebrated in legend.

I upend the flower cup to make sure there isn't a single drop of blushfruit juice left. Tek laughs and flings the spent petals behind him. A strange sensation begins to simmer in my stomach. I lay a hand to my bare skin and feel it flush with heat. A moment later, that single point bursts, spreading a delightful burn through my veins until my body thrums with something akin to the beginnings of the adrenaline rush that I experience after a performance.

Tek gathers me in his arms. "A few minutes more, then vigor restores." He nuzzles the skin behind my ear with his adorable button nose. "Shall I coo of my love to you, my dearest, Aurora? For I want nothing more than to lay all my truth at your feet. Share body, mind, and heart with the one who gives me joy unbound."

I turn in his embrace to face him. "I want to share the same with you."

I'm finished hiding my failures and fears. If our relationship is going to be open and honest, I can't hold back even if the news isn't good.

"Tek, I didn't make the cut."

He tilts his head to the side, a question in his eyes.

"*Saturday's Star* didn't call. I'm sorry your wonderful coaching went to waste." As hard as it will be to see disappointment in his eyes, I don't look away. I'm not quite prepared for the anger I see instead.

He rakes a wild gaze around the bower. Against my thigh, I feel Tek's hand close into a fist. "The stupidity of mortals confounds me."

I close my fingers around his fisted hand. "I was afraid you'd be disappointed in me."

His eyes go very round, almost unnaturally so. "The disappointment to be had here is *Saturday Star's* refusal to acknowledge your perfection." A flurry of ticks dance over his jaw and temples. "No, no, not so. Disappointment is too mild a term. I am murderous at their blindness."

His outrage overpowers any disappointment in myself. "Getting past rejection is not the pretty part of wanting to be a singer, but it's the reality of a creative life."

Tek rests his palm above my thumping heart. "My darling, Aurora, do not let rejection bruise your gentle spirit."

I lay my hand over his. “Bruises heal.”

He replaces our hands with his mouth to deliver a slow, reverential kiss above my heart that warms my bruised spirit more than any blushfruit nectar. Tek gazes at me with a look so tender, I feel a rush of what I’m beginning to suspect can’t be mistaken for anything but love for this indefinable man.

I guide his face to mine and offer my own kiss filled with a cocktail of complex emotions where the ingredients blend so perfectly together, they are impossible to examine as separate entities. We kiss until I wonder if the night has stepped aside for dawn.

Tek gently strokes his nose against mine. “Are you indeed spent beyond the gifts of the blushfruit, my beloved? Shall I return you to your world?”

I smile and borrow his phrase. “No, no, not so.”

Every craving for Tek I experienced during his devastatingly brilliant lovemaking reawakens in full force as the full potency of the blushfruit nectar kicks in. I slide my palms down his burned-butter chest, relearning the taut muscles he can’t hide from me anymore. I ease onto his lap, his cock the only thing separating our bodies. I dip forward pressing my lips to his for another slow kiss. We break long enough for me to run the tip of my tongue over those sweet fairy lips before I invade his mouth again as proof of my lusty restoration. Hopefully, I dispel any idea of my desire to leave Tek’s exquisite home.

My touch adds harmonies to the work of my lips as I grasp his shaft. Relishing skin as satiny smooth as the rest of him. Sliding my fingers along his length is as pleasurable as the mist that carried us through the bower to his bed and as arousing as the breath he used to launch my body into waves of fulfillment. I learn every inch and swell of his cock the way I explored his chest, tight stomach, and those deceptively slender thighs.

As his breathing deepens, Tek’s chest and hummingbird

heartbeat collide with mine. I take him in my palm and increase the pressure of my strokes.

"More," he rasps.

I angle my hips forward so he can feel the rising pulse of my slickened core against his base, and he gasps. The wine color of his lumen light bleeds into the air around us, turning our skins a matching deep sunburn. Tek shimmies to steal more of my body's eager reaction along his thickness. I push his shoulders until he's on his back. My knees trap his hips. I let my sex take over where my hands left off as I rub my begging flesh along his length.

Returning his tease of bringing me to the edge countless times before granting my body permission to let loose, I allow his tip the barest invitation to go deeper. Enough to tantalize but not to give in completely. As he sings high notes of pleasure, I paint him again and again with my silky wetness.

Tek palms my breasts, running the edge of a thumbnail over each nipple with the perfect balance of pleasure and pain. Once again, my lover beckons me to sink into the joy of my release. I hold back, refusing to fall without taking him with me.

Lowering onto his glistening chest, I attack his mouth, relishing the wet heat we exchange. Tek's hand sneaks between us, reaching for the perfect spot to set me off. Such a generous partner. How have I ever settled for anything less?

I surprise him by shifting so his tip sinks past my entrance. His sharp cry into my mouth makes me smile. He breaks the kiss to stare at me.

"Now?" He rasps. The question echoed in his eyes.

"Now," I say, running my thumb along his jaw.

He glides in slowly. I feel like one of his beautiful blossoms stretching to meet the morning sun. My body welcomes him as he tests my limits, slipping in and then easing out. Tek hums a sweet note with each new entry.

I allow him this considerate pace until I can't stand it anymore. Pushing back up, I slide down his dick the last few glorious inches to fully take him in. We join hands as I rock while he gently thrusts. At first, it's a slow dance as we learn our own unique fit through smiles and lingering kisses wherever lips can reach. Soon enough, we're cheek to cheek, unleashing a harmony of moans. When the pace turns mouthwateringly punishing, my core coils mercilessly, begging for release. We nip at shoulders and necks, bundling as many encouragements as possible into our joining.

Tek lets go of my hands and flips us over. I throw my legs around his hips and buck against him, unwilling to relinquish any of his glorious cock. His force against me quickens in contrast to the soft caresses of his hands across my face, neck, breasts. The mixed sensation wrings out the last of my sanity, and I lose myself again in the wonderment of making love with my fairy prince.

Continuing to ride my ripples of pleasure, I dig fingers into the hard curves of Tek's ass to jerk him even closer. The insistent touch brings him along with me into destruction. The notes of his pleasure song echo around the bower until fragments of light sizzle against our skin like tiny prickles of hot rain. I clench around him desperate to keep him inside. As methodically as he entered, Tek slides deep then retreats in a gentle pattern until we are once again separate entities. His thoughtful exit gives us both time to find our breath.

Face-to-face, bodies entwined, we trace lazy lines over each other's skin. I don't remember seeing Tek still for this long. I tuck my head under his chin.

His voice is low, body calm. "I lie with you; therefore, I will never lie to you. Love of mine, I give you the faithfulness of my body, and the light of my spirit." He takes a deep breath I long to drink in. "I have a confession."

I tilt my face to look at him. He swallows so loudly I hear a *thunk.*

"Rora, I entertained the option..." He wobbles his head. "For no longer than a moment, but I did consider using a spell stone to make you fall for me. Forgive me for allowing even a single thought of compromising your free will to cross my mind."

The guilty look on his face coupled with the way he asked permission to offer me that fairy energy drink is enough for me not to doubt he will keep the promise never to use magic against me. I'd be lying not to admit my foray into this magical and adventurous taste of a unique life with Tek isn't exciting. His touch and his home already inspire new songs.

"If you don't love me from the purity of your heart, it's because I do not deserve someone as wonderful as you, Rora."

"Tek, you don't need a magic rock to win me." My smile warms my cooling skin as I absorb the strange reality of lying naked in a fairy bower with a real prince. It's beyond daydreams.

"You're not the only one with a confession," I say, snuggling closer to him. "I've never been in love so I'm not a reliable judge of what's happening between us." I lay a finger alongside his lip. "But if this is what love feels like, I might be persuaded to go all in." I trace his well-exercised lips with my fingertip. My body hums not just with satisfaction, but happiness and a sense of safety I've never known. I begin to drift off but catch myself.

Tek brushes his nose along my cheek. "Sleep, Aurora. Nothing but sweet dreams and wonder can touch you here."

"I may already be dreaming. How can the wonder I've already experienced with you be real? Don't ever wake me, Tek. Let an endless sweet dream be the truth of my life."

He kisses my ear. "You've had but a taste of fairy temptation, the pull to stay in our world. I will not let you succumb to its call, my darling one. Sleep, dream, wish, but know I am the champion to safeguard your mortal life." The sound of the brook soothes every taxed place on my body as the bower's brightness dims to a shaded amethyst. Breaking through the canopy of blooms, diffuse threads of silver-blue moonlight rest around us.

I yawn. "Should I sleep? What about the time thing?" My eyes are already drifting closed.

His arms tighten around me. “Time thing?”

I mold my body to his. “Does time in a fairy realm pass differently than in mine?”

The buzz of Tek’s chuckle is soothing against my skin. “Not in the Emerald Spire, my silken petal of a thornless rose. Here, your world’s currents of hours flow in harmony with my kingdom.”

The sense of Tek’s warm mist encircles us as his breathing slows to match mine. We drift to sleep inside a coronet of fresh and fragrant flowers as a pair of moonlit dewdrops in Tek’s beautiful garden.

18

RESTORE YOUR WITS

TEK

AURORA GIGGLES AS I CLASP HER KNEES AND DRAW THEM UP, allowing the steady current of my bower brook to massage her delicate petals. She snuggles back against my chest as we cuddle in the cozy water. A night with only snatches of sleep between glorious lovemaking interludes has us both a bit weary.

My sunstone waves a hand over the water. "Turquoise."

I oblige her by changing the currently cerulean water into the color of her choosing.

More giggles. I adore her giggles. They show a carefree side of Aurora she seldom sets free in her world. Not tiring of my showy magic, she says, "Okay, let's go for steel blue."

Running my thumbs across the smooth skin of her thighs, I lightly caress her shoulder with my chin. "Are you sure?"

"Not your favorite shade of blue?"

It's my turn to chuckle. "Oh, I like it just fine. You however—"

Her hand reaches back to cover my mouth. "Steel blue. Go."

She squeals when the temperature of the brook plummets to

match its current hue. I subject her to the shock of frigid water for a heartbeat before I shift it to a more comfortable sapphire.

Aurora shivers against me. "You could have warned me."

"But you were so insistent."

She tips her head back to give me an upside-down kiss before resettling into our comfy position. "My tricky Tek." Her back expands with a deep breath. "How long before we need to leave?"

How I wish I could suspend time, stall the rest of the world from moving on while my delectable darling and I continue discovering new sensual adventures. I tell myself there will be time for that. Plenty of time once I vanquish the threats against her from my mother and the magic mortals.

My hands idly trail to her hips then wander inward to linger in her plush wet mound of golden curls. She rewards me with a pleasant sigh and runs her fingertips along my arms.

"If you'd told me your bower was also a spa, I would have come sooner." Rora purrs with satisfaction and tilts her head to dot a kiss to the underside of my jaw.

Such restraint I must practice not to pleasure her right now as the faint vibrations of her contentment run through my body. When my naughty thumb ventures close to her most sensitive spot, she shivers and guides my hands away.

"Tek, you promised me morning-after downtime."

I gently move a thick handful of damp yellow hair over her shoulder and brush my lips down her neck. "You enjoyed a full night of being carried away?"

She shifts her naked body to lounge across my lap and cups both hands over the back of my neck. "I've never been carried away so many times. Usually, I'm never carried away at all."

"That," I say, kissing the tip of her nose. "Is a great injustice." I burn with an urge to punch Demie for tormenting Rora with his sexual inadequacies.

She taps her lips with a finger, asking for a kiss. I oblige then she slides her hands across my bare chest. "I've never had a morning after either, Tek." She trills a long-satisfied note. "Or a free spa treatment to soothe my very happy lady parts."

Her touch, her ease with me, and mention of those very alluring parts makes my cock stir.

Rora gives the water a playful slap, splashing both of us. "Tek," she says in a half-hearted warning. "Are you capable of keeping your mind and your man parts off sex?"

I play with the small pile of spell stones sitting next to us on the low bank of moss. "Maybe. If you distract me." I'm afraid to let my magic pebbles farther away than arm's length. They're usually in a pocket, but at the moment pockets aren't an option.

She studies me as I clack the stones together in my palm. "Tell me about your pretty rocks." Aurora reaches for them. I nearly slap her hand away. No one but me has ever touched the limping dryad's gift. I've always feared contact might taint their magic or harm the one who lays a finger on a spell stone. Getting a handle on my panic, I slowly extend my arm, setting my treasures out of potential danger.

"They're full of dryad magic, Aurora. Best left alone by anyone but me."

Her brow wrinkles. "Why?"

"I bargained for them; therefore, I am their keeper."

She taps a finger to the knuckles of my hand clenched around the stones. "I promise not to touch. Please show me."

Slowly I unfurl my hand. Rora's eyes sparkle as her gaze pauses on each stone. "Smooth gemstones? No. Polished rocks? Fancy marbles."

My anxiety flitters away as Aurora keeps her distance from my treasures. "They're called spell stones. Each one holds a single magical purpose, except for this green one, the *Verdant Promise*." I hold the half-spent stone up to the diffuse light of my bower. "It is capable of twin spells."

She squints at the emerald pebble. "Why is it smaller than the others?"

I rub a thumb over the shiny surface. "I used one of its spells to create the Emerald Spire."

Her eyes widen, bright with astonishment. "You made the Spire with only half of a single stone?"

"And almost every ounce of magic I possess." I stare into her eyes. "I was sent to beg a trade with a crotchety, old, unstable fairy lord. The bargain was a rare fairy eaglet in exchange for a weaving spell to create a temporary homeland for my coterie. On the way, I met the limping dryad, and she offered eight spell stones. Any fool could see it was the better bargain." I clench my fist around the stones. "The King and Queen did not agree."

Aurora shakes her head. "But you built this amazing place for your people. Surely, they realized you made the right call."

I bow my head to hide the shame stinging my face. "Yes, but to create the Emerald Spire, we had to align with the powers of magic mortals."

She raises my head with gentle fingertips. "Why?"

How do I make her understand the symbiosis necessary between mortals with powers and fairies to keep the magic aspects of the Spire secret? Diving in is the only way. "Magic always requires a bargain and rarely a fair one. The *Verdant Promise* stone could only create this enchanted beanstalk with multiple dimensions if my folk accepted a sworn partnership with gifted humans." I snort. "In a sour twist of fate, the sorcerer and his witches became the conduit allowing the human/fairy dichotomy that is the Emerald Spire to thrive."

"Oh, Tek. You're talking serious shit." She smooths strands of hair off my face.

"Serious shit indeed." I force my lips into a half-smile.

Aurora taps the back of my fist holding the stones. "I hope your other stones don't have as high a cost."

I cradle my hand against my chest, cupping the stones in my palm. "Thankfully not. See this clear one. It used to be milky white, the *Pearl Tear*. It allowed me to form the shell to hide the Dark

Vinyl Artists when they come into Stalk." Rora presses her hand to mine, careful not to touch the stones. "Once I use a stone that holds a single spell, it loses its color."

"The red one matches the color of your lumen light."

My half-smile becomes whole. "Very observant. It's called *Claret Blood*."

She tilts her head. "A love spell?"

I snap my hand shut. "Of sorts. It accelerates blooming love or resurrects lost love if the partners still carry a whisper of affection for one another in their hearts."

Aurora narrows her eyes. "You considered using a stone on me."

I take a fortifying breath and let the truth out. "I considered how wrong it would be to do so. Does that count?"

She studies me. "More than you know." Her face relaxes into a smile warm enough to light the bower. A crinkle dips between her eyebrows. "So, *Claret Blood* can't make a person fall in love with something or someone they don't already have feelings for whether they admit it or not?"

I feign shock. "Some *thing*? Aurora, would you use a spell stone to make Demetrius fall head over heels with a pair of tongs?"

"I was thinking more along the lines of the donkey on the corner near Hotel Caliwood that kids take pictures with."

I carefully nestle the stones into a groove in the moss so I can pull her fully into my arms. "Naughty, Rora. With such thoughts, one might conclude you are kin to fairies."

She anchors her hands to my shoulders and stretches the rest of her body into the brook. "Part naughty—part fairy, what's the difference?" Our lips meet in a long, languorous kiss as bubbles tickle our skin.

Aurora rests her head against my collarbone. "If she is in danger, is there a stone to help the singer who the magic mortals are keeping?"

It's a fair question. My cherished darling senses a potential wrong and means to right it. Her kind nature would allow nothing less. "No obvious choice, but I will think on it."

Her head pops up. "I want to talk to her, Tek. Listen to her story and learn the truth. I felt a pull toward her and the undercurrent of sadness in her song."

"It was the sea witch's magic pulling you, Rora."

She presses her lips together until their pastel pink hue turns nearly white then thumps a finger in the hollow of my throat. "If the Dark Vinyl Artists have their eye on me to help her, we can use my meeting with the Harp to figure out if she needs rescuing."

I am uneasy at Rora's interest in the Golden Harp. It compounds her danger instead of alleviating it. "Perhaps she's happy with them and doesn't fit your vision of a maiden that dreams of rescue."

She does not buy this possibility. "Promise me you'll try to find a way for us to meet with her."

I smooth her hair away from her face with my thumbs. "I won't do anything to put you in more danger. That is all I will promise." I slip my body under hers and wrap my arms around her. We bob in the current. Her wet, slippery body chases all thoughts of stones and golden harps from my mind.

Her hands float next to us for a moment before she traces a path across my back. Suddenly her fingers stall at the pair of thin ridges beneath my skin running from my shoulders to the base of my spine. She shifts to stand in the brook, pulling me with her, and moves around behind me.

"Tek, what is this series of little flat bumps? I felt them last night but I don't see any scars." Aurora's fingers press harder against me.

I spin and capture her hands. "Once I had wings."

Her voice is a whisper. "Once? What happened to them?"

I lower my head so my lips meet her knuckles and stare at her through my lashes. "After the Brineborn salted our land, I flew back to see if there was anything to save, any seedling or blossom that had not been destroyed. I was careless." I huff. "Careless Tek. I fell backwards into a pile of salt. My wings were gone in an instant."

"Oh, Tek. How awful." Tears gather in the corners of her eyes. "Will they grow back?"

"Our home is blighted for a hundred years. When at last we return, I will seek help from our healers. Until then, I am as blighted as the land."

Aurora's tears, as bright as star drizzle, fall.

I kiss each trail streaming across her apricot skin. "Do not weep for me. I can still lumen travel."

"A hundred years," she murmurs and a weak smile finds its way to her lips. "Seems neither of our lives have been filled with light."

I ease us back into the soothing waters and summon warmer currents to combat our cooling moods. I've shared pieces of my darkness. I want to know hers so I can love all that has transpired to challenge my sunstone's light. "Rora, how did you end up dwelling in the shadows of Hollywood?"

"You're asking me to dump more sadness into your beautiful bower?"

"Flowers are more resilient than people give them credit for." I rub patterns across her scarless back.

Again, she lets her arms float atop the water. "I lost my parents just before I turned eight." Her voice catches. "Their car blew a tire on a high mountain road. They went over a cliff."

I stroke her hair. "It is nature's gift you weren't in the car with them."

She stiffens. "A cruel gift."

"Then you had no home?"

Aurora stacks her hands on my chest and rests her chin atop them. "I lived with my aunt and uncle who I'd only met once when I was super young. She was my dad's sister and a very challenging person. First, there was resentment she was stuck with me. Then near the end of high school, she accused me of tempting my uncle's inappropriate attention and kicked me out. No graduation. No diploma. No future."

My chest tightens with each bitter turn of her story. Her aunt is not challenging, she is unforgivable. Rora's nature doesn't allow her to tell a truth that diminishes another. "Did your uncle desire you?"

"Ugh, Tek. I don't even want to think about the creep. He always made me feel uncomfortable. I did everything I could to avoid him."

"The aunt was jealous of your beauty and goodness."

Aurora snorts. "What she accused me of was anything but goodness."

I kiss her temple and speak against the soft skin. "People with shadows in their hearts cannot abide those with light. They seek to demean, control, or destroy what they will never possess."

Rora's silence stretches. I should be protecting her, not coaxing her to relive such an ugly truth.

I lift her chin. "We will be each other's light."

Her answer is a sweet kiss. I swear the warmth of her sunstone heart flows across my skin. Slender arms snake around my body to grab my ass, and the kiss shifts from sweetness into unspent fury. We both pour the anger of our pasts into unspoken promises of a future together filled with the brightness and joy we are capable of offering one another. A fairy and a human cannot predict their path, but I know in that moment our hearts are pledged.

My tongue traces the seam of her mouth as I whisper. "Are you recovered?"

She rubs her cheek against mine. "I'll never recover from you, Tek."

We float under the bridge, our kisses growing more insistent. Up ahead, the mossy bank offers a conveniently low ledge. I lift Aurora onto it then press my body to hers. My happy cock teases her slick heat that the brook fails to cool. We are all demands and moans until my need for her sings through my veins.

"Let me take you back to my bower bed," I groan against one delightfully swollen plump nipple. "And serve you properly."

Her voice is clipped and adamant. "No. Take me here, fast and rough."

I share her desire and replace my cock with naughty fingers to circle and stroke until she arches, her body begging. Spinning my sunstone to face the depths of my bower, I cover her with my body, biting where her shoulder meets neck. My insistent groans are a tangle of music, lust, and a heart's confession. "I'm lost, Aurora."

"Lose yourself inside me, Tek." She lifts her beautiful bottom and angles her toasty core to present me with an irresistible invitation. My eager length plunges into her as the water churns around us, mirroring the turbulence of my desire. She sings a sweet note with every thrust, each sound higher and longer as she surges toward climax. I grab her hips and with a far from gentle push alter the angle of my path. Her notes shift into a wanton scream as I too find my oblivion.

For the briefest moment, I regret I gifted her with useless seed. To give Aurora my children and build a family with her is a daring dream. One I must banish. Unless...no. Using any spell stone without her permission to craft a future where Rora and I could be together despite our fairy/human challenges would be deceitful.

Foolish Tek.

Such a dream must forever be a dream. Mortals are to fairy kind as a feather is to an oak. One can be swept away by the slightest of breezes while the other stands steadfast into eternity. Dreaming of a life with Aurora beyond a short interval of human time is folly.

I've been called the Prince of Folly too often for my liking.

Rora is delightfully limp as she collapses against the soft streamside moss. Her hand reaches back to stroke my cheek. I slide out of her to tenderly fold my body around hers.

"I'll never recover from you either, my dearest sunstone."

We walk hand in hand through the fairy door that opens to a dark corner of Stalk. Once we're in the club, Aurora looks back at the black marble wall.

"Why can't I see the door if I could see the meadow, the forest, and your bower?"

I kiss her cheek. "Sensitivity and full sight are two very different beasts. The doors bear layer upon layer of protections."

She smooths her dress. "Bad planning not bringing a change of clothes." Her sharp laugh rings through the room. "I suppose it's not a walk of shame if no one saw you leaving."

I scowl. "Shame? Have I caused you shame by lying with you?"

Her soft palms cup my cheeks, and she gives me a quick kiss. "No, you silly man. It's just an expression." Rora's expression grows serious. "There is nothing shameful about making love with you."

When our next kiss flowers with passion, I ache to whisk her back to my bower.

We both jump when we're suddenly surrounded by floating silk and wings in four familiar pastel shades of pink, blue, lilac, and mint. Aurora crushes my hand as my mother's favorites brush wings she feels but cannot see over her body.

"The sunstone is sweetness," croons Chalcedony. "Just as our queen promised."

"And light," adds Galena.

"To be adored," purrs Peridot, pouring a little too much intention into her words as she boldly slides a wing across Aurora's chest.

"And adoring," snickers Tourmaline, spinning Rora.

My love backs into me, making shooing motions to the queen's favorites. "Hey!"

I wind a protective arm around her. "Hands off, ladies."

Aurora whispers fervently into my ear, not realizing the fairy quartet can hear the barest hint of a sound from her. "Why do they look like they're floating?"

The queen's ladies weave their quiet laughter together then speak as one. "You've knotted and bedded our prince. Trust expands your vision of our reality. Not completely, but more than other humans." The four join hands and fly in a circle around us, their next words a chant. "Once your knot breaks with this mister, Citrine claims you, dear sweet sister."

Aurora's fingers grip my arm hard enough to leave a bruise.

"With all due respect to my queen's favorites," I say with a bow of the head before spearing the quartet with my glare. "Fuck off."

They think I'm hilarious. Their tinkling crystal laughter dances around the club. "Lie with a mortal, curse like a mortal," snickers Tourmaline.

"The prince requests us to begone," says Galena, the closest thing to a peacemaker in my mother's girls' club.

"And so, we shall," says Chalcedony. "But first, dear prince, you're summoned to the royal chamber." Their signature lumen colors twinkle around each of the queen's favorites.

Faster than a blink, the four fairy women shed their flowing silks and don well-tailored blazers and pencil skirts that feature every tantalizing curve of their lithe human frames. Over Chalcedony's shoulder, I see the reason for the shift. Demetrius trudges up the staircase outside Stalk's arch.

"Don't make Ms. Citrine wait, or you'll be...*royally* fucked," says Tourmaline with a giggle, taunting me with her shift into insinuation-loaded human speak.

Our welcoming committee clacks away in heels spiky enough to be weaponized, and act as if they're heading to Citrine's office. Demetrius doesn't temper his gawking as the gorgeous foursome passes him under the arch.

I pull Aurora into my arms and pitch my voice too low for Demie-poo to hear. "I'm sorry about them."

Even though she's still trembling a bitty bit, Rora doesn't linger in the embrace. Her gaze sweeps the room. "Well, if that wasn't grounds for sexual harassment in the workplace, I don't know what is."

"Believe it or not, their, ah, attention was meant to be friendly."

Aurora crosses her arms. "So, all you fairies are a touchy bunch?"

I reach for her hips and pull her back against me, relishing the look of abject disgust on Demetrius's face. My lips brush the shell of Rora's ear. "We are very tactile, yes. A sense you humans fail to enjoy to its full extent."

To my surprise, despite our audience, she nips my earlobe. "Can you recommend a good coach to help me expand my tactile horizons?"

"I may know one," I say and delight when she answers my thorough kiss with equal enthusiasm as Demie smashes and crashes things behind the bar. I sigh when we part. "I have to go, light of my heart." Her smile fades at the seriousness in my tone. "Despite the inevitable unpleasantness, please stay near Demetrius. Go where he goes so you are never alone and vulnerable."

Rora exhales with a groan. "Goody."

I firmly grasp her shoulders. "I'm serious. You must stay in my presence or that of another mortal until I can dismantle the dangers waiting to catch you off guard."

Fear settles across her features. "I prefer your nervous rhyming instead of this face." She squeezes my cheeks in one hand. We mirror fearful expressions.

I grasp her hand to kiss her palm. "I will fly back to your side the moment I'm able, hopefully with a stouter promise from the queen to forfeit her desires to add you to her private court." After holding up two fingers, I put one down. "That cuts our worries in half."

She scoffs. "One fairy queen—check, four dastardly magic mortals to go."

I walk her to the bar and kiss her once more before gesturing to the blender. "Create something extraordinary, my magician."

Demetrius skulks at the far end of the bar, attempting to destroy me with his poison gaze. I throw him a salute before leaving Stalk and rounding the corner as if I'm off to Citrine's office. Once out of sight, I flick into lumen light and disappear through the closest fairy door.

When I travel to the entrance of the royal hall, the guard bows and cracks open one of the grand doors to allow me through. Slipping through in fairy silence, I survey the royal landscape. The full house I expect in the throne room does not appear. The king and queen alone pose before the dais. They are locked in combat with both words and looks, oblivious to my presence. I remain still inside the chamber doors. My happy heart, radiant with joy from a night with my beloved, shrivels into one of princely stone as the constraints of my station hit with full force.

I am a prince. They are my monarchs. My loyalties to them must always take precedence.

"It was folly to approach the unsavory Brineborn, Cinnabar. We might as well have invited them to destroy our coterie outright," seethes the queen in a voice penetrating enough to splinter glass.

"And you proved you would sell anyone's soul to gain their allegiance," roars Cinnabar loud enough to outdo her.

I must put aside smoldering resentment toward my parents and enter the fray. My feet seem to have grown roots. I remain motionless as their toxic banter escalates.

Citrine jabs a fingernail into the center of Cinnabar's armor-clad chest, raising a loud *ting*. It's then I notice the queen too wears her metal shell. They went to the Brineborn as warrior monarchs, not diplomatic dealers.

"If *my king*..." She spits the title at him. "Hadn't saddled the Arborborn with a history of slighting the Brineborn, there would have been willingness to strike a new bargain." She scrapes the nail down his breastplate, creating a horrible screech.

Cinnabar retreats two steps, waving a dismissive hand. "They are heartless connoisseurs of kelp. You are deluded to believe fresh negotiations from any royal Arborborn tongue would alter their adamant stand on previous unfulfilled demands. They will stand resolved to act as the grievously slighted are wont to do until we produce a royal bridegroom for their princess. They are deaf to any new bargain."

Nature, save me. The Brineborn's unfulfilled demand is the shadow with teeth ever-seeking my obeisance.

My mother's shoulders sag. "They are fairy. We are fairy. Surely, siding with us is in their best interest. Our salvation is finally honoring their former request, Cinnabar. It would put the feud between coteries along with the loathsome magic mortals to rest."

As usual, Queen Citrine has no qualms about using me as a bargaining chip.

The king steps closer and with courtly grace, grasps his queen's hand. "And what of our feud, wife? Are you not exhausted of this chasm between us? The Brineborn were not blind to our marital divide. That is what makes us weak." He lays her hand to his heart. "If we reapproach united and stand firm, I believe our fairy brethren will open their ears to new offers."

My mother's gaze falls to my father's chest and then slowly lifts to meet his eyes. "I cannot trust you, Cinnabar." To my shock, her eyes glisten with tears. Never have I witnessed the tears of my queen.

"You can, my dearest Citrine. I've suffered these eighty-eight years for my misdeed and yearn to suffer no more."

In a move most unexpected, my mother lays her head on my father's shoulder. In this quiet moment, I see the love that still binds them laid bare.

As fast as it appears, her tenderness vanishes. "We must honor their original request and repair the slight between coteries."

She will not listen to her king. She will not waver in her resolve. If not for the delicate connection I just glimpsed and the love she gives so freely to her four favorites, I would deny my mother possessed a heart at all.

Cinnabar's gaze flickers to me, and he nods at the doors. Citrine turns. Their stares summon me forward.

Adopting my usual air of borderline disrespect, I saunter toward them. "Bad news on the Brineborn front?" I swallow a nervous chuckle. My speech sounds more mortal by the day. "What did our salty compatriots think of reconnecting?"

The queen's glare is needle sharp, but it's the king who answers. "We are still in negotiations."

Citrine gapes at him for a heartbeat before her mask of ire is back in place. "Still lying. Still deceiving, Cinnabar." She shifts her terrifying expression to me. "There is no negotiation. You know what they demand, Tek Goodfellow."

"Ah, no one has snapped up their fair Princess Dioptase yet?" I nonchalantly study my fingernails while my insides clench tighter and tighter until I'm not sure I can draw breath.

The queen's slap to my cheek is as quick as a serpent's strike. "How dare you speak so callously of your part in our coterie's diminishment?"

My hand flies to my stinging flesh. Even in her perpetual disdain, my mother has never struck me. As Rora would say, this is next-level shit.

Cinnabar takes hold of her hand to prevent another blow. "Peace, my queen. There must be a solution we have yet to discover."

"Open your eyes, Cinnabar." Her gaze flashes to me. "Your son marries their princess, or the Brineborn will join with the magic mortals to supplant us." Those glowing lemon eyes devour the king. "We'll once again be forced to flee, a doubly disgraced coterie of fairy vagabonds."

"There is another way," roars Cinnabar, dark spirals swirling across his mahogany skin with such fury his features disappear.

"There is not," the queen answers with a war cry.

I can't endure this. Now that I love, truly love, witnessing spite between two souls who, no matter how deep they bury it, do still love, destroys me. I can end their estrangement by agreeing to the Brineborn's demands and join our coteries with a royal marriage. But what of my sunstone, our happiness, our love? Is that not as sacred as the love both king and queen deny?

There is another way.

Cinnabar's words circle through my spirit. My lumen light spins faster and faster until the spell stones in my pocket heat and singe fabric. A wisp of smoke rises from beneath my tunic. I plunge my hand to grasp my treasures in a cooling grip to discover only a single stone pulses with heat. I draw out the culprit.

The *Claret Blood* quivers between my fingers.

I hold in my palm the power that may possibly mend their fractured passion. Using the stone will not create love where it does not exist. It will restore a truth. Only with reconciliation will the royals have a sliver of hope to give each other the grace to search for a different offering to solidify a Brineborn alliance.

Up and down, up and down, I will lead them up and down. Tek Goodfellow's spells are feared in field and town. I must do this.

There is no other avenue to cure my parents' diseased love. Only then may I retain hope of a yet unseen solution where I will not lose my sunstone, my dawn light, my Aurora.

Pouring the other stones back into my pocket, I hold the *Claret Blood* stone aloft and speak the words.

"Joined blood and bone,
Afar you've roamed.
Seek to repair
Two heart's despair.
Embrace as one,
The love undone."

I squeeze the stone and it bursts into a claret mist, the exact color of my lumen light. My parents whip their attention to me a second before the gentle steam engulfs them.

"All is well, enact the spell."

I dare not watch the aftermath. Its result will find me soon enough. Hidden from the king and queen's sight by the deep red cloud surrounding them, I shift into lumen light and fly.

I've already left Aurora alone too long. I must be her protector before her foes close in.

I clench the remaining stones in my pocket. The *Claret Blood* may not work on beings as powerful as Queen Citrine and King Cinnabar of the Arborborn Coterie. If that is so, I will be forced to enact my own bargain with the royals to ensure my beloved's safety.

If every choice incites regret, the path to save my folk is set.

Once I am assured Aurora is beyond harm, and there is no other choice to preserve the well-being of my folk, I may be forced to face the reality of my duty and wed the Brineborn princess.

19

SOFT OPENING

AURORA

Where is Tek?

He loitered with a perpetual sulk on his face around Stalk's perimeter for a few hours in the early afternoon while Demie, aka *Mr. Prickly As Ever,* and I worked on final training prep with our trio of barbacks—Toby, Mia, and Cooper—for the latest soft opening of the club tonight.

Mr. Cinnabar and Ms. Citrine have also been uncharacteristically scarce today. I suppose it makes sense. We've polished Stalk as near to perfection as it's likely to get until we gather feedback from our preview patrons.

I've tried for a cordial level with Demetrius, but he's still playing wounded and wronged. Mia, is a super peppy woman around my age who definitely has eyes for Demie. I overheard the pair swapping stories about European cruises. Privilege puts the two on a level of common ground beyond what I could ever share with him. Maybe there's hope there. I want him to be happy with someone who's the right fit for him.

The lingering animosity from Demetrius gnaws at my heart. I hurt him. I hate hurting people.

I huff. Tek would tell me I'm being too nice—again. Putting others first is one thing but allowing them to reform you into what they want you to be, not who you truly are, is very different. Giving in to Demie constantly led him to believe I was onboard with being shaped into the partner he wanted.

I will not make the same mistake with Tek.

My lips curve into a smile thinking about Tek. From the moment he crashed into me weeks ago, I've felt an odd attraction to him. My smile fades as I shake off a fleeting thought. He swore he didn't use fairy coercion on me, but does he even realize when he's doing it? If magic is second nature or probably first nature to him, is Tek conscious of the inevitable effect he has on a human?

What is wrong with me? I had the most incredible, bordering on unbelievable night with a man that does things to my heart I've never experienced before. There is powerful truth in this feeling that I don't know if I possess the strength to turn away from. Is there truly a possibility if I dare to love, it will mean the same thing to a whimsical fairy as it does to me? I so want it to.

I'm dabbing at drips of champagne slush on my vest when my phone buzzes in the pocket of my black slacks. I slide it free but decide to ignore the call when I don't recognize the number. A voicemail ping follows quickly.

Before I check the message, Demie leans over my shoulder, being nosy. "Where's your fuck buddy? Lost interest already?"

I don't know if it's my unsettled nerves over Tek's absence or Demie's tone that set me off. I heave the bar towel onto the counter and dig my fingers into one of his biceps. "Come with me."

"Damn, Aurora," he protests and tries to escape my grasp.

"Shush, we're doing this." Dragging him along, we head for the farthest curved wall of Stalk away from the bar. I call over my shoulder to the barbacks. "Take your break. Be back in an hour."

Toby and Cooper set a speed record bolting from our

confrontation. Mia, on the other hand plants herself at the end of the bar and calls out, "Demie, should I wait for you?"

Before he can answer, I do it for him. "He'll be a minute. Meet him at the elevator." With a one-shoulder shrug, she strolls out of the club.

Demie peels my steely grip off his arm. "What the hell is your problem?"

I close my eyes for a beat to gather my thoughts. "Here's the deal. I am sorry the way things ended. I should have been honest with you about my unhappiness. If you need to dump a hundred percent of the blame for this—" I flick a finger back and forth between us. "On me for us not working out, then fine, but please pull your head out of your ass and be civil to me at work."

I expect a return volley, but instead he turns on the waterworks. "What didn't I give you, Rora? Tell me how to get you back, and I'll do it."

I believe he means what he says, but Demie is what he is and won't change. The urge to comfort nearly overwhelms me until I remind myself it's my default reflex and would send him an unfair signal. He's still grieving us when all I feel is guilt.

"You're asking to fix something that wasn't broken because we never worked in the first place. I'm sorry I ever led you to believe otherwise."

Demetrius bends to grip the edge of a low table and stares at its surface. "But you and the errand boy work?"

"Yes, Demie. Tek and I work. He believes in my talent and my dreams. You never supported either, and I allowed it."

Tek gives me so much more. He treats me as if I have value, a whole new experience for me. It's not only his support for my singing, but also his genuine encouragement, the push for me to be ambitious. My fairy prince has given me a taste of what a partnership can be. In my life, that's powerful magic.

Demetrius lifts his gaze to me. The tears are gone, and his familiar dismissive expression appears. "I was being kind by not encouraging you. It's not my fault you refuse to see the odds of you making it in the music business are a joke. I didn't want to see you crushed."

I press my lips together to cage rising anger. "Dreams don't work that way."

He throws his arms up. "Fine. Dismiss us, and I'll do the same." Demie spins on his heel to leave.

"Demetrius, stop." I'm sure it's the unexpected command in my voice rather than the words that cause him to turn back. "I want your word you'll be decent to me while we're at Stalk. Your constant snarking and digging at me in front of our assistants is not acceptable."

"Last time I checked, you are not my boss. If you can't handle the climate, quit." He jabs a finger at the stage. "Go sing on the streets and chase your ridiculous dream."

His cruelty burns, but I temper my voice into a cold, even level. "I will not quit. What I will do is go to Mr. Cinnabar and file a formal complaint for hostile work environment."

Demetrius splutters and his face turns an interesting shade between eggplant and fuchsia.

I untie the string of my black apron and yank it off. "I'm going on break." Playing the part of a confident woman, I stride across the club toward the storeroom, not looking back at Demie. As soon as the bar door closes behind me, my waterworks flow.

Why can't Demetrius accept a clean break and move the hell on? I know he's hurt. That's on me, but I can't make it any plainer we're over. Maybe he'll quit Stalk. Heaven knows he doesn't need this job.

When my cell buzz pesters me with an incoming text, I remember the voicemail. After using the sticky apron to daub my eyes, I click on the message.

"*Aurora Herman, this is Monica from Saturday's Star. We are delighted to inform you one of our finalists for tonight's sing-off to win the warmup spot at Stalk's opening night dropped out of the competition.*

That moves you into the vacant spot. I'll need a call back within the hour or we'll go to our next on the list. Congratulations, and I hope to hear from you."

I play the message twice more, speechless as tumbling thoughts form into something cohesive.

This—is—happening.

My hand trembles as I tap the return call icon. Monica of *Saturday's Star* ticks off the particulars. Once the call ends, I turn to the huge stainless-steel fridge and pound on it.

"Yes. Yes. Yes."

Abruptly, I stop hollering and rub my throat. I've got to baby the instrument. "No dairy. Sip tea with honey and lemon. Go talk to Mr. Cinnabar. And for heaven's sake, Aurora, no more crying." I don't need stuffy sinuses. Thankfully, I've kept THE dress I planned to wear for the performance to help me manifest success in my work locker. I lean against the fridge. Wow. I was going to take it home tonight. This is a lesson in *never give up*.

I grab my phone to call Tek. No, first I have to clear my brief absence from bar duty with Mr. Cinnabar. Demetrius and the barbacks can surely cover me for twenty minutes while I warm up and perform. I'll hum as I craft cocktails to keep my vocal cords nice and toasty.

It'd add to my confidence if Tek listens to me sing one more time before I go on.

I hug myself and squeal, before skipping out of the bar's stockroom and down the hallway to Mr. Cinnabar's office. I can't think of him as a king or Tek's father right now, just my boss.

I lift my hand to knock when I hear the raised voices of Mr. Cinnabar and Ms. Citrine inside. I grimace and slowly back away from the door. Clearly not the time to be asking for favors. Well, at least I know they're on-site. Tek can help me find the right time to approach Mr. Cinnabar.

I glance at my watch. There are mere hours before tonight's soft opening crowd descends. A drop of sweat trickles down the side of my face. I'll go to the empty wardrobe room, do vocal exercises, then come back. Hopefully that'll give them time to finish their fight.

I turn to go when a third voice crackles through the air.

Tek.

"Your Majesties, I've pondered well the solution you desire. If my wedding to the Brineborn princess brings hope, I quench all disobedient fire."

Wedding? Princess?

His words slither like a thousand tiny snakes through my blood. Tek, my Tek, the man I was willing to possibly fall completely in love with, just agreed to marry a fairy princess.

I wish I could travel via lumen light like Tek to get the hell out of here. Instead, I run back to Stalk. Slamming through the stockroom, I head into the service elevator to go hide in wardrobe.

To plummet from the high of winning a place in the *Saturday's Star* contest only to crash into the unforgiving reality of Tek's engagement scrapes my emotions raw and bloody. I lie on the long bench in front of the row of lockers and use an arm to shield my eyes and think.

My heart believed the knot Tek and I committed to was a legit relationship. It's obvious now it's nothing more than ordinary dating in fairy speak.

My naivete bites me in the ass once again. Tek's words of love set me on the path to my own thoughts of the same. I don't believe he is lying to me, but as I feared, love to a fairy is not what it is to a human. How could it be if he had a potential bride waiting in the wings? A royal bride, and a marriage that could benefit his people.

Tek is a fairy prince. Princes marry princesses.

I picture love as something with roots that can grow and thrive. To Tek, it's only a beautiful blossom to pluck and admire until its initial liveliness wilts and fades.

Love is transient to Tek.

I've lived mired in transient for too long. Yearning for stability led me to Demetrius and look where it got me—trapped to fulfill the expectations of someone else.

The problem is I don't want Tek to be transient. I'd be crazy to entertain any hope he's my forever, but I wanted to see where a relationship with a soul who saw me and valued me might go.

The answer is clear. Our relationship will stay exactly where it is and no further. Do I continue with Tek knowing full well we have an end date—his wedding? Do I enjoy this knot he claims between us until it is time to dissolve it or step away before I give any more of my heart to him? I freely gave Tek too much too fast, and now I will pay the price.

I pull my arm away to see a smear of black mascara across the white sleeve. It's strangely grounding to have such a mundane problem as needing to change into a new uniform shirt and wash my face. The jolt of Tek's future must be tucked away for now. It's my future that I must focus on. The one I build for myself by nailing my performance tonight and winning the slot for Stalk's opening.

I'm no longer a street kid. I am a self-sustaining adult with dreams. My affair with Tek will be a single chapter. A sweet chapter. One I have the choice to continue writing until the last sentence is complete.

I've pondered well the solution you desire. If my wedding to the Brineborn princess brings hope, I quench all disobedient fire.

I open my locker and unzip the garment bag. Yes, the dress is perfect. Sexy yet classy. Tek will approve. I picture it slung over the flowery hedgerow in his bower and wonder if I will ever see that private paradise again.

Zipping the dress back inside its cocoon, I grunt. At least this breakup won't fall to me.

Out of nowhere, dread intrudes on my self-pity. Tek told me not to be alone, and here I am utterly secluded. Irritation butts its way in. If he's so worried for my safety, why has he made himself scare when he promised to return?

This is the price of falling for a flighty fairy.

I'm careful not to splatter cocktail makings on my dress. Clingy black fabric with a slight sheen covered in tiny flecks of sequins celebrates my curves without being trashy and provides the look of a moving starfield. From the thin black shoulder straps, layers of silver organza kiss my upper arms and slightly flutter in the AC. My own fairy wings. Tonight, I will rival star drizzle.

Demie's eyes bulge when I step behind the bar. Nice confirmation the dress hits the home run I knew it would from the moment I saw it in the window of Flo and Edie's boutique. He's been cold but decent tonight even though I'm sure he's still stewing over our earlier conversation.

Mr. Cinnabar and Ms. Citrine arrived at the club not long after I returned from wardrobe. There were no visible signs of the shouting match I'd overheard. Ms. Citrine at least acted surprised at my news about being a *Saturday's Star* finalist, cooing and fussing over me. Mr. Cinnabar was generous, allowing me to vacate my cocktail magician duties for as long as I needed.

Neither of these royal fairies appears or moves like fairies at all. Both come off one hundred percent human. Apparently, my newly acquired fairy detector "sight" doesn't extend to them.

Thoughts of Tek threaten to darken the thrill of my anticipation. He still has not made an appearance. I almost texted him multiple times to share my *Saturday's Star* success, but I owe the entirety of my mental and physical energy to my performance, not an improbable future with the engaged prince.

I mix my tenth Frostywood of the evening. After handing it over to one of the servers, I watch her deliver it to the table in the center of the club. Five people—two men and three women—sit with tablets propped in front of them. The *Saturday's Star* judges are decked out in everything from gold lamé suits to watermark silk ball gowns. They furiously type as they take in each finalist's performance.

There's a lull in the orders, giving me a hot second to watch the current singer. He's built like Mr. Cinnabar, muscles barely contained in the midnight blue leather tux he's chosen for tonight's gig. Many a thirsty eye, both male and female, drink him in. His growl has too much grit and not enough purr for my taste. I can almost feel his throat muscles tightening with nerves. The lyrics of his song also try too hard. His musical plea for love is pathetic, not provocative.

Yeah, I can beat this guy.

"Rora, quit ogling the tool on the turntable." Demie quickly tempers his tone. "We need five *Hotel Caliwood Haunts* for table two."

I glance at the group seated next to the perpetually empty *reserved* table nearest to the bar and nearly swallow my tongue. Leonato Andante sits with two younger couples. Holy shit. The president of Caliwood, Inc. records is going to hear me sing tonight. I squint through the dimness to try to make out the others at the table. The combed-back white-blond hair of Benedict Boyd is a bright beacon in the dark club. The woman he's got his arm around must be...

Double shit, I'm looking at the other lead singer/songwriter of B&B+3, Beatrice Sharpe. They must be scoping the vibe of the venue for their opening night gala performance.

"Hey, Aurora," says the server, sidling over to the bar. "The curly-haired dude at table two said to give you this." He hands me a quarter with the image on one side smoothed away so it's blank.

I pop my head up to stare more closely at Leonato's table. My old bud and Robo Robbie's bestie, Santino Fedele, waves at me. Rand Diggs had me working for a short stint at Fedele Costumes a few years back. Even though the Fedele family owns an entire block of Hollywood Boulevard, Santino had shucked all of it for a while and had become one of Rand's street kids. Ever since then, he's been loyal to Rand and the incredible network of Boulevard people who've taken up the mission of helping lost souls like me.

I rub my thumb over the smooth side of the quarter. Rand gave us these special coins as a symbol to remind us we had the power to rewrite our future. I blow Santino a kiss. He couldn't have picked a more perfect night to send me his quarter. Ah, so the woman next to him is Leonato's daughter, Hero, Santino's fiancé. There's a wedding sure to be an epic event. I hope I get an invite.

After we create the signature cocktails for the Hotel Caliwood bunch, I remove my apron. The woman currently on stage dressed in a sheer, plum-colored, off-the-shoulder dress revealing a gold bustier beneath is the last singer before me. She was introduced as Desiderata, and like the poem of the same name, she has an ethereal, positive vibe while pulling off slinky and provocative. In my gut, I know she's my main competition. I study every move, every intonation of her phrasing. She yearns and grieves for a lost love. Her performance shines with hope for a different outcome.

Desiderata tells a story that deserves to be listened to.

I have a story too.

And it's time to tell it.

Ms. Citrine is resplendent in a gown of yellow metallic overlays that at first glance look like fish scales, but upon closer scrutiny are tiny leaves. It reminds me of Tek's fairy prince tunic. She flows onto the vacated turntable and starts my introduction.

The audience is wonderfully receptive when she gives me credit for designing many of the cocktails they've enjoyed this evening in addition to being their next entertainer. When she says my name and reaches a hand to me, I step from behind the bar.

A different hand clutches mine.

Tek.

He looks as if he's been dragged behind a bus with scragglier than usual hair and dark smudges beneath his eyes. Tek meets my gaze as he raises my hand to his lips, kissing it tenderly.

"You are perfection," he whispers. Then he drops my hand and gestures at the stage.

It matters he's here. In the last few hours, I tried to tell myself it didn't, but I was lying. Even as I give him a smile of thanks, I know sadness shadows my eyes. Is this our prelude to goodbye?

I carry that hint of melancholy to the stage and take Ms. Citrine's hand. She guides me onto the turntable and kisses my cheek. A second royal kiss for tonight's performance. As soon as she steps away, the turntable begins its glacial rotation.

I tell my story.

Love is lust. Love is wonder. Love is desire. Love is pain. Love is expectation. Love is fragile. Love is strength. Love defies definition. Love is deserved.

I make love to the audience. I give love and take it away with my body, mind, and soul as I sing. Each note wears a color to complement or oppose the next. I sing contradiction and despair and hope.

I tell my story.

I finish with my head down as the last note slides around the room, brushing every ear, every heart.

Exuberant applause lifts my gaze. My revolution brings me to face the Hotel Caliwood table. They all stand. Santino whistles. The turntable slows even more as I take my bow.

The entire room is standing.

Tears smear my vision. Ms. Citrine offers a hand to help me off the stage. She leans her lips near my ear. "You are perfection, my sunstone."

A gentle vibration runs through my body as her hand trails across one of my organza wings before she takes the stage for her closing remarks.

The faintest glow surrounding my hand draws my attention. Is this Ms. Citrine's doing or a trick of the light?

As I turn to exit, Tek is there, staring at me aghast.

"Curse my mother," he growls, snatching my hand to blow a

breath across my knuckles. I stifle a cry when shock rattles my body, and the weak light clinging to my skin evaporates like a raindrop in midday sun.

I'm shaken by how easily the fairy queen could release her magic on me.

"Come with me," he hisses and drags me toward Stalk's archway.

I pull my hand from his. My tolerance for anything fairy wears thin. I want to shout *where have you been all day* or *you're getting married*. All that comes out is, "I'm working."

Taking my place behind the bar, a hand lights against the small of my back. Demetrius gazes at me with awe. "I, I never realized how good you are," he says almost reverently.

I step away from his near-embrace. "You never bothered to listen."

He has the decency to look ashamed until Mia lays a hand on his shoulder. "Last call, Demie, and everybody wants something."

While the barbacks, Demetrius, and I create final drink orders in a whirlwind of alcohol, fruit, and flavor beads, Tek silently stands at the end of the bar as if on guard. Ms. Citrine ushers the *Saturday's Star* judges, tablets in hand, from the club and around the turn heading to her office. The servers flow in and out like the tide until every patron is served. The five of us on bar duty lean against the counter to catch our collective breath.

Mia lifts her foot with a squelching pop. "Ugh, the floor is disgusting."

Demie shushes her and nods at the guests.

Nervousness wedges in my throat. I fill a glass with water and guzzle. Cold drips meander down the exposed skin above my plunging neckline, and I shiver. Busying myself, I organize the supplies scattered across the bar, unable to look at Tek or Demie or anyone while we wait for Ms. Citrine to return with the judges. I can't think of her as Queen Citrine right now. She's the talent coordinator for Stalk who holds my future in her hands.

I toss the last rogue olive into the trash when the group struts back through Stalk's archway. Too fast. They were too fast, a jury deliberating for such a short amount of time guarantees they've found the defendant guilty.

I'm deluded to think I had a chance. The contest was probably decided from the videos before anyone sang a note live, and the winner certainly isn't me, the last-minute wildcard. My money is on Desiderata. She had the look and the goods to fit right in at the opening night gala of rockstars.

As I stare at the *Saturday's Star* folks making their way back to their table complete with refreshed cocktails, movement flashes at the corner of my eye. My gaze locks onto the empty table next to the bar in time to see a pair of sparks erupt then fizzle from behind the reserved sign.

I grab the counter to keep from falling. Are they there? The magic mortals. Good heavens, if they are, Tek's spell to keep the group hidden is extremely potent. I steal a look at him to find him staring at the table as well. I suddenly understand his vigil at the end of the bar.

He is protecting me.

Tek said if I wasn't alone, I wouldn't be in danger from his mother and my invisible enemies, the Dark Vinyl Artists. When I was angry at him earlier, I discounted his warning, but...

My stomach flutters. Did he want to take me out of here because I'm not safe even in a room full of people? Was the glow that disappeared when Tek grabbed my hand a sign that bad things are about to go down?

Get a grip, Aurora.

I might as well imagine vandals popping from beneath the tables to steal me into the shadowed alleys of Hollywood. Nothing will happen to me here. If I was truly ripe for the snatching, Tek's supposed villains would have grabbed me earlier when I was alone, getting ready for my performance.

Ms. Citrine calls for the crowd's attention. In her silky voice, a torch song itself, she reminds the audience of the *Saturday's Star* competition and the prize of being part of Stalk's gala opening night lineup.

"So, let us all raise our glass with a cocktail she most likely designed for you, to the newest *Saturday's Star*, Aurora Herman."

My first impression is that I misheard her. The second impression is the fingers twining through mine as Tek escorts me to the stage. A terse look passes between him and Ms. Citrine. More than terse. Tek's eyes flash her an unmistakable warning.

In moments, the *Saturday's Star* judges engulf me. I'm covered with kisses of every variety—air, cheek, and one on the lips with the kick of blood orange and chilis from a *Rampion Records Tower* cocktail. Applause, cheers, and the clinking of glass swirl around the club.

I find Tek through the curtain of people. Nothing resembling a smile sits on his face. His stare pierces me like a shard of ice.

Most guests are on their feet for a final mingle before leaving. My hand is claimed once again. This time, Santino helps me off the turntable and into his arms.

"Rora, you are truly amazing." He releases me. His smile could blind the room. It's the expression I want on Tek's face. "Rand and Robbie will go wild. Well deserved, my friend. Well deserved."

The slight, dark-haired beauty next to him beams almost as bright. "You are really something."

Santino pulls her close. "Aurora, meet my fiancée, Hero Andante."

I take one of Hero's hands in mine. "I'm glad to finally meet you." I hip-check Santino. "This guy is one of the good ones."

The look they share both warms and breaks my heart at the same time. It's love, and to think I almost had it.

A hand braces the small of my back. I expect it to be Tek, but Benedict Boyd towers above me. Next to him is his partner, Beatrice. "We need to up our game if you're the warmup act. Excellent performance."

Beatrice nudges him. "Thank you, Aurora. Your singing chops will get this one's ass back to rehearsals."

Over their shoulders, I swear there's another red-orange burst like a cinder rising from a bonfire at the eerily empty table beside the bar.

Behind the Caliwood, Inc. contingent, I notice Ms. Citrine attempting to make her way to my side. Before she gets there, my fingers are crushed in a vise as Tek deftly extracts me from the throng.

I try to reclaim my hand. "What are you doing?"

He does not relinquish his death grip. "We need to talk. Now."

I swivel back to Santino. "Will you be at the gala? I could use a friendly face."

"Wouldn't miss it," he says as I'm unceremoniously whisked away by Tek.

He's so determined that I decide not to fight him. I'll let him have his say then try to reclaim networking time with the *Saturday's Star* peeps.

To my utter shock, the moment we clear the arch and cross into the office hallway, Tek lifts me into his arms and snaps into lumen form. We're through a fairy door and onto his private skyscraping leaf before I can protest.

As soon as he sets me on my feet, I shove him backwards with both hands. "What the hell, Tek?"

"Sorry, sorry, sorry. No choice. No choice." He paces around me in a circle as if he's not sure in which direction I'll try to flee.

I'm no match for a frantic fairy. I cross my arms and wait for him to simmer down.

Tek tears at his hair as he bounces from foot to foot. "Their prize is rife with danger near. On opening night, you can't appear."

My patience snaps. "Don't you dare ruin this night for me. Stop with the fucking rhymes and explain yourself."

He practically claws at his face, puffing as if he's run a thousand miles without a break. "Aurora," he says and takes both my hands in his. "You cannot perform at the gala. It's a night of terrible danger. Arborborn, Brineborn, magic mortals—all go to war. No guarantee of the victor."

The hysterical doomsday shit he's spouting can't be true. How can Tek tell me to shuck my dream? "Stop. Right now. You know singing at the gala means everything." He reaches for me, but I slap his hand away. "You believed in me, in my dreams. How dare you rip them away?"

"It's what must be."

Tek's about-face is a coverlet of thorns.

"For what? For your benefit?" Am I so trusting that I've misread Tek's motives? Is allowing me to finally step into the spotlight not part of his plans for me?

I begin to fortify my emotional wall. It's happening again. If I don't stop Tek from preventing me from reaching for my dream, I'm repeating my pattern of letting men I have feelings for lead me into a situation that diminishes me. The solution is clear. To walk away from one dream in order to claim my chance at another.

I believed I was falling in love with Tek. The cold truth is that I got caught up in the novelty of his uniqueness and lowered my guard. Maybe deep down, attaching to Tek was my rationalization for leaving Demie.

A pang deep in my gut disagrees. It was an enchanting notion to picture a future with Tek, but not realistic. I should have accepted our impossibility the moment I learned the truth about him. We don't work. We never could. My feelings for him grew strong enough for his betrayal to crack my heart, but hopefully not strong enough to shatter it.

Asking me to walk away from this opportunity is a gigantic red flag I can't ignore. I am finished forfeiting my dreams.

"Tek, our time together has been special to me. More than special, it's been a gift. Thank you from my heart for your generosity in bringing my performance to the level that led to tonight's win. I can't tell you how much I appreciate your help in giving me the courage to break it off with Demetrius, and…" I gather my nerve and continue. "What we shared together in your bower—I'll hold it dear for the rest of my life, but it's best if you leave me alone from now on. Please take me back to the club."

"You're asking to break our bond, untie our knot?"

The look of genuine surprise on his face makes me waver until I remember he's engaged. I'm not the bond-breaker here. Even if there were nothing else in the *walk away* column, his future bride would be enough.

"Rora, how can you ask this of me?"

I suppose fairies aren't used to not getting their way. "How can you ask me not to perform?"

He holds his hands to me in supplication. "An untied knot between us renders me toothless to defend you. Open your eyes. You are the prize."

I've seen Tek in a nervous tizzy, but his current mood surpasses even that. He's unglued, darkly manic.

"I don't need a bodyguard. I'll take your warnings seriously. No more mystery doors or staying alone in the club." I don't know how much longer I can go on without dissolving into tears. I need Tek to see my strength, but I'm shaky. "Now take me back."

Tek's head slowly lolls to the side, his gaze digging into me. "Your hesitation screams of words unspoken."

My mouth goes dry. This is Tek. The fairy man who doesn't let anything slide. He's got a right to be baffled over my adamant retreat after the intimacy both physical and emotional that's been building between us. He may be withholding the truth, but I've got no reason to do the same.

"Aside from the fact you want to ruin my chance to sing for people who have the power to give me a shot at a career in music—which is reason enough in itself to walk away…" I swallow hard. "I heard you earlier in Mr. Cinnabar's office." Even in the dark, I see his face pale, but I forge on. "You agreed to get married. I don't know how it works in your world, but in mine, being someone else's husband is a definitive relationship killer."

His lumen light outlines Tek in a red sizzle. "Please do not take what you've heard as foulest fortune's final word."

He reaches for me, but I do not take his hand.

"Rora, I do not cease my search to seek other ways of overcoming the shadows closing in. Using pretense to agree to that repulsive marriage is merely a delay tactic until another solution presents itself."

"The statement I heard you make sounded more definite than just a delay tactic."

Turmoil is written all over Tek's face. He grabs the sides of his head as if he's in pain. "These are dark times for the Arborborn, Aurora. I am pledged to my coteries, to the Emerald Spire and..."

As angry as I am at him for disrupting my thrill of earning a place in the gala, I am genuinely moved by his conflict, his desperation. "Tek—" I try to say anything to comfort him and pause when he aims his damn otherworldly focus directly at me.

"...pledged to you, my sunstone, my dawn, my love."

I reel from the fervor of his declaration and find myself in his arms. Such sweet words, but what do they really mean? My voice is ragged. "You once warned me not to fall for you, Tek. I should have listened. I hear you now. The Emerald Spire, your people, they will always come first, and they should." I touch my forehead to his. "It's okay to let me go."

We're both still as if knowing once we move, this enchanted bubble we've been floating in together the last handful of weeks will pop.

Bubbles are never meant to last.

20

TRUE VISAGE

TEK

MY WORLD THREATENS TO COLLAPSE. INSTEAD OF PROTECTING Aurora, I damaged her faith in me. I've jeopardized the knot we agreed to, the mightiest arrow in my quiver to keep her safe.

Blind Tek.

As usual, I hurled myself forward without fully anticipating the effects of my actions. I knew how brightly Rora's desire to win a place in Stalk's gala glowed in her soul. In my panic, I did not temper my words and devalued her dream to protect her. It is clear she does not accept the gravity of her situation. There is a solution to shift her perception of danger from abstract to concrete, but I fear her mortal mind may not be able to withstand the enormity of truths surrounding her.

I cling tight to my sunstone when she tries to free herself from my embrace. "Aurora, before entertaining your desperate notion to dissolve the knot between us, I beg for a chance to prove what I say is true. My dire warnings of the forces gathering are not a ploy to hold you to obligation or to serve any agenda of mine." I stroke her glorious, thick, honey hair. "You must believe I am not the destroyer of your dreams. I am the man who cherishes your light and will not—cannot see it diminished by those who wish to seize your freedom for their own gain."

She lowers the top of her head to my chest. "It's too much for me, Tek. Your battles, your parents, and scary magic I can neither see nor understand."

I gently cradle her chin in my fingers, lifting her face. "Then I will show you all."

Aurora's expression wilts into melancholy. "Nothing you show me will matter. You are getting married. There's no point in continuing our knot."

The leaf beneath us rumbles in solidarity with my frustration to close this chasm growing between my sunstone and me. Rora's wide eyes dart to the green beneath our feet, and an idea flashes through my head.

"If you allow it, I will share one breath of my magic with you to grant you deeper glimpses of all things hidden to the unaided mortal eye." I suspect it won't take much of my influence for her to break through the shield fairies surround themselves with given the ease in which Aurora sees our world.

Her expression is skeptical. "You promised not to use magic to control me."

"And I hold to it, but for you to uncover what truly surrounds you, not just what we fairies choose you to see, I must use my power to gift you the means."

Conflict shines in her eyes. In their beautiful emerald depths, I see a lingering bead of trust. Aurora gives a single nod. I guide her lips to mine and release a prolonged puff of magic-laden breath. She struggles for a moment but then opens herself to allow my offering. Easy warmth radiates from her body as her skin gives off a faint sunstone-colored light.

When I pull away, her gaze softens. "I feel floaty."

Keeping a hold of her arm, I say, "Look down."

She follows my directions and draws a quick breath as she sees the leaf holding us for what it truly is, a living part of the world.

Rora crouches and pets the waxy surface. Beneath her touch, the leaf gives a contented shiver. "Wait. It's not metal." Her gaze darts to the tapering center of the Spire. She scurries over and presses palms to the stalk. "None of it is." She stares at me. "Tek, this is a real, living beanstalk."

"Created by me and the *Verdant Promise* spell stone. Within its secret natural state, the temporary realm of my folk thrives. The metallic behemoth humans see is due to the magic deception woven through every bough and curving tendril."

Aurora is stunned. "The entire Emerald Spire is from half of that tiny pebble?"

"And a great deal of fairy magic," I say, allowing myself a moment to revel in her wonder. "As more good faith, I have a confession. I spent the power of another stone this day, the *Claret Blood*."

She narrows her eyes. "Your love spell? Did you use it on the princess to get her to agree to marry you?"

My *no* is so loud, Rora recoils. "I used it on the king and queen to soften their hard hearts toward one another. I hoped in such a state they'd work in harmony, not opposition, to end our feud with the Brineborn. Beyond that, I wish to deter the royal pair from bartering my eternity as their *solution*." I take her face in my hands. "Aurora, I do not desire to marry the princess of the Brineborn. I do not love her and never will."

Her hands cover mine. "You used the love stone on your parents?"

The weight of my failure draws my eyes shut. "I spent the precious spell on two hearts refusing to reconcile. That is why you heard me agree to join our coteries through a marriage. It was a false promise cloaked in the guise of a last resort."

"What do you mean a guise?"

"My promise to wed another is an empty gesture as long as I am knotted to you. As of yet, the Brineborn do not know of the obstacle."

Rora takes a step back. "Are you saying I might be responsible for screwing up a deal to save your people? Damn it, Tek. That's worse than you trying to keep me from singing at the gala." She drops her head into her hands.

I close the distance between us and grasp her shoulders. "If I could end the danger to you by untying our knot, I'd do it before your next breath. Reluctantly, but I would. Unfortunately, things have become too complicated for such a simple remedy. Please, Aurora, will you receive more of my magic and its gift to look deeper? If once you know everything and still wish to separate your light from mine, then I will bargain with the king and queen to ensure your freedom."

"Is that possible?"

I grip her arms. "I will make it so." Releasing my hold on her, I pull the spell stones from my pocket and hold them on my palm. Starlight glints off their polished surfaces. "The king and queen covet the use of these." I close my fist around them and drop to one knee. "I will gladly forfeit every stone to protect you."

Rora's eyes glisten with tears. "You would give up all your leverage, for me?"

I tuck the stones away and stand to catch her falling tear with my thumb. "I've spent my life feeling inconsequential, a burden, and a disappointment. Let me be more for you."

Her gaze is pure kindness. "I certainly know what that's like."

This gentle soul before me understands what it is to be treated as less than her worth. She glances at the sky and then to the faint pearly trace of the Harp Star's gift upon her fingertip as she considers my proposal. It takes iron will to keep my energy at a level humans are able to tolerate and give her the peace to decide. I want to plead with her and swear promises I may not be able to keep.

I wait.

She ponders.

I concentrate on prolonging my silence.

Finally, her gaze returns to mine. "All right, Tek. I won't untie our knot yet. Give me more of your magic to see everything you claim is coming for me." Her lips part, inviting my breath.

"To give you enough to last the night, the ah, delivery will take a bit longer than before."

Aurora doesn't look away. "Do you need to kiss me, Tek?"

If only she understood my need to kiss her surpasses my heart's need to beat, my breath's need to fill my lungs. My entire being longs for the closeness we shared in my bower and that the promise of our togetherness might not be fleeting. I nod.

She loops her arms behind my neck, never breaking eye contact. "Then make it a good one since it might be our last."

I cover her mouth in a kiss with the sweetness of a candied breeze, pouring the light of my lumen, memories of mountaintop star drizzle, and the beauties of my realm into her spirit. Aurora takes the kiss deeper, molding her body to mine. The thrum of magic begins as a soft mew in her sunstone heart and then from there, spreads radiance through her body.

Her sunstone heart.

I picture the golden brilliance that bathed Stalk when Aurora sang at the club for the first time. Hers is not the gleam of a fairy heart. Such a truth I would have recognized. The source of this woman's personal shine remains a mystery.

Rora cups the back of my head to pull my mouth harder against hers, thrusting a greedy tongue to lap up every drop of my gift.

I wish there were a way for me to know how much of her passion is the same longing I feel for her, and what part is the human exhilaration of being filled with fairy essence.

How will I ever untie this sacred knot with Aurora and not lose myself?

I loathe to break the kiss, but when the soft melody of my magic begins to sing through her blood, I know it's time. Giving too much will put her under my control. As tempting as it is to cross that line to keep her safe, I swore I would never take such advantage.

Humbled Tek.

In the past, I would choose the trick and revel in the entertainment. Not with my Aurora. I am indeed more at her mercy than she is at mine.

Rora rests her head on my shoulder and gently sways, dropping her arms to circle my body. I'd love nothing more than to dance with her until the stars grow weary and morning light yawns awake over Hollywood. Contrary to my wishes, I hold her at arm's length. "How do you feel?"

There is new luminescence behind her garden-green eyes giving Aurora the shine of fairyglow.

She taps a finger to her lips and tilts her head. "Dizzy but not. Light, airy." Rora giggles. "I'm filled with warm feathers." There's an arch to her brow. "Is this what it's like for you, Tek?"

Sludge from the weight of feuding coteries, adversarial parents, and greedy magic mortals thwarts my own airiness. I muster a smile for Rora and brush a strand of hair from her eyes. "I'm glad my magic brings you pleasure."

Rora's gaze snags on my face. She studies me, drawing a finger across my cheekbones and along my jaw. Thankfully, at present, I only bear the subtly sharpened features of a common fairy, not a royal. When her expression shifts into one of solemnity, I prepare for the next move in her campaign to untie our knot.

"I am too, Tek." Her lips meet mine in a light tap, then she hugs herself. "Let's get this over with."

I chew on my lip. "Before we return to the club, you need to know that King Cinnabar and Queen Citrine's true selves are—"

"Stop, Tek. Let me see for myself."

For a moment, I glimpse the Aurora who refused to let forces in her life diminish her drive to succeed. She is strong and brave and...

Guilt claws my insides. I became one of those negative forces when I told her she couldn't sing at the gala.

Reprehensible Tek.

"I'll be there with you, Rora." It's killing me not to prepare her in more detail. The fairy queen's beauty is not of the variety she's used to in mortal terms. Not that of a flower, but rather the elegance of a mighty warrior's blade ever-poised to cut out a heart. "Are you ready?"

She moves close enough for me to lift her into my arms. In minutes, we've lumen travelled back through my petiole door, down the stairs, and to the threshold of Stalk. Aurora straightens her dress and hair then takes my hand as we prepare to reenter the club as a couple.

Cinnabar is schmoozing the last of the crowd under the arch, encouraging them toward the grand staircase and their glass elevator ride to the street.

Rora peeks at him and then takes a longer look. She whispers in my ear. "Are those black tornadoes swirling across his skin fairy tattoos?" Her hand covers her mouth as she gasps and stutters. "W-wings...enormous."

King Cinnabar is on full view in a royal pewter tunic that falls to his knees, form fitted to his intimidating warrior's frame. A crown of braided obsidian adorns his head, catching the deep blue and magenta spotlights of the club. Quicksilver flows in rivulets through every curve and angle of his royal wings bordered with overlapping panes of onyx diamonds. Their tips tower above Cinnabar's head while their lower extremities end in daggerlike points behind his knees. The lines down my back where my own wings should be pucker painfully at the sight of my father's magnificence.

The king whips around to stare at us. My oversight turns my muscles to stone. I forgot to warn her a whisper is a shout to a fairy. Cinnabar heard her plainly and immediately knows I've given her a taste of my magic. The burnt cinnamon tone of his eyes flares to vibrant red as he shoots a fiery look at me. I shrug and hold a finger to my lips while I give my head a shake.

He's on us in an instant. With a sweep of his hand, Aurora's face goes blank as he suspends her awareness. "Tek Goodfellow, this is an outrage. You go too far."

"It is a necessary outrage, Your Highness. I will not have my knotted darling blind to the dangers surrounding her." I lay a hand on Rora's cheek. "I beg you not to reveal to the queen I have shared the gift of fairy sight with Aurora. It is unfair for my dear knotted love not to understand who we truly are."

Cinnabar inhales with enough might to raise a gust that ruffles Rora's hair. "There will come a day, my careless young prince, when even I may not protect you from the queen's wrath." He lays a hand on top of Rora's head. "You desire to keep the mortal from peril but be prepared for your gamble to end poorly."

I meet my father's stare. "Will you keep our secret for this night alone?"

The fire in his eyes fades. "I will have no part in your deception." He glances at the magic mortals' table. His night-dark spirals spin furiously, appearing as ink pooling across his skin. "The cabal remains. Your queen approaches. Take heed."

He turns and strides out of the club. As soon as he's gone, Aurora's knees nearly buckle. I fling an arm around her waist so she does not fall. Quickly, I lead her to sit at a table. Resting my hands on her shoulders, I touch my lips to her ear. Unlike Aurora, no fairy can hear what I wish to keep masked.

"Rora, do not speak of anything you see. Learn what you must, but do not question aloud. Fairies and other magic folk are privy to the quietest whisper. I will answer all once we depart."

She nods. When she trembles beneath my touch, I dot her cheek with a reassuring kiss. Sweat drips into my eyes.

Negligent Tek.

I am a fool for not thoroughly preparing her. Such injudicious behavior could lead to my undoing and Aurora's.

"There's our sunstone," coos Citrine as she slinks over to the table.

Rora's heart beats violently enough to shake window glass. I should have spared her this level of shock and found another way to illuminate the depth of her predicament. What is common to me must be terrible beauty to my sunstone. A thousand limoncello strands of glass twist into swirls from the top of the queen's head before flowing down her back. The ten-pointed crown she wears is made of the same Citrine crystal that surrounds her royal heart. Its light bright enough to blind any human not protected within a fairy's gift. My mother's features while severe are yet lovely in her human form. Now Rora will see the queen's face as knife sharp and menacing. While my father's wings are mighty, my mother's are deadly. Serrated diamond edges promise to shred any unwanted touch while their substance appears as a breathtaking silken tapestry of gold, crème, and yellow hues. The apparent delicacy belies the raw power embedded in those wings.

"You charmed the room tonight, dear heart," says the queen, her fingertips gliding over Aurora's hair. "We celebrate your victory."

The queen shoots me a glare that barely disguises her dislike. I hear the strain in her voice. "You must be proud of your darling, Tek."

Rora blinks too rapidly. I ready myself to whisk her away if the queen's true presence is more than she can bear.

"I was the most enchanted dude in the club," I say. "Even though I already knew my babe would be the best." I strain to use my human phrasing even though I'm in the presence of my queen.

The monarch gives me a tight-lipped smile, then refocuses her charms on Aurora.

My sunstone swallows hard and forces herself to speak. "Thank you, Ms. Citrine. I truly appreciate you allowing me the chance to sing and any kind words you put in with the *Saturday's Star* people."

The queen purses her lips. "You should have been top of the

finalist's list. It's poetic justice no one from their ill-chosen original batch captured the prize."

A rattling of glasses behind the bar catches Rora's attention. "I should help get things in order." She stands, freezing as she catches sight of the perpetually unoccupied reserved table that is no longer empty.

Nature's scorn. She stares bug-eyed at the magic mortals tucked beneath their *Pearl Tear* shield. Luckily, Grant Gothel taps a finger against his wineglass deep in conversation with the three women sharing the table with him. No doubt Aurora follows music-related happenings closely enough to recognize the disgraced president of Rampion Records and knows Rubata Lear from her insipid reality show, "Kickin' it With Midas."

To disguise her shock, I twirl Aurora to allow her a reprieve from the queen's true form and the Dark Vinyl Artists. When I plant a possessive kiss on my sunstone's lips, she barely registers the affection. I cradle her face. "I don't think I've told you enough how fantastic you were tonight, Rora." I kiss her again, fearing she's on the verge of coming apart.

Citrine doesn't appear concerned about Aurora's near shock. She steals my sunstone, threading an arm around Rora's waist to guide her toward Stalk's arch. "The bar bunch can do without you, dear Aurora. There's someone I'd like you to meet."

Panic sizzles through me. What is the queen up to? Can my dearest maintain her charade? Rora throws me a worried glance over her shoulder.

I rush to her side and replace the queen's arm with mine. Since we're knotted, my princely touch will negate any devious charm Citrine attempts to use on Aurora. "Mind if I join you?"

Oh, the queen minds. The citrus light in her eyes sparks. I notice Rora's throat bob in fear, leaving no doubt, she saw the danger in Citrine's eyes.

"Will this take long?" I ask. "We have celebrating to do."

A familiar look of haughty disgust sharpens the queen's

features, but she flicks her wrist at me. "What of your work for Cinnabar?"

I add a spring to my step. "Finished." I kiss Rora's cheek. "I'm yours for the night, my sweet one." As long as our knot remains declared, my presence at Aurora's side must be tolerated even by a royal.

Citrine dons a placid mask to cover her rage as she beckons us to follow. She forces a casual tone. "Humor me with the quick introduction I've planned. Afterwards, you two will be free to toast our Aurora's success."

Our Aurora.

No, no, not so, dear mother. *My* Aurora.

"Yes, of course, Ms. Citrine," says Aurora in a dazed tone.

I twine my fingers with Rora's and give a reassuring squeeze. Her fragile state begins to worry me. It was essential to solidify my darling's caution by showing her the danger she was facing, but did I go too far?

When Rora finds a more confident stride, my fears dampen a little. We pause short of Citrine's office before a round-topped door. My chest tightens again. Behind the façade of dark wood, I sense the swirling glow of a fairy door. I sneak a glance at Aurora. Her eyes widen noticing the unnatural light. I nudge gently, reminding her to suppress her reactions.

There is no air of malevolence surrounding this door as there was at the entrance to the sea witch's quarters. I don't hesitate when the queen gestures us inside. We enter a circular foyer. Within five arches set into the walls are identical white marble staircases of a design similar to the one leading to Stalk's grand entrance. A blown glass vase nearly as tall as me filled with sprays of white star lilies is set beside each bottom step. The vases differ in color—purple, ice blue, cherry red, jet black, and the last, a sunflower yellow.

I've not ventured into this chamber. Traces of magic mark the nature of the place. These steps lead to the dwellings of the magic mortals. Indigo for the sea witch, the blue of glacial ice for the enchantress, cerise for the shapeshifting Lear witch, and onyx for the darkest soul of all—Gothel. As proven by the sea witch's attempt to lure Aurora, the Dark Vinyl Artists believe they have private fairy doors to their separate spaces. Of course, the king and queen would create secret back entrances such as these in case necessity arose to catch the magic mortals unaware.

The yellow vase is a puzzle until Citrine's lemony lumen glow is near it. Ah, the marker to the fifth staircase is not yellow at all, but gold. This is the route to the Golden Harp.

"Come," says Citrine as she leads us up the brightly lit steps next to the vibrant gilded vase.

Rora is careful to stay out of range of the queen's wings. A pang of despair catches me full in the chest. I had no choice but to show Aurora the real danger before her, but as usual I did not consider all the repercussions. Is she repulsed by the authentic visages of the royals? Besides my unremarkable fairy body, Rora's limited sight only allowed her to see Chalcedony, Peridot, Tourmaline, and Galena's fluidity as nothing more threatening than preening butterflies. Did she expect replicas in the royals and not variations that might very well appear as twisted mockeries of what she perceives as beauty?

Fairy kind can be as magisterial as they are terrifying. It is who we are, folk who bear the sharp edge of a crystal or the protective thorn of a flower alongside the beauty of its petals and leaves. Especially monarchs who for the very survival of their coterie must present as forces not to be challenged.

If the day ever comes when my mother accepts me, my looks will shift and sharpen into the countenance of a true Arborborn prince. Thoughts of Aurora repulsed by my potentially over-chiseled features are daunting.

My sunstone grasps my arm with her free hand as the faint sound of singing floats from above. In her apprehension, she presses closer. Rora's heard this voice before on the steps of the sea witch's lair.

The Golden Harp.

Does the queen plan to use Aurora's breath as a key to trespass into a place warded against her regal presence? I burn to scoop Rora into my arms and lumen travel out of here. What price will my sunstone pay if the queen bids her to open that door?

We continue to climb until we approach a familiar keyhole bathed in a stream of golden light. To my relief, the queen asks nothing of Aurora and merely knocks on the door.

If the Harp does not answer, will the queen then demand the breath of my beloved?

The singing stops. There is no sound for a moment then muffled footsteps no louder than fallen leaves blown across a forest floor approach.

"Who's there?" calls a voice as fresh as spring rain and as sweet as peaseblossom pudding. "Papa? Aunties?"

The queen presses her palm flat against the door, and wood shifts to amber glass.

"Oh," says the young woman with nothing more than vague surprise when she sees us through the transparent pane.

Magic is no stranger to her.

Citrine smiles at the woman as a small burst of mist, glittering like yellow diamond chips seeps through the barrier between them, to surround the doe-eyed singer. The queen's enchantment takes hold quickly, and the Harp opens the door.

"Hello, Ms. Citrine. Papa told me to expect you. Have you brought my new tutor?" The Golden Harp gleefully claps her hands and jumps up and down.

The Harp is strange. She looks barely younger than Aurora but behaves with a lack of poise similar to fairy children playing at hurling with their buttercup ball.

The Harp giggles, adding to her juvenile countenance. "Papa says it's time to take my singing to a higher level."

There can be only one Papa she's referring to—Gothel. How can such an atrocious sorcerer sire such apparent sweetness?

The Harp skips backwards. "Come in." She giggles again. "Oops, I forgot my manners. Hi, I'm Maisie Gothel."

Her truth confirmed does not make it less repulsive. Aurora lets go of my hand. To my surprise, she steps into the room first, positioning herself between Citrine and the Harp.

"Hello, Maisie. I'm Aurora, and this is Tek. You have a beautiful voice."

The woman/child throws herself at Rora, wrapping arms around her waist. "You're so nice and pretty." She dances backwards. "Please be my tutor." Maisie smiles. "I can already tell you'll be much nicer than Auntie Rubata or that cranky old man who makes me sing scales for hours."

I stare at the Golden Harp. There is something familiar about her voice and the way she carries herself. My mind flips through possibilities like shuffling a deck of cards, and then I land on the Ace.

Zeli.

Maisie reminds me of the singer, Zeli. I've seen the pop diva's videos many times on the flatscreen in Stalk. I know she's one of Aurora's favorites.

My wing scars twitch. Zeli/Gothel. I stare at the Harp and remember words straight from Gothel's lips about the Golden Harp.

She will be the first of the rekindled Opus crop to elevate Dark Vinyl Artists.

A crop. This odd human is a flower Gothel cultivates in his dark garden to replace the singer who betrayed him. Maisie is locked away for his gain, not her safety.

Rora smiles back. "I've never tutored anyone before, but Tek has. He has a beautiful voice too." She gestures for me to come closer. "We can both teach you." She nods to the stairs. "How would you like to come to Stalk and sing on the circle stage?"

Citrine stiffens.

It's clear what Aurora is doing. Even though I'm sure she's

completely unnerved by the queen, she's assessing Maisie's situation. My sunstone senses something is not right. Of course, Rora sets aside her fear out of concern for this young woman.

Maisie anxiously looks at the door. "I don't go anywhere without Papa or one of the Aunties. It's not safe. There are beasts and monsters outside."

Oh, such innocence. The beasts and monsters dwell inside these walls, not outside.

Fear rolls off the Golden Harp in skittering little waves. What rancid lies did the sorcerer and his witches feed the Harp? It's obvious she sees this collection of evil as family. Oh, so puzzling.

Citrine takes a step toward the pair of singers. "Aurora is excited to help you."

What in nature's promise is the queen up to? I reclaim Rora's hand before Citrine decides to unleash unwelcome magic. Devious is my queen. She covets the Harp to become the treasured daughter she's been denied.

Desire to protect the Harp seizes me. I sense the same in Aurora. There is an unnatural and exceedingly vulnerable air about the young woman. Is she stunted in ways of the mind apart from obvious talent and physical body because her life has been coddled and controlled?

Confusion shadows the Harp's eyes. "Will Aurora and Tek both work with me? Papa didn't tell me there would be two new music masters."

Citrine lays a hand on the girl's shoulder. "Do not fret." Again, the queen sends her magic to encircle Maisie. "Rest now. We will visit again soon."

The Harp yawns. "Excuse me. I am sleepy and must rest my voice."

Aurora's gaze follows Citrine's circling magic. I nudge her shoulder as a reminder not to reveal her ability to see the queen's enchantment.

"We're sorry to surprise you so late with a visit, Maisie." Rora produces an answering yawn. "I'm very sleepy too. I hope to see you again soon."

The Golden Harp treats us to the lazy smile of a kitten content with a patch of sunlight then staggers toward an archway with a bedroom beyond.

Rora heads for the door and whispers to me, knowing full well the queen can hear her. "Tek, I feel badly we surprised Maisie." She's first to the landing and waits for the queen to join us. "Ms. Citrine, these rooms are incredible. I'd never guess they were here."

Citrine spells the Harp's closed door back into wood. "These are private residences for very exclusive tenants." We walk down the stairs in silence until we reach the bottom, and the queen turns to Rora. "What did you think of Maisie? Can you work with her?"

I keep the fingers of one hand twined through Aurora's and lay my other on top for more contact. My mother's magic pushes against mine, searching for a way into Rora.

My darling lays her free hand on my arm, strengthening the contact even more. "She's very sweet and…" Aurora searches for the right word. "…innocent. I've never coached another singer before. I don't know if I'd be any good."

"Oh," says Citrine, stroking Rora's cheek. "You'll be marvelous, and who doesn't appreciate extra income."

I block yet another of the queen's sneaky volleys of magic at Aurora as we leave the magic mortals' domains behind. "And now, Ms. Aurora," I say in a seductive tone, flaunting my connection to my sunstone for Citrine's benefit. "We're overdue for our celebration."

She turns to the queen. "Thank you for your kindness and support, Ms. Citrine. I will definitely consider tutoring Maisie."

I see the effort it takes Citrine not to bare her teeth at me. "Congratulations again, Aurora." She leaves us in the hallway. As the queen powers her way to Stalk, her wings flick side to side with a crack in sharp, angry movements.

The moment the queen is out of view, Rora falls against me,

shaking. When she starts to speak, I lay a finger to her lips and then point to where Citrine vanished, reminding her not to speak.

When I give her the all-clear, a mix of exhaustion and fear colors her voice. “Please take me away from here, Tek.”

I brush the top of her ear with my lips. “Soon. I’m sorry, my love, but we’re not finished.”

21

REMEDY

AURORA

I WANT TO COLLAPSE ONTO THE PLUSH CARPET OF THE HALLWAY AND sob. Ms. Citrine...Queen Citrine and her battle-ready wings with edges like a thousand knives are worse than anything I could possibly have imagined. Even her hair isn't hair, but braids of crystal or glass. The electric lemon glow of her eyes nearly made me pass out.

And then there's the fairy king.

Cinnabar towered freakishly taller than any person I've ever seen. What the hell are those writhing black patterns across his dark skin that conjure visions of hellish monsters, not ethereal fairies? I swear his wings are a Gothic death painting covered in metallic black lace.

I squash Tek's shirt in my hands, afraid not to be touching him. He insists our knot protects me from those creatures. Not creatures —his parents. If those are the beings he came from, what did he inherit?

Tek reaches for me and I jump away. "You are safe, Rora. I swear it," he pleads.

I stop him with a look, then study the fairy before me from tangled corkscrew hair to shoes. He looks like my Tek. How can I be certain I'm seeing his reality? Does the magic he breathed into me only allow me to see what he chooses? His wings may be gone but is he hiding pointy teeth or freakishly jutting cheekbones?

I'm aching to ask, but I might as well be gagged. If I speak, the fairy king and queen will hear me. The best I can do is to fan an arm down his body and point to my eyes.

Tek grabs my hand and places it over his heart before yanking me against him to whisper in my ear. "You see a true Tek Goodfellow, your selfsame lover from the bower. Please, Aurora, do not fear me." He splays my palm over his heart. "If I thought you were afraid of me, it would shatter my woebegone heart." Lips press against my ear in a soft kiss before he gives me space.

I point to my lips and mouth *we need to talk*. Any notion I had about the ability to thwart advances from Citrine is long gone. She pursues me like a bee searching for exposed skin to sink her stinger. The fairy queen clearly has plans for me, whether it's to add me to her ladies or trap me with Maisie, the Golden Harp. Either way, I lose my freedom as Tek warned. My head pounds, unable to tease a single idea from my brain to save myself. I must rely on Tek.

Soon, he mouths and bobs his head toward Stalk. I shake my head no and dig my heels in. I'm not going back in there with those terrifying fairies.

Tek huffs and wiggles, becoming an out-of-focus picture. How did I ever think he was a regular guy? Finally, he points upwards to what I assume is his leafy penthouse and gestures his intention to carry me. I circle my arms around his neck. I'd rather go up there again than face the threats lying in wait for me in the club.

In a snap, he's carrying me within his lumen light. For a few heartbeats, my panic eases until I realize we are not on that welcoming leaf but hovering outside Stalk's windows.

"Aurora, we must return inside at once to learn what this visit to the harp portends." He nods at the table he's carefully shielded from human eyes. "I will ensure we are unseen. Do I retain your trust?"

Can I trust myself? My instinct is to run far and fast away from the reality Tek has shown me tonight. Except, the thought of running away from him leaves me hollow. Can I escape if the queen wants me? How far is fairy reach?

I've come this far with Tek. If I don't go the rest of the way, I could lose any control I have in my own story.

Tek snugs me closer. "You know of Gothel's evil, correct?"

I nod.

"The powerfully built woman next to him with the multitude of blues in her hair is Sulaa Kylock, she is a sea witch. At his other side is the enchantress, Tressa Divine. Do not underestimate her look of fragility or countenance of vapidity."

I squint at the blond dressed in white sequins and a tulle skirt that sparkles with its own light. Tek's right. She looks like a fancy doll.

"The enchantress wields the strongest magic of all."

When he gestures to the busty redhead in a curve-hugging minidress, I nod my head vigorously and mime singing. I know Rubata Lear, one of the trio of Irish witch sisters from the reality TV show "Kickin' It With Midas." She disappeared right after being convicted of conspiring to kill her aging rockstar father, Midas Lear. Dang, I used her line of cosmetics for years until her company went belly up after she vanished.

"Yes. Yes. You know her as Rubata, but she is also Brandy Winter, who sang before you at the soft opening last week. She can change her body to appear as different humans."

My gaze snaps back to Rubata. The Lear sisters mentioned serving Irish goddesses and crediting their musical gifts to those beliefs, but they never talked about magical chops like shape-shifting. I nearly laugh. Why would they? Can the other two sisters, Chorda and Glissanda, turn into whoever they want to? Dammit, will the cloud of weird enveloping me slow the fuck down so I can catch my breath?

He raises a finger. "My magic more you must allow if fiends be blind to where we dwell. When secrets all do leave their lips, my spell away from you will slip."

Tek's rhyming proves he's as jittery as I am. He's asking to douse me in more magic. There's no other way to go forward if we're going to learn their plans for me. I nod.

With the snap of his fingers, it feels as if a light blanket nestles around me. In the next blink of Tek's lumen light, he flies us flush against the ceiling above the perpetually reserved table I always believed to be empty.

"I hope you'll find the Aurora solution satisfying," says Citrine.

"Oh, very much so," says Gothel, flashing her a smile.

The fairy queen blows Gothel a kiss and leaves the club without a glance in our direction. He looks to the enchantress who tilts her head, eyes glazed in concentration before she nods.

"Okey dokey," trills Tressa Divine. "She's gone."

Gothel leans in, his eyes shifting side to side. "Are there others?"

She presses fingertips to her temples for no more than a second. "Nope. We're fairy free."

When I shoot Tek a questioning look, he answers with an expression of arrogant satisfaction. I have to believe he's got our stealth under control.

"What do we think?" asks Sulaa, her voice assuming a growly quality. "Do the fairies suspect our intentions?"

Gothel steeples his fingers. "It appears not. Citrine would not be helping us acquire the Aurora woman to mentor the Harp if she knew we plot with their Brineborn enemies." He taps his chin with a pair of middle fingers. "I believe with a new permanent in-house mentor, the Harp will be ready to make her debut earlier than scheduled."

Tek's grip pinches, and I bite my tongue to keep from crying out.

He mouths *sorry* but does not loosen his hold.

Sulaa scoffs at Gothel. "Ready? You're too eager, Grant. The Harp may possess the singing voice of the Zeli clone you insist upon recreating, but every other word out of her mouth sounds like the child she is."

Gothel's expression is condescending with streaks of malice. "Which is why I will script her interviews and limit public appearances to silent, choreographed photo ops."

I swear actual flames blaze in his pupils as he continues. "We'll control the narrative in the studio once we've rid ourselves of the brats who've overtaken my Rampion Records Tower. The Dark Vinyl Artists will be the biggest game in Hollywood and beyond."

The Sea Witch stares at the enchantress. "Is there nothing else you can do, Tressa, to speed up the Harp's mental maturity?"

This reeks of creepy.

The enchantress leans one elbow on the table. "You insisted I age the kid physically. I warned you she'd be a child in a woman's body. There's no fix except time." She huffs. "And etiquette lessons. Her ten-year-old, smart-aleck mouth could use a gallon of polish."

Tek and I share a shudder. Woman's body? Ten-year-old? What have these horrible people done to the Harp?

Sulaa scrapes a nail over her gold trident necklace. "You should seriously consider one of the older teens in your Opus crop as our debut artist. Let Citrine's singer work with the Harp for a while before you parade her around as your prize."

When Gothel's fingertips glow red-orange, I clutch Tek's arm.

"The Golden Harp will be the symbol of my triumph," Gothel hisses. "None other."

Rubata fills her wineglass. "You're all too uptight. Our little miss spouts the brainless chatter of any spoiled diva." She takes a long sip, then trades her glass for a compact, adding more blush to her already bright raspberry cheeks. "Claude's waiting on me for after-hours clubbing." The Lear witch pushes out her over-plumped lips in a pout. "Since tonight's his last night before you kick him out of the Spire to work with your Opus brats at the Caliwood, I intend to treat him to some unforgettable fun."

I stifle my cry against Tek's shoulder when Rubata's body blurs and Brandy Winter takes her place.

The shapeshifter wrangles her breasts to fit her new form. "Anything else about the big night we need to know, Grant, or can we enjoy the gala's champagne and charcuterie until we x-out our enemies?" Rubata over dramatizes the last word with a deep spooky voice.

Gothel surveys the club again, sending an inquisitive glance at Tressa.

The enchantress stands, turning in a slow circle.

When she pauses to listen, the muscles of Tek's arm around my waist go rock hard. I hold my breath. Does she sense us?

A moment later, Tressa shimmies as if trying to rid herself of clingy spiderwebs and settles back in her chair. "Still clear."

Wow. This bunch doesn't fathom the extent of fairy magic.

Gothel, with a cautious look on his face, pitches his voice even lower.

"When the king and queen are occupied, the Brineborn will use the fairy doors Tressa identified to break in and conquer the Emerald Spire's fairy dimension. King Cinnabar and Queen Citrine will once again find their coterie banished to the shadows of Hollywood. Our new allies will assist us as we enact our revenge on those who attempted to destroy us, and we, my dear witches, will be back on top."

Rubata raises her glass. "Here's to champagne, charcuterie, and revenge."

The quartet clinks then drain their glasses. Brandy Winter is the first to scurry out. Followed by the enchantress who whines to be included in the after-hours clubbing. Gothel stands, offering his hand to the sea witch. When she takes it, he yanks her against his body. He grabs her ass while savagely devouring her mouth. A moment later, he lifts her onto the table, hiking up her skirt as he shucks his jacket. The creep splits her legs apart to plant himself between Sulaa's thighs and grinds against her.

I've seen enough and duck my head against Tek's shoulder. Sensing my distress, he wraps his arms around me. In moments, we're encased in the safe shell of his lumen light.

I'm dizzy as I emerge from what felt like a deep sleep. My thoughts are a fuzzy cotton ball. Tek rocks me on his lap slowly, gently, until I'm able to lift my head and look at him. We're parked on his leafy balcony. The lights of Hollywood rise into the night until they become paint smears dissipating into a charcoal sky.

My cheek rests against Tek's chest. "How do you stand it? Seeing so much. Knowing so much."

He huffs a laugh. "You are assuming I do stand it." He tilts my chin to look into my eyes. "I do not. My world, my life, stands on the brink of tatters." Tek stares at the sky. "I believed when I made the Emerald Spire, my folk would be safe until we returned home." He levels a gaze at me so full of sadness, tears well in my eyes. "Am I a dreamer or a fool, my beloved sunstone?"

"You are an optimist in a world set against positivity." I stroke his cheek. "I understand that kind of hopelessness."

The gratefulness in his expression speaks to my heart.

Tek draws a stuttering breath. "I have approached my existence too lightly, always looking for the easy jest or game. The cost of a frivolous life has finally caught up with me."

I stare into his exotic eyes with their golden sun flare. The volumes I don't know about Tek weigh on me. Survival instinct should set off my flight response, but instead, I'm driven to dig into those unknowns. I want to know more of Tek, not less.

He kisses my forehead. His lips are warm and gentle as he speaks.

"I do not know how to protect you, Aurora."

The words snap me back into the true gravity of our situation. I wish he could lumen light me away from his mother and the vile group of magical jerks, but he can't.

His eyes go wild as his mouth bobs open and shut. Tek's version of tongue-tied.

"Deep breaths." I pat his cheeks. "I don't understand why Citrine wants me so badly."

Tek drops his head back. "A heart betrayed she still claims to be, to possess you promises sweet remedy."

I grip his shoulders. "No vague rhymes. Just tell me."

Tek looks drained. I prefer him buzzing around like an agitated dragonfly.

"The king promised his queen a daughter for their firstborn, but he used his seed to create me instead."

My mouth drops open. "He can control that?"

Tek nods. "A fairy king dictates what his offspring will be." He plows forward before I can unpack that unsettling fact any further. "When you sing, Aurora, you radiate the light of a sunstone. That quality draws the queen to you. I do not know if she desires you as a lover, pet, daughter, tutor for the Harp, or all those things. My mother chases her gratifications as well as her grudges with single-minded purpose."

"But she can't touch me as long as I'm fairy knotted to you, right?"

He gives me a tight-lipped bob of the head. "Yes, but you seek to dissolve our knot." Standing, he slowly approaches me. "We've each promised to be a light to the other. Is that not enough to stay our course?"

Is being each other's light what love is? I take a step back mostly to prevent myself from giving in and finding my way into his arms. "Tek, I was willing to see what happened between us until you showed me my dreams are nothing to you."

"Not nothing. Never nothing." As he jitters in small quirky movements, an idea flashes through my mind. Before he registers what I'm doing, I plunge my hand into his pocket and grab his spell stones.

Tek sputters and springs toward me, but I trap his treasures in my fist and hold them next to my heart.

"Aurora, don't—"

"Stay right there," I order and open my palm. Tek's pretty pebbles shine in the starlight. "I know you don't use these lightly. Can one of these spell stones derail the plans, putting us in danger? Is there a stone to stop the queen, Gothel, and the witches?"

Tek's gaze is riveted on the stones. His breathing grows ragged as worry raises line after line across his forehead and out from the edges of his lips. He looks as if I'm dangling his best friend over the edge of a cliff.

He stretches a shaky hand toward the spell stones. "Magic mortals, queen, and Brineborn too, the threat is thick, which oh which might do the trick?"

I pour the pebbles onto his palm afraid he might pass out if he isn't reunited with his pretty rocks. "Whatever you decide for me, it must protect Maisie, the Harp, too. She's in danger. I feel it in my gut."

"You first. You first," he wails.

His passion, his devotion is intense and terrifying.

He clutches the spell stones in one hand and wraps his other over them. His body shakes.

"It's okay, Tek." I lightly touch his arms, leaning in to kiss his cheek. "Let's figure this out." I sit on the rigid vein of the leaf to reassure him I'm not going to grab his magic pebbles again.

Cautiously, he comes to sit next to me and stares at the collection in his once again open palm. He lays a fingertip on the red-orange stone. "*Fire Melon* may chaos sew, but our solution, I think not so." Tek chews on his lip as he moves his touch to the canary yellow one. "*Saffron Ruse* will distraction feed, but much too fleeting for our need." His brow is knitted so thoroughly, it changes the shape of his eyes to narrow ovals instead of their usual roundness.

"And the blue one?"

His gaze lifts to mine. There's dreaminess in his eyes I could easily melt into and forget the dangers closing in on us. "A wish profound will that stone spend, its mighty gift shan't change or bend."

I wish he'd elaborate, but he's too unglued for me to press him. I'm afraid to ask about the obsidian one. Its color reminds me too much of the spinning black whorls on King Cinnabar's skin.

Tek plucks the purple stone between his thumb and index finger, scrutinizing it from several angles, a jeweler appraising a gemstone. He returns the rest to his pocket and holds it out for me to see.

"This is the *Iris Dreaming* stone." His lips form a straight line. "Risk indeed does its spell raise, loosed by desperation's blaze."

Its name may be enchanting, but after his warning rhyme, I eye the purple pebble like it's going to bite. "What does it do, Tek?" I quickly add. "No more rhyming. I'm too strung out to decipher your riddles."

He makes a distressed gurgling sound, then steadies himself. "It brings on enchanted sleep."

I raise my hands as if to keep the spell at a distance. Too many fairy tales of women getting duped into a comatose state ricochet through my mind. I'm vulnerable enough as it is without being forced into unconsciousness and completely at anyone's mercy. Being too trusting may be one of my faults, but I'm not a total shitiot.

"Absolutely not."

Tek deposits the deep indigo magic stone with the others and shows his empty hand to prove he's not preparing to douse me with a spell. He clears his throat several times, probably trapping rhymes.

"Hear me out, Rora."

I've gotten so used to his formal fairy speak, I nearly laugh at his human phrasing. When his explanation stalls, I twirl my wrist in a *get on with it* motion.

"The stone's spell will send you into peaceful slumber and hide you from everyone but me, its keeper. That gives us the chance to escape the dangers brewing on the gala night and wake you far from harm's terrible grasp."

The anticipation in his expression makes it clear the decision is mine. "Are you saying you would run away with me? Break your bargain to marry the Brineborn princess? Leave the Emerald Spire? Leave your people?" I press knuckles to my closed eyelids. "Become a fugitive fairy?"

Tek's tears burst and flow down his cheeks in streaks of moonlight blue. "I did not know myself until just now, but yes, my dearest love, I would do this for you."

An answering torrent of tears dampens my face. Never in my life has anyone made such a vow to me.

Tek clutches my hands as if I'll drift away. How can I ask this of him when my own feelings are such a mess?

I watch the stars. While I was in the sky with Tek, life felt limitless as if every path I chose would be the right one. Oh, to live a life filled with such possibility.

Is the strongest path calling to me music...or Tek? How do I choose between a secret life with him or one where I pursue my art, my human dream? Is that direction open to me anymore with unwanted forces trying to steal my freedom?

I reach for Tek's hand and twine my fingers through his. "If I can find the nerve to go through with your suggestion, I need a promise from you."

"What promise, my love?" He raises our joined hands to his lips and kisses my knuckles one at a time.

"Even though I believe your heart is in the right place, I will not be your captive. You must swear wherever we go, if I ever need to leave, you will let me."

Tek stares at me with utter devastation. "You do not love me?"

Strange desolation bleeds across my heart at the thought of not loving Tek. "I didn't say that."

His eyes brighten. "You do love me then?"

A debate peppered with his fairy directness is not what I need right now. "I want to love you. Is it enough right now?"

He beams. "Yes, my sunstone. You will never be my captive, though I am already captive by my love for you."

How often have I yearned to hear these words, but a chill along my spine reminds me it's not as simple as disappearing with Tek. My life is not the sole consideration.

"Tek, does the spell only work for one?"

He swipes at a fresh onslaught of tears. My fairy prince is a sloppy mess. I pray there will come a time when I can languish in this mushy side of him and kiss every tear from his sweet caramel skin. "Yes, it works but once."

I gently swipe at his soggy cheeks with the pad of my thumb. "That's not what I'm asking. Can you use the sleep spell on two people at a time?"

He considers it for a moment. "If they are physically entwined, the enchantment will see both as one." Tek levels his gaze at me. "But Rora, I cannot enter the sleep with you for escape to work."

I may be pissing away my safety putting conditions on Tek's offer, but I forge ahead. "I want to take the Golden Harp, Maisie, with us."

Tek's body shudders. "Into exile?"

"Into safety. Away from Gothel and the witches. Didn't you hear it in their conversation? She is a commodity to them, not a person. They're using her." I turn my body to face him. "I don't know how much you fairies are aware of, but Gothel was raising a bunch of kids on a ranch in the desert, forcefully grooming the poor things into becoming Rampion Record's singers. He called the detestable scheme, Opus. Gothel blackmailed famous rock stars like Mistress

Mango and Da Da Da Deacon, keeping them captive on his prison ranch to educate and coach the younger kids. There were murder charges involved. He's a demon on earth, dangerous and deadly."

"Fairies are well aware sorcerers are treacherous."

I scoff. "But not treacherous enough to refuse to bargain with them."

Tek looks pained. "Fairies can be equally treacherous. Our foul alliance was for the sake of the Emerald Spire."

"Tek, concentrate. You heard the enchantress say she made Maisie appear older than she is. It sure as hell explains her odd behavior. Doing that to a kid is all kinds of wrong. We've got to save her. Maybe if she's tucked away, the spell will break and she can be a little girl again."

He tugs at his bevy of corkscrews while his eyes wobble. His hand grips my thigh. "Yes. Yes. Your heart knows the way. We will steal the Harp. As soon as the magic mortals descend on the gala, we will take Citrine's stairs and go to the woman/child. I will use *Iris Dreaming* on you both."

"After I sing."

Tek rockets to his feet. "No, no, not so. You cannot be near the fray. Magic mortals seeking revenge portend unspeakable outcomes."

I jump to my feet to equal his power dynamic. "Tek Goodfellow, at least let me live my dream for one song."

"Aurora, please. The Dark Vinyl Artists named the targets they intend to extinguish, but magic tainted with malice is unpredictable. Others may fall during their storm of wrath."

I loop my arms around his neck to calm him. Hands cradle my hips as he pulls me close. When he moves to kiss me, I shake my head. "I'll be singing early while guests are still arriving. The group they're targeting for revenge might not even be there yet. It makes no sense for the Brineborn or Gothel and his witches to pull their evil shit until every table is occupied."

His fingers trace a gentle path through my hair.

"Tek? Are you listening?"

"Yes." He pulls me against his body. "Wise, beautiful—"

I lay a hand on his chest. "Focus, please."

His gaze falls to my lips.

"Think about it. If I don't show for my song, it might tip off Ms. Citrine and the Dark Vinyl folks something's up."

"I will not gamble with your life."

I rub his nose with mine to keep his attention from spinning off. "But you agree I'm being logical, right?"

Tek does not look happy. "For you, Aurora, I agree." He snorts. "Grudgingly."

I lay my cheek against his. "I'm going to believe there's still a good chance your coterie will come out on top."

His breath is hot against my neck. "It may be so, if not we go."

I nod. "As soon as I take my bow, they'll expect me to head to wardrobe to change into my Stalk uniform. You wait in the stockroom. Once I join you, lumen zip us to Maisie and use the spell stone."

He brushes his lips to mine and whispers. "On and on we go."

"Is that a yes?"

"This is my yes."

Before Tek begins the kiss in earnest, I smile against his lips. "I guess we haven't had our last kiss after all."

He smiles back and teases the seam of my lips with his tongue until I part for him. The kiss is not frantic or demanding. It's filled with joy and possibilities I no longer want to resist. Hollywood help me, I'm ready to face them. I sweep my tongue against his as if I'm sliding silk across skin. His hands stroke my hips as Tek's claret lumen light pulses around us.

No more letting past fears keep me closed off from the love I deserve.

I kiss Tek Goodfellow, Prince of the Arborborn Coterie, with a fully open heart. All my misgivings disappear. I will tuck my dreams of a musical future away for now until we find a place for them to be reborn. Tek believes in my dreams so I know they will not be lost forever.

I'm willing to give our love a chance, whether it be in exile or in an Emerald Spire free of danger.

This man is the life adventure I choose.

22

COUNTERFEIT SLEEP

TEK

Desperate Tek.

The walls of Cinnabar's office close in on me as bursts of tension pop off the king and queen like a lit string of firecrackers.

Why, oh, why did I agree to let Aurora sing? Terrible decision. When she grabbed the spell stones, it rattled me to my depths. I was so frightened she would follow through with untying our knot I ignored whatever good sense still floundered in my brain in order to agree to anything she wanted.

Unexpectedly, through my feelings for Aurora, I understand my parents more than ever before. Love changes the way you breathe, the way you think, every action you take. I was love-blind, then lovesick, and now love-conquered. Whatever I do, I do for her.

Never, never, never should I have agreed to let my sunstone to set foot on that stage.

Cinnabar voice is charged with volatile energy. "Tek Goodfellow, are you listening?" He slams fists against the desk with such force, I expect it to cleave in two. "The Brineborn will not treat with us. Nothing less than driving us from the Emerald Spire will sate them."

I fight to keep my voice steady. "What of my agreement to marry the princess royal?"

The king grimaces. "Your agreement no longer holds sway."

Despair and failure to my folk render me hollow. "Then our foes stand with the magic mortals tonight. Conquest and revenge served in tandem." This portends to be a dark night indeed.

The queen stands beside the king; their animosity shelved for the moment. I foolishly wasted the *Claret Blood* stone on two hearts who refuse to discard their steel sheaths.

"Our scouts confirm there is no sign of the Brineborn's usual moonlight debauchery," she says. "They are hidden, likely moving on us already." A knowing look passes between them. They anticipate battle.

"A gathering of humans will not deter them?" I clasp my hands behind my back to hide their trembling. My parents expect me to stand with them, not fly away with my sunstone and the Golden Harp. I am a defiant barb in the queen's side, but she would never suspect I'm on the precipice of turning full traitor.

I am torn body and soul. Leaving the Emerald Spire and betraying my folk will forever darken my spirit. For Aurora's safety, her freedom, I will endure diminishment.

"Tek Goodfellow," the king shouts. "Your gaze does flit and roam. Abandon your frippery on this night. As steward of the Emerald Spire, it is essential your magic protection must stand strong."

I bow. "I understand, Highnesses."

Citrine pins me with her stare. "Here is a chance to prove your worth, Prince Tektite."

I nearly crumple. The queen has never uttered the word *worth*, my name, and royal title in the same sentence before. Too long have I been discounted and despised to trust the queen is capable of truly accepting me.

Rora has always seen me as more. Her love and trust fuel my spirit, making me believe I do have worth.

I clench my teeth. Does the queen suspect my strongest loyalty has shifted from duty to my folk to the woman I love?

Doubtful.

The queen does not value love and therefore does not realize its true power. If she did, the *Claret Blood* spell stone would have reconciled her with my father.

The king stands with feet spread and arms straight at his sides. A commander poised for battle. "If the Brineborn breach our lines to join with the magic mortals, it is essential to weave a hasty stasis spell over every human in Stalk to protect them and preserve the secrecy of fairy existence."

I'm hollow inside. "The magic mortals will use violent charms to murder those who stand against them. A stasis spell will not offer their victims protection."

"Death within Stalk is unthinkable. It cannot be," shrieks Citrine in a banshee wail.

I shake my head. "The fiends plan to spread the seeds of falsehood through the human realm to explain their target's demise. None they spoke of point to Stalk."

The king's expression is inscrutable. Here is evidence of the dire cost of bargaining with the spoiled souls of the Dark Vinyl Artists.

Citrine glowers, whether it is at me or the situation, I can't tell. "I shall not dwell on the death of humans. Assure us the fortifications you have woven around the Emerald Spire will hold fast."

I nod. "I communicated warnings to our beloved beanstalk and fashioned barriers within barriers to hold Brineborn aggression at bay." Genuine sorrow wearies my muscles. "Every leaf and stalk will do what it can to protect our coterie."

The queen continues to stare with her vibrant eyes. "And none of your pretty pebbles can add to our defenses?"

To my surprise, Cinnabar lays a gentle hand on her arm. "If Tek had any more power to give, I have no doubt he would."

My spirit is laden with goodbyes that cannot be spoken. I take a last lingering look at my parents who only have eyes for one another, never their ill-begotten prince. If given time, would my mother's hatred of me soften? It is a gamble I will not take. Aurora is the dawn I will follow into day.

The gears of fate turn, and there's nothing left to say. I leave them.

The marble staircase leading to Stalk's shining arch is packed with press. An emerald carpet infused with fairy magic to set it twinkling adorns the steps for celebrities and high-powered guests alike to enter the club. A legion of servers bearing trays filled with flutes of effervescing champagne waits to greet each elevator that arrives packed with guests.

Aurora, Demetrius, and their crew work at a fever pitch to fill orders of the signature cocktails designed for the club. The set of her shoulders and the way she keeps glancing at the table reserved for the magic mortals tells me Rora is on edge.

Tonight was to be her triumph, and it has been stolen from her. Near murderous rage burns inside me. Curse Queen Citrine for coveting Aurora and those viperous magic mortals who desire to rip my sunstone's freedom from her. She deserves a life as luminous as her heart, not the shadows closing in around her.

I finger the *Iris Dreaming* stone, our only choice on this choiceless night. Next to it in my pocket is a steadfast acorn from a silverwood tree. Once they slumber, I will hide Rora and Maisie inside the vessel where no one can find them.

Amidst the clinking of glass and the cacophony of chatter in Stalk, I nearly miss the entrance of the Dark Vinyl Artists as they arrive within the shell of the *Pearl Tear*. Their attire matches this blackest of nights. Gothel's fitted suit gives off the sheen of a black opal. The witches wear variations of inky evening gowns. Rubata's dress is made of material that mimics overlapping vinyl records. Tressa dons cascading layers of smoky chiffon that flounce from her chest to her thighs. The sea witch is encased in a metallic fabric reminiscent of tight-fitting chainmail.

A string quartet is set up on the turntable. Their music provides a soothing undercurrent to the rattletrap of club patrons. Cinnabar and Citrine circulate like a couple at their wedding festival. Not a single crinkle at the corner of an eye or the tightening of a lip mars their suave countenance.

I play my part, hovering at the edges of the gathering, ever alert for signs of the Brineborn. In truth, I'm standing guard to whisk Aurora away at the first sign of the impending confrontation.

Glancing over at the shrouded table, I see Gothel checking every patron and shadowy corner of the club between noxious glares at the tables where Justin Time, Zeli, Rora's friend Santino, and the other artists who will perform tonight cluster. The creatives smile, sipping my sunstone's brilliantly crafted cocktails.

Bitter anticipation cinches the tektite around my heart, making every breath an ache. Too soon, the live music ends, and the band retreats. Citrine dazzles in a gown of spun gold sprinkled with chips of her signature citrine crystal as she saunters to the center of the turntable.

"Welcome to the opening of Stalk," she purrs. The crowd answers with an energetic swell of applause. "On behalf of the club's manager, Cinnabar Woods, and myself, Citrine Fairley, your director of talent, we welcome you to a night of celebration, uniquely designed cocktails..." She nods toward the bar where only Demetrius and the barbacks remain since Aurora's gone to change into a dress worthy of her torch song.

The guests break into a fresh round of clapping and table thumping. I'll share this grand appreciation for her inspired beverages with Rora once danger is behind us. She dedicated herself fully to being a cocktail magician and deserves to know her efforts are indeed celebrated.

"...and a spectacular parade of your favorite performers. We're pleased to welcome Justin Time and Zeli from Rampion Records, Midas and Chorda Lear from Golden Pipes, Rai Cloud and Azure Tempesta from Cloudpath Music, as well as Benedict Boyd and Beatrice Sharpe from the chart-topping B&B+3 to add their signature dazzle to our long-anticipated launch of Stalk."

The patrons, now more tipsy than sober, roar their approval. The air is laden with undercurrents of hatred, seeping from the magic mortals.

Citrine continues. "To begin our evening of stellar entertainment, we've partnered with *Saturday's Star* to treat you to a peek at a few up-and-coming artists destined to shine in the Hollywood sky." She gestures to the vista outside the curved glass windows.

Beneath the grand arch, the lineup of *Saturday's Star* singers waits. Aurora stands at the front of their gathering in the same stunning gown she wore the last time she graced Stalk's stage. The diffuse lights of the arch reflect off the sequins of the dress. My lover looks truly kissed by the stars.

I'm so mesmerized I miss Citrine's introduction. Wearing what I recognize as a mask to hide her nerves; Aurora takes her time approaching the stage.

Good girl.

She's making sure every eye in the room is on her as she traverses the distance from arch to turntable. For a moment, I forget my trepidation and languish in Aurora's perfection. When Citrine kisses her on both cheeks I tense, wary of my mother's tricks, but the queen yields the stage without mischief.

Few borrowed moments remain before Rora will safely slumber inside the silverwood acorn shell. I startle when her music rises from the ring of speakers embedded in the turntable. It's not the right song.

No, no, not so. The incompetent sound techs have cued another singer's music. Rora's composure will be thrown off. The moment is here for her dream to come true and some nitwit mars her triumph.

Aurora is unfazed. She steps up to the mic as if approaching a lover. The lights focused on her shift from a delicate white to a deep red, a claret red. Her finger caresses the mic before bringing it to meet her lips.

Anticipation of danger propels me to the edge of losing my mind, but possessiveness for this woman may be what sends me over the brink. I shake with a jealous urge to blind every man and woman in the room ravenous for Aurora's seductiveness.

As the turntable slowly revolves, her gaze finds mine. The lazy smile and subtle wink are for me alone, her knotted love. Rora's voice awakens with a low sultry hum, then she begins to sing.

"He flew me to a cloud,
The lover, the dream of my heart.
Lights below faded, faded, faded,
Until starlight danced with us.
I asked a single blaze,
To meet my waiting touch.
Within the kiss of starlight's fire,
My passion learned of true desire,

In a daze, I step between two tables to be closer to my sunstone. The new song is about us, our night on a cloud. A time of truth telling and shared desire.

"The lover too was seeking,
The one to see his worth.
Together separate journeys,
Melted melted melted into one fulfilled.

Hearts of crystal, blood, and truth,
Know their match when once it's found.
In nighttime skies or sun bright days
Love-blind, lovesick, at last allayed.

Aurora's gaze finds me with every rotation of the stage. She sings to me. There is no power beneath the sky that could pierce my changed heart so dearly. I am no longer Tek the trickster, Tek the maker of mischief, Tek the unrestrained. I am Aurora's Tek for everything she needs me to be—lover, protector, maker of dreams. I finger the spell stones in my pocket until I feel the halved *Verdant Promise*. I will create a new Emerald Spire far away and safe to provide my sunstone a peaceful haven hidden from the evils of any world.

"But happiness is fleeting,
And soon the spell was broken, broken, broken.
The world decries that too much joy,
Must often be diminished.
We fought to keep our knot untouched,
Safe from powers threatening."

Her song of sorrow feathers my tektite heart with cracks. She's sexy and heartbreaking, a soul laid bare for the scrutiny of the room. I hear every fear, every doubt as she sings. A torch song must bare its wounds, its pain. I pray she believes our knot will hold enough strength to outrun the predators at our heels.

As our story unfolds under the saturated beams of stage lights, I hear Aurora's truth. A thread-thin saffron beam stretches from her heart to mine.

She is indeed a sunstone. The light to pierce any darkness.

I search the room, striving to see if her light is a gift of fairy sight alone. Fear weakens my knees when my gaze lands on the unrelenting expression of hunger on Gothel's face. Not far from the magic mortals table, the queen locks her stare on Aurora with a greedy look to rival the sorcerer's.

I'll lock you in an acorn shell then all our foes can go to hell.

No one will touch my sunstone. I fight to draw breath as our time to flee draws nearer. Her lyrics tell me everything. We are two discarded souls who discovered their value in the arms of each other. I am not a worthless prince and she is not an inconsequential human. Together we will paint our own dawn light. With Aurora's love, I will no longer be nature's misdeed, but its brightness.

The room holds its collective breath as the song winds toward its end. Stirrings of awe weave through the air from every spirit in the room. My own stronger than any other. It is no misstep giving Rora this moment to prove she deserves the dreams she chases with passion and perseverance. I hate to rip her from those dreams. If there were any other choice...

"I choose belief, a light revered,
That what is true prevails,
Vows will find no oath's defeat,
Knotted souls do cherish still,
A love.
A dream.
A life fulfilled."

She raises her chin and gazes beyond the window glass. I alone know it's a last look at the world she leaves behind. Not one clink of ice disturbs the silence. Slowly, slowly with head bowed, Aurora settles the mic in its stand.

The club erupts, breaking the spell my sunstone wrapped around everyone in the room with her performance.

I hear Zeli's voice through the applause as I make my way to the door behind the bar. "Who can follow that?" she says, nudging her husband, Justin Time.

On stage, Aurora dips into a humble bow as the turntable stops for her exit. I don't linger to hear Citrine's praise or Gothel's words of possession. I'm panting with anxiety, staring at the door, willing Rora to walk through before the Brineborn arrive or anyone stops her. A moment later, she slips into the storeroom, face beaming.

Before a word is spoken, I scoop her into my arms and the cocoon of my lumen light. My lips cover her face in a thousand kisses as I murmur praise against her skin. "There is no greater magic than the power of your newly born song."

We fall into a kiss for the few breaths it takes to fly through Citrine's private fairy door and up the stairs to the Golden Harp.

When I set Rora down, she lays a hand on my chest, delight setting her skin aglow. "The song switch surprised you then?"

I laugh. Even though we're about to undertake a task with no guarantee of success, I share this moment of joy with my love. "I look forward to a lifetime of surprises from you, my cherished dawn."

The lightness fades from her face as we stare at Maisie's door. "Tek, what if something happens to you while we're asleep in the acorn?"

It is a fear that's squeezed my heart as well. I have no soothing answer for her. "I will fly and I will hide to keep you both tucked safe inside." I take her hands. "Slipping away if I must, is a thing I can do. Keep faith with me, Aurora."

She clings tightly to me. "I do have faith, but I'm also afraid. What if I don't wake or I do wake and don't remember you?" A light sob escapes her lips. "How will you protect the acorn if things get really bad?"

"Banish your worries, my dearest love." I pull the silver acorn from my pocket and hand it to her. "Here is your bower. I shall be the briars to surround and protect, be it for an hour or a hundred years." I wave my hand and conjure a gauzy image of layer upon layer of thorny vines around the acorn until only a glimmer of silver can be seen within.

Aurora barely gets her words out. "A hundred years?"

I stroke her sunstone yellow hair. "Time will not touch you while you sleep. Dream of me in starlight and tether to our love. Our knot is true. Trust in that. I will find you...once upon a time."

She stares deeply into my eyes. "I do love you, Tek. I truly do." A light sob escapes her bow lips as her hands slide to the scars where my wings should be. "Swear one last promise to me with your lips, and I will do the same. A kiss is the courage I need to believe I'll wake from the stone's enchanted sleep."

There is no time for debate. I will gift her courage the joining of willing lips do promise. We fall into the kiss until it reaches the core of our spirits. We are breath, the shared beat of loving hearts, and souls knotted in promise.

"I love you, Aurora."

Her gaze is transfixed on mine. "You are my dearest dream," she says with the light of a thousand sunstones blazing in her eyes.

"And you mine," I answer as we steal one last frantic kiss.

The moment our lips touch this second time, the crystal shell around my heart ignites, sending a blinding glow through my skin. The claret of my lumen is replaced with multiple shades of tawny tan and deepest earthen brown as my tektite essence mixes with the rays of her sunstone glow.

We are more than a knotted pair. We are love.

All too soon, we part, knowing there is no time for more tender words or caresses, neither is there a need. When we are far from here, there will be time to puzzle out mysteries such as the source of Rora's brilliant light and our future. One that I am determined will be filled with the beauty of her songs.

I nod to the golden gleam pouring through the keyhole. "On and on we go?"

Aurora gives me a smile laced with melancholy before she sends her precious breath through the opening. The door swings aside.

We slip into Maisie's bedroom where she sleeps under a quilt of powder pink. Hand in hand we move to her side. In repose, the

Golden Harp's face is not the face of a young woman, but clearly that of a child. Innocent, but sadly not carefree. Unrest lies within her.

Rora squeezes my hand and slides her finger down her own cheek beneath her grassy green eyes, then gestures to Maisie. I spy the thin lines of tear stains on the girl's face and gasp. The dual tracks glisten like a rivulet of gilded moonbeam.

With a feather-light touch, I dab a finger to the shallow pool of the liquid and lick it from my skin. My eyes widen as I taste magic. Is this child of Gothel's a sorceress in the making? I pull Rora from the bedside to whisper so as not to disturb the Harp.

"Her tears hold power. For good or ill I cannot tell." I shake my head. "We shall not risk her joining you in enchanted sleep." I start to tug Rora toward the door, but she digs in her heels.

My love whispers as not to wake the girl. "Friends from the Boulevard told me Zeli cries magic tears. If she and Maisie share such a gift, labelling the poor thing the Golden Harp and keeping her secreted away is exactly what a controlling creeper like Gothel would do." She eyes Maisie with renewed fear. "Gothel thinks he's created another Zeli." Rora's eyes glisten with tears. "She absolutely must join me in the acorn, Tek."

I chide myself for not learning more of the magic mortals. Aurora's expression is steel. She knows much more about the shock waves created by the sorcerer and the witches in the human world than I do. In this I must trust her.

I steal one last tender kiss from my sunstone and nod. "Are you ready?"

Rora shakes her head. "I want to be." A stitch of panic starts to overtake me, but she lays her palm on the side of my neck. "I'm okay, Tek. What do I do?"

I lead her to the bed. "Slowly cradle the Harp with your body. Best if she does not stir."

Rora's fingers slide through mine as she carefully crawls onto the bed, curling her body around Maisie. Thank goodness for the deep slumber of innocence.

"Now close your eyes, my love."

She does, and I immediately miss her nature-green gaze. Drawing the *Iris Dreaming* spell stone from my pocket, I touch it to my lips and breathe the words of the spell.

"Dreams will shroud your sacred sleep. Cherished beauties do slumber keep." When I finish, I lay it on my open palm. The stone liquifies and I squeeze drops into Rora and Maisie's eyes. "All is well, enact the spell."

I do not move as I watch the two women melt into deep sleep. My sorrow in the necessity of this act wars with relief that I have found the means to keep my Rora safe. I open the acorn as if its two halves are held together with a hinge.

"Into this vessel I draw Aurora, my eternal dawn, and Maisie, the Golden Harp." Even though I knew what was to be, watching Rora's body shift into a thin wisp of mist alongside the girl's as they flow into the silver acorn devastates me. Lovingly, I seal the vessel and hold it to my ear.

At first, silence rolls over me, but then as peaceful as a breeze kissing a meadow vine, I hear the twin breaths flowing within. A spell stone well spent.

Before burying the precious acorn in my pocket, I encase it in layers of spells as staunch as the protective briars I showed Aurora.

I'm seized with great emptiness at my darling's absence. I weep as I snap into a being of lumen and speed to face the oncoming tempest.

23

VILLAINY

TEK

In my heart, ages not minutes have passed since Aurora and I left Stalk. As soon as I emerge from the storeroom, I seek the king and queen. They stand together, her arm linked through his, exquisite royal faces scarred with worry.

Within the *Pearl Tear's* protection, the magic mortals lean close to one another, heads nearly touching. They hiss and grumble like wild animals, hand gestures flying. I can't decipher a single word until finally Gothel lifts his face to flash a seething glare at Citrine and Cinnabar.

The sorcerer looses a gritty growl. "They suspect something."

I'm not surprised his mistrust is triggered. I've never known my parents' public expressions to be so lacking in poise.

The sea witch taps her trident necklace as her eyes roll back, exposing an excessive amount of white. "I sense a tumultuous wave. The Brineborn approach."

Tressa Divine has traded her usual smug expression for one of solemnity. "Fairies," she sighs. "They don't know the meaning of the word subtle. Cinnabar and Citrine will clue in any moment."

Forcing a casual pace, I saunter over to the king and queen. "The Brineborn are soon upon us."

To my surprise, Cinnabar lays a hand on my shoulder. "Stand true, my son."

In an unexpected happenstance, the queen's gaze lingers on my face, her features lacking their usual stony edge. "Hmm," she sighs. "I do indeed live as a splash in your eyes and on the tips of your lashes and locks." She looks away in an instant, as if it pains her to acknowledge any connection between us. It takes the precipice of doom for the queen's motherly carapace to crack even a little.

I should run now with Aurora and the Harp before the Brineborn arrive. Why aren't my mighty parents braced for battle? Do they not intend to stand against our enemy?

The magic mortals focus on their cornered victims. Stretching tall enough to match my parents' heights, I dip my head to complete our trio. "The Emerald Spire will shield our folk from the Brineborn until the last leaf falls." I speak low even for a fairy. "You will fight then, will you not?"

You, not we.

Cowardly, self-serving Tek.

Guilt over my decision to abandon the cornerstones of my loyalty, the Arborborn Coterie and the Emerald Spire, gnarls my spirit. I must not falter in my devotion to Aurora.

"We will defend," says King Cinnabar. "But not sacrifice our folk."

The message is clear. They will flee. My final shreds of doubt disappear as I read their devastation. There is no shame in my leaving a battle already lost. In time, our coterie will find a new place to wait for our land to heal without being tied to the Dark Vinyl Artists, and I will be off and away to begin a life with my sunstone.

This is the crossroads where I part from my kin. Without my presence as a bitter reminder of betrayal, perhaps a king and queen who were immune to the *Claret Blood* spell stone will find their way back to the love they once shared.

Citrine breaks away to usher the final warm-up singer off the stage. Zeli and Justin Time leave their table to retrieve a pair of guitars, one pink and one black, from their man waiting near the arch.

Electricity arcs through the air from the approaching Brineborn. A glance around the club tells me the humans do not notice it. My heart thunders, and I check that the spelled acorn with Rora and the Harp is secure in the sealed pouch at the bottom of my pocket.

With every step Justin Time and Zeli move closer to the stage, my head feels as if it's being crushed in a coralberry press. Through bleary vision, I take in the movement of the Dark Vinyl Artists. They've risen to their feet and stand in a rigid line before the table at the edge of the *Pearl Tear's* mask. Gothel's hands glow a deep spoiled orange. Oval discs on Sulaa Kylock's shoulders swirl in menacing deep opalescent shades. Sparkles like tiny licks of blazing white cinders surround Tressa Divine, while Rubata Lear's cherry red locks blow as if caught in a restless wind.

Nature, spare us these evils.

The magic mortals ready their attack. To generous applause, Justin offers his hand to help his doll-sized wife onto the turntable then follows her up. The pair secures guitar straps around their shoulders, readying their instruments.

My parents have disappeared. I frantically search the club to warn them we're poised on the verge of cataclysm. Will it be the Dark Vinyl Artists or the Brineborn who first shatter the night with malignant mayhem?

Justin Time pulls the mic stand between Zeli and him as he leans into it. "Congratulations to all the folks responsible for setting this fabulous venue ablaze in the Hollywood night." He flicks his hot pink damask tie. "It takes a lot to get me to bust out one of these." The crowd titters. "Anyone want to guess who chose it for me?" He bobs his head at Zeli, who wears a gown studded in various shades of pink crystals dripping down her small frame. The adoration of the guests reaches a raucous level. Oh, if only this evening of celebration was not to be spoiled by the machinations of venomous spirits.

Justin continues. "Here is the song that brought me the love of my life." He winks, leaning in to kiss Zeli. Before their lips touch, an inferno of super-heated air blasts across the room. The *Pearl Tear's* power dissolves, and the sorcerer and his witches stride to the stage. Distorted waves of magic surround the disgusting group like rings of a lunar halo.

I snap into lumen form, preparing to sprinkle a stasis spell over every human before a vision of these fiends sear themselves into innocent memories. Preempting my action, enchantment from a different source casts a delicate net of sleep magic over most of the guests.

But not all.

Justin and Zeli rush off the turntable to their friends. The doomed mortals pool together, backing toward the curved expanse of windows to create distance from their foes. Expressions of shock and terror flow across blanched skin as victims recognize the true danger before them.

My fears are made real as reflections in the glass reveal my lumen light is surrounded by a flurry of speckles hovering just below the velvety black ceiling of Stalk. Myriad pinpoints of jewel-tone lumen lights ranging in color from raspberry and deepest sea blue to every shade of citrus fruit pepper the air.

The Brineborn are here.

It's they who charmed unsuspecting mortals into slumbering sculptures. To my utter horror, I spy my parents under Stalk's magnificent arch. They are surrounded by our rival coterie's soldiers.

My moment to escape is now. I must fly before my enemies detect my presence and entrap me along with the king and queen. Deep-seated loyalty roils through my blood. I swore my protection to Aurora, but faced with the choice to abandon my parents, my coterie, and the Emerald Spire to the Brineborn looming raw before me, I cannot summon the strength to flee.

I must find the path to stay true to those I am pledged to, my knotted love and folk alike. With painstaking slowness, I float to the ceiling, heading to the outskirts of the Brineborn legion, and pray they do not notice one Arborborn lumen amongst their ranks. For once in my impulsive existence, I must pause and plan before acting.

I eye the fairy door in the corner. Do I escape to muster help? I may very well be walking into despair. What has become of our dimension within the beanstalk? Did my protections fail? Have the Brineborn driven my people from their home? Does salt cover our new realm where we'd begun to plant seeds of hope? My gaze darts to the window, searching fearfully for any sign of displaced fairy lumens who wander in woe through the unforgiving landscape of a Hollywood night.

Nothing but the glare of the human realm below floods my fairy sight—a small hope all is not yet lost.

The Dark Vinyl Artists gather on the still turntable. Gothel waves his burning hands through the air, sending a thin stream of flame cycloning through the club.

The sorcerer's voice carries the malice of a hundred readied swords. More horrible still is the serpent's smile he aims at his targets. "Welcome to Stalk's magnificent gala. It would be a night to remember for the rest of your lives if..." He raises a finger wreathed in crackling flame. "...tonight wasn't the finale of your insignificant yet irksome existences."

A sturdily built man with iron gray hair and bushy mustache steps in front of the tangle of terrified humans. "Don't you dare touch anyone here, Grant Gothel. We buried you once, and we'll do it again."

Rora's friend Santino steps shoulder to shoulder with the older man much to the dismay of a slight, brown-haired woman, bunching handfuls of his jacket in her fists.

"Rand is right," says Santino. "Your power over us is long gone." He runs a finger along a nasty scar on the side of his face. "You're not the only one who came back from the dead, you bastard."

I shudder remembering the story Rora told me about Santino being caught in a horrible explosion when he and a squadron of bikers bent on saving Zeli destroyed the electrified fence around Gothel's Rampion Ranch.

As nonchalantly as if batting a fly, Rubata flicks her wrist, sending a wall of wind against the two men. They stumble backward a few steps before regaining their balance.

Lightning crackles in the black sky outside as a male figure to rival Cinnabar's mighty build joins the front line of defense. I feel the man's magic whip around the room in unyielding currents of power. Here stands a sorcerer and not a weak one.

"Hello, Prospero, or should I say *lover*," croons Sulaa. "Pity our affair must end like this. I always did enjoy your power." An indigo bolt shoots from the sea witch's trident aiming straight for the sorcerer's crotch. He meets the onslaught by conjuring a blast of water. The two supernatural assaults collide in a blast of steam.

Yes. Yes. Yes. I know of this magic mortal, Prospero Tempesta. He is the selkie Stormbringer. The royals once considered courting him as their conduit for the Spire's protection but deemed him too volatile.

"Enough," thunders Gothel then addresses the collection of lumens above him. "Contain our enemies for their trials."

Sparks rain down around the terrified humans, snapping into Brineborn fighters as they reach the ground. They form an impenetrable circle around Gothel's targets. Sneering with victory, the Dark Vinyl Artists leave the stage to perch on a quartet of seats set in front of the turntable.

I skitter along the edge of where wall meets ceiling, dimming my light. Soon, I've positioned myself behind the magic mortals and closer to my parents. I fear surprise is my only weapon. I'll create a distraction to allow the royals to act. But what can they do?

Gothel, ever the showman, stretches a hand toward Tressa Divine. "My dear, enchantress, the first revenge goes to the latest wronged."

The flouncy witch stands and crooks a finger at Benedict Boyd. He moves on stiff, uncooperative legs as he is magically forced to approach the stage and nearly trips climbing onto the turntable. There's a feminine cry from the humans as Beatrice Sharpe is restrained by the Brineborn.

Tressa flits over next to him, skimming a finger under his chin. "Oh, Benedict, you should have chosen me instead of the harpy to join your band."

Benedict jerks his head to avoid her touch.

"We might have been lovers." Her teasing touch trickles down the center of his chest until she dips it inside the waistband of his suit pants.

"Get your hands off him," Beatrice shouts and breaks the Brineborn's hold, rushing between the enchantress and Benedict.

Her bravery seizes my heart. This is what love does. Sets aside fear to protect the light of your soul. It is a beautiful gesture, but I fear for her.

Tressa glares at Beatrice. "Once a monster, always a monster. I'm sure you've missed your feathers, Beast. Time to wear them for good."

Benedict shoves Beatrice behind him as white dots of magic begin to coalesce into a ball between the enchantress's petite hands. When she pulls back the sphere containing a spell reeking of vindictiveness, a mighty voice shakes the room.

"Now." Cinnabar, the King of the Arborborn Coterie, my father, thunders and the Emerald Spire quakes beneath our feet.

A sheen of white like the froth of a great wave surrounds the Dark Vinyl Artists as the Brineborn soldiers abandon the mortal targets to reform around the sorcerer and his witches. Flames, indigo bolts, wailing wind, and sizzling white ice daggers attempt to assault the fairies, but to no avail. The fiends are caught.

My father acknowledges me with a nod as I snap out of lumen form to appear in my royal garb, sword present but sheathed, to join my king and queen. We stand united, radiating regal invincibility alongside King Cavancite and Queen Aventurine of the Brineborn Coterie. Deadly wings on full display boldly stretch behind the four monarchs. All subterfuge vanishes so every unspelled human, magic or not, in the club will witness the totality of fairy might.

The Brineborn king and queen share flickers of distaste registering my wingless inclusion in the lineup. Royal condescension is of no matter. Whatever is about to transpire, their ire will not prevent me from contributing to a united Arborborn front.

Unrest exists between the coteries, but thank nature, in this moment, they stand as allies against the Dark Vinyl Artists. An influx of Arborborn soldiers take up positions to join the Brineborn and bolster the protection around the monarchs as well as those menacing the magic mortals.

Cinnabar takes a step forward, Citrine's hand never leaving his arm. "Esteemed guests." He gestures to the shaken humans. "Be at ease. No harm will touch you. Instead, we extend the offer of fairy justice against these..." The king wrinkles his nose in disgust. "Tainted villains."

Citrine lifts her chin. "Do you accept?"

The once-targeted mortals are ill at ease. Prospero returns to the forefront of their group. He wears a wary expression. "An offer or a bargain?"

The Brineborn royals reform the line with us. "We two fairy coteries have joined to curtail the treachery of these magic mortals," says Cavancite, the briny king, with the strength of a breaking wave. He's swathed in aquamarine armor with a crown of brass driftwood and sea stars. He inclines his head to Gothel and the witches. "The advances of the sea witch to treat with us against our kind portended a foul future indeed."

I sneak a glance at Sulaa, who clenches her trident necklace in her fist.

Cavancite's voice rolls over the room with the power of a sea storm. "For their offenses previously known to us, we sought to banish these mortals to an eternal fairy stronghold until far more insidious tidings of their deeds found our shores."

Gothel tries to speak but the Brineborn king cuts him off. "It seems such mercy does not equal your quartet's trespasses. Darker punishment stands at the ready."

Queen Citrine's eyes blaze with otherworldly citrus light. "Victims of Gothel and his witches, share with us what you've endured, so that we may deem the extent of justice to be dealt."

I pity any human daft enough to disagree with my mother. Prospero turns to his folk. The hum of conversation lasts a few moments with furious glances thrown over shoulders at the Dark Vinyl Artists, who still writhe and push against the magic of their Brineborn cell.

The shape of Stormbringer's face flickers, hinting at the enraged selkie hidden beneath his human form. "We accept as long as *you* agree to carry out the punishment."

Cinnabar's brows furrow. "You would forfeit the satisfaction of vengeance?"

Prospero's gaze flicks over his people. "These human hearts will scar committing the violence you may prescribe. They have already suffered enough injury from the deeds of these horrors."

Fear and rage crack through the air in a violent dance.

Cinnabar waves a hand to the stage. "Then bear witness, and

we will see justice done." He widens his stance, crossing Titan arms.

Justin, Zeli, and Santino step up together. Their story of Zeli's imprisonment in the Rampion Records Tower, Gothel's toxic tea that provided his stable of stars fame until it ruined their voices, the captive children at Rampion Ranch victims of his Opus scheme, the harvesting of Zeli's magic tears to fuel Gothel's sorcerer's powers, and Santino's tragic injuries spill out in a diatribe of doom for Grant Gothel.

Humans do not possess fairy sight, so they cannot see that each of their accusations manifests as wavering images in the air. We folk alone observe the atrocities words describe. I clutch the hidden acorn in my fist as if I can shield Aurora from these nightmares.

Gothel's face is rage incarnate as his accusers meet his fiery stare.

Midas Lear is next to the stage. He calls to his daughter, Chorda, to join him, but she hides within the embrace of a dark-haired, gangly man, who I assume is her husband given their matching wedding bands of gold etched with sunflowers.

Midas never takes his stare from Rubata. As he tells the tale of his daughter's bargains with a malevolent goddess and the witch's attempt to poison him with malachite, his eyes radiate the deep sorrow that shadows his very soul. With obvious reluctance, Chorda joins him, holding tightly to his arm as between sobs, she corroborates his story of familial dedication reduced to rot and avarice.

"Oh, Ruby," cries Chorda, reaching hands to her sister. Rubata for once, drops her toxic petulance as tears pour from her eyes. The shapeshifter lays a hand over her heart and mouths, *I'm sorry*. Remorse from any of the Dark Vinyl Artists is unexpected. Will they all share the same measure of fairy justice? Gothel surely is a greater evil than Rubata.

Prospero Tempesta ushers a blue-haired woman in a silken green dress and a tan-skinned man with three black braids trailing down his back to the stage. The magic wafting off the sorcerer and the woman is palpable. I would guess she was Brineborn except there is no fairy tell about her. Another selkie perhaps?

Their story images unfurl in vibrant hues above their heads. The woman is Azure, a mermaid. I swallow my sound of alarm when the blue-haired beauty reveals the sea witch is her mother from a union with Stormbringer. That explains the kiss of the sea I sense from her.

"I have five half-sisters, cursed with painful deformities from my mother's experiments to breed a mermaid." She threads one arm through Prospero's and the other through the steadfast man at her side. "My father and Rai are their family now."

The mermaid pushes herself to continue. "Sulaa Kylock not only imprisoned spirits of innocents, but she gave Grant Gothel and Rubata Lear sanctuary knowing full well of their crimes." She stands taller. "Even though she is the mother I once loved, any goodness she possessed was abandoned in her lust for power."

Prospero raises a fist. "My daughter omits Sulaa's intention to sacrifice her own child, Azure, as well as Rai Cloud, the love of Azure's life, to gain wealth and power." Images of waves magicked to deliver killing strikes erupt in the air above the sorcerer's head. The Brineborn king's jaw clenches at the abuse of the sea's power.

Fury roils off all four fairy royals. The magic mortals disgraced and distorted the very core of nature's gifts. These are not actions that will bear even a glimmer of tolerance from fairy folk.

Santino takes the stage again with his partner at his side. An elderly man joins the couple as well as Beatrice and Benedict, who were to be Tressa's first targets. The slight, pretty woman is first to speak. "I'm Hero Andante and this is my father Leonato. For too long those evil pricks..." She jabs a finger at the Dark Vinyl Artists. "...controlled his mind. Before they hid in the Emerald Spire, these vermin skulked in the shadows of Hotel Caliwood."

"Are her words true?" asks Citrine of Leonato.

The man looks exhausted as well he should if one half of his mind battles the other in an attempt to discern reality from evil.

Leonato bows his head to the royals. "Yes. I never retain memories or awareness of my dealings with Gothel and his group. For that I will always carry great guilt."

"No," says Hero. "It's on them. You had no say."

Leonato strokes his daughter's hair. "You are too generous, my sweet Hero."

Beatrice glares at the caged DVA. "Tressa Divine laid a curse on Benedict and me because he didn't choose her as the female vocalist for his band. When the curse took hold, I was turned into a Beast, a harpy."

This human exudes sting and spice to rival Queen Citrine.

"And then all four of those fuckers kept me captive in the library of the Hotel Caliwood and forced me as Beast to terrify a beautiful little girl so she'd cry the magic tears that fuel Gothel's fire fingers." Her bravado falters. "We, we..."

Benedict continues the story. "We tried to save the kid, Maisie, but—"

The stream of Benedict's memory is the most jarring of all with the Harp's imprisonment, then images of transparent blue figures wearing faces frozen in terror.

Ghosts.

What beings have not been ravaged at the hands of Gothel, Rubata, Sulaa, and Tressa? The Beast in Benedict's narrative—a strange, giant bird woman—wears a look of such sadness, my throat tightens. The creature presses a pink bottle to catch a small girl's golden tear. I recognize the child. She is a younger version of Maisie, the Golden Harp.

My thumb caresses the silver acorn as if I'm wiping away the Harp's tears. The brilliant streaks I saw on her cheeks as she slept are evidence enough. She is not a contented or happy soul.

Anger and disgust roll off the fairy royals. The Brineborn king narrows his brows as he faces Cinnabar and Citrine. "And this is the filth you bargain with?"

The patterns along my king's skin swirl with his mounting outrage as he glares at his rival. "Desperation provided limited choices after your cruel destruction of our homeland."

Citrine clicks her long fingernails. "We may stand together now, but do not discount your part in bringing us to this moment. The crimes you inflicted on our coterie contributed to the need of a collaboration with these vile magic mortals."

For the first time, the Brineborn queen speaks. Her skin is as light as a whitecapped wave, a striking contrast to her husband's sun-worn coloring. Deep blue hair very close to Azure's long tresses is twisted through a crown of sea green pearls. "Our alliance is fragile but in the pursuit of justice may we now be joined." In a gesture as graceful as a light summer current, she extends an arm toward the victims of the Dark Vinyl Artists. "These humans both plain and magic, present a litany of grave offenses indeed. Before we pass judgement, let us venture into the memories of the accused."

As one, the two pairs of royals turn and raise fisted hands at Gothel, Sulaa, Tressa, and Rubata. Four thin streams of lumen light in crystal colors of citrine, cinnabar, bright blue cavancite, and seafoam green aventurine, surge from between clenched fairy fingers, each targeting a different Dark Vinyl Artist.

Agony pinches the faces of the sorcerer and witches as their dark deeds flow in a stream of translucent images above their cage. Much of it has already been shown from the witnesses' points of view, but from Gothel, the deepest horrors emerge. Pregnant women are forced to eat mountains of green leaves piled onto plates. These same women birth scores of children who are immediately stripped away and the mothers disposed of. The word *Opus* flickers above his head. Lines of young children sing to fields of the same green leafy plants that flourish at the sound of their voices. Gothel cradles one wailing tiny blond babe in his arms who spills tears of gold. The sorcerer's eyes blaze with victory. The child could be Zeli or Maisie, they are so alike.

Aurora's image flickers into these poisoned thoughts. I see how they covet my dear one and planned to lock her away with the Harp.

They will not touch her.

Gothel's impressions collide with Tressa's. A girl of less than ten years old cries out in pain, weeping golden tears. Her body contorts, writhing and shifting into the young woman I know as the Golden Harp.

This last abomination is damning enough for the royals to snap the crystal strings that probe the Dark Vinyl Artists' memories. The fiends collapse to the ground, drained. One by one, kings and queens grasp the wrist of another until locked arms form a four-sided square. With eyes closed, their voices murmur the chant of fairy justice.

A quartet of judgement to parallel a quartet of villainy.

There is a loud *pop* as a curl of black smoke rises through the middle of their conclave. Four sets of royal eyes open as they speak as one.

"Death."

Chorda Lear screams her sister's name and tries to run to her, but the sorcerer, Prospero restrains her. In his face, I see reverence for the power of my people. None of the other humans apart from Stormbringer take the fairy sentence well. Despite the wrongs done to them, they are not vicious folk.

Death is vicious.

Four sets of royal fairy wings shiver as they prepare to rise and render death, honoring Prospero's request to spare the humans from enacting the terminal strokes. I study the terrified faces of Chorda, Midas, Leonato, Santino, Hero, Rand, Beatrice, Benedict, Rai, Azure, Justin, and Zeli. What if Aurora and her kind heart were among them? She could not bear the blatant slaughter of even the most despicable foe. Aside from Stormbringer, the group of wronged possesses frail hearts. The impending act of fairy vengeance will indeed scar those hearts.

My love for Aurora gives me the strength to protect them.

"Stop." I step in front of the royals and hold the black spell stone, *Viper's Onyx*, aloft. "As prince of the Arborborn Coterie, and one-half of a knotted pair with Aurora whom these villains sought to harm, I beg for the honor to carry out the sentence to send these poison souls into oblivion."

My father's eyes gleam with pride, but instead of gratifying, his expression is a dagger through my heart. He perceives I am embracing my royal responsibilities when my intention is to spare the magic mortals' victims the horror of a ruthless, bloody fairy execution.

The Brineborn's appraisal unnerves me. Does my action mark me once again as a fair bargain for an alliance between our coteries? My mother's face radiates suspicion, but she nods along with the rest of the fairy monarchs.

I walk with solemn purpose until I am in front of the magic mortals. Gothel, Sulaa, and Tressa eye me with loathing. Only Rubata shows weakness. I will not allow her tears to sway me. The Lear witch bestowed a death sentence on her father and was complicit in the unnatural life inflicted on the Golden Harp. Her display of remorse is not for deeds which I do not doubt she would repeat, but for her failure to succeed in every heinous act.

I hold the *Viper's Onyx*, the stone of destruction, to my lips and speak. "For deeds both vile and malice great, before these eyes reveal your fate. Now fade from sight so all may heal, for nevermore you'll goodness steal."

A shield of black glass pulses around the stone as it sits on my palm.

"All is well, enact the spell."

The glass shatters releasing a plume of black smoke as wide as a mighty silverwood trunk that races toward the magic mortals. Cries from the group behind me echo through Stalk as an acrid smell fills the room. The haze encases the Dark Vinyl Artists, condensing them into a writhing mass that diminishes swiftly to the size of a fist. The last hint they remain is a flash of fire, Gothel's final attempt at escape before the horrors are no more.

There are neither blood nor blows. A more merciful death than they deserve. Smoke settles, and the stench disappears.

Grant Gothel, Rubata Lear, Sulaa Kylock, and Tressa Divine are no more. Only a wisp of black dust remains where they once stood.

The souls now freed from danger gather in a sobbing tangle, except for Prospero Tempesta who faces the royals. "They are destroyed then?"

I walk over and hand him the clear, spent spell stone. "The *Viper's Onyx* does not fail. They will plague you no longer."

Stormbringer returns the stone to me. "I have no qualms over the obliteration of these serpents." His eyes flash over his folk and soften. "But it is a bit much for them."

"As it should be," I tell him. "Ending any life is no easy matter."

He scoffs. "To you perhaps, but I can't say the same of those wretched horrors we are now well rid of."

I do not disagree with the selkie sorcerer.

"Santino, your scars," cries Hero, touching his face. "They're gone." Zeli, Justin, and Rand rush to his side, gawking at his unmarred skin.

The sorcerer levels an untrusting stare at me. "Is this your fairy doing?"

I think back on the words of the spell.

Now fade from sight so all may heal, for nevermore you'll goodness steal.

By destroying the powers that inflicted the injury, the harm itself has been undone. I underestimated the *Viper's Onyx*. Its spell was not solely of endings, but also of righted wrongs.

"It is the spell stone's gift."

Beatrice catches my arm. "Maisie? Where is Maisie?"

My hand wraps around the acorn as I give her an encouraging smile before returning to my king and queen. "She is safe."

Safe, but what is she? Woman or child? Did my protections thwart the reversal of the wrong against her? Is Tressa's aging spell still in place?

Prospero speaks again. "Your Majesties, all of us here exist in the company of magic and freely acknowledge it. What thanks can we offer for your abolition of the evil that shadowed our lives?"

Cinnabar answers with no hesitation. "For our survival, the Arborborn Coterie was forced to enter into a dread arrangement with the Dark Vinyl Artists. We offered sanctuary to these magic mortals in exchange for their use as a conduit connecting us to the human world in order to disguise the Emerald Spire's fairy dimension. Desperation blinded us to the depth of their schemes."

Prospero wears an expression of grim understanding. "Your conduit is lost."

Citrine waves a hand. "It wanes. We've always maintained a limited quantity of temporary magic to prevent the conduit from failing. It will hold until the Golden Harp and the sunstone, Aurora, become our new resources." Her gaze flits around the room. The queen frowns when her quarry is not to be found.

"No." My voice shakes the room. "It's true the Harp possesses magic tears of gold, but Aurora is merely human. She cannot be a conduit. Neither deserves to be shackled to our needs."

The queen's pitying look enrages me, and I lash out at her. "Would you entrap them as Gothel and the witches have done? That marks us as vile as they."

Judging from the switch of her expression into volcanic rage, this may be the moment my mother strikes me dead. I squeeze the silverwood acorn in my pocket.

"On the contrary, *prince*." She forces my title through her lips. "We would not entrap but rather bargain with them, offering great rewards for their service." Citrine schools her features. "Do not act as if you are blind to the sunstone's gifts."

Gifts? Aurora? What in the name of blessed nature is the queen talking about? Then I think of the ray of light that emanates from Rora when she sings, and the way her sunstone aura blended with my lumen light when we made love. Of course, I have mused over her mystery, but I will not expose what the queen knows of my beloved's nature in front of those gathered.

Queen Citrine narrows her eyes at me. "Where is Aurora?"

Stormbringer doesn't hesitate to boldly enter the fairy discourse, saving me from answering my mother's question.

"I have a proposal, or rather a bargain as your folk prefer to term it," he says. "You erased the dangers from lives dear to me. As my part of the bargain, and as thanks for your deeds, allow me to act as your magical conduit."

"Me as well," says Azure, joining him. "I am not as powerful as my father, but magic runs in my blood."

"I will too," says Zeli. "My tears are an enchanted gift."

"Count on our connection to magic as well through the power our Irish gods and goddesses, Manannán Mac Lir and Bríg," adds Chorda Lear as Midas nods along with her words.

The group of five stand shoulder to shoulder. Cinnabar takes Citrine's hand and they approach, expressions unreadable. This is an unlooked-for boon. If the royals accept, Aurora and the Harp will indeed be free. I roll the acorn in my closed fist, willing the king and queen to seal the proffered bargain.

The Brineborn queen frowns. "Are these disparate wisps of power enough to maintain your Spire?"

Citrine waves her hand in an arc, encircling our new potential collection of enhanced mortal allies with a rope of her light. I stare breathlessly as her magic begins to pulse, expanding until it forms a luminous golden bubble around them. Suddenly the orb explodes into a rain of brilliant droplets.

The queen smiles. A real smile, not one tainted with regal contempt. "Their combined power will serve."

Cinnabar inclines his head. "The bargain is struck." His gaze shifts to me. "Prince Tek Goodfellow will instruct you in the days to come on the way to fortify the bond between human and fairy to allow our worlds to live side by side in the Emerald Spire."

Citrine claps her hands. "Our business is concluded." With a graceful twist of her wrist, the dust that was once the Dark Vinyl Artists disappears. "The time is nigh, please retake your seats. Justin and Zeli on stage, please."

My mother splays her fingers as her arms slice through the air in a scooping motion. "'Tis time to bury confusion in mortal minds for soon our bargain will be tended. As for souls who slumber here, the night shall soon be mended."

My mother calms the collective minds of the sleeping humans. Before the queen can lift the spell, Beatrice winds her way to the front of her group. "Wait. I need to see Maisie. Right now."

Benedict joins her in solidarity as the other erstwhile victims collapse onto padded chairs. "We'll give the kid a home and love her as our daughter."

My mother betrays a slight wince at the word *daughter.*

I grip the acorn tight enough to crush a weaker vessel.

The queen locks her stare on me as she speaks. "Where ere you've tucked the treasures deep, I do implore to see them plain. Safe shall they be within our care, free to live sans fear or pain."

Slowly, as if it is difficult, Citrine speaks in tender tones. "Take my hands, true son of mine, I freely bless our bond divine."

Tears blind me. My mother holds her palms up, inviting me to touch her. My wounds from years of her heartless dismissal prevent me from returning the gesture. I neither trust nor understand the reversal of her affections. Why now? Is this the queen's ultimate trick to steal my sunstone?

My gaze wanders past her to Cinnabar. When our eyes meet, he gives a gentle nod of reassurance then looks to his queen.

Citrine is patient, a state never before directed at me. She waits, hands poised in the air between us. Her eyes glow a soft sunflower hue, not a terrifying lemon blaze.

If I'd fled, her olive branch would have been lost to me. I do not want to forfeit this chance. Trust in my estranged mother is threadbare, but the hope of it lingers in my heart.

I lay my palms to hers, and she immediately closes her fingers around my hands. The queen's touch is warm and soft. My magic stirs and reaches out to her power. She accepts it and for the first time, I feel a connection begin to sprout between us.

"I vow to nurture trust between us, Tek Goodfellow," she says in a voice for my ears alone. "Will you bring forth your knotted and the Harp?"

Sliding my hands free, I dig into my pocket for the acorn and cradle it against my chest. I will not hesitate to protect my sunstone if this is but a royal ruse. My mother's gaze does not waver from mine. I detect no deception.

With a heart pounding in anticipation, I hold the silver acorn in my palm. Slowly, I spin a finger around its shape, shedding every layer of the briar protection spell I swathed my Aurora in. The silver sheen brightens as its shroud disperses. Cupping my hand, I bring the silver acorn to my lips. "New dawn arrives and with it peace, from fairy slumber, you now release. And as I am an honest Tek, your precious life I do protect."

With a snick so faint only fairy ears could hear, the clasp on the acorn opens. Two streams of delicate light, one saffron and the other gold, rise from the shell, spinning faster and faster until they fall away to reveal Aurora and the Golden Harp locked in an embrace. Maisie is not the young woman whom the magic mortals held, but rather a child with hair of yellow gold and eyes the color of a perfect summer sky.

I catch Rora as she sways, not releasing her grip on the little one. She turns her head to look at me. "Tek?" Her gaze flashes around the club. "Are we safe?"

I kiss her hair. "Yes, my darling Aurora."

She moves to kneel in front of Maisie, but Beatrice is there first, running her hands over the child as if to convince herself the girl is real. "Maisie, oh, Maisie."

The Harp widens her eyes at the sound of Beatrice's voice. She pivots in Aurora's arms and tilts her head, studying the woman. "I know you."

Beatrice smiles through her tears. "And I know you."

Maisie lightly rests a finger under each of Beatrice's eyes. "You are my beautiful bird." Benedict drops to Beatrice's side, catching Maisie's attention. "And your name is Ben. You loved the beautiful bird too."

He wraps an arm around Beatrice. "I still do. I always will."

Aurora clutches my arm. "She's a child."

I hold her close. "The enchantress's aging spell is broken."

Rora shivers as her gaze whips to the table where the magic mortals lurked. "Where did they go?"

I kiss her temple. "To the darkness that made them."

"Citrine," she hisses low in my ear, pressing closer to me.

"Stay by my side. I will explain all ere long."

Benedict and Beatrice each hold one of Maisie's hands as they lead her to their table. At a nod from Queen Citrine, the Brineborn and Arborborn soldiers flick into lumen lights and fly over the sleeping Stalk guests, dusting every human with a waking spell. Citrine and Cinnabar fade into their mortal shells. The Brineborn royals have disappeared from where they lingered beneath Stalk's archway.

Cinnabar lets loose a single sustained note, and everyone in the room snaps back to life, applauding madly at the last words Justin Time spoke before enchantment seized them.

To their credit, Justin and Zeli break into song as if the events that just concluded were nothing more than a dream. Their courage is a marvel.

Twining my fingers through Aurora's, I lead her toward Stalk's entrance with every intention of whisking her off to my bower as soon as we're out of sight. We're a single step away from crossing beneath the silver arch when Queen Citrine blocks the way.

"Our business is not concluded," she says, capturing both Rora and me in her steely citrus stare.

Four of Cinnabar's guards/lovers, each bursting the seams of their tuxedos, surround us.

The queen issues a command, the warmth in her tune restored to ice. "Escort Tek Goodfellow and his knotted lady to the throne room."

Beside me, the catch in Aurora's breath is thunder to my ears.

Foolish Tek.

A moment of counterfeit tenderness from my mother blinded my reason. We are caught in the queen's trap.

24

A PRINCE'S HEART

AURORA

I'd believe I was still dreaming if Tek wasn't crushing my hand. We stand in the middle of an honest to goodness throne room. The space is alive with twirling flowers and veins of metallic liquid flowing through marble walls. Queen Citrine and King Cinnabar stand at the foot of a dais housing a pair of spectacular thrones made of twisting branches and a thousand leaves of glass. They're facing off with another impressive fairy couple. The crowns on their heads suggest they too are royals, but they are as unlike Tek's parents as trees are from an ocean tide. Gusts of wind from beating wings I can see as clearly as my own hands and flashes of light streak between these four powerful fairies.

It's intimidating as hell.

My head is still woozy from my acorn nap as I try to put a coherent question together about the new royals. I sway, my hip bumping the very real silver sword at Tek's side. His lips graze my ear as he fills me in, anticipating my confusion.

"You see King Cavancite and Queen Aventurine of the

Brineborn Coterie. Their daughter, Princess Dioptase, is the fairy maiden standing off to the side glaring at us." He flicks his gaze to a dark-haired woman so beautiful I wilt in her presence.

My throat bobs as I attempt to swallow, taking in the Brineborn princess's frigid stare at Tek. "Is she..."

"Yes. The match I rejected that brought about the great salting."

Princess Dioptase, who looks to be of an age with Tek and me, is encased in a blue-green glow that casts a sheen across her caramel-colored skin like light reflecting off water. The princess's gown is dark burgundy silken lace, rippling like a current as it hugs her tall shapely figure. Woven into the straight, shiny black hair cascading over her shoulders almost to the floor are ribbons of tiny, braided shells. Her features are a collection of delicate curves. She's stunning. I'm a mouse to her peacock.

I clutch Tek's arm with my free hand and ask the question I'm afraid I already know the answer to. "Why is she here?"

Tiny currents of energy flow off Tek and hit me in a series of little stings. "I fear the past has reared its head. A bargain shunned my heart now dreads."

I feel as if my insides have been removed and set aflame. I heard Tek tell his parents he would honor the former marriage bargain to save the Emerald Spire. The cruelty of these fairies to insist I be here to watch this man ripped from my arms stuns me. This man I traded my future for. This man who taught my fractured heart to love will be lost to me despite our plans to see where a life together might take us.

I wish I'd never set foot in the Emerald Spire.

The combative conversation between kings and queens comes to a halt, and the four regal fairies stand shoulder to shoulder with ramrod-straight postures.

Cinnabar is first to speak. "Prince Tektite come before us."

Tek takes a step closer to the royals, dragging me along.

"Alone," says the king, not a shred of sympathy in his voice.

"Please approach as well, daughter," says the Brineborn King to Dioptase.

With a hair flip and look of practiced boredom, the princess flies next to where Tek stands, facing his parents. Her wings are a breathtaking art piece of abalone-colored satin stretched inside a border of crushed seashells.

Tension in Tek's bunched shoulder muscles is evident beneath the same magnificent leafy tunic he wore when he took me to his bower. A flicker I've come to know as magic draws my gaze to Queen Citrine. She watches me with gentle kindness. It fills me with anger. These fairies are cruel, dragging me here to witness Tek's sacrifice to calm the animosity between their people.

I understand the stakes for him. He is the key to broker peace between sworn enemies. Marrying the princess saves his coterie so they can one day return to their ancestral kingdom. Plus, it protects his revered Emerald Spire from the same type of heartless attack that ruined their Griffith Park homeland. Part of me wishes I'd never insisted on singing at the gala. We could have run, but what would abandoning his people have cost Tek?

Perspective bites me in the ass. Losing Tek is a small sacrifice in comparison to the great gains for his folk, but damned if I'm going to stand here and watch it all go down.

"I'd like to leave." The strength in my voice surprises me as I become the center of attention. "I want nothing to do with this." I flick a finger to where Tek and his bride-to-be stand.

Instead of eyeing me with distaste, the princess casts an interested glance in my direction.

Tek starts toward me, but Citrine lays a hand on his shoulder to stop him. Her wings flow in one graceful undulation as she flies to me. Her touch is gentle against my cheek. "My dear Sunstone. A knot must be terminated by both souls pledged to it." She sighs. "I'm sorry to cast this shadow over a heart as bright as yours."

I back away, thoughts spinning. If Tek can't wave his fairy fingers and break up with me, is there a chance I won't lose him? I meet his gaze, but the agony on his face snuffs out any dwindling ember of hope. His suffering echoes mine. He has no choice.

The queen's lips burn against my ear. "The prince may keep you as a lover even after the knot is untied."

This is insanity. I'm not going to watch Tek marry someone else and be his bower buddy on the side.

I face Citrine. "Not acceptable."

To my surprise, the queen flashes me a look that might be interpreted as respect before she returns to Cinnabar. She threads her slender hand through the crook of his insanely muscled elbow.

The Brineborn King clears his throat. "On with it. King Cinnabar and Queen Citrine proclaim that their son, Prince Tektite, has renewed his offer to wed our royal daughter. Such a union will restore our coteries to a state of peaceful coexistence." He dips his head toward Tek. "Is this so, Prince Tektite of the Arborborn Coterie? Will you untie your knot with the sunstone mortal and accept the hand of Princess Dioptase of the Brineborn Coterie?"

My breath comes in short bursts. Why do they all insist on calling me a sunstone?

Tek turns to me, clutching his stomach as if he's been stabbed. His tears run freely. "Aurora, please forgive me. We should have run. I destroyed us."

My heart splits at the pain on his face. I've never been loved the way Tek loves me. Our story isn't ending happily, but it is ending with love. I rush into my fairy prince's arms. "I understand, Tek. I hate it, but you have obligations I can't begin to comprehend. Your loyalty is only one of the reasons I love you."

Our kiss is the brutal farewell of two souls destined for a love that cannot be. We brand one another with the passion that should have been ours to keep. Tek's gentle touch on my shoulders separates us. "You will always be my dawn light, Aurora." With a final kiss to my forehead, he pivots to face the royals. "King

Cavancite and Queen Aventurine, I hereby untie my knot with Aurora and accept Princess Dioptase in marriage."

Tek's words destroy me. The cracking sensation in my chest drops me to the marble floor of the throne room. I press both hands over my heart and wail. I dared to imagine I'd found someone to love who wouldn't leave me in pieces, yet here I am shattered, watching the dream of my heart slip away.

I believed my greatest wish was to live a life of song. It isn't until now I realize life will be incomplete without the love Tek freely gives me without judgement. His only expectation was that I give him a chance to win my heart.

Tek's words to destroy our knot only cement the truth that my heart is forever his. My dream of Tek is the longing of a soul, a wish granted, a life filled with light.

Light.

Light.

Soothing warmth begins to bathe my battered heart until its heat can no longer be contained. Streams of yellow-gold light burst from my chest and between my fingers, soaring toward Tek. Royals and guards alike gasp as shining beams encompass him, spinning in a frenzy until they flare to form a buttery wrapping, shielding him from view.

I stare at the hands still pressed to my chest that glow with the same color as Tek's shimmering coverlet. What have I done?

The princess rushes to her parents as the three shield their eyes from the blaze.

"What is she?" demands the Brineborn King, pointing his finger at me.

As I lay panting, unable to move, Cinnabar and Citrine kneel at my side. The queen lays a cool hand to the side of my neck. Her eyes glow with lemony brilliance as she assesses me. Cinnabar strokes my hair with a calming touch as their eyes meet.

Their smiles are as radiant as sunbeams.

"Can you not see the traces upon her spirit?" says Citrine. "I have suspected them since the night I first heard Aurora sing and hints of a sunstone lumen shone from her breast."

Cinnabar nods. "I perceived an uncommonness to her, but did not look as closely as you, my insightful queen."

Citrine's gaze washes over me. "By which Coterie I know not, but it is clear that at the time of her birth as is often done to honor a rare debt owed to mortals, three of our kind bestowed gifts upon this woman. She is thrice fairy blessed."

I barely process their words. Fairy blessed? Me? Gifts? How can this be? A much-faded memory suddenly sharpens in my mind. There was a favorite story my mother used to tell me.

There once was a babe named Aurora. When she first met the world, her parents made three wishes for her future. The girl would possess a sweet nature freely given. Her voice as lovely as a songbird promised happiness to a world that could always use a bit more of it. Most dear of all, Aurora's light will never cease to shine upon those she loves. With these desires spoken aloud, three brilliant dots of light shone above the cradle. From each, a thin stream of star drizzle fell upon the babe to forever dwell in her spirit.

Could the long-ago story be more than a story? Have fairies been part of my life from the beginning?

The king lifts me into his arms. My body thrums with wave after wave of a strange energy, brightening the whipping strands of light streaming from me to Tek's casing. Cinnabar sets me down next to where my darling fairy is hidden from view. I throw myself on the glowing shell, sobbing Tek's name.

Citrine and Cinnabar stand on either side of me to face the Brineborn king and queen, but Tek's royal mother leaves one hand resting gently on my hair. "Aurora embodies gifts of kindness, song, and a heart with the radiance of sunstone."

The hard-hearted rival Brineborn queen pierces me with an

unforgiving stare that slowly melts as her shoulders sag. "Ah, 'tis true. The prince's knotted holds unique gifts. She bears untainted goodness that glows with the power of the sun's first light. This woman is not fairy kind, but nonetheless, has received these blessings. This Aurora is dawn, the herald of new beginnings, of new possibilities."

The Brineborn king crosses his arms. "Knotted they may be, but she is still mortal. This union will not enjoy the longevity of years that a fairy binding offers."

Princess Dioptase shakes her head. "No matter the time of this union, I will not be the destruction of their knot. Prince Tektite is not meant for me. I condemned his rejection, but I see now it was a blessing none had the foresight to understand. Our union would have become a curse of sorrow once the sunstone came into his life. Their knotting is one of fated hearts."

The princess, who I mistook for a haughty entitled thing, nods to me. "Thank you, sunstone, for showing me the beauty of a true knot."

I have no idea what to say, so I nod back. My arms still press against the pulsing light holding Tek.

Dioptase looks to her parents. "I reject Prince Tektite's proposal." She extends her hands in my direction. "Let this mortal's goodness that she cannot hide even in the company of fairies be a lesson." The princess raises both her hands. "The connection between our coteries should be repaired by friendship, not a forced marriage. Let the Arborborn and the Brineborn once again work toward harmony."

Cinnabar smiles at the princess. "The lesson here is to trust in the wisdom of our progeny."

The royals bow to one another. In a flash, the Brineborn royal family along with their guards burst into lumen form and pass through the throne room doors in a stream of multi-colored light. In their wake, Cinnabar signals the Arborborn guards to leave the throne room.

"Aurora," Citrine coos my name.

I lift my head from where it rests on Tek's prison of light. "Please, please. Tell me what I've done to him. How do I bring him back?" Tek was loving and careful when he sent Maisie and me into the silver acorn. I blasted him into this version of fairy shell with the finesse of a car wreck.

Gentle hands pull me to stand. Citrine meets my gaze. I'm not used to a softer version of Tek's scary mother. "He is no prisoner. The goodness in your heart continues to knot him to you and none other. Simply call. His heart will hear."

I shudder. This could have ended very badly. Tek tried to untie our knot, but my heart refused to be parted from his. If the princess hadn't stepped up, no doubt I'd have been smacked with ugly zaps of fairy magic.

That doesn't matter now. I need Tek in my arms. Lowering my lips to the yellow-gold shell, I whisper. "Tek, come back to me. Please. Tek, it's your Rora. I love you. I do. You are my greatest wish, the forever dream of my heart. I love you. I love you. I love you."

The light sparks into a vivid corona then fades, revealing a stunned Tek lying flat on his back.

"Aurora?" he asks, eyes straining to focus.

"Tek." I fall to my knees, gripping his face to kiss him. Our last kiss was a farewell. This kiss is a promise renewed.

Tek, still dazed, breaks the kiss and glances frantically around the throne room. "The Brineborn? The princess?"

Queen Citrine flutters to his side. "Gone."

He stares at me. "You refused to untie our knot."

I shake my head. "When you tried to break it, I thought I was going to die." Grasping my chest in an attempt to feel the glow living within my heartbeats, I continue. "Then yellow streaks flew from me and trapped you in a shell of light. I don't know how I did it."

Tek looks at his mother. "Was it the sunstone light that wakes when Aurora sings?"

Citrine's smile is radiant. "The very same."

Cinnabar joins his queen. His gaze, overflowing with love, locks on Citrine. "Aurora, you radiated the light of your goodness and love for our prince, but it was not you alone who protected him." He kisses the queen's hand, then looks at Tek and me. "It was my queen, *my* dearest love, who joined with the beam of your sunstone heart to shroud our son. Her magic prevented you from untying the knot with him."

I stare at Queen Citrine. "You saved Tek from marrying the princess?"

Tek sits up, bringing me with him. "I am confounded."

Mother and son stare at one another. Citrine is first to break the standoff. "I should punish you, mischievous prince, for using the *Claret Blood* spell stone on your king and queen without our consent."

Tek juts his chin at her. "Why bother when it was useless against your hard hearts?"

The queen reaches out to lay one hand on Tek's shoulder and the other on Cinnabar's. "Not so, son of mine. Your sleight of hand, did hearts rebind."

Tek's mouth hangs open as he gapes at his parents. "You are reconciled?"

Cinnabar threads an arm around Citrine, pulling her close. "We decry the errors of our ways, again in love we'll pass our days."

Their kiss is so intense and passionate, I should turn away. Cinnabar brings his queen flush against his body, and she growls with pleasure.

Tek clears his throat.

Cinnabar's sensuous smile could melt the clothing off anyone. "Thanks to you, our fine prince, we were able to stand united and treat with the Brineborn against the magic mortals."

"Joyful I am that you, my king and queen, are to the same bower bound, but—" Tek crushes my hand. "What becomes of my promise to wed the princess and the promised peace between our coteries such a wedding would bring?"

Citrine's face is grave. "Once reminded of the gracious beauty true love gives to the heart, how could I doom my son to a life without it?"

Tek's voice shakes. "Son?"

To my surprise, the queen's already milky skin pales as she speaks. "For nearly nine decades, I punished you for what I deemed your father's hubris. The *Claret Blood* spell stone allowed my mind to open and understand the desires of Cinnabar's heart. My own need for gratification blinded me to my husband's dreams and the beneficence of compromise."

Wow, there were serious communication issues between Tek's parents. Nine decades is a hell of a long time to hold a grudge. Then again, I have no concept of how the passage of fairy seasons or years translate to human ones. It's only one of the thousand questions buzzing through my brain.

Cinnabar idly strokes the queen's wings. "And I accept blame for overpowering the dearest wish of my queen and bringing forth first a prince upon her."

Tek's teeth are clenched so tightly tics dance along his jaw.

The queen looks at Tek with surprising vulnerability. "I hid my love for you to punish the king, but it was always there. Forgive me for making your life a misery. You will never know another day without seeing the truth of your value to me." Citrine bends to where Tek and I sit and kisses his forehead. "I will be patient until your heart is able to trust in my promise." She smooths a hand through his forest of corkscrew strands then returns to Cinnabar.

Tek's eyes bobble as he calms enough to meet Citrine's gaze. "I have no rhyme or riddle to offer you." He tries to keep speaking but a sob chokes him.

When I slide my hands around his back to gather him close, two blunt ridges descend from shoulder blades to hips, stretching his tunic away from his body.

"Tek, you're hurt." I run my fingers along what used to be a line of bumpy scars from his missing wings. Did Citrine's cocoon or my light harm him?

"No," he says, shaking his head as if waking from a deep sleep. Tek cranes his neck to stare at his back, then in one swift motion rips off his tunic.

"Nature's gifts and blessings," gasps Citrine, tugging Cinnabar to stare at Tek's back.

Replacing the parallel scars I reverently touched while we made love are what appears to be a pair of tight shiny green scrolls. The throne room is silent as I gently brush fingertips from top to bottom of Tek's new adornments. "What are these?"

In a graceful pas de deux, two dazzling emerald wings unfurl. Their texture is like metal hammered so thin I'm afraid if I press too hard my finger might pierce their delicate surface.

"So very strange," says Cinnabar, but Citrine shushes him as I help Tek to his feet.

Behind him, the wings stretch to their full size to reveal themselves as a pair of enormous leaves, exact replicas of those gracing the Emerald Spire. Never releasing my hands, Tek waves both wings through the air, marveling at them. Beams of light stream in through the windows to ignite a million pinpoints of sunstone yellow glitter glass scattered across the metallic surface of his new wings.

"Tek, they're beautiful," I say, squeezing his hands.

He looks to his parents. "How can this be? These are not the wings I lost in the great salting."

I lay a hand on Tek's bare chest, the boy then man who spent his life as a punching bag between warring parents. When he described his missing wings to me, they were made from elements of both the king and queen. The incredible pair at his back are a sign of Tek's devotion to the Emerald Spire he created to save his people. I'm gratified they wear a sprinkling of sunstone chips to blatantly declare his love for me, the mortal who dared to fall for an extraordinary fairy.

My lips graze his with a reverent kiss. “These are the wings of a man who knows his own heart.”

Tek’s hands slide around me. “You are my heart, Aurora.”

Normally, I’d be embarrassed to kiss Tek luxuriously in front of the king and queen. Not today. They can all fly away if they don’t want to watch the way my body molds to his as we tie our knot so tightly it will never be undone by human or fairy.

“To my bower?” he asks against my lips.

“Yes, my sweet prince.”

In one graceful movement, Tek lifts me into his arms and those gorgeous wings flow behind him as gracefully as his bower’s brook. We fly toward the huge double doors of the throne room.

“Prince Tektite, our audience has not come to an end,” says Cinnabar with firm formality.

Tek glides to the floor and releases me. “May Aurora and I take our leave of you, Highnesses?”

I suppose I’ll need to learn fairy formal speak to talk to Citrine and Cinnabar. Since Tek and I remain knotted, they’re my king and queen too.

“Not yet,” says Citrine.

Hand in hand, we approach the royals who now sit on their thrones. The queen pierces us with the cold stare I’m used to instead of mushy motherly Citrine. She leans forward. “The fact remains you, Aurora, possess too much knowledge of our fairy realm.”

Cinnabar’s melancholy look jolts my heart as he speaks. “Knowledge is vulnerability.”

Tek’s hand tightens on my waist. “Aurora will honor our secrets as she has proven thus far.”

“I swear I’ll continue to respect your world,” I add.

“Nevertheless, we now enter a new chapter with the next cadre of magic mortals, making the safety of our existence even more fragile," says the king.

"Aurora, your awakened fairy blessings and knot with the prince allow you to see much of our realm. You cannot continue as you are," says Citrine.

I tremble. When Tek released me from the acorn and told me Gothel and the others were gone, I also assumed I was free from Citrine's intentions for me. Doesn't the strength of my knot with Tek protect me from the queen's plans?

The queen reads the strain on both Tek and my faces. She wipes a hand through the air. "Have no fear. I once desired to tempt Aurora to join my favorites and to keep her as both mentor to the Harp and conduit for the Emerald Spire." She turns to Cinnabar, desire flaring in her eyes. I wouldn't be surprised to see her jump him right in front of us. "I no longer have need of either outcome."

"A knot by its very nature while strong and true holds the caveat of a transient agreement," says Cinnabar. "Because you are burdened with our secrets, sunstone, we need a more permanent solution."

I do not like where this is headed. Are they going to force me to marry Tek instead of the princess? I love him and can't imagine ever loving anyone else. But insta-marriage? Holy Hollywood, our relationship is still new. Even though my heart pleads with me to shun logic, good sense insists on more mileage before wedding vows. Marrying Tek should be the culmination of a beautiful journey, not an ultimatum dumped on us by royal fairy control freaks.

Tek's voice is laced with trepidation. "It is unjust to limit Aurora's freedom to our realm alone."

Fear sizzles up my middle. I was only stressing over a forced marriage. "I can't disappear from my world." Robbie, Santino, Rand, and my other friends from the boulevard fill my thoughts. They'll try to find me. Fear for me. Miss me. They are more than friends. Those people are family.

"We are willing to bestow upon you the gift of fairy life," says Citrine. "It ensures an unbreakable promise of loyalty to our kind and our secrets. The goodness of sunstone you already carry will become the crystal guarding your steadfast fairy heart. You'd dwell with Prince Tektite in our lands for the same bounty of years fate allows him to draw the sweet breath of life."

Cinnabar weighs in. "Your knot then transforms into an oath to remain with our prince."

"Turn me into a fairy?" My head swims. A life tied to *Hollywood knows* how long of Tek's fairy destiny? What if I agree and things go wrong between us? His parents spent decades hating each other. How would fairy Aurora change? I don't want to become fickle and flighty. I look at Tek, the fairy prince who was the definition of fickle and flighty before he loved me. "What about my dreams? I want a career as a singer. I've only taken my first step to success. I'm not ready to walk away."

"If that is what you wish, my dear sunstone, then our next action will be grave indeed," says Citrine.

"No," says Tek, putting his body between his parents and me.

Is this it? Am I going to be turned into sparkles because I'm a fairy liability? "Please don't hurt me," I beg, burying my face between Tek's outstretched wings.

He swivels, wrapping his arms around me. "No one will harm you. The choice they offer is to cleanse your mind of all you've seen of our kind, our home. You will be the Aurora you were before our knot was tied. You will only know us as Mr. Cinnabar, Ms. Citrine, and their attendant Tek Goodfellow."

I snap my head up. "And forget everything between us? The joy you've brought to my life." I shake my head. "I can't live with that choice either."

Movement catches my eye. Tek fools with the spell stones in his pocket. What is he thinking?

"This will not do," says Citrine with traces of the bitter

dismissal I'm used to. "We offer you the gift of two choices, Aurora sunstone. Denying both is not possible."

How can I gamble on becoming a fairy who could end up broken and miserable? What if something terrible happens to Tek and I'm alone in a world completely foreign to me? But the alternative of having no memory of Tek's love...

I pull him away from the king and queen. "If I choose to forget, will you come to me again, Tek? Win my love a second time? Give us a fresh future?"

He looks so sad, tears well in my eyes. "I would still be fairy and you human. The glories of my world by ancient decree must be sealed from your sight. They..." He nods to his parents. "...will cast restraints upon me, preventing any transgression I may attempt to once again share my truth with you." Tek cradles my face in his hands. "Aurora, this stolen time together will always be the most precious of my existence. I will continue to love you even after you forget what we have been."

My tears slide over his thumbs. "How can I condemn you to such sadness?"

He gently kisses a path through my tears. "Rora, choosing your human dream will be my reward as well."

Tek is letting me go. He is not a selfish princeling, but a man who reveres and protects the life of the Emerald Spire as he reveres and protects mine.

I touch my forehead to his. "I'm lost, Tek. With either choice I make, I am lost."

Tek's body trembles. "Choice," he cries. "Yes, yes. To future bleak we shall not steer, when perfect joy does dwell just here." He releases me and stabs a hand into his pocket. A moment later, a vibrant blue spell stone as clear as a perfect Hollywood afternoon sky rests in his palm. "The answer true with me has dwelt, yet foolish blindness masked its spell." Tek clasps my hand, trapping the stone between us. "We are not lost, my sunstone."

I stare at our joined hands that hold the shiny pebble. Can so small a thing save our future? "What do you mean?"

"Here is the *Celestial Gift*, most powerful of the spell stones. It creates a path born of desire, not a future dictated by decree or magic." He opens our hands, laying the blue beauty in my palm. "Once we speak the desires we choose in the spell, they cannot be undone."

My hand quivers. "If you use this stone to keep us together, how is that any different than using a love spell on me?"

He shakes his head. "No, darling Aurora. I do not speak of one outcome. Let our stated desire be a future with unlimited choice. As human and fairy, we will choose to stay together or honor freedom if our hearts should find themselves seeking other paths. Continue your dream to be a singer in terms of human success. The royal offer of a fairy heart and years to match mine will always be waiting as a choice for you to embrace. The king and queen need not fear our choices, for your agreement to partner with this stone's spell proves your heart will be true to keep the secrets of the fairy realm. Even their magic, powerful as it may be, cannot override this most sacred of all spell stones."

I feared the magic of the Dark Vinyl Artists, the fairy royals, and spell stones, but when Tek is the one guiding the mystical power, I see goodness. The *Iris Dreaming* stone saved Maisie and me. Proof that magic can possess benevolent intention.

Tek's excitement fills the room with vibrant energy. "Choice without these limitations my parents press upon us, Aurora, that will be the destiny we ask of the *Celestial Gift*."

I press my forehead to Tek's. "Oh, Tek. That's perfect, our gift from the stone will be to make our own choices."

"Tek Goodfellow?" asks Cinnabar. "What are you about?"

The king's voice is distant. Tek and I pause in our own cocoon. Can this be true? Will we be able to shape our future without fear of the fairy royals dictating our lives according to their narrow perspectives?

"Tek, can the stone's spell override your parents' magic?"

"Even their magic, powerful as it may be, cannot countermand this spell." His smile is broad and confident. "They thought me a fool and a failure when I bargained with the limping dryad for these stones. No, no, not so. I created the Emerald Spire as their home, vanquished their foes, restored the love trapped behind pride in their spirits, and now will ensure our knot may continue without threat to their Arborborn Coterie." He pulls away and tilts his head to one side. "A careless prince I seemed to be, 'til love's bright goodness woke the truth of me."

I rest my head on his bare shoulder. "A heart alone did life portend, 'til fair Tek Goodfellow that fate did end."

"I love it when you rhyme." Tek steals a kiss before we face the fairy royals. He raises the *Celestial Gift* above his head.

"Time before us simply lays, choices vast will be our play. What we decide will shape our paths, with hearts united, a promise cast." He breaks the stone between his fingers, covering us in sapphire mist. "All is well, enact the spell."

Tek and I are thrown together as a rumble shakes the throne room. The king and queen leap to their feet.

"What have you done?" bellows Cinnabar.

With one arm firmly around me, Tek holds out the empty spell stone for the royals to see. "What does your magic tell you?"

Queen Citrine closes her eyes while the king stares at her. Suddenly her lids pop open, liquid lemon light shining from her fairy form, which I see with perfect clarity, lethal wings and all. She whips her head to face the king. "The prince has seen what we did not. Aurora sunstone may be human, but the power of the *Celestial Gift's* influence coupled with the fairy blessings at her birth, mark her as friend and no threat to fairy kind."

My prince bows. "Exactly, wise queen. The *Celestial Gift* stone allows us both to embrace the reward of endless choice. My beloved chooses to see and accept you as you are. You have nothing to fear from Aurora. Her devotion to our kind matches the strength of any fairy in our coterie."

I bow. "I understand how vital your secrets are. You can trust me. I honor both my human dreams, and..." I take both of Tek's hands in mine. "...the knot I've tied with Prince Tektite of the Arborborn Coterie."

Tek and I see nothing but one another. In his eyes are every love story I've ever dreamt of. I will be able to choose my path through life and love in any world. I turn to face the king and queen.

Cinnabar smacks his hands together. "Our son bends rules to best his kin, wise and true his fate does spin." He shrugs. "It seems, dear Citrine, our business with the sunstone and the prince is concluded." The king draws Citrine against his body, caging her in his beefy embrace. She leans her head back, the lust sizzling between them roils in waves of heat across the room as they kiss. They're going to make up for decades of separate bowers right here in front of us if we linger.

Tek pulls me toward the doors. "I celebrate a love rekindled, but there are things a son should never see."

To my surprise, the royals break the kiss. Citrine calls after us. "My dear ones."

Tek speaks out the side of his mouth. "That's going to take getting used to."

"Do not leave without my blessing," she says.

We turn to the dais and the lusty royals.

Citrine opens her arms. "All in our coterie shall hop as carefree as a bird on a gilded branch at this outcome. May you sing and dance hand in hand with fairy grace in all that you desire. We will sing and rejoice along with you in this our home, the Emerald Spire."

"Thank you..." Tek hesitates for a moment. "...mother."

A pained smile escapes the queen's ironclad demeanor for the briefest moment before her regal superiority is back in place. It hurts my heart a reconciliation between mother and son will not be a path of daisies and sunshine after so many adversarial years, but at least it's begun.

Cinnabar's hands roam his queen's body. My face heats at their bold display.

Tek scoops me into his arms. "As you showbiz folk say—" He nods at his groping parents. "That's our cue."

His Spire-gifted wings beat once, twice, and a third time, barely disturbing the air around us as we rise almost as high as the fluted columns in the throne room. Tek flicks his wrist and the doors open to let us through.

Before we fly deeper into Tek's magnificent world, Citrine's voice slides through the room behind us.

"And this time, my king—a daughter."

EPILOGUE

TEK

We lay upon a mattress made of thousands of petals I beckoned to rain upon my bower bed. Rora brushes her lips across my jaw then shifts her route to leave a sumptuous trail down my chest. I'm going to be the one to need restorative nectar from a blushfruit flower to match her stamina.

For once, there is no danger. For once, time does not demand our parting.

Aurora chooses to step away from her duties as cocktail magician and dedicate her days to making music. It is a heady wonder to be the sovereigns of our time.

"Tek?"

"Mmmm?" I lose my fingers in the thick waves of her hair.

"What's the next step after a fairy knot?"

I chuckle. "After only a few nights of uninterrupted love-play, you're ready to take us to the next level?" I enjoy using casual human speech to tease. Locking my hands behind my head, I smirk. "I am lord of love, Tek doth roar, since unsated Rora begs for more."

She smacks my chest. "Of talents wild my Tek does boast and fine though they may be." Her palm presses over my heart. "'Tis here within this noble chest the deepest treasure lives, not jest or trick masks precious love his shining spirit gives."

I roll over on top of her, bracing myself to look into her beautiful Emerald Spire green eyes. "You have me at a disadvantage. I can't resist a rhyme."

She pops up to dot a kiss on my lips then settles back down. "Speaking of which, I need you to help me write a killer song."

"Who do you intend to murder, my sunstone?" I brush my nose along her collarbone.

"I finally agreed to let Robbie arrange an audition for me to sing for Justin and Zeli."

I capture her in my arms and roll us through my bower bed, sending a shower of petals into the air. "That's wonderful, Rora."

She giggles with joy at the profusion of color and my enthusiasm. I am a proud Tek to see my beloved walking a path to her dream. Her naked skin flushes with every shade of pink. We are a pair of willing, love-conquered fools.

"You know," she says, pinching my ears. "I'm going to need a coach to get ready for the performance."

I grip her legs and wrap them around my waist. "I know someone perfect for the job. This fellow—" My hands cup her round bottom. "Knows how to coax a very sexy performance out of his pupils."

"Does he?" she whispers then reaches around and strokes the ridges of my furled wings. Words disappear as we join again. If I could stop time, it would be now with eyes and bodies locked. There is lust and love, desire and promise as we pause seared together. In the eye of our sexual storm, I find the sense of belonging I want to keep forever.

And maybe we will. I lay a hand to feel the beat of a heart that may one day wear a case of sunstone crystal and beat alongside mine for the length of a fairy life.

Afterwards, we sink deeper in my bower bed as downy petals caress our bodies. I tickle Rora's skin with a single tulip bloom. The sun streaks making their way through the verdant layers above us remind me time continues to forge on outside our private garden.

"As much as I'd prefer to continue testing the limits of our endurance..." I produce a pitiful sigh. "It is time to garden, and there is news I must report to my king and queen," I say, kissing the tip of her nose. The Emerald Spire is due for another sprinkling of my magic to keep its secrets safe from human eyes. "And you mentioned retrieving items from your mortal dwelling to bring to our bower."

Rora smiles. "Our bower, huh?"

I prop myself on an elbow. "My home is yours as long as you desire it."

She tucks in closer. "Ummm, let's take this slow."

I roll onto my back and groan. "You and your painful pace."

Rora slides on top of me. "It's not because I doubt you, Tek. I want to enjoy and be present in every step we take together. Celebrate each one as it happens."

I wrap my arms around her back. "I am a greedy, impatient Tek. You will have to teach me how to endure your slow and tortuous ways."

"My pleasure," purrs my sunstone.

We fall into a lazy kiss that she ends without warning. "Wait, what is this news you need to report to your parents?"

I flash my most mischievous smile. "The same I now report to you, my love."

Rora's brows knit in suspicion. "No riddles."

I lay a hand over my heart. "I shall break the news that I will not take up my mantle of royalty." I place my other hand over Rora's heart. "Instead, I shall wear the mantle of happiness."

She covers my hand with hers. "But you're a prince. How can you just turn your back on who you are?"

I shake my head. "My loyalty is unwavering, but I shan't allow the king and queen to now yoke me to royal responsibilities heretofore denied me. Our coterie has managed without a prince for nearly a century. No doubt, Citrine and Cinnabar will soon produce royal heirs better suited to the task than I."

Rora frowns. "This feels awfully sudden. Don't you want to think about it before you dump this on your parents?" She grimaces. "They're going to blame me."

"It is they who have withheld my station, and this is the conclusion those seeds of denial have sprouted. The blame is theirs alone." I stroke her hair. "This Tek need not renounce his ploy, the life I choose doth promise joy." I brush my thumb over Aurora's pout. "I shall be gardener to the Spire and lover to my sunstone. The day will come when woods, streams, and flowers all in our Griffith Park homeland will require my skills of nurture to flourish as they once did. That and not royal pomp is the true purpose for which I was born."

Aurora's face is aglow with love. This blessed friend of stars shall always be my dawn, my day, my moonglow.

"If, you're sure. I want this for you, Tek. We both deserve our dreams."

Before our passion builds again, I break from her. "Rora, there is something I must do before seeking a royal audience." I smooth the hair from her face. "Will you come with me?"

An hour later, with my sunstone in my arms, we lightly touch down at the edge of the Field of a Dozen Shimmers. When the gaggle of children playing a game of hurling spot me, a lad with long ginger waves quickly stows the buttercup ball under his tunic.

"Come here, you passel of mustard seeds. I've brought you gifts."

Rora hisses in my ear. "They're afraid of you."

"Not long ago, I was quite the ass to them." I snicker. "Now they stand awestruck by wings as magnificent as mine."

Aurora slaps my biceps. "Why am I not surprised about the ass factor in that explanation?"

I capture her hand and nip her knuckles then set the basket on the grass. "What do you think of these, seedlings?" I turn to show the full glory of my leafy metallic wings dusted with sunstone sparkles.

In the uninhibited way of children, they approach and poke my new acquisitions. "You've got wings," says the boy with a tunic bulging from the buttercup ball. "Is the great salting over?"

I shake my head. "No, young ones. My wings are a gift of the Emerald Spire and a sign of hope."

One of the smaller girls takes a tentative step toward Rora, peering around to her back. "Who is your wingless lady?"

I wind an arm around my sunstone. "This is Aurora—my true love." A few children roll their eyes, but others gaze at Rora with interest. "Now to my purpose. I am here to make amends for disturbing your merry game some time back."

They look warily at the large basket as I wave them forward. "Come, now. Your prince orders you to approach and dive into this mountain of lemon ginger tarts from Beryl's Bakery."

I guide Aurora away from the oncoming hoard of sugar-dazed fairy children as they attack the basket of favorites. Her face is soft and lovely as she watches them.

"What?" I ask.

"They're beautiful. It's as if they're lit from within."

I stare at the little ones until I understand what she sees. "Yes, they yet retain the luminosity of innocence."

She spins to me in a flash, and I almost lose my balance. "Do you want any? Kids, I mean." The shock on my face makes her laugh then Rora shrugs. "You didn't exactly grow up in a happy home, so I wondered."

For the first time, I notice a faint first-blush peachy glow shining around her. First-blush peach, the lumen of possibility. Seeing the light of my folk embrace Aurora is an unexpected gift. "Neither did you, and you deserved so much more."

Rora's laugh is a nervous trill. "Wouldn't it be interesting to do...

the family thing...with kids." She darts an accusatory glance at my crotch. "Not now, but someday?"

I gather her close and thank my fairy spirit for Aurora, my true dawn. "Now there's a choice for our future I've no doubt the *Celestial Gift* would approve."

To the twittering sound of fairy children, upon a field of a thousand shades of dancing green, I kiss my sunstone and celebrate the miracle of being loved.

Thank you for reading! Did you enjoy? Please add your review because nothing helps an author more and encourages readers to take a chance on a book than a review.

And don't miss more from Leslie O'Sullivan with HOT SET, a romantic comedy, available now. Turn the page for a sneak peek!

You can also sign up for the City Owl Press newsletter to receive notice of all book releases!

SNEAK PEEK OF HOT SET

If dread is ground glass shredding your stomach, then I'm digesting a set of eight crystal goblets. As I ready my opening shot on the seventeenth hole, Lanie Blesch's giggles rise from the golf cart parked alongside the tee box. Aglow in her fifteen minutes of fame as the spokesmodel for everything from moisturizer to orthotic inserts, Lanie flirts with abandon. Her target and cart buddy this morning is my boyfriend, Treat Graham.

This woman who holds the gold medal for stellar BMI is everything I'm not—tall and curvy with negative body fat in all the right places. I flick one strawberry blond braid over my shoulder and wonder if I could pull off Lanie's fluffy chocolate bob with strands of amber peeking through at strategically stylish locations. Next to her overflowing sexuality, I come off like Treat's tomboy sidekick.

When Lanie adds another lipstick smudge to the collar of Treat's gaudy, neon pink polo, I take a step back from the tee and drop my lethal glare to the grass before anyone notices. It's hard to justify visually disintegrating Lanie since she has no clue the man next to her is off limits. Per an agreement I'm rapidly losing patience with, my two-year relationship with Treat is a secret.

Bobby Provost, who shares my golf cart, takes a break from destroying every blade of grass on the tee box with his practice swings. He sidles up next to me. "Gillian, you okay?"

Ironic question from the man who's responsible for half the pulverized goblet glass sitting in my digestive system. I toss Bobby a smile that would register as less than ten percent genuine to anyone who knows me. "Rethinking my club." *And the gag order on my relationship.*

A gust of wind knocks my newly acquired *Chieftain's Son* baseball cap off my head. As the showrunner bringing the most anticipated series of historical romance novels in a billion years to television, Bobby is a swag dispenser. Everyone in this charity golf tournament is outfitted with *Chieftain's Son* logo caps, jerseys, and metallic water bottles.

"I've got it," says Bobby, chasing my cap as it skids down the rise next to the tee. Definitely a gentleman, for more reasons than one. Thankfully, for the last sixteen holes he has diplomatically ignored the giant elephant riding between us in the golf cart. Nearly a year ago, our mutual literary agent approached me with Bobby's interest for me to possibly join the writing staff of *The Chieftain's Son*. An opportunity so unexpected and frightening it came from whatever territory is out beyond left field.

Treat's words ring in my head from our discussion about whether or not I should even entertain Bobby's request to take a meeting.

"Why put yourself through it, Babe? You've never written a script in your life. Face it, Gilly, you are master of the short game. Copywriting for my company is your sweet spot."

Treat is blunt, but I know he only has my best interest at heart. Raw truth—my agent couldn't sell my book; therefore, I live in the stable reality of being the reigning queen of clothing blurbs for Lawson Graham Premier Sportswear.

I shake out my hand, numb from gripping the club too tight. If penning catalogue copy is my career, at least it involves writing. Is the definition of a career what you do to pay the bills when you're two years shy of thirty?

When Bobby Provost, gentleman, and I did meet face to face this morning, I managed what I hoped was an appreciative "thank you" for even considering me for the position on his show, followed by an apology that things didn't work out. We shook hands and

Treat whisked him away to talk business, but something about the look Bobby's jade-colored eyes shot in my direction didn't feel like a period at the end of a sentence.

Thankfully, in less than an hour, Treat will finish selling Bobby on the crossover marketing benefits if our companies pair up. The Irish Country Lass clothing line will shoot on Bobby's company property in Ireland, featuring show locations. *The Chieftain's Son* will get some dandy print exposure for its premier season.

Bobby waves my rescued cap like he's starting the Indy 500. "Victory."

"Good catch," I say, fitting the hat back on my head as Bobby salutes.

I clear my head by ripping a handful of blades from the grass and let the wind carry them to calculate my shot. The faster we play these last two holes, the faster I'll avoid any talk with Bobby about his offer, and the faster I can pull the pin on the *what the hell* grenade I plan to heave at Treat for his flirting overdrive with Lanie.

My tee shot hits the fairway dead center. To my delight, momentum carries it forward a gratifying distance.

"Brilliant," says Bobby, applauding. "One fairway shot, a chip, putt, and you're the birdie queen of the day." He pulls off his own logo baseball cap and trains his hair back. "How many so far?"

"Nine birdies," I say, and head back to our cart. I'm behind the wheel before Bobby finishes his tee shot.

He pops onto the seat next to me. "I chunked it. Is it driving you nuts to play with a duffer like me?"

I muster a smile. "You're far from a duffer. If we didn't have Lanie and Treat dragging us down, we'd own this tournament."

Bobby is the type that perpetually moves and chatters. Luckily, a sweet, candy-coated personality keeps his hummingbird vibe from being irritating. He's the geeky big brother that all my friends would confide in. Treat actually expected me to flirt with him. I'm a good little soldier for Lawson Graham Premier Sportwear and loyal girlfriend, but I have my limits. It's awkward enough spending this much time with Bobby after rejecting his job offer. Given our age gap, which has to be at least ten years, any attempt at flirting would reek of insincerity. Treat's the game player, not me.

Treat and Lanie blow by in their cart, barely missing ours. She drives like an idiot, trashing shrubbery as she rips down the cart path. The flirty laughs between them threaten to bring up my breakfast burrito. Treat doesn't even wave at me.

The jerk can't spare one measly, reassuring smile. Less than six months ago, we were together in Oregon eating his mother's homemade chicken marsala while his stepdad reminded him daily that he'd be a fool to ever let me go.

On the drive back to L.A., Treat professed a dozen times how much he adored me. *Adored*, not loved. Here in reality, *adored* translates to undercover relationship. Treat made it clear from the beginning that if our situation ever became breaking news at Lawson Graham Premier Sportswear, we'd get the axe. I'm certain that axe would only swing my way since Lawson Graham is Treat's father. Lucky me. I get to carry on a hush-hush relationship and watch my boyfriend play gigolo every time Daddy needs someone to court a spokesmodel or female designer.

A pang of disappointment stabs as I relive the joy of living as a non-secret couple with Treat up in Oregon. People take handholding and quick kisses for granted.

After his next shot, Bobby lopes over to me like a deer. The entire cart lurches when he leaps in. "Well, that drive made up for my previous chunkage."

My face heats. "Full disclosure, I missed it."

"I'm sure I can repeat it—never." He laughs.

Before I step on the gas, he raises a hand. "Hold up. I don't intend to waste the serendipity of sharing this golf cart with the author of *Traipse of Moonlight* because her boss wants to use my property."

The serious look and tone of his voice set off a warning klaxon in my brain. *No, not now. Don't do it, Bobby. Throw the elephant in the cart some peanuts and call it a day. Please kill off any mention of our awkward history when we're so close to the finish line.*

"Why in the hell is Gillian Bettencourt wasting her talent writing banal clothing descriptors for a Ralph Lauren wannabe company?"

I'm not sure how many times per minute one is supposed to breathe, but I don't make the quota.

Bobby continues. "In the spirit of full disclosure..."

I remember to breathe but forget to blink.

"My offer still stands for the author of *Traipse of Moonlight* to join my writing staff for *The Chieftain's Son*."

I swallow a very unladylike gulp. This is not a conversation I ever wanted to have, but he's got me cornered.

"*Traipse* never made it."

He stares me down. "Awards and landing the literary agent that we share say otherwise."

I attempt to match his intensity. "It's a decent novella that became a novel she couldn't sell."

Bobby holds up a hand to stop me. "It sold me. From the day Jen passed it to me last year when I was reading everything in sight about Irish history and folklore, *Traipse of Moonlight* has been a major tonal inspiration in my development of *The Chieftain's Son*."

He gestures so wildly I have to lean away to keep from getting whacked.

"The way you juxtapose the despair of the villagers with the unrelenting possibility of hope is gorgeous. Your story shares DNA with Deidre LaRochelle and her *Chieftain's Son* series."

"*Traipse* isn't a romance."

I must present like a shock victim because Bobby speaks with slow and succinct phrasing. "It is a love story. The passion those parents feel for their sick child and the bargain they make with the Otherworld...grand stuff."

His energetic dance calms. "And my dear Miss Bettencourt, *The Chieftain's Son* series is so much more than a romance. It's got historical gravitas and a timeless message." He runs a finger across his chin. "As does *Traipse of Moonlight.*"

I rub my hands together, shoring up courage to reject Bobby a second time. His offer is nuts. I barely survived converting *Traipse* from a novella to a novel.

Bobby knocks on the roof of the golf cart. "I don't invite people lightly to be on my creative team, Gillian. Your story has stuck with me. I see raw talent in you. Talent to be cultivated."

"My novella version of *Traipse* is likely a one hit wonder."

He points at me. "How will you ever know if you don't take a shot?"

My damp hands slip off the steering wheel. "I'm not good enough for something this huge."

"'Not good enough,' says the woman whose prose about trekking in flagstone jackets raises Lawson Graham stock prices."

"I'm good at the short game." Treat's words feel sour on my lips. "I'm not a fool, Bobby. I know writing for your show is a once-in-a-lifetime offer. It's just one that would be a better fit for someone else."

Bobby dismisses my embarrassment with a flick of his wrist. "I disagree."

I can't deny the rush I get from this guy addressing me as a writer. My pilot light to become a novelist sputtered out shortly after *Traipse* fell flat and I landed the blurb writing gig at Lawson Graham Premier Sportswear. Bobby's offer makes my light spark for a moment but then die. Except for witty descriptors, my writing muscles have atrophied, and I know zilch about screenwriting.

My mind flashes on the trio of manuscripts I wrote in grad school hiding on my hard drive. The stories I never raised enough courage to even show my agent.

"What can I say to make you reconsider, Gillian?"

I fidget instead of answering.

Bobby leans in closer. "I dare you."

I slide away. "I don't know the first thing about writing a screenplay...teleplay? See, I don't even know what to call it."

"No one knows how to write one until they do it. We'll teach you. My writing staff is as generous as they are talented, and I'm betting you're a fast learner."

I can only imagine how big of a thorn a green writer with no experience would be in the side of a staff trying to condense a twelve-hundred-page novel into thirteen episodes. I'd resent the hell out of me. I'm not eager to flaunt any more insecurity, so I go with the practical argument. "You shoot in Ireland. I live in L.A. Bit of a commute."

He shakes his head. "You're a hard ass, aren't you? I'm used to people begging to get a foot in the door of *The Chieftain's Son*. We're on the brink of a five-season pick up, and I've no doubt we'll add five more to that, a season per novel. What's not to love?"

"The offer is flattering, but I just don't see myself joining a television writing staff. Too intimidating. I'm sorry."

A muscle on Bobby's jaw twitches, and his fingers tap the dash of the golf cart. The hummingbird perks up. "What if I find a way to ease you more slowly into the picture?"

I nearly take the bait but stop myself so I don't give the impression of false interest. I need to veer away from this subject and resuscitate the Lawson Graham Premier Sportswear agenda.

"Continuing our trend of full disclosure, what will it take for you to agree to Lanie Blesch over your leading lady as the spokesmodel for our line?" I ask.

Bobby's eyes narrow at my skittish change of subject. The way he appears to be reading me like a cheap novel is disconcerting. I fully expect him to reject my new choice of topic and launch back into his campaign to unhinge my life.

"My green Irish hillocks are ripe for the picking if Mr. Graham signs my star, Niks Tellefson, as spokesmodel."

Relief softens my stone-hard muscles. The elephant has been

evicted from our cart as we shift back into conversation that doesn't force me to take stock of my existence.

The corner of his lip sneaks up and his pupils flare. "Hmm? Then again, Mr. Graham wants my land, and I want his writer. Dare I say there may be a bargain in the making?"

And Jumbo plonks back onto the seat between us. I sputter like a kitchen faucet coming back on after the water's been turned off. Treat will have an apoplexy if my repeat rejection of Bobby's job offer gets in the way of his plans for the Ireland shoot.

Someone hollers behind us, and I realize we're stalling the tournament. I hit the gas to drive the cart up to where my ball landed. "That's not where I was going with the conversation," I say as I hop out and grab my six iron. "You know that one has nothing to do with the other."

Bobby chuckles. "I didn't get where I am without testing every available angle."

Every available angle to bait me again. His business with Treat and his job offer to me exist on two entirely different planes. There's no leverage crossover between them, and Bobby Provost will not bamboozle me into thinking there is.

As I line up my shot, I notice Lanie and Treat are nowhere in sight. *They must already be on the green. Damn, how long were Bobby and I yakking?* I'm equal parts flattered by his kind words and jittery from his pressure. A golfer's worse enemy, distraction, clutches the back of my neck, and I slice my shot into the trees.

"Damn it."

It takes my entire reserve of self-control not to stomp back to the cart or snap my club in two. That was my worst shot of the year.

Bobby leans with his back against the cart. "So, you are human."

"Tragically human." I pick out a few clubs. "I'll go find my ball and meet you on the green."

He tugs at the sleeve of my newly acquired *Chieftain's Son* jersey. "New deal. If I can't convince you to join my team, which I'm not giving up on yet, how about this? I'll agree to let Treat Graham use *The Chieftain's Son* property for his shoot and go one more round with him over the spokesmodel stand-off, if"—he holds up a finger —"you join *The Chieftain's Son* foursome in our charity golf tournament at the end of the month."

"Which course?"

"Gal Tré in Kerry."

I stumble on the cart path. "As in Ireland?"

Bobby nods. "Expenses paid by the network. It's a good cause."

I should say yes. The showdown for the Irish Country Lass model will be over by then, and I can settle back into my clandestine but adoring relationship with Treat.

The thought of putting the Atlantic between Treat and me feels perilous. The shattered goblets in my stomach tinkle a warning, but I shake it off. A night in my apartment in front of the fireplace with Treat and a bottle of wine will wash away this rising sense of doom. He cozies up to women for business, but at the end of the day, it's my bed he's in. Or *was* in. It's been over two months since he's been in town long enough to spend couple time with me, our longest separation so far.

Unwelcome thoughts percolate in my head. What scares me the most? Treat not showing up at my door or seeing his face next to me on the pillow while I continue to invest in a relationship that only goes in circles?

"You're sweet, Bobby, but this is a crazy time for me with looming Irish Country Lass deadlines. I can't get away." With what I intend as a kindly wave, I head into the trees to find my errant golf ball. It sits on a tidy patch of grass between two sycamores in a direct line to the green. I may pull off a decent score on this hole in spite of my godawful slice. As I address the ball, a familiar giggle fouls the air to my right. Shadows dominate this makeshift forest but don't obscure everything. As I turn toward the sound, golf becomes the least of my problems.

Shafts of sunlight filter through the trees to feature Treat pressing Lanie against a nearby trunk. His hands twist her hair in a way I know all too well. My boyfriend's lips devour Lanie's mouth, neck, and single exposed breast. Treat's hand travels down her ribcage, over a hip to disappear under a Lawson Graham Premier Sportswear golf skirt. The two rock and slide together in a rhythm that fills me with the chilling certainty that this isn't their first encounter.

When she hooks her leg around his hip, I bite back a scream. To make the nightmare vanish, I whip around, execute a violent backswing, and strike my ball with gale force intensity.

Frantic commotion explodes from the green. I lift my head in time to see Bobby Provost, showrunner of *The Chieftain's Son*, crumple onto the grass.

Don't miss more of the *Rockin' Fairy Tales* series, coming soon and find more from Leslie O'Sullivan with HOT SET available now.

Gilly Bettencourt is almost as fed up with writing witty descriptors for a sportswear catalog as she is with her on-the-sly workplace relationship with the CEO's son that makes her feel like a dirty little secret.

After catching her boyfriend with another woman, Gilly leaps at the opportunity to head to Ireland as a writer's assistant on the much-anticipated TV show, *The Chieftain's Son*, an Irish historical drama based on an insanely best-selling series of romance novels.

When Gilly meets Jack O'Leary, star of the series, passion blazes between them. Unfortunately, the show insists on branding Jack as an available heartthrob—landing Gilly in the type of hush hush relationship she crossed an ocean to forget.

Can their love affair survive the demands of the show's PR machine, or is Gilly doomed to be typecast as the girl behind the scenes?

All reviews are **welcome** and **appreciated.** Please consider leaving one on your favorite social media and book buying sites.

Escape Your World. Get Lost in Ours! City Owl Press at www.cityowlpress.com.

ACKNOWLEDGMENTS

My gushing gratitude to all the readers who have supported and stuck with the *Rockin' Fairy Tales* since the beginning when Justin Time first fell from the sky in *Pink Guitars and Falling Stars*. It's been amazing to connect with you through social media and at book events. Your support is truly the stuff of fairy tales. Thank you to all the TikTok, Instagram, Threads, bloggers, and Facebook folks who've spread the word through posts, comments, likes, shares, reviews and all the things.

This series would not have been possible without the loving support of the creative team at City Owl Press. Obnoxiously loud shout outs to Tina and Yelena who have championed this series from day one and continue to do so. Squeezy hugs to the brilliant editor, Heather McCorkle, who helped shape the first Rockin' Fairy Tale, and the wonderful editor, Lisa Green, who deftly guided the rest of the series into its shiniest form. Heartfelt appreciation to Lisa C. for being part of team Rockin' Fairy Tales through her flawless and generous copy editing.

So much love to my amazing ARC/Street Team, A Company of Readers, and the magical Sav. You all make this writing journey a joy.

Special thanks to Sarah, the best beta reader in the known world.

Kudos to the readers who found the Shakespeare Easter eggs in each book and shared your discoveries with me. I am in debt to Hollywood itself for its inspiration not only as a real place but also as the land where so many dare to dream.

Beloved family and friends, thank you for always believing my stories would find a place in this world, and being there to help me navigate my creative sailboat through both calm and stormy seas.

ABOUT THE AUTHOR

LESLIE O'SULLIVAN is the award-winning author of *Fae Destiny*, a romantasy series that explores the collision between the real world and the Irish Faerie realm. Her *Rockin' Fairy Tales* romantasy stories shine a new spotlight on favorite fairy tales set against the backdrop of a fictional Hollywood music scene. The completed *Behind the Scenes* contemporary romcom series peeks into the off-camera sizzle of a wildly popular Irish television drama. She's a UCLA Bruin with a BA and MFA from their Department of Theater where she also taught for years on the design faculty. Her tenure in the world of television was mainly as the assistant art director on "It's Garry Shandling's Show." Leslie is a voracious reader who loves to connect with other book lovers and indulge her fangirl side at cons.

www.leslieosullivanwrites.com

facebook.com/leslie.osullivanauthor
instagram.com/leslieosullivanwrites
tiktok.com/@leslieosullivanwrites

ABOUT THE PUBLISHER

City Owl Press is a cutting edge indie publishing company, bringing the world of romance and speculative fiction to discerning readers.

Escape Your World. Get Lost in Ours!

www.cityowlpress.com

facebook.com/YourCityOwlPress
x.com/cityowlpress
instagram.com/cityowlbooks
pinterest.com/cityowlpress

www.ingramcontent.com/pod-product-compliance
Lightning Source LLC
LaVergne TN
LVHW010557100826
845148LV00014B/2751

* 9 7 8 1 6 4 8 9 8 5 5 4 6 *